Hide
Her Name

NADINE DORRIES grew up in a
working-class family in Liverpool.
She trained as a nurse, then followed
with a successful career in which
she established and sold her own
business. She has been the MP for
Mid-Bedfordshire since 2005 and has
three daughters.

Also by Nadine Dorries

The Four Streets

NADINE
DORRIES

Hide
Her Name

HEAD
of ZEUS

For my late father George, the gentlest and kindest of all men, and my inimitable and beloved Irish nana, Nellie Deane, who stole me away from Liverpool in order that I would love Eire as much as she.

I went out to the hazel wood,
Because a fire was in my head,
And cut and peeled a hazel wand,
And hooked a berry to a thread;
And when white moths were on the wing,
And moth-like stars were flickering out,
I dropped the berry in the stream
And caught a little silver trout.

When I had laid it on the floor
I went to blow the fire a-flame,
But something rustled on the floor,
And someone called me by my name:
It had become a glimmering girl
With apple blossom in her hair
Who called me by my name and ran
And faded through the brightening air.

William Butler Yeats
selected verses from
The Song of Wandering Aengus

Chapter One

'STOP LYING ON his pyjamas now, Peggy, and let yer man out to earn an honest crust!'

Paddy's next-door neighbour, Tommy, impatiently yelled over the backyard gate as he and the Nelson Street dockers knocked on for Paddy. They stood, huddled together in an attempt to hold back the worst of the rain, as they waited for Paddy to join them.

Much to her annoyance, Peggy, Paddy's wife, could hear their sniggering laughter.

'Merciful God!' she said crossly. 'Paddy, would ye tell that horny fecker, Tommy, it's not us at it every five minutes.' She snatched the enamel mug of tea out of Paddy's hand and away from his lips before he had supped his last drop. There was not a second of silence available for him in which to protest.

'The only reason he and Maura have two sets of twins is because he's a dirty bugger and does it twice a night. I'll not have him shouting such filth down the entry, now tell him, will ye, Paddy?'

Peggy and Paddy had spawned enough of their own children, but Peggy had never in her life done it twice on the same night. Every woman who lived on the four streets knew: that sinful behaviour got you caught with twins.

'I wonder sometimes how Maura holds her head up

without the shame, so I do. Once caught doing it twice, ye would know what the feck had happened and not do it again. He must be mighty powerful with his persuasion, that Tommy. Answer me, Paddy, tell him, will ye?'

'Aye, I will that, Peggy,' said Paddy as he picked up his army-issue canvas bag containing his dinner: a bottle of cold tea and Shipman's beef paste sandwiches. Rushing to the door, he placed a kiss on Peggy's cheek, his shouted goodbye cut midway as the back gate snapped closed behind him.

Each man who lived on the four streets worked on the docks. Their day began as it ended, together.

It took exactly four minutes from the last backyard on Nelson Street, down the dock steps, to the perimeter gate. The same amount of time it took to smoke the second roll-up as ribald jokes and football banter rose high on the air. When the sun shone, their spirits lifted and they would often sing whilst walking.

The same melancholy songs heard in the Grafton rooms or the Irish centre on a Saturday night sunk into a pint of Guinness. Melodies of a love they left behind. Of green fields the colour of emeralds, or a raven-haired girl, with eyes that shone like diamonds.

The Nelson Street gang was often delayed by Paddy at number seventeen and would pause at his back gate and stand a while.

Each morning, wearing a string vest that carried the menu of every meal eaten at home that week, Paddy sat up in bed, picked up his cigarettes and matches that lay next to an ever-overflowing ashtray on the bedside table, and lit up his first ciggie of the day.

Paddy smoked a great deal in bed.

He would often wake Peggy in the middle of the night with

the sound of his match striking through the dark, providing a split second of bright illumination.

'Give us a puff,' Peggy would croak, without any need of the teeth soaking in a glass on the table next to her. Not waiting for nor expecting a reply, she would warily uncoil her arm from under the old grey army blanket and, cheating the cold air of any opportunity to penetrate the dark, smelly warmth beneath, grasp the wet-ended cigarette between her finger and thumb, put it to her lips and draw deeply.

'Ah, that's better,' she would say. 'Me nerves are shot, Paddy,' and within seconds she would drift back to sleep.

This morning, the squall blew across the Mersey and up the four streets, soaking the men waiting for Paddy. They stood huddled against the entry wall, trying in vain to protect their ciggies from the downpour.

Paddy appeared through the gate, Peggy's words at his back pushing him out onto the cobbles.

'Yer fecking bastards, ye'll get me hung one day, so yer will,' said Paddy only half seriously to Tommy and the rest of the gang.

'I was only joking, Paddy, I've seen a better face on a clock than on yer missus,' said Tommy. 'I knew ye was just stuffing yer gob with another slice of toast.'

'Leave Peggy alone or I'll set her on yer,' joked Paddy. 'She was kept in a cage till she was five. Ye'll be sorry if I do.'

They all laughed, even Paddy.

Tall Sean, a docker by day and a boxer by night, joined in as he struggled to light up.

'Never fear, Paddy,' he laughed. 'Yer a lucky man with your Peggy, her titties are so feckin' big, ye could hang me wet donkey jacket off them with a bottle of Guinness in each pocket and it still wouldn't fall off.'

They roared with laughter and with lots of matey reassuring pats on the back for Paddy, they continued on their way down the steps to face another day of hard graft on the river's edge.

Boots on cobbles. Minds on the match.

From an upstairs window in the Priory, Daisy Quinn, Father James's housekeeper, studied the dockers marching down the steps towards the gate, just as she had done every single morning since she herself had arrived from Dublin during the war.

In an hour, once she had cleared away the breakfast things, she would take her damp duster and move to another room, across the landing and look down on the mothers and children from Nelson Street as they walked in the opposite direction to that of the dockers, towards the school gates.

The Victorian Priory, large, square and detached, stood next to the graveyard and from each of the upstairs windows Daisy could alter her view: of the docks, the graveyard, the school and the convent, or the four streets. Daisy had her own panoramic view of life as it happened. There wasn't very much about anyone or anything Daisy didn't know. They all turned up on the Priory steps at some time, for one reason or another.

'Daisy, have ye any coal to spare? We have none and the babby is freezing.'

'Do ye have any potatoes or bread? A coat for the child to go to school?'

They were always wanting something and, sure enough, Father James could often solve the problem. They had cupboards in the Priory stuffed full of the clothes people donated for him to hand out to the poor.

But the father never gave. Mothers had to ask.

'I am here to do God's work, not the corporation's,' he would often boom in a bad-tempered way when Daisy asked should he take a coat or a pair of shoes to a family, after she had noticed the welfare officer knocking on their door.

But pride never stood in the way of a mother needing to warm a child, so beg they often did.

Occasionally people came for happy reasons – to ask for the father to perform a christening or a wedding – and when that happened, the father would take them into his study and Daisy would carry in a tray of tea and a plate of her home-made biscuits, just as Mrs Malone had taught her.

She almost always took back an empty plate. Hardly ever had Daisy returned a biscuit to the kitchen.

If ever a mother was too polite or too scared to allow her children to take one, Daisy would press a few into her hand at the front door, wrapped in greaseproof paper and tied up with string.

'Go on now, take it,' she would say. 'Have them for later.'

Daisy would have loved to have had children of her own.

She had arrived in Liverpool from Dublin to take her position at the Priory whilst still a child. She became an assistant to the fathers' cook, Mrs Malone, and like most young girls she had a head full of dreams and plans.

Father James had disposed of those faster than a speeding bullet.

'You will have one day and one night off per month,' he told her, within moments of her being summoned to his study.

Daisy was a little disappointed by that news. She had been told by the sisters at the orphanage in Dublin that she would have one day a week to herself and a week's holiday each year, during which she could travel back to Ireland and visit the only place she knew to be home, the orphanage where she had been raised since she was a baby.

Now, all these years later, Daisy could count the days off she had taken on one hand.

'You must work hard and help Mrs Malone in the kitchen,' the sisters at the orphanage had told her. And, sure enough, working hard was what she had done every day since.

Without a moment's pain or illness and certainly without any warning at all, Mrs Malone had dropped dead, almost ten years to the day following Daisy's arrival.

Mrs Malone had often told Daisy what a good worker she was.

'I don't know how I would manage without you, Daisy,' she said, at least once a day. 'The sisters may have said you were simple in the head, but I didn't want you for brains, brawn was what I was looking for and you have plenty of that.'

Daisy smiled with pleasure. Being told that she was simple was not news to her, sure, she had heard it so often before. But the sisters had also said, 'You can hold your head up with no shame, you were born to a very good family, Daisy Quinn.'

Daisy never thought to question why she was in an orphanage and not with her family. She had no real understanding of what a family was.

Being a good girl and coming from a good family must have been why she was sent to take up such an important job in England and for one of the fathers too.

'You have simple ways, but they can be put to good use if you can be protected from the sin that preys upon girls like yourself,' the sisters had told her. Daisy had no idea which sin would prey upon her or what it would do, but she was grateful for the protection.

Neither the sisters nor Mrs Malone had ever mentioned to Daisy the other reason that she had been sent to the Priory.

Daisy presumed that they could not have known, because

Father James forbade Daisy to speak to anyone about it.

'To speak of anything that occurs in this Priory would be the greatest sin for which no forgiveness would ever be forthcoming. Ye will be left to burn alone in the eternal flames of hell and damnation. Do ye understand, girl?'

She was asked this question on a regular basis and her answer was always the dutiful same: 'Yes, Father.'

Daisy took over the housekeeper's role in full. She coped well and never took nor was offered a day off.

However, there had also been a number of welcome changes following Mrs Malone's death.

Neither Father James nor any of his friends had bothered her again, and the nuns began to invite her over to the convent for tea.

She had only the bishop to tolerate now.

She sometimes wondered if Father James would have preferred someone other than herself as housekeeper, but on the night of Mrs Malone's funeral, on her way to her modest room, she had overheard raised voices coming from the study.

'The money for the Priory would stop if she left. It must follow her wherever she is and, anyway, the sisters in Dublin would have too many questions to ask should she be moved.'

That was the bishop speaking. A fat man, distinguishable by his thin, weedy whine, which as it whistled into the air struggled past the blubbery folds of lard gathered under his chin.

'I suppose we are safer if she is here,' said Father James in a tone loaded with disappointment.

'Aye, we are that, but anyway, she is simple. No one would ever believe a word she said. I will write now that she is happy and improved. That she is running the show and, sure, isn't that the truth? Wasn't that just the grandest bit of rabbit pie we ever ate for supper?'

Daisy grinned from ear to ear with pleasure. They had loved her rabbit pie.

On this wet morning, Daisy padded across to the south side of the empty house. Sister Evangelista had popped a note through the door late last night to let her know she would be visiting the Priory this morning to help Daisy pack up the father's room, ready to send his belongings to his sister in America.

The murder of Father James in the graveyard had taken place only feet away from the Priory and everyone was still in a state of profound shock.

Everyone except Daisy, that was.

Daisy wasn't sad and didn't miss the father at all. Not in the way she had missed Mrs Malone when she died.

In fact, Daisy missed Mrs Malone a great deal. She had always told Daisy what she could and could not do, and with no one to guide her, Daisy was lost.

Father James had told her what she could and could not say.

What should she say now and who to?

Her mind was in torment.

Daisy pressed her forehead against the cold window and, looking down, watched the children walking to school. She saw Sister Evangelista close the convent door, make her way down the path and turn right along the pavement towards the Priory. The Reverend Mother waved to Kitty Doherty from number nineteen, who was making her way towards the school steps on the opposite side of the road to the convent. Kitty was herding along the two sets of twin boys and that lovely girl, Nellie Deane, from number forty-two was helping her. The girls waved back to Sister Evangelista, all smiles.

The Kitty girl. Daisy had often seen Father James visit her house, very often at night, but he never visited Nellie's.

Nellie, whose mother, Bernadette, had died so tragically young and whom Daisy still saw sometimes in the dead of the night, running up and down the four streets.

It was Nellie's Nana Kathleen who had woken Daisy late on the night the father was murdered. She had been talking to Bernadette as she left the Keating girl's wedding and followed the river, down towards Nelson Street.

Daisy wasn't scared to see the ghostly Bernadette with Kathleen. She often saw her in the graveyard and up and down Nelson Street, as she flew straight through the wall into what had once been her home, number forty-two.

Daisy, uneasy, had been unable to return to sleep on that particular night. She had wandered out of her bedroom, the static from her peach, brushed-nylon nightdress crackling and snapping at her feet as she walked. She had leant over the dark, swan-necked banister that swept away steeply, and gazed down the long stairwell. The hall light was still on. The father had yet to return home from the wedding. He would switch the light off when he returned to the Priory.

From the window, Daisy had watched Nana Kathleen and Bernadette, and waited. And then she had seen the father in his large hat and cloak, turning the corner into the back entry just ahead of them both. He hadn't come back to the Priory as ususal that night.

Daisy knew she should tell someone what she had seen. But Daisy wasn't allowed to tell anyone anything.

'I might be simple,' she had said to herself as she got back into bed on that fateful evening, 'but I'm not an eejit. There's no way I am spending eternity stood in the fires of hell.'

When the bell pull rang, Daisy almost fell down the stairs as she ran to open the Priory door for Sister Evangelista. She had been unhappy sleeping in the huge house on her own since the murder. Today she would beg Sister Evangelista to take her to the convent right away. She would be safe there, just as she had been at the orphanage.

'Morning, Daisy.' Sister Evangelista sounded brighter than she felt.

She was dreading this job but the bishop had been very strong indeed on the telephone.

'Make sure you clear up every single thing that belonged to Father James, Sister, and I shall be with you later in the morning in my car to cart it all away to send on to his sister in America, everything, do ye understand?'

Of course Sister Evangelista understood. Did the man think she was witless?

'Yes, Father, there will be no problem. The housekeeper Daisy will help me and it shouldn't take long.'

'Ah, yes, Daisy, the girl is a bit simple, is she not, Sister?'

'She is, Bishop, but she is a good housekeeper, Mrs Malone trained her well.'

'I am sure she did, but she is bound to be very upset indeed and may be prone to rambling. We must be careful to protect her, as she has no family of her own, except for us. I wonder if a spell in the peace and quiet of the convent might be a good idea?'

This had never crossed Sister Evangelista's mind and she was far from happy. Disruption in the convent always upset the nuns' routine and, sure, didn't she have enough to do with a school to run as well?

However, even she dared not argue with the bishop.

'Aye, well, I'll see how she is, Father, when I get there,

shall I? She will need to prepare the Priory for the father's replacement.'

No sooner had the words left her mouth than her throat began to thicken with emotion and tears swam across her eyes.

'I mean, what are the arrangements, Bishop? Where is Father James to be buried? We need someone in authority here. Everyone is dreadfully upset. Will you definitely be coming soon?'

The bishop had promised to visit days ago. But something both mysterious and urgent had occurred daily to prevent him. Sister Evangelista had carried the entire burden alone and now she felt exhausted.

She had almost broken down earlier in the morning when speaking to her friend, Miss Devlin, a teacher at the school.

'Our own Father James, found murdered in the graveyard, and the bishop still hasn't arrived to help deal with the police or bring some authority to the church, and now, here I am, about to pack up all his personal possessions in the Priory with only simple Daisy to help.'

Into one of her hands Miss Devlin had quietly placed a hankie, and into the other a cup of tea with a couple of Anadin on the saucer.

Tea and Anadin, hailed as a miracle cure by all of Liverpool's women. A headache? Take a cuppa tea and two Anadin. A toothache? A cuppa tea and two Anadin. A priest found murdered in the graveyard? A cuppa tea and two Anadin. Anadin sat on the wooden shelf next to the Woodbines in the local tobacconist's and they sold almost as many of one as the other. Acknowledged as an effective alternative to gin to help with the pains of afterbirth, mastitis, monthlies and the constant headaches brought on by looking after a dozen unruly children.

Miss Devlin had spoken in her customary gentle tone. 'It has been very hard indeed on yourself. Drink the tea and take the Anadin now, Sister, and it will all be easier to face. The bishop will be here soon.'

Sister Evangelista's distress on the telephone had been apparent. Sensing that she was losing patience, the bishop had tried to pacify her as an adult would a three-year-old child.

'I will be there this afternoon, so keep calm now. Everyone must remain very calm. We cannot bury the father until the police release his body, but we know how the police can behave. Remember how pushy they were about coming into the school and upsetting the children. You must say nothing to them about anything. They will be looking for someone to blame and we mustn't let that be us, Sister. Of course when I say us, I mean the Church. This is all a dreadful mess but be sure, Sister, we have a responsibility to protect our work.'

Sister Evangelista was speechless. She had no idea what the bishop was talking about. The police didn't have anyone in their sights? He was right. In fact, they had taken themselves down a few embarrassing blind alleys, but none of them had led towards the school or the convent.

She replaced the receiver with a prayer that the bishop would make haste. As God was her judge, if she had to deal with much more on her own, likely she would go mad.

Now at the sight of Daisy's relieved face, she was glad she had come.

'Hello, Sister.'

Daisy grinned from ear to ear in that inane way she had. Her dark hair with its thick fringe was kept short and tidy with the help of a pudding basin and the kitchen scissors. Her nose dribbled slightly, as though she had a cold, but she seemed not to notice and her eyes always appeared bright, as though full of tears.

Sister Evangelista sighed. Her heart suddenly felt very heavy. Daisy would be of little help.

'The bishop is arriving this afternoon to remove Father James's belongings, Daisy. We need to pack up the father's room and all of his personal possessions. I hope to God he sends another priest to us soon to take charge. Everyone is in such a state.'

Daisy's heart sank into her boots. Whenever the bishop visited, he slept over at the Priory and often popped into Daisy's room before retiring for the night. Father James had accompanied him the first time, but ever after he had visited her alone.

Daisy's expression never altered, and she didn't speak.

'Have you any sacks, or the father's suitcase, Daisy?'

Sister Evangelista's mind was already focused on the task ahead. Daisy nodded. 'We have hessian flour sacks folded up in the scullery and there's a suitcase on top of Father James's wardrobe in his room,' she said.

'Good girl, bring them to the study, we will start in there. And, Daisy, you had better bring a tray of tea for us both, we could be a while.'

Daisy disappeared into the kitchen, as Sister Evangelista walked across the highly polished parquet floor of the square hallway and, in a businesslike manner, threw open the study door.

The gust of a breeze created by her sudden entry sent a cloud of dust particles flying upwards where, trapped, they swirled and glittered in columns of weak sunlight. It took her eyes a moment to adjust. She caught her breath and dragged the courage from somewhere deep within her to take the next step.

The courage to walk over to his desk. To begin the process of parcelling up the life of the man she had known well and worked with for over twenty years. This was daunting, even for someone as efficient and strong as she was. The father, whom she had loved and who had had such a passion to help the poorest children in the community. She silently vowed he would never be forgotten and that a mass would be said for him every day at St Mary's, for as long as she was alive.

As Sister Evangelista approached the murdered priest's dark-oak desk, she crossed herself.

As she surveyed the surface, she noticed his diary was open on the day he had died. Pushing her thin wire-framed spectacles to the top of her nose with one hand, she placed the other on the open page and let it travel across the words, as though they were written in braille.

The police had not yet gained entry to the Priory. They required permission from the bishop, which was one of the reasons he was arriving today. Everything was just as it had been on the day the priest had died.

It now crossed her mind that maybe Father James's belongings held a clue as to who had murdered him and that maybe packing away his personal effects might not be the right thing to do after all.

But the bishop had been most insistent. 'We must protect the Church,' he had said. What had that meant exactly?

Father James would have done nothing other than protect the Church, surely?

'Oh, Daisy, you and that tea are a welcome sight. Bring the tray here, dear,' she said, as she looked up to see Daisy standing in the doorway, the sacks rolled up and tucked under her arm. Daisy laid the tray on the table.

'Who was Austin Tattershall, Daisy?' Sister Evangelista

enquired. The name glared up at her from the diary page. Four o'clock, Austin Tattershall. The diary entry had jumped out as the name wasn't Irish and was certainly one Sister Evangelista had never heard before.

'I don't know, Sister,' Daisy said. 'He came here sometimes to see the father.'

Daisy was whispering, almost into her chest, as she poured the tea.

Sister Evangelista looked squarely at Daisy, who avoided her gaze as she handed over the cup and saucer, keeping her eyes fixed firmly on the desk as she did so.

'Did the father keep his appointment with him at four o'clock?' she asked.

Daisy still kept her head down as she replied, 'He didn't, Sister.'

A silence fell between them.

Sister Evangelista had spent her life being lied to.

The reasons given for why children came to school with no food in their bellies, shoes falling off their feet and lice dancing on their heads had to be heard to be believed. Sister Evangelista could smell a rat a mile away and she smelt an enormous one right here in this room, right now. Either Daisy was lying, or there was something she wasn't telling her.

She flicked over the diary pages, feeling worse than a thief. Father James was dead and these earthly possessions were of no use to him now, but, even so, she felt extremely uncomfortable. She had always been an intensely private woman herself, raised to have impeccable manners.

Now she saw that there was a diary entry on the same day each week with names she didn't recognize. Arthur, Stanley, Cyril, Brian. Who were these men?

'Manners won't get his belongings to his family, I suppose.'

She suddenly spoke her thoughts out loud as she snapped the diary shut, making Daisy jump.

'No, Sister,' said Daisy, unfolding one of the small sacks.

Sister Evangelista placed the diary carefully in the hessian sack.

On top she laid his silver letter opener and a leather-bound volume containing his precious stamp collection, which he often brought children into his office to view.

'The stamp collection is so beautiful. The children would never have seen anything like it before,' she had often said to Miss Devlin.

Sister Evangelista had always thought Father James the most patient of men. She had repeatedly said so to Miss Devlin.

'He is so busy, with barely a moment to spare, and yet he always finds the time to share his knowledge of the world with the children through his wonderful collection of stamps. He never minds them visiting him in his study. I just don't know where he finds the patience.'

Sister Evangelista surveyed the contents of the bookcase on the opposite side of the room and realized she couldn't place the precious stamp collection in a sack along with the books.

'Daisy, I think we are going to need some newspaper. Are there any old rag sheets we can rip up to wrap things in? I would like to protect his stamp collection, at the very least.'

As Daisy left the room in search of dust sheets, Sister Evangelista slowly lowered herself into the father's chair behind the desk. Tears that had never been far from the surface since the murder now threatened once again to pour down her cheeks.

She felt a hum. A sizzling static in the air.

Daisy's receding footsteps had taken her downstairs into the kitchen and could no longer be heard. Sister Evangelista felt as though the father were standing in the room, objecting to the use of his chair. It was a real presence.

The air smelt of the last time it was occupied. An odour trapped by locked windows and doors.

Musty. Ink. Hair grease and man.

He was there.

There was another smell too. Faintly familiar, of lavender floor wax and polish. Daisy may have been simple, but Sister Evangelista acknowledged that the Priory was spotless.

He was there.

'Don't cry,' she whispered to herself, clasping her hands together in front as though in prayer. She was a nun, unafraid of ghosts. She was protected by God's light. 'Just get through this as quickly as possible,' she whispered, defiant, challenging the empty space. Father James might have been a saint in her eyes, but he was no Lazarus.

Distracting herself, she glanced down at the desk drawers. Each one was locked. A small bunch of keys lay on top of the desk next to the open inkwell.

There was still no sign of Daisy. Should she wait for Daisy to return before opening the drawers?

Picking up the keys, she tried first the top right-hand drawer. The key turned easily. Feeling bold and moving quickly before she could think about what she was doing and hesitate, not waiting for encouragement from Daisy nor permission from the bishop, she swiftly opened the drawer and pulled it out as far as it would extend. It was stuffed full of bundles of white envelopes stacked in three neat rows and tied with string.

She lifted the first bundle and flicked her fingers down the side, revealing the addresses printed on the front. All of the envelopes, she noticed, were addressed to people she did not know and had been sent to a PO Box number. Some coincided with the names in the diary entries. The first one was addressed to Austin Tattershall.

Sister Evangelista took out the envelope and lifted the flap, revealing a wad of black-and-white photographs.

What she saw made her feel as though she had been punched in the heart.

Winded and breathless, in a state of acute shock and creeping numbness, she examined the photographs, one by one.

When she considered the events in her mind later that evening, she wondered to herself how in God's name she hadn't fainted. How had she managed to behave as though she was looking at photographs of a beautiful rural landscape, instead of the most vile and depraved images of young girls and boys she had ever seen?

Some of the photographs had been taken abroad, that much was obvious by the name stamped on the back. Most were of men with children, girls mostly and the occasional boy. Some were obviously taken in a hospital setting. Others were of very young girls. With horror, she realized that one picture had been taken in the father's study and it was of a child she recognized from the school.

She furtively glanced at the door to see if Daisy had returned and hurriedly slipped the pictures back into the envelope, scooping the remaining envelopes in the drawer onto her lap.

Daisy walked into the room with what had once been a large sheet now torn into squares for dusting cloths.

'Thank you, Daisy. I think maybe there are some things I had better take to the convent for the bishop to deal with. Could you begin lifting the books down from the bookcase?'

Sister Evangelista felt as though her head were spinning but she knew she had to remain calm.

Daisy noticed that the Reverend Mother was breathing

faster, that perspiration stood out on her top lip, and that her forehead and her cheeks were burning red. Daisy was not quite as simple as people thought.

All the sister could think about was how much she and the entire community had loved Father James and yet all the time this filth was sitting in his drawer. She was out of her depth and had no idea what to do. She had to speak to the bishop as soon as she could, ask him to finish the remainder of the packing up himself. She felt as though the ground were shaking beneath her. She must ask the bishop, should they show this to the police?

'*We have to protect the Church*,' he had said.

She placed the diary and the envelopes on a square of white linen and tied up the four corners.

'Daisy, I don't want to do this just now, I have to speak to the bishop. We will finish all of this later.'

Daisy had never seen the sister so agitated. This upset her. She didn't like to stay at the Priory. She wanted to be at the convent and had hoped to talk to Sister Evangelista about maybe leaving with her when she had finished the packing. Daisy had only ever lived with nuns or in the Priory with the priest, and she knew she preferred to live with the nuns. There were no men in the convent.

'Who came here to visit the father, Daisy?' Sister Evangelista spoke rapidly. There was an impatience and roughness to her voice that hadn't been there before. 'Who visited him here that I wouldn't know of?'

Daisy remembered what she had been told by the father. Her lips were sealed. She looked silently down at the floor. Daisy always did as she was told.

'Daisy, tell me, who did the father see that I do know? He used to visit lots of people on the streets, didn't he, Daisy? Sure, I know he was mad busy, always calling in on the sick and the poor. Was there anyone he saw more often than others?'

Sister Evangelista was running on instinct. She recognized the child in the picture as a little girl from Waterloo Street who had been in Miss Devlin's class last year. She was no more than six years old. Her mother had been seriously ill and when she was bedbound, Sister Evangelista knew the father had visited daily to take mass at home at her bedside.

'Well, I cannot say who came here, Sister, but where the father went is a different question altogether. He liked to visit the Doherty house a great deal, Sister. He visited lots of folk but he was regular to the Doherty house.'

The Doherty house.

The image of Kitty Doherty, one of Sister Evangelista's star pupils, crossed her mind.

Ten minutes later, Sister Evangelista ran down the street towards the convent, hugging a large parcel to her chest with Daisy at her side. On the way she almost bumped into Nellie Deane with her arm round Kitty, leaving the school gates.

'Nellie, where are you off to?' she said, alarmed.

'I have to take Kitty home, Sister. Miss Devlin sent for me. She doesn't feel too good.'

Then, without any warning whatsoever, Kitty threw up all over the pavement.

Sister Evangelista stared at the child who had turned a ghastly shade of grey.

Kitty had been sick in the playground yesterday morning. As she grappled with the realization of what may be happening, she felt as though the vomit-strewn pavement was opening up beneath her.

She needed to help Kitty, but she was frozen to the spot.

She could hear Kitty's voice somewhere in the background, as she said, 'Sorry, Sister, I'm so sorry,' but she couldn't reply.

The world as she knew it and all that was familiar to her was collapsing around her and she along with it.

Daisy, a forced keeper of secrets, was staring at her. Her expression was unfathomable.

Sister Evangelista focused her attention on what Nellie was saying.

Kitty's innocence with her wet eyes and pale skin brought her to her senses. Only yesterday Miss Devlin had said how sickly Kitty had been in the mornings.

'If the child wasn't so young and an angel herself, I would swear she was pregnant.'

Oh Holy Mother, this cannot be true, she thought, and then suddenly, pulling herself up, she addressed Kitty.

'It is all right, child, you go home for the rest of the day. I will send the janitor out to clean the pavement. Are you sure you are all right, Nellie?'

Nellie put her arm round Kitty once more and smiled weakly at Sister Evangelista, who realized she could no longer wait for the bishop. This was beyond either of them. She knew what she had to do.

Howard sat at his desk, drumming his fingers and staring at the array of police notebooks before him. It was only ten o'clock and he was already lighting up his fifth cigarette of the day. Not one of the notebooks held a single clue.

They had no witness or a shred of motive but they did have the superintendent breathing down their necks, urging them to find the priest's killer as soon as possible.

Simon walked into the office with two mugs of tea and a message that made Howard feel weak.

'The super wants a meeting at twelve and an update on the priest's case.'

'Have you any bright ideas?' Howard threw across the table to Simon as he picked up his mug.

'Apart from the fact that we both have a gut feeling Jerry Deane knows something, we have absolutely fuck all to go on. Not a single frigging lead. The whole lot of 'em are either ignorant or stupid. No one knows owt,' said Simon unhelpfully.

Howard picked up his tea and groaned.

'Well, sergeant clever dick, we have got two hours, so what do you suggest?'

The black Bakelite phone on the desk between them began to ring.

'There you go, it's a message from the dead priest.' Simon began to laugh to himself. 'He's sending you a little clue from above.'

'Shut the fuck up,' said Howard as he flicked his cigarette stump at Simon. Picking up the handset, he turned to face the wall before speaking into the mouthpiece.

Less than thirty seconds later Simon almost spat out his tea as Howard spoke soothingly into the phone.

'Now, now, Sister, you must not upset yourself. We will be at the school in less than half an hour. I can assure you, you have done exactly the right thing calling me and we will make sure the bishop knows that.'

Howard replaced the receiver with far more enthusiasm than he had picked it up.

'That was Sister Evangelista, she's got news, good news, full of clues news. It sounds as though she has got our motive, mate. Drink up, one very upset nun seems to want to tell us all.'

They both banged their mugs down on the table and two minutes later were whizzing through Liverpool city centre in a pale blue and white panda car, heading up towards Nelson Street school.

Chapter Two

LIFE ON THE four streets had very slowly returned to a normal routine. After all, the women could only last so many days without baking bread.

From the second the news had broken, floor-mop handles had banged constantly on kitchen walls, summoning the women to a conference in whichever home had the freshest piece of gossip first.

As they ran up and down the entry and in and out of one another's homes, with babies on hips, holding half-full bottles of sterilized milk for the tea or a shovel of coal to keep a fire burning, they became engrossed by the most intense speculation. Who on this earth could have done such an awful thing and why?

The women talked of nothing else and almost wore themselves out.

Even the children playing on the green huddled into groups and repeated the whispered conversations they had heard at home. Rehearsing for the future. Dealing in the currency of the streets.

'The Pope is in such a rage, so he is, he is coming from Rome to Liverpool to kill whoever did it with his own bare hands,' said Declan, Maura and Tommy's little rascal, to his rather serious twin brother, Harry.

'No,' said Harry, shocked at the thought of the Pope strangling someone. 'That cannot be true, ye liar, where did ye hear that?'

'It is so, I heard Mammy say it to Sheila in the kitchen this morning.'

If his mammy was telling Sheila, then it must be true for sure. Harry gasped and put his fist in his mouth before he ran off to tell his mate Little Paddy, who had been a bit down of late, having caused such a fuss himself.

He had been at the very centre of his own storm in relation to the murder and was now maintaining a low profile.

As a result of what Little Paddy had blurted out, the police had taken in one of their own, Jerry Deane, for questioning. Everyone agreed this was a fanciful notion on the part of the police, who must have been desperate indeed. And all on the back of Peggy and Paddy's stupid Little Paddy, looking to make a name for himself as the clever one at school. Claiming he had seen Jerry Deane running down the entry on the night of the murder, skulking like a thief in the night.

As if anyone would ever believe anything Little Paddy said.

Jerry Deane had been back at home within the day. Following the beating he took from his da, Little Paddy struggled to sit down for a week.

'That is one child who will never be described as clever,' said Molly Barrett to Annie O'Prey, just loud enough for Little Paddy to hear, as they both stood on the pavement to sweep their front steps.

'As if any child from that family could know anything,' Annie O'Prey replied, not breaking her stroke with her broom.

Little Paddy's da might have thrashed the living daylights out of him, but Little Paddy knew what he had seen, and he

knew it was true, and no matter how many thrashings he was
given, he knew he was right. He had seen Uncle Jerry running
down the entry in the middle of the night. How was he supposed to know that he was only off to Brigid and Sean's house
for a card school and to tuck into the wedding whiskey they
had all been given as a present by Mrs Keating's publican
in-laws on the morning her daughter got married?

Not that he would ever say it again, mind. Next time his
da might use his belt and Little Paddy idolized his da. He
didn't want that to happen. Little Paddy would keep his gob
shut in future.

The reaction of the families on the four streets to the murder
of their own priest had been powerful and all-consuming.

Some of the women had cried almost constantly since
hearing the news. Others had become so upset that Dr Cole
had to be sent for to administer a sedative.

'Sure, it must be the mystery of the century, so it is,' said
Annie to Molly, as they both swept away.

Annie was as skinny as Molly was fat. Both wore the tra-
ditional uniform of the four streets: a wraparound floral
apron and hair in curlers tucked away underneath a hairnet.
Annie possessed no teeth and had long since given up pretending to own any. Like many others, she had dentures that
lived in a glass on her bedside table, but one morning, instead
of putting them in, she decided to leave them where they
were. With her husband long dead and both of her precious
boys inside Walton gaol, who was there left to put the teeth
in for?

'Sure, I never liked him meself,' replied Molly with a flick
of the broom as she swept up the dust, across the pavement
and into the gutter.

This was the same Molly who had baked the priest a batch of scones every Sunday morning and had dutifully delivered them to the Priory for eighteen years.

As she knelt to pray, the scones would sit on the pew next to her, filling the church with an aroma of fresh baking, competing with the smell of incense.

Some weeks, she barely had enough flour to make a decent batch, or enough coal to heat the oven on the range. Her own children had often gone hungry and didn't see fresh baking for weeks on end. But she never missed her gift for Father James, her bribe in exchange for a place in heaven.

Now that he was dead, it had all been in vain. He was years younger than she. Who would ever have thought this would happen? Eighteen bloody years of scones, all in vain, she was heard to mutter to herself more than once a day.

'The biggest mystery to me is what was me cat doing with the father's langer in his mouth? Now that truly is a riddle – he had been fed twice that day.'

'Who had? Father James?' asked Annie quizzically. 'How do ye know that?'

'No, Jesus, Mary and Joseph, not Father James, me bloody cat. I have no notion at all what he will bring me next. Sends the shivers down me spine, so he does, every time he wanders into the kitchen. To think, he saw it all. If cats could talk, so.'

Molly had yet to recover from the fact that her cat had proudly returned from his nightly graveyard prowl with a murder trophy.

The news of the priest's death was already speeding round the streets when Molly realized what the cat had deposited on her kitchen floor. Her screams could be heard as far as the butcher's and beyond.

'Aye, true, Molly, if Tiger could talk, we would know who had murdered the priest and ye would be a very rich woman indeed, so ye would.'

They both laughed as they finished sweeping into the gutter and walked back to their respective front doors.

'Well, Annie, now the cat can't talk, but I will tell ye this for nothing. There is one woman on this street who I thought we would see being carted off in an ambulance with the grief when she heard that the priest was dead, and yet I saw her more upset on the day Rita O'Neil's lad was made altar boy and not their Harry.'

Mrs O'Prey shuffled closer to Molly's step, crossing her arms and looking around furtively before she spoke. 'Do ye mean Maura Doherty? Because I was thinking the very same thing meself!'

Both women huddled in close.

'Aye, I do. She looks upset all right, but given that the father was never out of her house and she being all pious, high and mighty so, I thought she might have taken to her bed an' all, but not a sign of it. Kathleen Deane is the same, but I never would expect her to be upset. It was no secret she didn't like the priest and never went to mass. She always took herself off to confession with Father Donlan in Bootle.'

For a brief moment, they both lapsed into silence as, leaning on their broomsticks, they watched Kathleen Deane, with her daughter-in-law Alice and the baby Joseph in his Silver Cross pram, head across the cobbles towards the entry, to Maura Doherty's house.

Once Kathleen and Alice had disappeared from sight, Molly examined her broom head with the bristles almost worn down to the wooden block.

'Well, Mrs O, a rich woman I am not. But I know this, if I

don't buy a new broom head today, ye'll be sweeping me step tomorrow along with yours.'

'Wouldn't be the first time,' Annie replied, 'and ye has done mine often enough, Molly me love.'

Molly sniffed in acknowledgment and, without another word, wobbled across her step and closed the front door.

'If ye ate a bit less, ye fat lump, ye could afford a broom head no trouble at all,' whispered Annie to herself as she closed her own front door.

The police car glided round the corner of Nelson Street almost unnoticed. Just a few short weeks ago, the police had been virtually mobbed by neighbours asking one question after another with children constantly circling every policeman and car.

Howard and Simon each took out a fresh cigarette and lit up, squinting through the haze of blue smoke to survey the houses on both sides of the road.

'Where shall we start?' said Simon.

Both men were feeling more confident than they had first thing that morning. That hadn't been difficult given what little information they had and despite their initial optimism, the sister hadn't given them a huge amount to go on.

What they didn't know was that as soon as Sister Evangelista had put the phone down on Howard, she had picked it up straight away and spoken to the bishop, who had been very, very angry when she told him she had called the police. So strong had he been in his opinion, regarding what she should and should not say and do, that he had left Sister Evangelista shaking in fear and in desperate need of something much stronger than a cuppa tea and two Anadin.

Sister Evangelista had no choice but to obey. She answered

to the bishop and, much as it went against her better judg-
ment, she would be obedient. Almost. She would not keep to
herself her suspicions regarding Kitty. She was fond of the girl
and she felt sure that at least must be her godly duty.

It took more than a few slugs of the holy mass wine before
she could face Howard and Simon, having hidden the disgusting photographs in her office safe, as the bishop had ordered.

Simon fixed his gaze on Maura and Tommy's house as
Howard spoke.

'Well, as Sister Evangelista was worried about the eldest
Doherty girl in number nineteen and as the priest spent more
time in number nineteen Nelson Street than any other, we
should visit there last and question all the others first. Let's
not mention the Dohertys or the girl,' he said. 'Just ask, did
the priest have any favourites around here, that kind of thing,
and let's see what happens. I had no idea priests did home
visits, so we have something we didn't have yesterday. And
then if that bloody bishop arrives today and we finally gain
entry into the Priory, maybe we will find another clue. If we
keep shaking the tree hard enough, Simon, something will
eventually fall.'

Before they left the car, they both took another long pull on
their cigarettes as they watched Mrs O'Prey and Mrs Barrett
bang the dust from their brooms and waddle back indoors.

Chapter Three

NELLIE'S BEDROOM WINDOW, at forty-two Nelson Street, overlooked the backyard. Earlier that morning, as she had drawn back the curtains, she had spotted her Nana Kathleen and Auntie Maura down in the yard, whispering furtively over the gate. They were too engrossed to look up and see Nellie, so she pressed her ear to the cold glass window to catch what they were saying. Their behaviour was unusual and Nellie supposed it was yet more gossip about the priest.

Nellie had never attended Father James's church, but always took the bus into Bootle with her Nana Kathleen to attend the mass held by a friend's cousin from back home in Bangornevin.

She felt a strange detachment from the upset, but the fact that someone had committed a murder was truly shocking. None of the mothers had allowed their children to walk to school alone since.

So much had happened of late, it was as though someone had thrown a hand grenade into the midst of their lives and they were all still flying through the air.

Since that awful night when all the Doherty children had piled into Nellie's bedroom in the dark small hours and she had heard crying and talking downstairs, she had felt as though Nana Kathleen and her da were holding out on her and keeping secrets.

She was especially worried about Kitty who was more of a big sister to Nellie than a best friend. For the past few days she had been so ill and this morning had even thrown up all over the pavement, in front of Sister Evangelista.

She had dropped the poorly Kitty back at Maura's and had popped home to tell Alice and Nana Kathleen what had happened.

'Well, glory be,' shouted Kathleen as Nellie walked in through the back door. 'Is school on a half-day now or what? Why are ye back home so soon?'

'It's Kitty, Nana, I have just taken her to Maura. She is so sick, the poor thing.' Nellie had leant against the range as she talked and helped herself to a chunk of the hot barm brack freshly removed from the oven.

Nana Kathleen playfully whacked her hand with the end of the tea towel. 'Away with ye,' she half shouted. 'Off to school and stop shirking. There is nothing wrong with ye, miss.'

Nellie's stepmother, Alice, was sitting on a chair next to the fire with Nellie's little brother, Joseph, on her knee. 'How are the sisters this morning, Nellie? Are they still as upset as they were?'

'Oh my gosh, you should have seen Sister Evangelista,' Nellie exclaimed through a mouth full of the hot fruit bread. 'She was running from the Priory with Daisy, clutching a parcel to her chest, and she looked as though she had seen a ghost. I don't know who looked the most sick, her or Kitty. In a right state, she was.'

Kathleen and Alice exchanged a worried glance, which Nellie missed as she made her way to the door with a sneaky slice of the brack in her hand.

'See yer later, alligator,' she shouted as she closed the door and headed back to school.

'Put Joseph in his pram,' said Kathleen to Alice, 'and let's get over to Maura's.'

Kathleen sensed that they were running out of time. They might need to act more quickly than she had thought.

Maura and Kathleen had already decided between them that Kitty should be told that she was pregnant, before they told her own father, Tommy. After all she had been through, she had the right to that.

Once Tommy had been told, a decision would have to be made. What in God's name were they going to do about the dead priest's bastard child?

Maura had hoped that maybe one day she would wake up and it would all have been nothing more than a nightmare.

As she walked into Kitty's bedroom each morning, she crossed herself and prayed to the Virgin Mary for a miracle. The first thing she did, once Kitty was out of bed, was to pull back her blanket and look hopefully for a sign of blood on her sheet.

Father James had not destroyed her faith in her God. Father James was the devil himself. This she had recognized. Satan had tricked his way into her home.

Maura's faith was the stronger for it. She would not let the devil win.

But the Virgin Mary never answered her prayers and as Maura pulled back the blanket every day, her heart sank into her boots.

There was a murdered priest, and his baby was growing in her daughter's belly.

Could there be much worse to wake up to than that?

Wasn't life hard enough as it was, trying to make ends meet and keep everyone happy? Declan wore his shoes out every week and Maura had no idea how she was going to manage to keep him in school. The sisters had asked to see her to talk about Malachi's demon behaviour in class. Angela needed glasses. Niamh had what looked like the beginnings of Harry's asthma. She had lent Peggy some of her family allowance and now might not have enough for her own family. Tommy would go mad indeed if Declan went without shoes because she had been too quick to lend to those who did not manage their money as well as she did.

And on top of all this, she now had something to deal with that eclipsed everything else. A problem so big, so vast, it was almost incomprehensible, so she pushed it firmly to the back of her mind each morning before her feet had even touched the floor.

Tommy would often wake and find her staring at the ceiling. Without speaking he would pull her into his arms and they would hold onto each other tightly.

Maura would weep into his chest and Tommy, blissfully unaware, had no idea that each day his wife was saving him from further heartache and anguish than that which already tormented him.

'God, Tommy,' Maura sobbed, 'I was happy he took himself up the stairs to the kids' bedroom to bless them, I even encouraged him. How can I live with meself, what kind of mother have I been? How could we have known he would follow her to the hospital?'

It was the same question every day. She knew the reassuring answer off by heart.

'The very best, queen, the very best,' Tommy would reply, swallowing down his resentment of Maura's unquestioning acceptance of a priest he had never much liked.

The image of a gallows and a swinging noose burnt into

his mind as he lay awake, holding Maura, and stared at the stars through the bedroom window.

Kathleen was all too well aware of the power of the Church and the impending crisis of Kitty's pregnancy. No matter who had put that baby there, it was still a sin of the highest order. The fact that it was a priest's bastard made the situation doubly worse and it would be Kitty who would be labelled the sinner.

There was no separation between the Catholic Church and the local neighbourhood. They were one and the same. The control of the community by the Church was absolute.

Maura had cried each time the subject of Kitty's pregnancy was raised. Kathleen knew she had to allow her time to come to terms with what was a living nightmare, but now she would have to put her foot down. She was finding it hard to believe that Maura was unaware of the danger Kitty's condition presented to them all.

'If we don't act quickly,' said Kathleen to Alice as she took her coat down from the hook on the back of the kitchen door, 'the hounds of hell will be chasing after us and I am not about to allow that to happen when we have other options.'

She fastened a headscarf over her curlers and held Joseph, whilst Alice reached for her own coat. Alice was a Protestant. The power and the ways of the Catholic Church were all a mystery to Alice, but she had learnt enough over the last few years to know that you didn't argue with Nana Kathleen.

Sister Evangelista and her sisters of the Sacred Heart convent ran the school and sustained the children with messages of faith, obedience, guilt and fear.

Whilst the children were in school praying, each mother on the four streets attended mass at St Mary's every single day, some twice, morning and evening. The hold of the Church and its grip on the community were unbreakable. A forgiving exterior hid a steadfast dogma. There was no escape.

Kathleen was relieved to find Maura alone in the kitchen with her latest baby and she appeared to be happy to see them both.

'Oh, thank God it is ye two. I have told everyone I feel unwell, to try and stop the knocking on. I swear to God I am terrified of being in the company of the others and blurting out something that shouldn't be said. My nerves are in pieces, Kathleen.'

Maura didn't need to tell Kathleen that; she could see it for herself. She walked over and took the baby from Maura.

'Is she fed?' she asked, lifting the baby up to her face and blowing a raspberry at the same time.

'Aye, she is,' Maura replied, 'and Kitty is in bed feeling like death.'

Kathleen shifted the baby onto one arm and, with her free hand, picked up the baby's shawl from the top of her sleeping box. Expertly wrapping it around her, she took her outside to the pram in the yard. Moving Joseph over a little, she laid the baby next to him and then covered them both with the blanket.

'Alice, love, take them both for a walk to the shops and give me a while with Maura, will ye now?' she said.

Alice nodded. 'Of course I will. How long shall I be?'

'Give me half an hour and bring me back a packet of five Woodbines. I think we may all need one soon.'

As Alice passed through the back gate with the pram, Kathleen looked in through Maura's window and saw her wiping her eyes with a handkerchief.

Holy Mary, there is more to come. How is she going to cope? thought Kathleen as she closed the gate behind Alice and moved back indoors to Maura.

When Maura was sitting down with a cup of tea, Kathleen began. It wasn't often the Doherty house was quiet and Kathleen had to seize her moment.

'Listen, Maura, Kitty's abuse at the hands of a man of God will present us all with a terrible threat, so it will.'

Kathleen looked at Maura as she spoke, leaning forward so that she could lower her voice. Even with just the two of them in the room, Kathleen still felt the need to whisper.

'Kitty's pregnancy will lay bare Father James's hypocrisy, Maura. It will reveal the truth, that our priest was an impostor, a despicable human being, not a man of God. But who will listen, Maura? Imagine if it weren't Kitty, but Mrs Keating's daughter. What would happen? Who would ye and Tommy have thought was to blame? Your precious Father James? Or the Keating girl? Would anyone talk to the Keatings again? And what would the Church do and the nuns? Would they support her, or do ye think the Keating girl would be labelled a liar and a whore overnight? Would the Keatings even stand by her or would they throw her out? And by God, Maura, here's the worst of it. When Kitty's belly starts to show weeks after the priest was murdered, Kitty becomes a liability. She becomes a motive. Do ye understand me? Kitty's belly will point the finger at you and Tommy. Do you see what that means?'

Maura hadn't said a word. She sat at the table looking at her hands, then began to sob.

'My poor Kitty, she doesn't stand a chance, does she? What in God's name can we do?'

'Maura, when that child's belly starts to show, people around here are going to put two and two together. That's not a baby, it's a motive, and we have to get Kitty out of the way before anyone guesses.'

'Oh my God,' said Maura as she sank back into the chair. 'Oh, Holy Mother, of course it is, I had not realized that.'

Kathleen now put her own arms round Maura's shoulders.

'Aye, two events of such an extraordinary nature would have to be linked, Maura. Once Kitty starts to show, the police will be round here in a flash. We have to get her away, and for now, something is pulling me back home to Ireland. I must leave and take her with me.'

'We cannot put the shame on either of our families in Ireland, Kathleen, are ye mad? They would be scorned and become outcasts themselves. No one would speak to them. We cannot do that.'

'I know, but there has to be somewhere for the poor child to go and, God knows, no one round here must know what is going on. I have to think, Maura, and I cannot do it here. That kid needs a rest, she looks so sick. I'm taking her with me and I'm going to take Nellie, too. Make it look like a grand little holiday now, in the middle of all the upset and all that. What could be more natural, with us all distraught by the priest's death? It is just the sort of thing a nana with a nice farmhouse and family in Ireland would think of doing, especially as I won a handsome amount on the bingo last week.'

Maura smiled for the first time in days.

Kathleen was a legend down at the bingo; she won more often than all the women on the four streets put together.

'Before I take her, Maura, we need to tell Kitty she is pregnant. And we will do that as soon as Nellie gets home from school. She hasn't got a clue. Best to tell them both at the same time.'

Maura nodded. She could not trust herself to speak. Both women turned their heads to look at the flames flickering around the coke cinders in the grate and became lost in their own thoughts. Upstairs, Kitty rolled over in her bed, exhausted and sickly, deep in her second sleep.

Kathleen mused that if it was this difficult reasoning with Maura, how could they even begin to explain it to Kitty?

Kathleen felt a huge sense of responsibility. She was in it up to her neck and it appeared to her that she was the only person who had a plan to save Tommy and Jerry from the hangman's noose.

She had discovered the priest in Kitty's bedroom, about to carry out his wicked deed, and had smashed him over the head with the poker. She hadn't killed him, but she felt as though she had.

'I hated that evil man with his vain and pompous hat and cape from the day I arrived on the four streets. He made the hairs on the back of me neck stand up on end, so he did.'

She had said the same thing to Jerry, every day since the morning Father James had been found as dead as the corpse on whose grave he had been discovered.

She should have known. Why had she not acted on her instincts?

He had been in and out of every house on the four streets that had daughters. It was staring them straight in the face.

Every night since, when she gave Jerry his tea and Nellie was in bed, she vented her spleen.

'Why had not one of us ever noticed that he never called on the Shevlins, with a house full of boys, eh? They're so holy, Maisie Shevlin's knees are rheumatic with the praying she does, and yet it never occurred to us. We never even questioned why the filthy priest did not once knock upon their door or why his vile shadow never darkened their doorstep. Jesus, we must all be bloody eejits.'

Kathleen had barely stopped punishing herself since that fateful night.

'Shush, Mammy, what's done is done now. He'll not be harming any other child,' said Jerry, trying to calm his mother down.

Jerry, who gave the same reply each time, wondered when his mother would stop beating herself up.

'Mammy, how were ye to know? How could ye possibly have known what he was up to? No one knew, not even Maura and Tommy, and he was at it under their very noses in their own home. Shush now or ye will make ye'self ill.'

Aye, but ye don't know all the facts, thought Kathleen as she placed his steaming bacon ribs and cabbage on the table in front of him. When ye do know that Kitty is pregnant, ye will be feeling as bad as I do. Kathleen would not be pacified.

'When I saw him coming out of Brigid and Sean's house, a home full of little red-headed daughters, I should have known. The dirty bastard.'

Kathleen probably should have known because she had the gift. A gift that was aided and abetted by the Granada TV rentals man, and his comings and goings in and out of every house: that was the truth of it. Nevertheless, she did have the gift of prophesy, manifest via reading the tea leaves.

Most of the women on the four streets visited Kathleen on Friday mornings to have their teacups read. Kathleen knew things. She could tell the women what their future held. She knew when most women on the street were pregnant before they did themselves. And yet the biggest danger of all had slipped past her. She had suspected Father James was a bad man, but she had kept her own counsel.

She was convinced she had let them all down and none had been more let down than little Kitty, who would have to be told the worst news of her life.

Early that morning, unable to sleep, Kathleen had tiptoed down into the kitchen to put the kettle on what was left of the heat in the range embers, before stoking up the fire. She looked up at the statue of the Holy Mother on the shelf above. Kathleen often talked to the figurine. They were both mothers. She thought, as she often did, of Bernadette, the woman who had loved the home Kathleen cared for.

Beloved Bernadette. Still thought of and missed every day.

Kathleen set the kettle down on the black range and, with her hand still gripping the handle, bent her head in prayer.

'Bernadette, ye will be in heaven, queen, and so, please God, don't ye mind if I pray to ye both. Help us today with little Maura and Kitty. I know that man wasn't a man of God, he was a man of the devil, deceiving us all. Don't let him win. Holy Mother, the mother of all innocence, be with us today, for the child's sake.'

It seemed fitting to Kathleen, halfway through, that it should be the Holy Mother she prayed to. Having had an unusual pregnancy herself, she might understand.

As Kathleen and Maura drank their tea and stared at the fire, each lost in their own thoughts, the back door flew open and Alice, breaking the silence, rushed in. Rushing was a new experience to Alice. Kathleen was worried that she was rushing a bit too much.

Alice, her difficult daughter-in-law, who had tricked her son, Jerry, into marriage following the death of his wife, Bernadette, had come on in leaps and bounds over the last few years.

Alice had been the reason Kathleen had left the family farm in the West of Ireland to live with Jerry and Nellie in Nelson Street, to save them from the horrors of living with a woman who was obviously, as a result of her own abnormal upbringing, mentally unwell.

Alice, who had been the housekeeper at the Grand hotel until she had married Jerry, had known their Bernadette. When Bernadette had first arrived in Liverpool, she had been a chambermaid at the hotel. That was how Alice came to set her cap at Jerry. As soon as she heard of Bernadette's death, she had her feet under the table before any other God-fearing Irish lass stood a chance.

Alice was now almost entirely weaned off the Valium tablets and each day she felt more alive.

She knew that Jerry and Kathleen, and even Nellie, were watching her closely, but she would never slip back to the dark years. Nana Kathleen had rescued her. It had taken years of patience, but she had got there. And then Alice had rescued herself. Which had felt even better.

'They are both asleep in the pram and I have got the Woodbines. Shall I make a fresh mash of tea, or shall I reuse them tea leaves again?' Alice trilled, without pausing for breath.

Kathleen didn't know why, but today Alice's voice grated.

Alice had proved her worth in recent weeks. She had dispatched the police from their door with a flea in their ears and provided an alibi for Jerry when the police had taken him away for questioning. As an innocent man at the scene of the crime, doing nothing more than trying to protect Tommy from himself, Jerry had needed one.

Kathleen rose from the chair to help Alice make the tea.

The normally happy, laughing, vivacious Maura didn't move her vacant gaze from the fire.

'I've just seen the police on the street,' said Alice cheerfully.

Now Maura stirred. Both she and Kathleen looked at Alice, neither speaking, both waiting for her to continue.

'It looked like Molly Barrett was inviting them into her house. The poor woman must be feeling lonely if she wants a cuppa with the coppers.'

It seemed to Nellie that she was the sick-duty child today because she was now on her second journey out with an ailing pupil.

This time it was little Billy from the Anchor pub. He was so poorly he wasn't fit to walk and Nellie squatted down so that Miss Devlin could lift him onto her back, then she carried him in a piggyback all the way to the pub.

Billy's da was grateful. 'Come and have a glass of sarsaparilla before ye walk back to school. Our lad is heavy, so he is.'

'I'd love one, thanks very much,' said Nellie.

She liked drinking sarsaparilla. Sometimes, when the pop man brought it round with his horse and cart after church on Sundays, her da would buy a bottle to have with their Sunday lunch. It was sweet and black and made her feel grown up, as if she was drinking a glass of Nana Kathleen's Guinness.

Gratefully drinking the whole glass full almost at once, Nellie handed it back empty with a polite thank-you and made her way down the pub steps to run back to school.

Just as she turned the corner at the top of the road, she saw

Alice, standing outside the shop with the pram, in what looked like a deep conversation with Sean, Brigid's boxer husband. The only man Nana Kathleen had said was nearly as good-looking as Nellie's da, Jerry.

Alice threw back her head and laughed, as Sean bent down to look inside the pram.

As Nellie watched, Alice placed her hand on his arm, chatting all the while.

The women on the four streets never really talked to the men. They talked to one another.

Men talked about football and sex.

Women talked about the other women on the four streets and sex.

Nellie didn't know this. She knew only that the warm feeling of happiness that had arrived with the sarsaparilla evaporated, faster than the bubbles that had danced on her nose as she drank.

Chapter Four

ALICE WAS A new woman, so much so that she was often flooded with feelings of exhilaration, partly due to her growing love for her baby boy, Joseph. The baby she had never wanted.

These days, Alice laughed out loud.

When Jerry commented upon it, she announced proudly, 'I have opinions now and everything.'

Jerry laughed and said to Kathleen, 'Jesus, Mary and Joseph, between you and Dr Cole, you have worked a miracle, Mammy.' As he spoke, he glanced at the unopened bottle of Valium tablets, standing on the press.

'It's like Alice has broken free and now we have no idea where she will end up. Each day I wake up to a bolder Alice.'

Kathleen wasn't as impressed as Jerry by Alice's transformation.

It had all been very gradual and welcome to begin with, but lately Alice was presenting Kathleen with cause for concern. She had moved from moody to giddy in no time at all. Sometimes, it appeared as though Alice couldn't sit still, or stop talking.

Alice and Kathleen were now both returned from Maura's to their own house, waiting for Nellie to arrive home from school, when they would pop back over to Maura's and break the news to Kitty.

'I have given the floor a mop and washed the dust off the sills,' Alice announced as she bustled out through the door to Kathleen who was now in the yard.

'Aye, well, 'tis just a novelty now. I'll enjoy it while it lasts,' said Kathleen, but she had laughed, despite herself. They both had. And Kathleen counted their blessings. As little as a year ago, no one would have imagined that Alice could laugh.

Kathleen turned Joseph's nappies in the copper boiler, using the long wooden paddle.

Electric-mangle washing machines and twin tubs were all the rage now, but in a two-up, two-down there was nowhere to put one. It mattered not a jot to Kathleen. She thought the copper boiler and the big mangle, kept in the outhouse, did a grand job anyway. It was her routine and Kathleen didn't like change.

As Nellie came through the gate from school, Kathleen wiped her hands on her apron and announced, 'Right, we're off, so we are, Nellie, no need to step on Alice's clean floor,' and within minutes, with Joseph once more tucked up in his pram, they were on their way back across the road.

Molly Barrett twitched her net curtains and craned her neck to take a clearer view of the top of the entry.

She had just made a cuppa for Annie and given her chapter and verse on her conversation with the two police officers. Both had said that her scones were absolutely delicious. She had given them an extra one each for later.

'Well, what would ye know,' she said to Annie, 'they are off again. Now tell me there's not something bloody funny going on with that lot. They were all over at the Dohertys' not hours since.'

Annie O'Prey jumped up to look through the nets herself.

Most families on the four streets lived in the back of the house and used the back entry and gates. Not Annie and Molly. They both preferred the front. They liked to see what was happening and just who was visiting who, and this was by far the best place to do it. Molly had placed a folded-down dining table in front of the net curtain, with an aspidistra pot plant in the middle and a chair on either side providing an excellent and unhindered view of who came and went. This was where they both had a cup of tea whilst they did an hour's knitting, most afternoons. On fine days, they took the chairs outdoors and sat on the pavement underneath the window.

'Oh, my giddy aunt,' exclaimed Annie, putting her hand over her mouth in shock as she watched Alice pushing the pram, with Kathleen and Nellie behind, crossing into the entry again. 'Do you think they killed the father, Molly?'

'What? Kathleen? No, you silly cow. How could she do that? It would have taken more than a handbag or a hairpin to take his bloody langer off. No, I don't think she killed him, but there is something very suspicious about the comings and goings at number nineteen and that's a fact.'

'Did you say that to the policeman when he was here?' Annie's voice was loaded with suspicion.

'I might have done,' said Molly in a tone that invited no further questions.

Both women picked up their knitting. There was nothing more to see, but the fact that Molly Barrett's cat had played a part in detecting the murder imbued in her an inflated sense of responsibility. Molly, via her cat, was now involved. She had told the police she would tell absolutely no one, not even Annie, of the fact that she was now officially helping them with their enquiries and had promised to maintain a vigilant watch on the comings and goings across the road.

*

As Kathleen, Alice and Nellie walked in through Maura's back door, the kettle began to whistle on the range. Maura jumped up to fill a large metal teapot that she placed on the table, along with the milk jug and the cups and saucers. She had been dreading this moment, but she knew there was no alternative. Kitty had to be told.

Kathleen was glad to be getting on with what they had to do. She couldn't explain it with any degree of meaning to any of them but she was weighed down with an overwhelming sense of urgency. It was her gift, helping her, and she knew she had to move fast. The appearance of Bernadette in her dream last night, doing exactly what she had done on the night of the murder – urging Kathleen along, pushing her, faster – had not left her thoughts throughout the day.

As they drank their tea and sat round the table chatting, Nellie looked out of the window over the kitchen sink, steamed up from the boiling kettle.

There she was. Nellie knew she was somewhere, she could sense it. She could see her outside, standing in the yard, looking in. Nellie knew it was her mother, Bernadette. She had seen her often since she was a child and the visions didn't scare her. She never told Kathleen or Alice.

She felt Bernadette's love so strongly that she could have scooped it up in her arms and held on to it.

Bernadette never missed her birthday. Nellie would enter her bedroom and be overcome by a heady smell of flowers. There were no flowers anywhere in the house. None even within a mile of the four streets. Nellie knew it was her mother, the woman no one ever talked about, not even her da.

Nellie didn't always see Bernadette. Sometimes she could only feel her. On the night Nellie had been discharged from hospital following the accident when she and Kitty had been knocked down, she had been curled up on her da's knee, reading the paper with him in front of the fire, when Bernadette came, or at least the feeling did.

As she arrived, her presence washed over them, gradually at first and then wrapped around them both. As Nellie rested her head on her da's chest, she looked at Jerry and they smiled. They hugged one another tightly and watched the flames leaping in the fire, not making a sound nor moving a muscle, not wanting to scare Bernadette away. And then she left slowly, in gentle waves, just as she had arrived, until she was with them no more.

Jerry softly kissed the top of Nellie's head and she felt his hot tears drip through her hair onto her scalp.

Nellie knew her da still missed Bernadette and that, when she joined them in these special moments, it was painful for him, even though she had died on the day Nellie was born.

Nellie knew that if she looked away from the kitchen window now, Bernadette would disappear in a flash. Her eyes began to water – she was scared to blink.

'What are ye gawping at, miss?' said Nana Kathleen, swivelling round on her chair to see what it was that Nellie was staring at.

She blinked. Bernadette left, leaving Nellie alone again.

Maura, timorously, began to speak.

'Kitty, we have a problem, child, and it is something we need to talk about and sort out before we tell Daddy. He will be distraught when I tell him the news and so we must be well prepared, so we must.'

Maura began to cry. She was never going to get through this.

Her Kitty. Maura had dreamt of her daughter taking the veil. Kitty, who was like another mother in the house, so good was she with all the little ones. With two sets of twin boys, Maura found life hard and Kitty had eased her burden by half.

But Maura wasn't selfish. She didn't want to keep Kitty to herself. She wanted to share her with God and thereby elevate the status of the Doherty household above that of her neighbours. Maura craved status; in fact she craved anything that would reward the family for her endeavours. She longed to be looked up to and, indeed, many a less holy neighbour already did look up to Maura. If there was a problem on the streets it was Maura or Nana Kathleen they went to. But that wasn't enough. Maura wanted one of the Doherty clan to do something, to be someone. She yearned for her household to be set above and apart from the others. What could achieve this more than having a child become a nun or a priest?

She had prayed about sharing her children with God. About giving God back some of the issue with which she and Tommy had been blessed.

Kitty had been shared with God.

Just not in the way Maura had prayed for.

Maura knew that what she now struggled to say to Kitty flew in the face of every motherly instinct. Earlier in the day she had questioned Kathleen.

'Once I have spoken those words, there will be no going back, Kathleen. Are we sure?'

'Aye, Maura, we are sure, queen. I wish to God we weren't

and I have prayed that every day you would run up this entry to tell me Kitty was started, but you haven't. There is no use us putting it off any longer or denying it: the child is with child, God help us, so she is.'

Now that they were here and the time had come, Maura lacked the strength to speak. Her mouth felt as though it were stuffed full of wool and the words she had rehearsed so well were lodged somewhere deep in her throat. The tears began to pour uncontrollably down her cheeks.

Everyone round the table stared at her expectantly, but she couldn't make out their alarmed expressions as their faces swam in a blurred haze through her tears.

Maura was weak. She was lost. Events had knocked the stuffing right out of her and she was as close to done for as it was possible to be.

Nana Kathleen decided it was time to take over. Twenty years older than Maura, Kathleen had also been crushed by events but it was not her daughter who was about to suffer. They were her closest friends facing a problem to which there was almost no answer.

Nellie sensed something utterly catastrophic was about to take place.

Had they all stopped breathing? They had. They had.

Fear gradually wrapped its icy tendrils around Nellie's heart and slithered down into the pit of her stomach. Under the table, she slipped a hand across and met Kitty's, searching for her own.

For a heartbeat of a moment, a drumroll of domesticity filled the silent kitchen.

Maura's gentle sniffling into her hankie.

The click of Alice's knitting needles.

The tick-tock from the clock and the slow, repetitive drip

from the tap pinging onto an enamel bowl in the sink.

As the coal burnt in the fireplace, it hissed and spat in accompaniment to the slow bubbling simmer of a pan of broth, warming on the range.

Kitty looked at Nana Kathleen and knew that whatever she was about to say had something to do with the night the priest had raped her in her hospital bed. Nothing had been the same since. Then, after years of abusing her, he had elevated his depravity to a new level and was about to do it again in her own bedroom when all were at the Irish centre and dancing at a wedding. But Nana Kathleen had caught him and then the priest was found murdered. He had never bothered her again.

Kitty had been stunned by the reaction of her da. She thought he was going mad with the rage. Tommy, normally mild-mannered and gentle and who loved them all to distraction, had been torn apart by the knowledge that the priest had been helping himself to his precious daughter, in his own house.

The man they had trusted above all others – the Holy Father of the community, whom everyone revered as though he were God himself – had abused their trust. And Tommy, whose only job was to protect and provide for his family, had let down his first-born and closest in a way he could never have imagined, not in his very worst nightmares.

Just when Kitty had thought the horrors of the past were about to fade, she had now begun to throw up every morning and most of the day.

Kitty really couldn't remember normal any more.

Kathleen found the words hard. Kitty was still only fourteen but she looked just twelve and, sure, wasn't that the reason

Kitty and Nellie got on so well? Kitty was still an innocent little child, hesitant to embrace her teenage years, while Nellie, having faced adversity at such a young age, was older and wiser than most.

'Kitty, my lovely one,' said Kathleen in a soft voice.

She rubbed the top of Kitty's hand, a thin, pale hand of innocence, held in a plump, warm hand of wisdom.

Kathleen raised her gaze and looked her straight in the eye.

She wanted Kitty to fully understand each and every word she was about to say. There was no room for ambiguity once it was spoken out loud.

All eyes rested on Nana Kathleen.

Kitty waited. Mouth open. Licked dry lips. Heart beating.

Tense expectancy cast a spell and drew them in closer.

'Kitty, we have to tell ye important news, my darlin'. Ye need to know now. We cannot keep this in the dark any longer. Yer mammy and I, we are very sure ye is having a babby.'

She held Kitty's hand more tightly.

'Ye is pregnant with the priest's child and we have to decide what we are going to do about it.'

All eyes were on Kitty and silently they witnessed the moment when her childhood died.

'No,' she screamed loudly, as she dropped Kathleen's and Nellie's hands, pushing the chair away and staggering backwards towards the range – desperately needing to put as much space as she possibly could between herself and what Kathleen had said.

Space, so that the words would not touch her, but would fall to the floor and shatter before they reached her. Space, to protect and save her.

But the words had been spoken. They were crawling all

over her, already inside her, screaming in her head, piercing her heart.

It was too late. No escape. She had become what the words had made her.

'A baby? Oh God, Mammy, no, not me. I can't!' She looked to Maura with her hand outstretched.

And then they all died a little as Kitty howled with both her hands clutching at her abdomen as though testing to see if Kathleen were telling the truth.

Everyone in the room began to cry, even Alice.

But Kitty knew. As the words slowly filtered deeper and settled into place, she knew. She had seen Maura and other women on the street in the same situation often enough. Her mind was recoiling. Her heart sank and the fight, which had quickly flared up in her, took its leave and left.

It was true. Really, she already knew.

Within seconds, Maura was at her side, shaken out of her stupor by Kitty's distress. Her child needed her.

Kitty made a sound like that of an animal in pain as they stood and rocked together, Maura absorbing Kitty's agony, holding her upright.

Kitty, in her torment, provided Maura with a reason not to fall apart.

Nellie hadn't moved from her chair and had begun to cry quietly to herself, stunned by the news and shedding her own tears for the loss of Kitty's childhood.

Alice had jumped up and was making another pot of tea while Kathleen began washing the pots in the sink. Ordinary tasks, ushering normality back into the room.

Kathleen could hear Joseph stirring in the large box Maura used as a baby basket. Kitty's crying had woken him. Time to put things back on an even keel, she thought, as she watched

Alice pick him up to change his nappy. Now, as she dried the wet cups and saucers, Kathleen felt a sense of relief that Kitty now knew.

Kathleen had won at the bingo twice this month. The money had been placed straight into the bread bin with the money she was paid for reading the tea leaves at her kitchen table on a Friday morning.

She was not short of money. Joe had been a clever and hard-working farmer and they had done well, because they were careful and had saved. Now Kathleen spoke again.

'Sit down now, Kitty,' she said kindly. 'Nothing can alter the facts, but we have to find a way to deal with them.' She gestured towards a chair at the kitchen table. 'Ye may be pregnant, Kitty, but really, 'tis our problem too. We will sort it and don't ye worry about a thing. This is one for the grown-ups.'

Kitty's crying subsided and an expression of desperate gratitude flooded her face.

'Maura, pull yourself together now. It could be worse, the child isn't dying.'

Kathleen knew the worst was over. Now they had to plan.

Nellie jumped up to help her nana and put the teapot on the table. Alice had Joseph in her arms. His little face lit up at the sight of Nellie and Kitty, now sitting next to each other at the kitchen table, with Nellie's arm round Kitty's shoulders.

Alice walked over to the range to fetch Joseph's bottle, which she had placed to warm on a range shelf. She pulled up her sleeve and shook the milk onto her bare elbow to test it was the right temperature and then sat amongst them to feed him.

The atmosphere was subdued. The only noise was the

sound of Joseph sucking and the snuffles of his blocked nose. Kathleen began to talk.

'Kitty, I have an idea if ye can just hear me out. I don't think we should tell the men just yet. I don't think we should tell anyone. What we need is some time to think about how we are going to manage this. What about if I take you and Nellie away back home to Ireland to the farm for a little holiday and try to think of a plan from there? What do ye think, girls? Would ye like that? We can go when the school breaks up for the holiday in a couple of weeks.'

Amazingly, both the girls smiled. Even Kitty. The excitement of a holiday together had for a few seconds wiped out the shock of Kitty's pregnancy.

Kitty had never had a holiday. It would be her first.

'Let's run upstairs now,' whispered Nellie to Kitty. Nellie had visited the farm many times. She wanted to share every detail with Kitty, in private.

'Holy Mother, Kathleen, would ye look at them smiling,' said Maura. 'It's a fairground ride of emotions all right.'

Alice began to pack up the pram. She had her own ideas about what to do.

'Have ye thought of an abortion?' she whispered to Maura and Kathleen, so that the girls upstairs didn't hear. 'You can get one easily. The chambermaids at the Grand used to go to a woman on Upper Parliament Street.'

No sooner had the words fallen from her lips than Alice felt bad. When first pregnant with Joseph, she had visited the same woman, though she had baulked at the offer of surgery. She had witnessed some of the chambermaids return to work in agony and be laid up for days. One girl had been taken into the Northern hospital after having an abortion and had never been seen again. Alice had no idea what had happened to her, but she knew she had been very ill. That was the old Alice.

The Alice who couldn't have cared less.

Alice, shamefully, had taken various concoctions and potions. But to no avail. Joseph was determined to make his entrance and look at him now. None of them could remember life before he had arrived.

However, this was different. Kitty was a child, and Kathleen was right. Her growing belly was a danger to them all.

Maura turned pale at the mere mention of the word abortion. Maura, who had wanted her daughter to become a nun, was now having to discuss whether or not Kitty should commit the biggest mortal sin imaginable, that of taking a life.

A second life.

A second murder.

My God, what and who had they become?

'Do ye think I want two murderers in the family, Alice? Do ye not think one is enough?' she hissed back coldly. The old animosity between Alice and Maura was never far from the surface.

Neither of them could quite forget the closeness there had been between Maura and Bernadette.

'I'm sorry,' whispered Alice. 'It just seemed like a good idea to me. And a quick solution too.'

'Aye, well, I think not. It only seems a good idea to you, Alice, because ye don't have the faith. No abortionist is sticking a dirty coat-hanger up my daughter. That's the path to three lives lost.'

Maura wanted to stop this loose talk of an abortion as quickly as possible and shouted up the stairs for Kitty to come down.

Alice looked to Kathleen, who put her finger to her lips.

The recovery of Alice had been a welcome one, but Kathleen could see that, with each day, her new boldness brought a fresh challenge.

'The offer of a holiday for Kitty is a kind one, Kathleen,' said Maura, walking back to the table, 'and one I will accept gratefully.'

Maura turned to Alice, guilty for her harsh tone a few seconds ago, when she knew how much Alice had done to help them. Alice had done her bit. She was on their side.

'Some way, we will sort this out and, Alice, I know ye think I am wrong, but I can tell ye now, there will be no meat for anyone in this house this week. I'm off to buy some Epsom salts and a bottle of gin. I'll be trying a few methods of me own.'

Alice smiled. She couldn't work out why that would be acceptable, but her suggestion of an abortionist wouldn't. She had heard that all the girls in Liverpool were doing it.

Kathleen felt lighter. Despite the reason why, the thought of returning home to Ireland had cheered her. The school holidays couldn't arrive soon enough, so that she could get on that ferry to Dublin. It wouldn't have been possible a couple of years ago to leave a baby of Joseph's age in Alice's care.

So much had changed.

There was also another dimension to the holiday. While they were away it would be the first time Jerry, Alice and the baby had been alone in the house together. Maybe that wasn't such a bad thing.

Kathleen put on her coat to head home. She would call in at the Anchor pub to use the phone and ring the pub at the back of the butcher's in Bangornevin. Days ago she had already let them know they would be coming home. Kathleen had known all along that it was the only thing they could do. She just had to convince everyone else.

They had made the decision to return to Ireland, she felt they had no time to lose and that feeling was exhausting her.

'I know the answers will come to me in me own kitchen,' she said to Alice. 'I'll get everything sorted from there. Just a few weeks to wait.'

Nellie and Kitty were now standing next to Alice, stroking baby Joseph's feet whilst he bounced up and down on Alice's hip. Nellie was now comfortable in Alice's company. A miracle, considering that, only a few years ago, Nellie had been terrified of her.

Simon and Howard had finished knocking on all the doors in the four streets and had retired to the car. They both lit a cigarette whilst they drank tea from the thermos flask provided by Howard's landlady.

'So,' said Howard, 'the sister's magnificent revelation is that the father spent a lot of time in number nineteen and now the eyes and ears of the world, Molly Barrett, tells us Maura Doherty should be knocked out with grief, but she isn't.'

'Fantastic, solid, wonderful leads. The super will be so pleased,' Simon replied in a voice dripping with sarcasm.

'They may not be strong leads, Simon, they may even be weak, but they both come from different people and both point to the same house. Something is better than nothing and, anyway, was it just me, or do you think the sister was hiding something?'

'Bloody hell, was she?' Simon replied. 'She looked like a scared rabbit. Didn't look me in the eye once, and her hand was shaking, did you notice that?'

'I did. Something or someone had taken the wind right out

of her sails in between her calling us at the station and our arrival at the convent.'

Howard wound down the window of the panda car and shook the remaining contents of his cup out into the gutter, then screwed it back onto the top of the flask.

'Come on then,' he said to Simon, who was in the process of rolling up a cigarette, 'let's knock on number nineteen and give that tree a good shake.'

Alice covered Joseph with his blanket just as the Doherty kids burst in through the back door, looking for their tea. Maura's second daughter, Angela, was the first in and began to strop about the fact that Kitty had had yet another day off school. This was nothing new. Angela found a new subject to strop about at least once a day.

'I have had to sit in that classroom with Sister Theresa all day long,' Angela yelled, pointing at Kitty, and they all stopped dead as they heard a knock on the front door.

A loud knock. Three long, fierce bangs on the front door. They sent a shiver of fear like a trickle of iced water straight down Maura's spine.

Alice had heard the knock before. She knew exactly who it was.

Even the twins, in the midst of helping themselves to a plate of biscuits, were frozen in mid-raid and looked towards their mother.

The three knocks came again a second time and made each one of them flinch.

As deafening and as threatening as a death knell.

Chapter Five

STANLEY WHEELED THE empty oxygen cylinder into place, on the end of a long line of huge spent cylinders waiting for the truck to arrive with full replacements.

He looked across from the hospital stores entrance to the large door of the kitchens on the other side of the yard to see if Austin was about to emerge. He would have to hurry. Stanley wanted a ciggie and they couldn't have one here without blowing themselves up.

Stanley had been a wreck since he had read the news of the priest's murder. He had hardly slept since. His mother had commented over breakfast that morning that he was looking sickly.

'They work you too hard at that hospital. Look at the state of youse. Mind you, I always say it must be harder working with them sick kids. Why don't you see if you can transfer to the Northern hospital or somewhere where it's adults, like, rather than them poorly littl'uns?'

Stanley stared at his mother. What would happen to her if she ever knew the truth?

The thought churned his stomach as he pushed away his plate of bacon and eggs.

'I've just got a bug, Mam, I'm OK,' he said with a hint of irritation.

Last night Stanley had walked into the kitchen to find his mother standing in front of the television with a tea towel in her hand, staring at the screen.

'I'm just plating up yer dinner, lad,' she said, without even turning round to look at him. 'They've got no one for this murder of the priest, yer know. Bloody shocking it is. I reckon there's more going on in there than they are telling us.' She nodded at the television, as though the investigation were taking place somewhere inside.

Stanley looked at his place set at the table and the folded-up copy of the *Liverpool Echo*, which his mam left for him to read as he ate.

The headlines glared at him. 'POLICE SHOCKED BY EXTENT OF INJURIES IN PRIEST MURDER AND APPEAL FOR WITNESSES TO COME FORWARD.'

The now-familiar hand of fear caressed his neck and shoulders as he shivered slightly and took his seat. It slithered down his spine and lay heavily on his chest, pressing down hard, making him work to draw breath.

Not again, he thought, as his face became hot and flushed, and pins and needles ran down his arms, but this time he was spared. His breathing slowed and he didn't pass out. His mother had walked in and, with one eye still on the TV, placed his supper in front of him. She had noticed nothing.

Eventually, Austin ran across the yard, the tan-brown tails of his porter's coat flapping in the wind. His round, dark-framed glasses were as opaque and as greasy as his grey Brylcreemed hair, which was slicked back and hadn't been washed for weeks.

Not for the first time, Stanley wondered how Austin could see where he was going.

'Come on, there's no one in the porters' lodge now,' said Austin, 'let's have a brew.'

Stanley tipped up the sack trolley, shuffled the next cylinder into place and ran across the yard into the wooden lodge with Austin, who placed the kettle on top of the electric ring.

'Have you seen last night's *Echo*?'

'I have,' said Austin.

Stanley stared at his back. Was the man mad? How could he be so calm? Did he not realize the danger they were in?

'What are you being so fucking calm about, eh?'

Stanley had almost shouted at Austin, who now turned round with a look of anger.

'I'm not fucking calm, I'm fucking working hard to make sure no one knows I am terrified of looking up and seeing the coppers walk in through the door, which is more than you are doing. All you need is a fucking sign on your head saying kiddie fiddler, priest's friend, police, please arrest me.'

'Have you collected the photographs?' Stanley asked as he handed Austin a mug of Bovril.

'Yes, of course I have. Did you want me to leave them sitting there, you stupid twat?'

Austin put his hand into his top pocket and handed Stanley a white envelope with his share of pictures inside. Tailored to his taste.

'Arthur is in a bit of a state. Wants us to see him after work tonight. I don't reckon that is a good idea. We need to disperse. It is only a matter of time before they get to us. We can sit here and deny everything or do a runner. I am going to stay put. I'm too old to run.'

How could Stanley run? Austin thought to himself. It would kill his old mam.

'I will stay put too,' Stanley croaked. He took a sip of the steaming-hot Bovril, which burnt his insides as it went down.

'I think Arthur is taking off tomorrow. Locking up the flat and visiting his sister in Cornwall. He will stay away until everything dies down. The PO Box is registered to him. They have nothing on me or on you. We will be all right, Stan.'

Stanley took another sip and then, taking a deep breath, looked up at Austin. He almost cried with relief. He had been the one who had let the priest into the children's ward at night, but only the three of them – the priest, Austin and himself – knew that and now one of them was dead.

'Do you really think so?'

'I do. They have nothing that can lead to us and we didn't bloody kill the priest, so stop acting as though we did, soft lad.'

Stanley felt much better as he opened the envelope and began to look at his pictures.

'There's a new little girl arrived on Ward Four this morning,' said Stanley to Austin. 'She's really lovely.'

Austin smiled. 'Is there now? Well, me and me Kodak Brownie need to visit Ward Four today, to check the oxygen cylinders, eh, lad?'

Chapter Six

TOMMY WALKED BACK up the steps from the dock to Nelson Street with a lighter heart than he had for days. The men were often louder on the way up than they were on the way down.

Whilst the others chatted about football, Tommy made plans in his head for the weekend.

Since the dark night, he had been planning non-stop.

'Got to keep busy,' Tommy had said to Maura. He had to ensure his brain was occupied, holding at bay the images he would rather not see, suppressing them somewhere in the back of his mind.

He had already taken the boys to the baths in Bootle. They were the only boys on the four streets ever to have tasted chlorine.

Little Paddy was sad that his best friend Harry was deserting him. 'Learn to swim?' he said to Harry. 'Why would I want to do that? I'm never going to need to swim. Are ye not playing footie on the green, then?'

Harry would much have preferred playing footie on the green. Everyone at home had been behaving in a very strange way and this thing Tommy was doing, taking them to the swimming baths and then to the shore for a walk afterwards, was odd behaviour indeed.

It was no different for the girls. Maura had taken them to the jumble sale at Maghull church, Maura's own secret shopping haunt. She had cannily obtained, for nothing more than a shilling, the entire contents of a new brown-leather holdall, including the holdall itself, which the kindly stallholder threw in for free to pack the clothes in, so that they could carry them home on the pram.

The jumble sale was at a Protestant church, but Maura didn't care.

'I like going to the Proddy church, the women in there don't look down their noses at ye like the women in the pawnshop do. They can be very superior indeed and who knows what for? I have no need to work in a shop.'

Maura had spent years hiding from the other women, and from Father James, the fact that she went to the Proddy church sale in Maghull.

Now that the priest was dead, she no longer cared a jot.

Besides, Maghull was a posh area and some of the clothes in the jumble sale were very decent. Maura was particularly pleased with the coat she had bought for Kitty, which was cream with large wooden buttons and a wide belt around the hips. It looked almost brand new. Maura thought it would do for Kitty later on, too, although she wouldn't mention this to her just yet.

Kitty also had two skirts, a pair of brown boots that were exactly her size and fitted well, which Maura had promised she wouldn't have to share with anyone else, two jumpers and the coat. It was a couple of sizes too big, but Kitty didn't care.

'I will keep this all me life, Mammy,' said Kitty, as she tried it on. ''Tis is the grandest coat I have ever seen, it is so gorgeous.' Kitty stroked the coat across the front and up and down the arms.

Maura laughed.

Angela had a fresh pair of leather boots in shiny leather that was all the rage. The heels and the soles were worn down, but Maura knew the boots would be as good as new for a trip down the cobbler's. They were slightly too large, too, but Angela could put on a second pair of socks.

'And, sure, won't ye grow into them in five minutes now,' said Maura to hush Angela's grumbling.

After the jumble sale, Maura had taken the bus with the pram wedged onto the front platform and then walked Kitty and Angela the rest of the way into town. The twins were out with Tommy and they had no rush with time. As they alighted from the bus, Maura had what she thought was a brainwave.

'Let's make it a really special day and stop at a café for our lunch shall we?'

Neither Kitty nor Angela had ever heard the like or ever been to a café before.

'Why is Mammy acting so crazy?' Angela whispered to Kitty.

Kitty shrugged her shoulders and made no comment, causing Angela to look at her strangely.

Angela drooled as the meat and potato pies that Maura had ordered for them, with bread and butter and a large pot of tea, arrived at the table.

Whilst they were eating, Maura announced that they would be buying new underwear for Kitty.

'God almighty,' said Angela so loudly that everyone in the café turned to look at her. Kitty had taken the first mouthful of her pie at just that moment and it hit her stomach like a hot rock. The familiar feeing of nausea gripped her. She stopped eating and stared at the table in shame.

'Why is she getting all this stuff and clothes and the like, and I'm only getting a pair of boots?'

Angela had yet to be told that Kitty would be taking a holiday to Ireland with Kathleen and Nellie. Maura felt her temper snap.

'Hush now, ye cheeky article, and if ye don't, I'll make sure ye won't sit down for a week. Only a pair of boots? They are of the highest fashion and ye are damned lucky to have them. Now shut ye big ungrateful mouth.'

Then she turned towards the window. Kitty watched Maura take out her handkerchief and wipe her eyes.

Maura cried.

Maura smiled. Maura laughed. Maura cried.

No one knew these days what Maura was going to do next.

Kitty stared at Angela. They had never seen Maura so mad. Angela looked scared stiff. She didn't utter another word of complaint for the rest of the shopping trip.

Woolworth's on Church Street was bright and busy and the perfect place to buy toiletries.

As they walked in through the door, Kitty was amazed to see display after display of lipstick and hand cream, perfume and a huge variety of different soaps.

Maura bought Kitty a pale pink washbag and soap box, patterned with sprigs of white and darker pink carnations with delicate green leaves. This was almost more than Kitty could take in. She felt incredibly grown-up, having her own possessions.

Inside was a bar of lilac soap that smelt like lavender, a toothbrush, a pink facecloth, toothpaste and a tin of talcum powder.

Maura's spirits had lightened. She had become overcome with sympathy and love for her eldest daughter. She wanted to spoil her. To shower her with treats in order to cushion the blow of the knowledge she had to carry.

Maura went mad in Woolworth's and bought Kitty a small

tub of lily-of-the-valley scented hand cream and a bottle of Pears shampoo. Kitty left the store with a bag full of belongings, never before owned by anyone else. What was more, they were hers and she didn't have to share them with Angela.

Back at home, Kitty had sat on her bed and looked again and again at her fancy possessions.

When the twins and the girls arrived home from school, Kitty made them sit on the bed with the baby propped up between them, as she took everything out to show them, one gift at a time. The four boys, who could not have been more bored if they tried, began to make their own amusement.

'Look at me, oh la-di-da, I am a very posh English lady,' said Malachi, the most mischievous of the four, as he grabbed the talcum powder, opened it and shook it all over himself, filling the room with a grey cloud that smelt of peaches.

'Mammy,' screeched Kitty down the stairs, 'Mammy,' as she chased Malachi round the room to grab back her beautiful white tub of talc.

Malachi, throwing the cannister down the stairwell, took the stairs two at a time all the way down and burst into the kitchen as Maura tried to intercept him on his way to the back door.

'Malachi, would ye come here now, you little divil, while I slap yer legs, ye horrible child, ye. Leave Kitty alone, do ye hear me, now leave her alone.' Maura was screeching down the back entry as Malachi was long gone and already sprinting across the green.

'God, that lad will be the death of me,' she said to Peggy, who was in her own backyard, putting her sheets through the mangle.

None of the children knew why Kitty was being treated so and Maura couldn't explain.

*

On her return from town Maura had said to Tommy, 'I'm plain worn out, Tommy. We don't have to keep filling every minute with things to do because of what happened. We will both be exhausted and broke at this rate.'

Tommy sighed. 'But I do, queen. I do.'

Tommy couldn't rest in the house. He hadn't placed a bet on his precious horses or read the *Echo*. He couldn't concentrate long enough to read past the first few lines.

He had to keep busy.

Daisy Quinn stood at her window that night, watched the lights extinguish in number nineteen and then slipped into her own bed. It had been a long and tiring day and she was exhausted.

The bishop had arrived as promised and had brought with him all manner of activity to the Priory.

Daisy couldn't help thinking that she had never in her life heard the sister talk so much in one day nor with as much agitation as she now did. She had always liked Sister Evangelista, who had been an efficient but kind Reverend Mother.

Daisy knew what had made the sister mad. It was the photographs in the drawer. Daisy had seen them too, lots of times.

She was sitting outside the sister's office, when she heard her on the phone to the bishop, asking him what she should do.

'I have already called the police, of course I have. These pictures are the devil's own work and surely they must have something to do with his murder. How can they not? Bishop, ye need to get here, fast.' Daisy heard the sister lower her voice even further as she hissed, 'They include one of our own children, taken in his office, so help me, God, it is a depraved picture. Ye will not believe it or understand what I am talking about until you see for yourself.'

Again, there was a long silence before the sister replied.

'Yes, Bishop. I will say nothing to the police until you get here and see the pictures for yeself, but what will I say to the police? I will always protect the Church, Father, yes, Father, I will, Father. I have to speak with you, though, urgently.' Her voice dropped even further to a rasp. 'I will send them to the Dohertys'. Daisy says the father spent a lot of time there and I swear, as God is true, the daughter Kitty is pregnant, but I'll not tell the police that, now, shall I?'

Daisy heard the sister replace the receiver and let out a big sigh, just as the police car pulled into the drive. Daisy peeped through the door and saw the sister wiping her eyes on her hankie, just as both doors of the police car clicked shut.

An hour later, when the police had left, Daisy boldly and nervously asked her own question.

'Can I stay here, please, Sister, at the convent?'

'Stay here, Daisy? Are ye mad, girl? The bishop will need somewhere to stay. He has to be looked after. Do you think it would be proper for him to stay at the convent, now?'

Crestfallen, Daisy looked down at her hands folded in her lap and replied with a voice loaded with sadness, 'No, Sister.'

'No indeed, Daisy,' said Sister Evangelista. 'Now, off ye go back over to the Priory, there's a good girl, Daisy, and I will pop back myself later with the bishop.'

Daisy was in the Priory kitchen, peeling potatoes for the bishop's supper, when he and the sister rushed in through the front door.

There had been a great deal of banging of doors, and of drawers and cupboards opening and closing.

The sister had brought the convent car, a Morris Traveller, to the front and she and the bishop ran in and out, loading up the back with one box after another.

Daisy couldn't help noticing how anxious they appeared and that there was little conversation between the two. They were very brisk with Daisy, shouting at her to go away when she went into the room to offer them tea.

Before the sister left, they told her that tomorrow the bishop would be receiving the police at the Priory and that they might want to ask Daisy questions, like the ones the sister had from time to time since the other day, and hadn't Daisy found that all very easy now?

Well, the truth was, she hadn't.

Daisy's head was hurting with the amount of questions she had been asked today and she thought it was funny no one had asked her any that she could answer without breaking the rules. Daisy saw a lot of what went on outside the Priory, but no one had asked her about that.

Whilst the sister and the bishop banged and clattered about the Priory, Daisy made the bishop his supper, and dusted and aired his room.

Later that evening, when the bishop returned from mass, the police were waiting for him. After they left, he had asked for his supper to be served in the small sitting room, on a tray in front of the fire, which Daisy had lit for him, with the television news on very loud.

When she entered the room with his tray of hot lamb scouse and steamed jam pudding and custard, he did not even look at her, fixing his gaze on the television screen. He said, 'Thank you, girl.' He said thank you, girl, often.

Just as she always had every meal since Mrs Malone had died, Daisy ate her dinner alone, in the vast basement kitchen at the big wooden kitchen table.

The bishop thought Daisy hadn't seen the bottle of whiskey on the floor, hidden down by the side of his chair, with the glass half full of the amber liquid tucked behind it.

He was wrong. Daisy saw everything.

As she nestled into her pillow and closed her eyes, Daisy heard his footsteps climbing the wooden stairs, slowly and heavily, towards her room on the top floor. The bishop was so fat, he struggled up the four flights, but Daisy knew he was coming to her and with every step she flinched.

She had thought that maybe, tonight, she would be safe.

As always, he sat on the edge of her bed whilst he struggled to catch his breath and, once recovered, he began to speak.

'Girl, the police will be here tomorrow and I am going to tell them that you are simple, do ye understand?'

Daisy nodded, but she didn't speak. She never spoke when he was in her room and he never called her Daisy, always 'girl'.

'If they ask you questions, girl, questions such as, has anything been removed from the Priory, you say no, nothing has. Do you understand?'

Daisy nodded.

'And if they ask you did any men ever visit the Priory you say no. Do ye understand that?'

Again, Daisy nodded.

'And as Father James told you, girl, it would be a grave sin to tell anyone what takes place in this room, even the police. You know that, don't you, girl?'

The bishop stopped talking and looked at her for a long, long time, as though a battle raged inside his head. Then, with a look of anguish, he pushed back the blankets covering Daisy, just as he always did.

Chapter Seven

As TOMMY OPENED the back gate he could see Maura through the kitchen window, standing at the sink; on her face she wore a tense and warning expression. His heart sank. Something was wrong.

The first thing he saw as he came in the back door was Howard and Simon, sitting at his kitchen table, each with an enamel mug of tea.

'Evening, Mr Doherty,' said Howard, as Tommy removed his jacket and hung it on the back of the kitchen door.

Tommy didn't speak but touched the peak of his cap in acknowledgment and looked over at Maura.

'That cuppa for me, love? What can I do for ye, gents?' With a smile that took every effort, he looked at both men and beamed.

When Tommy finally closed the front door on Howard and Simon, he and Maura peeped through the parlour window nets and waited for them to drive away.

A group of children had gathered around the car. Howard and Simon stopped and spoke to Little Paddy. Tommy watched as Howard raised his hand, waved a greeting and exchanged pleasantries with Molly Barrett, who was standing on her front step, hairnet in place and arms folded, chatting to Annie O'Prey.

As Maura and Tommy looked up and down the road, net curtains furiously twitched back at them.

'Look at that hard-faced Deirdre knocking on Sheila's door,' hissed Maura to Tommy. 'When did you ever see that slattern out on the front street pretending to look for her kids? They wander loose and free from dawn to dusk, without a crust in their belly, and suddenly she's all Mary good-wife, finding any excuse to see why the coppers are at our house. The nosy fecking bitch.'

'Hush,' Tommy replied. 'Don't let the children hear ye. We did all right. They have bloody nothing. I gave exactly the same story I have before. They have nothing, Maura.'

He put his arm round Maura's shoulder.

Deep inside, he was truly worried as they observed their neighbours, people he thought of as his friends, openly gossiping in the street. He no longer felt safe.

There had to be a reason the police had called again at Tommy's house. Something had put a spring in their step and a note of confidence in their voices, leading them straight to his door.

Maura knew Tommy was trying to protect her, but she was too canny to be fooled. She had to act fast. They had to spirit Kitty away from here and as quickly as possible.

Maura returned to the kitchen, wrote Kathleen a note and called Harry down the stairs to take the message across the road right away.

Maura didn't want to be seen outdoors. She knew she wouldn't make it far before a nosy neighbour called her across for an inquisition.

She could hear Peggy already shouting over the back wall, 'What did the police want, Maura? Getting mighty friendly with you and Tommy, they are now,' as she walked back into her own house. Peggy was a harmless friend, but Maura knew that even her idle gossip could be dangerous.

Later that evening, Jerry stepped into Maura's kitchen, just as she put the bread dough onto the side of the range to rise. Tommy had settled down in front of the television and opened the paper on his lap for a night-time read. He had decided it was time to make an effort. Having learnt to read only a few years ago, he didn't want to forget. It was one of the few things he had in his life to be proud of.

He leant forward and shifted the cinders around in the fire with the poker as he motioned to Jerry to sit in the chair opposite.

'Hello, Jerry, what's brought ye over here, mate? Has Alice whipped ye with her tongue then?'

Tommy began to giggle. He always laughed at his own jokes before anyone else did.

In months gone by, Jerry would have burst in through their kitchen door, cracking his own jokes as he came. But that was before.

When Kathleen had told Jerry Maura wanted him to pop over to the house, his heart had sunk. He felt sick and couldn't eat his supper. As soon as it was dark, he made his way down the entry to number nineteen. The sooner he knew what was wrong, the better. There had been too many nasty surprises of late. Kathleen promised she would follow him a few minutes later.

'Hello, Tommy.' Jerry lowered himself into the chair and held both of his hands out in front of him to warm before the embers, which had begun to glow with the heat. 'Apparently, Maura wants to talk to me.' Jerry rubbed his dry, crackling hands together, looking from one to the other.

Tommy looked surprised and glanced over at Maura as she took down from the press the tea caddy and the best, large, earthenware, blue-striped cups.

'Well, 'tis a mystery to me, Jer. Maura, do we want to talk to Jerry?' he said.

Tommy tilted his head to one side as he spoke, as though trying to see around Maura, to pick up a clue from her face.

'Aye, we do, but both of ye just sit while I make us a cuppa, and wait for Kathleen. We need to talk.'

Maura still hadn't turned round to face Tommy. She didn't dare. Without realizing it, she was allowing time for Jerry's presence to settle in the room.

'Well, this sounds serious altogether,' said Tommy, standing up and tipping the last of the coke from the scuttle onto the fire.

Maura felt calmer than she had earlier. Jerry was like a brother to her. In fact, he was closer than her own brother. She genuinely loved Jerry. They both did. Just by being here he had made the atmosphere lighter. She was glad she had asked Kathleen to send him over.

For a few moments, in hushed and whispered tones, the two men talked about the visit from the police.

'It is all just guesswork, Tommy,' said Jerry, leaning forward with his elbows on his knees and his hands clasped together, as if in prayer. 'No one saw us, no one was there, we are safe. You can't hang a man on the back of guesswork.'

Jerry had spoken the word no one else dared to. Hanging.

'No one would think hanging good enough for the murder of a priest, Jerry,' said Tommy, his eyes filling with tears of fear.

Jerry saw the distress on Maura's face. There was a moment of silence, until Jerry deftly moved on to a lighter subject, one guaranteed to alter the mood of the room. Football.

Tommy handed Jerry the *Echo*. The Liverpool football team manager, Bill Shankly, was all the talk in the football world.

'He's a Scot, a Celt. He will never stop being a problem for Everton, mark my words,' said Tommy.

'Aye, so everyone says,' Jerry replied.

Maura was pleased they were discussing football. She loved to hear the two of them natter. It made her feel warm inside. If Tommy was happy chatting football, she was happy. That was how it worked with them both. Maura took as much pleasure from Tommy's enjoyment as he did from hers.

It worked both ways. Each felt the other's pain and pleasure.

Or so Maura had thought.

The depth to which each had sunk into their own private world following the priest's murder had surprised her and added to the trauma. At the time when she needed Tommy the most, they had been the least able to communicate.

Touch, not talk.

Neither wanting to hear the other's opinion.

No analysis. The answers to unspoken questions burnt inside them, too painful to articulate. The knowledge and silence creating a vacuum.

But they had survived the first shock. The aftermath. The adjustment. Now they had to survive the second tsunami. As it rolled towards their kitchen, Maura took one of the hardbacked chairs from the table and dragged it over to the fire.

Jerry and Tommy looked at Maura. She was behaving strangely. Both felt their hearts sink as they waited for her to speak and they jumped when Kathleen burst in through the door.

'Thought it less obvious if we walked over separately,' said Kathleen. 'Molly Barrett's curtains have been twitching like a feckin' ferret all day. What did they want, Maura, what did the police have to say?'

'All the same questions we have been asked before,' said Tommy. 'They have nothing new.'

'Right,' said Maura, feeling much stronger now that Kathleen had arrived. 'I have to tell ye something and, Tommy, ye must not kick off, because Kathleen has the answer to the problem and I need ye to be strong. We all do, especially Kitty.'

Tommy's eyebrows knitted together. He lifted his backside up from the chair ever so slightly and, picking up the dark-green, flattened cushion on which he sat, slipped his newspaper underneath, for reading later.

'I'm ready,' said Tommy.

'I knew it,' Jerry said. 'As soon as Kathleen said you wanted me over here, I knew something was wrong.'

Tommy was suddenly fearful. He felt the change in the atmosphere and wanted time to stand still. He didn't think he could cope with anything else on top of all that had happened. Things were improving. Moving forward. Getting better. Why couldn't it stay that way?

He felt resentment brewing inside towards Maura. A feeling that was a stranger to the man who thought no ill of anyone.

He didn't want Maura to speak.

The coke in the fire was by now a red glow. They waited.

Maura took a deep breath. She spoke the words.

'Kitty is pregnant with the priest's child.'

She had said it. The words were huge, the biggest she had ever spoken, filling the room and polluting the air they breathed.

Before Tommy or Jerry could react she added, 'Before either of you think of gobbing off with an opinion, hear what Kathleen has to say, because she has more sense than all of us put together, so she does.'

Tommy couldn't have given an opinion. He was in shock. His bottom jaw had dropped and there it remained, gawping. Jerry rubbed his hands through his hair and was the first to speak.

'The fecking bastard. He's still here tormenting us. The fecking bastard.'

Maura didn't know where she found her strength. It came from nowhere and surged up in her. As she began to speak, she hardly recognized her own voice.

'Before either of you say another thing, I have children upstairs, and the baby is asleep and I will not let her be woken. They are not going to hear either of you raise your voices and they are not going to know what is going on, just because neither of you two can control yourselves. Do you both understand?'

For a split second, Tommy wasn't quite sure what had shocked him most. The news that Kitty was carrying the dead priest's child, or the fact that Maura was laying down the law when, as Kitty's father, he was more than entitled to kick off. He instantly understood why Maura had asked Jerry to come over.

'Whilst Kathleen explains, I will take some money from the bread bin and buy four bottles of Guinness from the Anchor. Not a word until I get back. I want no argument over this, it is too important.'

Neither man spoke. Jerry watched Maura as she put on her coat and fastened her headscarf over her curlers. The back-door latch clicked shut and Jerry listened to her feet tip-tapping over the yard.

Not for the first time, he admired her. She would fight for her family and here she was, laying the law down in her own kitchen to calm the two men she was closest to.

Tommy tipped his head backwards, stared at the ceiling and let out a large sigh.

His eyes focused on a stain that spread outwards from the light bulb in the centre. Within a dark-brown outline, shaped like a perfect cloud on a summer's day. The type you see drawn in the children's books from which Kitty had taught Tommy to read.

He remembered the first book they had read together. *Janet and John*. When he had told his five-year-old princess that he had never really attended school and had spent all of his childhood with his father, helping him with the horses, she had set her goal: to teach Tommy everything the sisters had taught her at school.

'Come on, Da, up,' she used to say to him when it was time for her to go to bed.

They had decided that it would be their secret. Sometimes, if he was tired after a hard day, he would make an excuse but she would stand there, one hand on her little hip and the other pointing up the stairs, her face set into what Tommy called her school-marm expression.

'Oh no you don't, Da, up you come right now,' she would say and it was all he could do not to burst out laughing. She was the image of Maura.

Sometimes he fell asleep on the bed next to her as they practised their letters. One memorable night, he opened one eye and saw her serious little face right next to his as she pulled the blanket over him, clambered back into the bed and, putting her little arms around his neck, fell fast asleep.

His first-born. His princess. His favourite.

Kathleen, who had not wanted to intrude on his personal grief, began to speak, softly.

'Tommy, we have to move her away from here. Her belly is trouble, a straight link in time to the priest. Two major events in one street would have to be connected. It is another reason for the police to visit your house. I don't know what has brought them here today, but I have a feeling that I just have to get her away. I have already rung home. I'm taking her and Nellie to Ireland for a break while we try to figure out what to do, but I do know this, Tommy: no one around here must have even the slightest notion that the child is pregnant.'

He still couldn't speak. His child was pregnant with the child of a man he had murdered with his own hands. How much worse could it be?

He made no attempt to halt the tears. He didn't care that he was breaking the unspoken code that real men didn't cry.

Jerry didn't speak. He offered no words of comfort. To do so would be to acknowledge Tommy's distress. Jerry had shed many tears of his own and knew that the best thing to do was to let Tommy cry them out.

It seemed only moments before Maura arrived back in the kitchen and was handing each of them a bottle of Guinness.

With a nod of appreciation to Maura for the bottle, Jerry asked Kathleen, 'When are you leaving, Mammy?'

'Tomorrow night, Jer. Well, at three in the morning, when it is at its darkest. We will leave the street without anyone seeing us go.'

'Tomorrow?' Maura almost shouted. 'I thought we were planning for the school holidays?'

Kathleen continued, 'Once we have left, you have to put the story about that my sister is ill. I had to rush back home and the girls came with me to help. I've made enough phone calls from the Anchor and given that story to Bill on the bar. I also used the phone tonight and told them we were leaving soon. I called Maeve the other day when I already knew in my mind what I was planning and she knows what's what.

'We have family in Ireland we can trust, Tommy, we all do. The streets here are on fire with the chinwagging and we need to be out of it. If we aren't here, we can be forgotten. Out of sight, out of mind. If they see us all leaving together with bags in hand, moving off for a sudden holiday, the gossip will run riot around the four streets and might reach as far as the police station.'

They were silent with shock at what Kathleen had planned. Each raised their bottle at exactly the same moment and took a long gulp of the Guinness.

But Kathleen hadn't finished; there was more.

'Now, Maura, we have to put on the act of our very lives, like we have nothing to hide and the fact that we have gone away is just a coincidence. Bring all the girls in tomorrow, even Peggy. Let's have a hair night. We need everyone to think all is fine and dandy in the Doherty house and that we haven't a care in the world. Don't even tell Kitty that she is being taken the following morning. The less she knows, the better.'

The following evening, after a few knocks of mops on kitchen walls, Sheila arrived in Maura's kitchen and transformed it into a hairdressing salon. Nellie had her hair washed, with her long locks tied tightly in rags ripped from an old nappy, which the following morning would leave her a head adorned with beautiful red ringlets.

Brigid had brought with her a jam tart she had made to accompany the copious cups of tea, as well as a baby tucked inside a blanket sling tied across her chest.

In her bag she had a pair of eyebrow tweezers and a jar of Pond's cold cream. This she had smeared thickly over everyone's eyebrows, in preparation for her session of plucking and shaping.

Peggy had settled herself by the fire with a packet of ciggies and an ashtray.

The kitchen was a buzz of activity as Kathleen, Kitty and Brigid took it in turns to have their hair washed over the kitchen sink by Alice as Sheila set about transforming them all into visions of beauty.

Nellie and Kitty were enjoying the excitement. Hair nights in the kitchen happened about once a month, in one house or another. It was the only time Peggy ever washed her hair. Very few could afford a hairdresser and Sheila was a dab hand with a pair of scissors. The shillings she earned from her scissor skills made a difference to her life. Sheila also owned a rubber hose, which divided in the middle and connected to the kitchen taps, just as they did in the hairdresser's. They all loved the atmosphere of the girls' night in. For the first time in weeks, Kitty laughed at Peggy who grumbled and shuffled as usual as she came in through Maura's back door.

The smell in the kitchen changed perceptibly as Peggy walked in. They were all well used to the distinct Peggy perfume and managed to ignore it.

'I swear to the Holy Father I was never meant to marry that fat slob and the midwife definitely slipped someone else's kids, which were devils themselves, into the cot, and gave the good ones I had to someone else. What have I done to deserve that lot next door, eh, Maura?'

'We often ask the same question ourselves, Peggy,' said Maura in a sympathetic tone with a twinkle in her eye as she winked at Kathleen. Everyone stifled their giggles.

Kitty knelt on a chair with her head over the sink, a towel wrapped around her shoulders, with Alice using the hose to rinse the shampoo out of her hair. Kitty's shoulders shook and she felt Alice's belly shuddering with laughter as they both leant over, trying not to be unkind and hurt Peggy's feelings.

That happened often enough when sometimes the little ones called her Smelly Peggy out loud and she heard them.

Kitty was feeling better by the minute. The old Kitty was returning, restored by laughter.

The new Kitty was fading, suppressed by denial.

Kitty loved her hair.

Long, thick and just like her mother's.

Brigid had plucked and shaped everyone's eyebrows, and the kitchen had been full of screams and laughter at Kathleen's antics under the tweezers.

Maura had sat Kitty on a chair in front of the fire and taken the curlers out. Then Sheila had backcombed the life out of her hair, piled most of it up on top of her head and swept her fringe dramatically across, almost covering one eye.

When Tommy walked into the kitchen, he pretended not to recognize her.

'Jeez, Maura,' Tommy shouted in mock surprise. 'What is Marianne Faithfull doing sat in our kitchen and where the hell is our Kitty?'

'Shut up, ye great eejit, this is our Kitty.'

'Holy Mary, how was I to know that? We had better be careful, someone might snap her up to appear in a film or something.'

Kitty threw one of the curlers at Tommy, but she was grinning shyly from ear to ear, beside herself with pleasure.

A grand show it was as the kitchen rocked with laughter and women tripped in and out of the back door, just as they always did. Hardly a word was mentioned about the police and when it was, Maura answered with confidence, 'Well, sure, there was no one the priest was closer to than us, now. Only natural so, that they be looking to us to help.'

Everyone nodded as kindly Brigid, who knew almost as much as the Dohertys, said, 'Sure, isn't that the truth.'

No one other than Nellie saw the smile slip from Kitty's face.

It was pitch-black outside and Kitty felt as though she had been asleep for only an hour when she was woken by Maura, gently shaking her shoulders.

'Wake up, queen,' she whispered, 'come downstairs.'

When Kitty staggered into the kitchen, her clothes were ready warming and Maura had poked some life into the fire. There was a candle lit on the mantel, but Maura hadn't switched on the lights.

As Kitty moved towards the switch, Tommy hissed, 'No, don't, queen, leave it.'

'What am I getting dressed for?' asked Kitty, dazed and only half awake, blinking at them both as she rubbed her bleary eyes.

'You are going to Ireland now, Kitty,' said Maura. 'Hurry, your da is taking you down to the Pier Head to meet Kathleen in ten minutes, so you don't have long.'

Kitty checked the clock on the mantel above the range. 'Mammy, 'tis only half two,' she said.

'Yes, and that is why we have to be extra careful and quiet and leave separately, so as not to wake a living soul. It's why we are meeting Kathleen at the Pier Head, do ye understand?'

Kitty nodded, but she didn't understand. Thoughts of her friends and teachers were flitting through her brain. How would they know where she was, if she hadn't had the chance to talk to them and explain what was happening?

She was too tired to talk. Maura forced her to take some tea and toast, which was the last thing she wanted, but as she drank, the excitement of the adventure began to filter through and drag her up through the folds of sleep.

Ten minutes later, with the new, brown, jumble-sale holdall clutched in one hand and Kitty's hand in his other, Tommy was tiptoeing across the cobbled entry, hugging close to the wall, slipping away into the dark night. Kitty's secret, their secret, was at last leaving the knowing, prying eyes of those who lived on the four streets.

Chapter Eight

JERRY'S BROTHER, LIAM, was waiting to greet them when they arrived in Dublin.

It was a dark and wet night and the girls kept their heads bent low as they disembarked to keep the driving rain from directly hitting them in the face. They had sat at the Pier Head for most of the morning as one crossing after another had been cancelled due to the choppy Irish Sea until at last, a ferry was allowed to leave.

Now, they were officially on holiday.

Both girls were still reeling with the shock from the suddenness of their departure. It had all happened so quickly.

'Ye'll get used to the rain,' shouted Kathleen who led the way as she bustled on ahead. 'It rains so much in Mayo, Kitty, that people who stay here for too long grow a set of gills.'

'They don't, do they?' Kitty said to Nellie.

Nellie laughed. 'Not at all, it's Nana Kathleen's joke. She tells it all the time. I must have heard it a hundred times, but me and Da, we just laugh so she feels like she's being funny.'

Both girls began to giggle, more from the excitement of setting foot on the soil of a foreign country than Kathleen's jokes, which they could no longer hear above the sounds of people greeting each other and car horns beeping. Suddenly, they thought they could hear Jerry shout, 'Mammy,' but they both looked up and realized it was Liam, who appeared and sounded as much like Jerry as it was possible to.

'Well, well, well, would ye look at the grown-up colleen now,' Liam shouted as he scooped Nellie up into his arms. 'Here, would ye let me take a look at ye. What a big miss ye are. The absolute image of yer mammy with that long red hair. I bet ye don't remember Uncle Liam, do ye?'

Nellie didn't know why, but she was overcome by a strange shyness. Maybe it was because Kitty was witnessing this very open display of affection. Or perhaps because he had spoken of Bernadette. She felt stupidly proud to have been compared to her own mammy, the mammy that no one in Liverpool ever spoke about. She did remember Uncle Liam. He was loud, gregarious and always playing practical jokes.

Nellie loved him. She loved him twice over for speaking about Bernadette as though she were still alive.

He was the funniest man she had ever met. She hadn't seen him for two whole years but she certainly did remember him.

She loved the farm and everyone on it. She often thought about them all. What she loved most was that it was where her daddy was born, and where Nana Kathleen had also been born, and her daddy before her and his before him. Uncle Liam had built a new house on the same land as the old house, so for a long time there had always been a Deane on the farm. The new house had a fully fitted indoor bathroom. That was a novelty on the four streets in Liverpool. It was a novelty in Ballymara and in the main village, Bangornevin, too. Nellie knew there were lots of people in the village and out in the country who were envious of what a good farmer Liam was and of how well the Deane farm fared.

Nellie had also been taken aback by the suddenness of

their departure. Last night she had sat on Jerry's knee in front of the fire for a cuddle. Jerry had played with her ringlet rags and wrapped them round his fingers as they both stared into the fire.

Jerry whispered so that Alice couldn't hear.

'Yer mammy, Bernadette, had loved the farm so much, she used to swing on the big five-bar gate to the yard and do nothing more than gaze up the hill opposite and dream of you. Yourself, little miss, were just the twinkle in her eyes back then.'

She gave Jerry a big hug to try to make him smile. His expression was wistful and sad but she knew that wherever it was he vanished to when he mentioned her mammy, it was somewhere Nellie couldn't reach. She could feel the ache in his heart but it was his ache and his alone, untouchable and not one she could heal.

Uncle Liam placed a kiss on her cheek and put her back down as he bent to greet Kitty. 'And you must be Miss Kitty?' he said grandly as he took off his cap and bowed in an exaggerated manner.

Kitty blushed a deep pink and took the hand Liam proffered.

A self-conscious Kitty had never shaken anyone's hand before.

'Now,' said Nana Kathleen, 'if ye would stop play-acting, Liam, and take these bags, I'd be very grateful.'

Kathleen playfully hit Liam across the back with her umbrella. Liam pretended it had hurt much more than it actually had and began to walk doubled over as though he were in great pain, lifting up the bags and howling with agony.

Kitty and Nellie were in fits of giggles.

'Here, Nellie,' shouted Liam as he threw her the keys.

'Would ye drive? Me back is so bad now thanks to that Nana Kathleen.'

Nellie squealed loudly as she caught the keys, but she and Kitty were laughing so much they could barely protest that Nellie was too young to drive.

Liam, affecting a miraculous recovery, lifted up the tarpaulin on the back of the van and placed the bags underneath.

As Kathleen shuffled herself across the van's bench seat to sit next to Liam, she shouted, 'The rain is playing merry hell with my wash and set, so get in quickly, girls.'

As Liam passed the girls to reach the driver's seat, with a wink he slipped them each a brown ten-shilling note. God, how can he afford that? thought Kitty. The reason most of the Irish were in England was to make money, but Nellie and Kitty's first impression was that they had more money in Ireland. No one on the four streets owned a car. A ten-shilling note was a huge amount of money, enough for two days' shopping at home.

'Flippin' heck, we are millionaires,' whispered Nellie to Kitty, as they scrambled along the bench next to Nana Kathleen, to begin the long journey in the rain across Ireland to the west coast.

Kitty had never before travelled in a car, a train or a boat, and in the space of a day, she had experienced all three.

She had never visited the land of her parents' and her ancestors' birth, yet here she was with her feet on Irish soil and, inexplicably, it felt like her soil. The furthest distance she had ever travelled had been to St John's market with her mam at dusk on a Christmas Eve, to buy a fresh turkey and some bacon from the meat hall at the end of the day at a knockdown price.

To date, that had been the most exciting journey Kitty had ever made. She loved the sawdust-covered, wooden floorboards and the Christmas atmosphere amongst the butchers, cheekily calling out to the women from behind their market stalls.

But that was as nothing compared to the last forty-eight hours.

Everything about this trip was a novelty, such as sloping off in the dead of night to the Pier Head to catch the ferry before the buses were even running. The sandwiches Maura had made her for the journey contained tongue. She had never before in her life had anything more exotic than jam or Shippam's fish paste.

Meanwhile, as Liam drove slowly away from the port towards the streets of Dublin, back at number nineteen Tommy and Maura were clearing up the kitchen following supper.

Angela had been in a foul mood, a seamless continuation from her bad temper at breakfast, when she had discovered that Kitty was taking a holiday to Ireland.

'I cannot believe this,' she had screamed. 'Why her and not me? It's desperate, Mammy, that I am being left behind, it is, desperate,' she sobbed.

Angela wailed and cried at the unjustness of it all, adding to the load of Maura's day.

'Every cloud has a silver lining, Angela,' Maura replied. 'Ye become the eldest child whilst Kitty is having her holiday.'

Maura had no idea that that was exactly what Angela was dreading.

'Thank God Kitty's gone,' said Tommy wearily when he and Maura were preparing for bed. 'She needs this holiday. The air on the farm will put the colour back in her cheeks. They say a change is as good as a rest, don't they?'

With a sigh, he pulled up the sash window. The night sounds of the tugs on the river filled the room. Putting his head outside to blow away his cigarette smoke, with a heavy heart he whispered, more to the moon and the stars than to Maura, 'I only wish I was going with her.'

Hardly a day passed without Tommy thinking of Cork and the village where he had been born and raised. He thought now of his own family – his mammy, daddy and those of his siblings – who had travelled on to America rather than stay in Liverpool. Whenever someone mentioned Cork within earshot of Tommy, he always repeated the same comment: 'Aye, God's own county, and there is no finer a place on this earth, so there isn't. No better people, no finer horses, nor more beautiful women.'

Tommy spent some of his day, every day, dreaming of Cork.

'I sometimes wish we had gone on to America, Maura. We both should have done what my brothers did. Maybe this terrible thing wouldn't have happened in America.'

Maura listened to him, all the while keeping her own thoughts close. How glad she was that she had indulged and spoilt Kitty over the last few days.

'Come to bed, Tommy,' she whispered.

Maura was exhausted from having to wake at two o'clock to spirit Kitty away into the night and coping with the demands of her children. Malachi and Declan ran Maura ragged on the best of days and today was no different. Maura was already missing Kitty in so many ways.

'She is with Kathleen and Nellie, and no doubt having great craic while we are here worrying ourselves stupid. Come to bed,' she said softly.

Tommy pulled the window down and the curtains across

before he slipped into the comforting arms of the woman who loved him as no other ever would.

Who was not from Cork.

Kathleen and Liam chatted away as they drove across Dublin, with Nellie throwing in the odd comment or question. Kitty could barely understand what they were talking about. She knew none of the names or the places they were discussing. Liam had a list of deliveries to collect, which would make the journey longer.

Kitty stared out at the wide river and the tenement buildings. Had it been only three days since she had found out what was wrong? Now she knew why her period hadn't arrived. She had started only a year ago and had not thought anything of having missed. She'd had no idea what this meant until Maura had explained it to her last night in furtive whispers, as she sat her in yet another scalding-hot bath before Sheila and the other neighbours called round.

On three occasions over the last three days, Maura had almost boiled her alive in a bath while making her swallow a weird-tasting drink. Her nausea had been replaced by the most awful diarrhoea.

'You need to be purged, Kitty,' Maura had whispered. 'Your guts making all that movement in the outhouse will bring your monthly on, so it will. And you have to drink the Epsoms whilst you are sat in the hot bath, it doesn't work else.'

Kitty had been well and truly purged and, heavens, had a cleaner child ever visited Eire? Her monthly had remained stubborn, clinging to the lining of her womb for dear life.

Kitty pressed her face against the window and looked out into the Dublin night at the women gathered on the tenement building steps under an overhead canopy, smoking pipes and wearing headscarves, with black knitted shawls draped around their shoulders. In long black skirts, they sat with their knees wide apart. By the light of the glass-domed street lamps, she saw children walking in the pouring rain, wearing barely any clothes. They couldn't have been more than two years of age. It was late and yet the streets were incredibly noisy. Through open doors she glimpsed long counters of polished dark wood in bars heaving with customers, drinking the black-velvet Guinness.

They drove past a group of men fighting in the street.

'Dublin is the capital of sin now, Mammy,' Liam said to Kathleen. 'No one comes here unless they have to. It is a bad state of affairs all right.'

'Sure, it always was, Liam, nothing has altered there. Dublin has always been a bad place, which is why I never allowed any of you to come here when ye were growing up.'

The capital of sin? Kitty and Nellie looked at each other and then outside with renewed interest.

Kitty had never even been into Liverpool at night and now, here she was, in the heart of Dublin, driving through the capital of sin.

It felt as though each minute there was a new sensation or experience. Kitty felt time shifting. Her foundation of stability, all she knew and understood, was slipping away from under her. This journey, with every mile they drove, drew a line under her life as the old Kitty. She tried not to think about what was happening but she realized that, from this night on, nothing would ever be the same again.

Already homesick, Kitty wanted to return to Liverpool to her mammy. To sit with Maura and Tommy, just the three of them together, as they sometimes did at night when the younger children were asleep.

Tommy would tell jokes about what the men had done and said on the docks and they would usually laugh about one of the twins' antics. They would worry out loud about Harry's asthma, and all three would have a drink and a bite together before Kitty went upstairs to bed.

Before she did, she would kiss and hug both her parents goodnight. Kitty would walk over to her da and bend to kiss him on the cheek. He would pretend to be reading his paper and then, at the last second, as she bent her head, he would turn quickly and steal a peck on the lips. He did it every night, but the three of them always laughed as though he had never done it before.

Kitty wanted to be there right now, in the warmth of her kitchen with the people who loved her best of all.

She was a young girl, pregnant, in a strange country with people who, kind as they might be, weren't her own.

Exhausted, she leant her head against Nellie's shoulder and slept.

Chapter Nine

A LICE AND BRIGID had become good friends.
They shared a secret. They had both become bound
by events which took place following the murder.

Brigid had helped in her own way to throw the police off
the scent away from number nineteen following the murder.
Her and Sean had provided Tommy with an alibi. They were
parents of daughters and although they didn't fully know all
the details neither did Alice, not completely. The only people
who really knew what took place in the graveyard that night,
were Tommy and Jerry. Or so they thought. On the night of
the murder, they had all raised their whiskey glasses and
made a vow. Not one word was to be spoken about that night,
to anyone, not even to each other, ever again.

No one other than Tommy knew of the torment that now
woke him in the middle of the night and left him staring out of
the window, wondering how in God's name he had gone from
a peace-loving family man to a murderer in one fateful hour.

Tommy would rewind the evening over and over in his
mind, as though on a loop. Images of the hangman's gallows
haunted him as he tried and failed to somehow make sense of
the extraordinary events that had taken over his very ordinary life.

It was no surprise, really, that the first real friend Alice had ever made, other than her mother-in-law Kathleen, had been Brigid. They had plenty in common, besides the secret. Brigid had daughters around the same age as Joseph.

There wasn't anything Brigid didn't know about child rearing. There was nothing Alice did know.

They both had the best-looking husbands on the four streets, if not in all of Liverpool.

Sean, like Jerry, was able to make even the elderly ladies on Nelson Street giggle in a flirtatious way and both men hammed it up outrageously.

'Evening, Mrs O'Prey,' Jerry would shout if he saw Annie on her step on his way home. 'God, ye look gorgeous today, so ye do. Lock the door tonight or I'll be desperate to get across into your bed if my Alice turns me away and says no.'

Mrs O'Prey would flash her gums at Jerry and disintegrate into a fit of giggles.

'Oh, away with ye, Jerry Deane, ye bad lad, wait until I tell ye mammy.'

Jerry knew there was very little in Mrs O'Prey's life to make her smile.

If Tommy was with him he would shake his head.

'Nothing wrong in making them laugh, Tommy,' Jerry would say.

'Aye, you just made her day all right, Jerry, you did.'

'What about ye, Tommy, will ye be comin' over after he's finished?' Annie O'Prey shouted cheekily across.

'Oh no, not me, Annie, my Maura never says no,' Tommy shouted back.

Sean on the other side of the road would join in the banter. 'Oi, keep yer hands off my woman, Deane, or yer a dead man. She's mine and if ye want her, see me in the ring on Friday night.'

The street was filled with laughter as Jerry whispered to Tommy, 'If Maura ever hears you telling Annie O'Prey that she never says no, you're the one whose feckin' dead.'

Blowing Mrs O'Prey an exaggerated kiss, the three men separated and walked on to their own back doors.

Sean and Brigid weren't as badly off as other families in Nelson Street.

Sean won money at the boxing ring each Friday night, which he put into the bread bin.

Some of it went to buy the meat and eggs Sean needed in order to remain fighting fit.

Some went towards the housekeeping and to feed his many daughters. And the remainder was for the day when they had enough saved to emigrate to America.

Sean had plans and dreams.

He and Brigid received a letter every fortnight from his sister, Mary, in Chicago.

Mary and her husband, along with Sean's brother, Eddie, had established a small building company and, by all accounts, were doing well. In every letter they pleaded for Sean and the family to travel and join them, to work with them because the business was growing so fast. They could barely manage and were having to employ large teams of Irish builders from home. It galled Mary and Eddie that their very own brother worked as he did on the Liverpool docks, when a life of prosperity and opportunity was waiting for him and his, right there in Chicago.

Sean was desperate to set sail and join them. His work in Liverpool was only ever meant to be temporary and a means of saving for the passage to America.

Mary and Eddie, who were both older than Sean, had travelled on ahead of him to Liverpool, worked for three years and went without, so determined were they to save every penny they earned.

Eddie had taken two jobs: for six days a week, Sunday excepted, he worked as a brickie on the new housing estates on the outskirts of Liverpool, and for four nights as a barman.

Mary had trained as a nurse and lived in the nurses' home, eating on the wards and barely spending a penny of her salary. Within two weeks of qualifying, she and Eddie realized they had enough saved and had boldly booked their passage across the Atlantic.

Their single-minded determination had paid off well.

Sean would have left the day after every letter arrived from America, but for two problems.

The first was that Brigid would have none of it.

'England is far enough away from Ireland and from my family and your mammy too,' she said reproachfully, every time he brought the subject up. 'Now that Mary and Eddie have selfishly gone to America, who will be here for your mammy, should she be sick? Ye know the rules, Sean. The nearest does the looking after and that's me and you.'

The second was that, even if Sean could talk Brigid round, he didn't yet have enough fare money for all of them. He was too proud to ask his sister for help.

Mary's last letter had included a black-and-white photograph of their house in Chicago and a picture of Mary and her husband in front of their fireplace.

Sean had placed the picture on the press. He picked it up and looked at it at least once a day.

It wasn't Mary he looked at, nor her husband, despite their clean, wholesome well-fed expressions and fine clothes.

'It was the size of the marble mantelpiece with the gilt-framed mirror above it and the solid brass fender round the fire. Alongside, a small polished wooden table held an over-sized lamp with a fringed lampshade. On the mantel stood an ornament of a sailing ship and a shire horse, with photographs in silver frames.

He studied them all. Such fine things.

Sean would not even have been able to afford the large brass coal bucket at the opposite end of the fender, never mind the house.

'They have everything, sure, there's no denying that, all right,' he said to Brigid.

"I desperately want us to be with them. I know we made the wrong decision to stay in Liverpool. I cannot see a way forward out of the four streets for us all and quick enough too."

Brigid never replied or returned his enthusiasm.

'Sure, she never stops giving out about America and how great it is, does she?' Sean said when he finished reading the latest letter.

'She makes me laugh, so she does,' replied Brigid. 'She always signs off, "From the land of the free". Sure, we are free too. Does she think we are all prisoners in England?'

'We are, aren't we, though, Brigid?' said Sean. 'I can't earn any more money than I do. They seem to be free to do whatever they want to over there. If you want to set up a business, you can. If you want to buy your own house, you can get money to do it. America is growing and bursting with opportunities that we just don't have here. No one cares where you came from or what class you are. There is no class in America, don't ye understand? Everyone is the same. If ye can work ye can win.

'We aren't even the same when we go to the grocer's. All the shite gets loaded into our baskets. Ye heard what the grocer told Paddy in the pub when he was pissed. The best potatoes go to the English, the second-best to the pigs and the rest to the Irish.'

Sean walked over to Brigid and put his arms round her.

'I just don't want our kids to live our life and repeat our hardships every day. We have to keep saving, Brigid, and I have to keep fighting to bring the extra money in.'

He pulled away and looked down at her, seeking reassurance.

Brigid broke free of his arms and refused to meet his eyes. She could be bolder when he wasn't touching her.

'I want to be wherever you are and if you think America is better for our kids, when we have the money for the fare, we will talk about it then, but I'm not making any promises, Sean.'

She was holding him off, playing for time. She turned back to the kitchen sink.

Sean put his arms round his wife's waist and hugged her.

He beat the shite out of three men every Friday night in order to earn the money they needed to save. Brigid would never know how that felt. She would never understand that, knowing she was with him, supporting him and sharing his dreams, would make getting into the ring easier to bear.

With Brigid beside him, he could dive over the ropes and see nothing ahead but their future.

Punches easier to take. Bruises quicker to heal.

Brigid continued washing the dirty dishes.

'I do think about it sometimes, ye know,' she said, with a lift in her voice. 'When Kathleen read me tea leaves on Friday, she said we would be visiting foreign shores before long.'

Sean didn't believe in prophecies found in the tea leaves, but Kathleen's endorsement made him feel surprisingly good.

'It won't be long now before we have enough money for the fare. Two more steady years on this lucky winning streak and we can be off, all of us.' His voice was loaded with a false brightness, but dropped as he added, 'Providing we don't have any more babies.'

Brigid didn't reply. She had no desire to move further away from home. She was happy enough, but Sean was always restless, wanting more and better, and looking to see how green was another man's grass. Sometimes it wore her out.

Nothing wore Sean out.

Winning in the boxing ring was a foregone conclusion for him, driven by his personal goal. Every waking hour that he wasn't working on the docks, he was training in the ring. There was no doubt in his mind that he would have the money within two years.

They were fine the way they were, mused Brigid. She comforted herself with the idea that he would soon grow tired of wanting to leave. Sean was someone in the community. He enjoyed his reputation as a big and powerful man. When he walked down the street, the kids shouted out to him, 'Hey, big man Sean, will ye show us how to throw a punch?'

They would run along beside him, begging and chanting. Often he would stop and spend time on the green, showing them how to jib. He truly was the big man and, when he realized that, pride alone would be enough to make him stay.

Better to be a big fish in Liverpool and not a little fish across the other side of a very big pond.

The adults on the four streets were in awe of Sean's size and strength. Even Kathleen, who had wondered at the arrogance and the cheek of Father James, who had often tripped in and out of Brigid's house. Kathleen liked to imagine what Sean would have done to the priest if he had caught him up to anything.

If neighbours on Nelson Street ever thought one of their own had murdered Father James, they would naturally have assumed it was the big and muscular Sean, not the short and kindly Tommy.

Little did they know.

It took rage to kill a man, not strength.

The night before Kathleen left for Ireland, she had popped down to see Brigid, to tell her they were having a hairdo night at Maura's.

'I haven't time to beat around the bush, Brigid,' said Kathleen, breathlessly, almost as soon as she walked in through Brigid's back door.

As Kathleen looked around the kitchen, she was overcome with admiration. A wooden box sat on the floor to the side of the fire, padded with hand-crocheted blankets, and inside, top to tail, slept two babies. In the pram just inside the back door slept two more. The kitchen was spotlessly clean.

'Brigid, I am here to ask ye a favour,' said Kathleen, 'and I didn't want to do it tonight in front of the others, especially nosy Peggy.'

'Oh, for goodness' sake, sit down,' Brigid said, concerned. Kathleen was bright red and panting. Brigid had always thought Kathleen did too much and should be taking things a bit easier.

'Brigid, I need ye to help me, but I also need you to keep it quiet, between the two of us. I am away to Ireland with Nellie and Kitty. Would ye please keep an eye on Alice and the baby whilst Jerry is at work and I am away? But please, Brigid, please, could it be our secret?'

Brigid pressed a cup of tea into Kathleen's hand and sat down next to her.

'I would be happy to, but Alice seems a different woman altogether these days. Sure, I know it was necessary, but remember, after the murder, she came into my kitchen, all by herself.'

'Aye, I know,' said Kathleen, 'and that is grand and a great improvement, so it is, but it would just make me feel better if I knew ye was keeping an eye out. Things aren't quite right, Brigid. I wouldn't worry if I was here, but I have to travel back home for a little while and I would feel much happier if ye was keeping watch for me.'

'Won't Maura be put out by ye asking me?' Brigid enquired.

'Maura has enough on her plate just now and, besides, they never seem to be able to move beyond Bernadette. Alice can't forgive Maura for being Bernadette's best friend and Maura can't forgive Alice for taking Bernadette's place. I don't think either of them will ever move on. What can I do? One minute they are fine, the next, for no reason what-soever, they flare up like a pair of entry dogs fighting over a scrap.'

Kathleen drank her tea and the two women chatted on until Kathleen realized she had been away for too long.

Brigid gave Kathleen a hug at the back door.

'Have a rest, Kathleen, will ye? Everything will be fine here now.'

'Aye, I will that, but keep your eyes peeled. Alice isn't herself, she's so bold now. Or maybe this is herself, I have no idea, but I can't help thinking that she probably needs to go back on her tablets. I have other things to deal with right now and I don't want to worry Jerry. Oh, and bring yer tweezers and Pond's round tonight. Me and the girls, we have good reason to need to look a little groomed.'

And with a last smile through the back door and another

promise from Brigid that not a word would be spoken about her visit to anyone, she was gone.

As Kathleen walked back, she thought to herself that Brigid, with all her kindness, was the one woman on the street they could trust with the news of Kitty's baby. She was the one person Maura could lean on whilst Kathleen was away, but Kathleen wouldn't dare tell her. She couldn't. No one must know.

Brigid dutifully called in on Alice, the following afternoon. She decided that asking had they got away all right was a good opening line. Alice was not known for gossip. She didn't speak to anyone as far as Brigid knew, but she was determined not to let that put her off.

Alice was slightly hesitant; she had never had visitors of her own.

'Hello, Brigid, you know Kathleen has left for Ireland, don't you?' she whispered, as though someone else could hear.

Brigid decided she had to be bold and make herself at home. She could see Alice was not at ease.

'You don't mind if I put these two on the mat next to Joseph, do ye?' she asked Alice, as she lifted her two youngest out of the pram and put them down on the rug besides Joseph.

Joseph kicked his legs frantically and began to chatter in baby language, which made both Brigid and Alice laugh.

'Would ye look at him,' exclaimed Brigid in mock indignation. 'Still in nappies and trying it on with my girls. I will tell Uncle Sean about ye, little man, so I will. Aye, I know Kathleen has gone home. I just thought I would pop in and see yerself and the little fella, in case ye was feeling a bit deserted.'

Alice put the kettle on and the two women chatted about babies until Jerry arrived home.

As Brigid left, she made a suggestion.

'Do the two of youse fancy coming down to the club with us on Saturday? Would Angela look after Joseph for ye? We have Sean's mammy here and Sean has no fight on, so we are desperate to get out and she doesn't mind stopping in to let us go. It would be a break for me to get away from her and Sean talking about how great America is all the time. They drive me crazy, the two of them. They would have us all packed up onto the boat for New York in the morning if they had their way. I need to remind Sean it's good craic around here too and there's more to life than the boxing ring and work.'

Alice looked at Brigid in amazement.

'Do you not want to go to America then?' she asked, almost incredulous. She could think of no prospect more exciting.

Alice had never planned to remain on the four streets. This was not the future she had imagined for herself when she had married Jerry. She knew she had not been well for a very long while but now she was absolutely sure she was fully recovered. She would never again need the little yellow tablets sitting in the glass bottle on the press. Alice was now her own woman. She could be like others and do whatever she wanted to do, whenever she wanted to do it. Alice felt as if she was truly alive for the first time ever.

She was no longer a spinster housekeeper working in a hotel. Even though it had been the most prestigious hotel in Liverpool. Facing the prospect of spending the remainder of her days alone in an old bedsit with only the rats for company was her future no more, but still, she was slightly disappointed that liberation from her old self had not presented more challenges than how to make a packet of butter stretch the whole week.

Alice had dreamt of living in America for many, many years.

'Oh, I will make up my mind if we ever get to that point,' Brigid's voice pierced her thoughts, 'it's what Sean says he wants and so I have to want it too, I suppose, but I will miss everyone and it's so far from home. Anyway, like all men, he's full of big ideas, but when it comes to it, if I turn on the tears he will maybe change his mind.'

Brigid grinned and winked at Alice, who returned a weak and thoughtful smile.

The following night, whilst Jerry was eating his supper and Alice, wearing Kathleen's apron, scrubbed the pans at the sink, she found her mind full of Sean and how lucky Brigid was.

How could Brigid complain about having a man who wanted to be something other than a docker?

Someone who wanted better than to remain in a house listed for slum clearance?

Alice wondered, did Sean feel like an outsider within the community, as she did?

'I'm an outsider because I'm an English Protestant and I was a sick one in the head at that, not that anyone ever mentions it, mind. Sean may feel the same because he wants better than the rest are prepared to put up with and that makes him different.'

'What's that, queen?' said Jerry, looking up from his plate whilst glancing at the *Echo*, which was propped up on the table against the milk bottle.

'Oh, nothing, just thinking out loud,' said Alice as she turned the cold tap on full to rinse the pan and drown her stray thoughts.

*

That night, Joseph slept in the room Nellie shared with Kathleen.

When it was time for bed, whilst Jerry switched off the television and the lights, Alice popped in to settle Joseph, who had been slightly restless in the new room.

As she stood at the window, rocking backwards and forwards with Joseph on her shoulder, Alice spotted Sean walking down the street, returning from one of his boxing nights. She felt a thrill in her belly and, without any warning, a flame lit somewhere in her heart.

He must feel exactly as I do, thought Alice.

As he walked under her window, Alice slipped backwards into the shadow of her old self.

She hadn't done it for so long. She had been fixed. She was fine. She was totally in control. She was free. Now that Kathleen had left, she felt the feelings of the past return. She was her own woman again.

As Sean passed she noticed how broad his shoulders were and how tall and proud he was when he walked, not like Jerry, who almost slouched along with his head bent.

She would tell Brigid they would love to go out tomorrow night. She wanted to be in the company of a man who thought just as she did, and who made her pulse race because of it.

Joseph fell asleep and Alice laid him down gently in the cot. She walked back to the window to gaze out on the street for another glimpse of Sean's receding back and then, suddenly, she stopped herself and stepped away.

Oh God, Alice, no, you idiot, she thought to herself. What are you doing?

She felt vulnerable, as though she were tumbling. She

realized Kathleen was her prop and that, without her, it was going to be difficult.

She needed to make more of an effort. But it was so hard as it was. Every day the bottle of tablets on the press were a reminder that the familiar pattern of obsessive behaviour lurked, waiting for her to slip.

As Alice walked into their room, she could sense Jerry was still awake.

For the first time ever, Alice wanted to have sex, a feeling she had never experienced before. She slipped into the bed and encircled Jerry in her arms. She felt his body stiffen. She was naked. She could hear his brain working, wondering what was happening and why. She had never before come to their bed without her nightdress.

Jerry rolled over onto his side and looked at her. His eyes were asking her a million questions she couldn't answer. How could she tell Jerry that what had excited her was catching sight of Sean walking down the street? Knowing that just down the road lived a man who shared her secret thoughts and who was talking to his wife about the life Alice wanted? That she had never been crazy and that just a few houses away someone else wanted the grander life she had yearned for too?

There must have been a mix-up, thought Alice. I wasn't meant to be here, I was meant to be down the road, with Sean.

The edges of reality were once again becoming blurred. The fact that Sean worked as a docker and a boxer, that he spent every day and evening working hard to realize the dreams he had for himself and his family, was lost on Alice. Once again, she imagined herself dressed just like one of the ladies who stayed at the Grand, the hotel where she had been the housekeeper. She saw herself surrounded by the leather luggage that had belonged to others, waiting to board the passenger steamer to New York.

New York. Just the thought of it sent a thrill down Alice's spine.

Every guest at the Grand who had been travelling on to New York had spoken beautifully and had dressed impeccably. They could barely contain their nervousness or excitement. Why should they? They were leaving for a great adventure. America.

And now, in the bed she shared with Jerry in the two-up, two-down on Nelson Street and with her thoughts full only of Sean, Alice gave herself up willingly. Jerry looked deeply into her eyes as he gently stroked her arms and breasts and then he kissed her, with longing and passion. For the very first time in seven years of marriage, Alice moved with him, but in body alone. In her mind, it was Sean caressing and entering her. And as she quivered and shook in his arms, Jerry felt that at last, for the very first time since the day they had married, they had truly made love.

Chapter Ten

MAURA AND TOMMY had a tough night settling the children. All were perturbed by Kitty's absence. Malachi had been playing up and Angela hadn't stopped complaining; Harry cried more than usual because it was hard for him to catch his breath. Each one of the children had a problem which at any other time, Kitty would have shared with her mother.

Malachi and Angela could give out enough for a dozen kids and Kitty knew how to deal with them. Both Maura's arms and belly had been full of a baby since a year after she had married.

Maura left the boys to Tommy and when she had finally calmed the girls, she lay on her bed to calm the baby on her breast.

After half an hour and with the baby still grizzling, Tommy put his head round the door. 'Just popping down to the Anchor for a quick one, Maura,' and with a wink, he was gone.

Tommy was crafty, knowing Maura wouldn't say a word in case she disturbed the baby. He was safe to sneak out when she was feeding.

Maura would never have objected anyway. Tommy hardly ever went to the pub. He was a family man who preferred to spend his nights in with her and the kids. She knew what he was doing.

This was the first occasion, since the day she had been born, that Kitty had been out of their sight. Oh, sure, she had spent lots of nights with Bernadette and Jerry when she was little and they had been waiting for Nellie to come along, but she was only across the road and within arm's reach. Not like now. Not like this. Not taking her first holiday with someone else's family.

Poor Tommy, he deserved a drink. Maura knew the visit from the police and the removal of Kitty to Ireland had worried him sick.

'Oh, Jesus, Mary and Joseph, please keep him strong,' she whispered into the top of her baby's downy head.

The Anchor was quieter than it would have been on a weekday night before the scandal of the priest being found dead without his langer, but the usual regulars were in and Tommy knew them all. As he walked up to the bar, men he worked with all day shouted their greetings. Most were standing round the fire, their backs to the flames, warming their rear ends.

For many of them there were no fires at home and the ranges were cold. Bill, the landlord, benefited from the money spent on Guinness, which would have provided a bag of coke in many a house.

The men were half-cut and had obviously been there since the end of their shift. Tommy had walked past children sitting on the steps outside, looking pale and perished. They were under instructions from their mammy to bring their da home before he had spent all the money.

Children, no more than five years of age, sent to do a man's job. Tommy knew one of the lads, who was a friend of Harry's.

'What are ye doing sat here, Brian?' he asked the lad, who was shivering so much he could barely speak through chattering teeth.

'Uncle Tommy, could ye send me da out to come home, please? Me ma says I can't go back home unless I have him with me.'

'Have ye eaten any tea tonight, Brian?' said Tommy, bending down so that he was at eye level with the lad.

Brian looked down and shook his head.

Tommy felt an anger he was now becoming familiar with burn into his gut. He put his hand in his pocket and took out a coin.

'Here's a sixpence, lad. Go to the pie hut and get a hot meat and potato pie and then go home after ye have eaten it. Don't tell anyone I gave ye a sixpence. Tell Ma I am bringing ye da home with me soon. Now away, lad, quickly.'

As Tommy walked into the pub, he cast his eyes around and saw Brian's da sitting by the fire, playing dominoes for money and nursing his Guinness.

With one hand thrust deep into his pocket and the other holding his own pint, John McCarthy hailed Tommy as he walked past him towards Brian's da.

'What d'ye think then, Tommy?' said John, looking around him furtively and dropping his voice. 'Go on, yer Maura, she and the priest was as thick as thieves. Who did for him, Tommy?'

'Sure, 'twas Molly Barrett's cat,' said Tommy with a forced laugh as he turned towards the bar and put his money on the long, highly polished wooden counter. He was about to order a pint and join John after he had put Brian's da out on the street.

Tommy had felt like a night of talking about the horses and football to take his mind off worrying about the police and missing his little queen, Kitty.

When he had left her with Kathleen at the wooden hut on the Pier Head, it was all he could do to keep his tears at bay, to be the big man and tell her to have a fabulous time.

He had given her an extra-long hug and she had clung to him, with her hands clenched behind his back. He had kissed her forehead and pressed half a crown into her palm.

'Be a good girl, queen, and bring me back the smell of the wet grass, with a rainbow's end sat on it for me as a present, now, would ye?'

As he made his way back up to the four streets, he turned as he reached the last street lamp and, through the window of the lit hut, he watched his little girl press her face against the glass and wave to him and despite the rain beating down, he could see the deep sadness etched on her face.

Tears blurred his eyes as he raised his hand and returned her wave. He wanted to run back to the hut and tell Kathleen it was all a mistake. That the only place any child could be truly safe was at home, with her ma and da. He had let his Kitty down, they had not kept her safe and now he had to pay the price.

As Tommy looked at Kitty he realized that this was the saddest moment of his whole life and he would always remember her face just as she looked tonight. During the day, he tucked under his cap the very thought of Kitty crossing the water on the boats he watched all day. His feelings swamped him, threatening to drag him down, so he kept them at arm's length and he focused his mind on the trivia of dock life.

Knowing she would not be there when he arrived home didn't make it any easier.

The house was quieter. It was darker. A light extinguished.

Her absence left a gaping hole, which the noisiness of all the others put together failed to fill.

He had to abandon his own thoughts and escape to the pub.

The men round the fire had heard Tommy's comment about the cat and sniggered.

John McCarthy whispered to Tommy, 'Aye, Tommy, keep yer fly buttons done up tight. If ye have to go into Molly Barrett's, put a shovel head down yer trousers and over yer langer, the fecking cat's a lunatic, so it is. It should be hunted down and shot.'

Feelings still ran too high for the men to laugh openly about the death of the priest. After all, some of the men still weren't allowed out in case they should meet the same fate. Tommy realized he couldn't stay in the pub. There was no light relief here.

The landlord began to pull Tommy a pint of Guinness.

'Hold it there, Bill,' said Tommy. 'Four bottles to take out, please.'

Whilst the barman descended into the cellar to fetch the bottles, Tommy walked over to Brian's da.

'Aye, Tommy, howaya?' said McGinty, looking up from his dominoes. 'Do ye fancy a game, Tommy?'

'No, McGinty, I don't and I will tell ye this right now, neither do ye. Get your arse back round home and see to ye wife and kids, else pay me back the ten shillings you borrowed from me to pay the rent.'

McGinty looked at Tommy with his mouth wide open and then began to laugh. 'Don't be an eejit, Tommy, I'm in the middle of a feckin' game.'

Tommy moved over to the table, put his face close to McGinty's and held his hand out.

'The ten shillings, right now.'

McGinty slowly rose to his feet, swearing under his breath.

"I have no feckin' ten shillings as well yer know, yer bastard."

Tommy walked back to the bar as the barman came up with the Guinness.

'Well, that's unusual, Tommy, I thought 'twas only the ladies who drank the bottles on your street.'

'Aye, and me and the missus too,' said Tommy, counting out his coins on the counter.

As Tommy turned right towards Nelson Street, he looked left and, through the mist, saw McGinty, staggering down the street towards home with Brian running from the pie shop to catch him up.

Maura couldn't have looked more surprised when Tommy walked in through the back with the four bottles. Her eyes filled with a ridiculous pleasure at seeing him home again. She shared his sadness. They both ached. She had been sorry that he had gone out to the pub, but at the same time she understood why. She was tidying away discarded shoes and children's cardigans and jackets that had been scattered all around the kitchen, placing each on its own peg on the door to the stairs, when Tommy walked in.

'Sit ye down, queen,' said Tommy kindly, as he put the poker in the fire to heat and took the bottles to the opener that hung from a piece of string next to the sink.

Maura flopped into one fireside chair and Tommy into the other. As she kicked off her slippers, Tommy plunged the poker first into her Guinness and then back into the red embers for his own.

As they lifted the bottles to drink, they grinned at each other for the first time in weeks. Maura left her chair and sat down on the rug in between Tommy's legs, with one arm on his knee. She looked up at him as they chatted and drank their Guinness in front of the leaping flames for an hour before bed.

Not about the evil that had swamped their lives and divided them, but about the things that held them together.

Their families in Ireland and America.

Tommy's work. What to do about Malachi? Who in the family did Angela take after and had someone snuck into the house and swapped babies when they were sleeping? They talked about the things Kitty would see and do in Ireland, and the kindness of Jerry and Kathleen and the entire Deane family to help in this way. For the first time they talked about everything and anything other than that awful night. That night, Maura realized, was beginning to drive them apart.

Night-time chatter had always been a part of Maura and Tommy's routine. Tommy always sat in the fireside chair, or at the table with his paper, while Maura nattered away to him as she cleared the dishes and tidied up. The ritual had stopped abruptly the night Father James was caught in Kitty's bedroom and it hadn't resumed since, until tonight.

'Bed,' said Tommy, draining the last of his second bottle.

'You go up,' said Maura. 'I want to sort the washing for the morning.'

'I bloody won't,' replied Tommy with a huge grin. 'Get ye'self up those stairs, missus, ye are in for a treat tonight. It's been over a week and that's not natural for any man, especially not this one.'

Afterwards, as Tommy slept a sleep of deep contentment, Maura slipped out of bed. The washing still needed to be sorted for the morning. She sat on the edge of the mattress and looked back at the man she loved, who had fathered their beautiful and loving children. He was the best husband. He didn't deserve to be in this position of guilt. Before she left his side, Maura prayed to God to forgive them for defending their child and asked him to bring them peace.

Maura prayed a great deal.

After all, it was not as if she could take confession.

Chapter Eleven

HOWARD AND SIMON had not been able to gain entry to
the Priory until the morning after the bishop had arrived.

At first, Howard had been furious at the nuns' refusal to
allow them in immediately following the murder. He and
Simon had tried to be as gentle as possible, explaining the
reason why it was very important that they have free access.
As gentle as it was possible for two hard-nosed Liverpool
detectives to be.

They had visited the Priory the morning after, but there
was nothing to be seen, other than a gaggle of nuns in a state
of high distress.

Miss Devlin, the teacher for whom Howard had a soft
spot, was in the process of comforting the housekeeper. She
told them no one had been near the Priory and that for all of
the previous day the priest had been away, along with everyone else, at the church and the wedding breakfast.

The Priory had felt cold and flat, unyielding of what it
knew.

The wailing and crying of the nuns, uninviting.

'There's nothing to see here,' Howard had said, finding the
tears of a nun particularly disturbing. 'Let's concentrate on
the school.'

And, sure enough, they had got lucky, or so they thought,

when Little Paddy had blurted out what he thought he had seen from the window that night.

Although the lead had crumbled away into dust in their hands, it had kept them busy for days. But although the lead hadn't held firm, both Howard and Simon felt that nothing was quite as it appeared.

'I can smell a great big dirty rat,' Howard said. 'I just can't bloody see it yet, that's all.'

The superintendent had begun breathing down their necks with threats of demotion and castration if they did not solve the case. It was now time to begin turning over even the very smallest stones.

The bishop had led them both into the study and dispatched Daisy to the kitchen to fetch a tray of tea.

Howard had no idea where to begin without causing offence. As he took his notebook and pencil from the inside pocket of his jacket, he cast his eye around, looking for an object of interest in order to stimulate a casual conversation.

But the study was deadly dull with no ornamentation to elicit his admiration nor painting to be commented upon. Heavy drapes hung across the windows as a mark of respect and the only light shone from a standard lamp in the corner, throwing eerie, creeping shadows onto the high ceiling and the tobacco-stained walls.

The murky-brown sofa and chair had seen better days and, apart from a small table in front of the sofa, the only other piece of furniture, in one corner, was the priest's large dark wooden desk, with one tall hard-backed chair behind it and two smaller chairs opposite.

Tall dark-oak bookcases partly lined the walls, the books appearing not to have been read for many years.

Only a circular dark-burgundy rug with a deep-grey fringe

provided any colour. Howard sighed. The room depressed him. There was something on the edge of the aroma, in the smell of musty old books and forgotten sermons, that made him feel intensely uncomfortable. Having been keen to gain entry into the Priory, he now couldn't wait to get out.

Howard ran his finger irritably around his collar, easing it away from his neck.

'May I look through the father's desk, Bishop, whilst we wait for the tea?' he asked.

'Of course, Detective Inspector,' said the bishop, 'but I am afraid it is quite empty. We removed all the private papers yesterday.'

'Really?' said Howard, with a note of surprise in his voice.

Simon raised his eyebrows. Howard's intuition was kicking in. 'What private papers?' he asked.

'Well, there were his sermon notes going back over some years and he had kept all his prayer requests and mass cards and his confirmation lesson notes.'

Howard immediately felt stupid.

'And what about his bedroom, his clothes and personal possessions?'

'Clothes?' The bishop stood before Howard, looking slightly confused, his brow deeply furrowed. Howard reddened immediately, feeling stupid and keener than ever to leave.

'The only personal possessions in his room were his watch and personal bible, with his coat and hat and a few other personal books. They were dispatched today, to his sister in America.'

'That parcel will be a bundle of laughs to open,' said Howard under his breath as he turned away.

Daisy tapped on the door and, once the bishop had shouted for her to enter, crossed the floor with the tray of tea.

Howard felt the familiar feeling of despair. They were heading nowhere fast, again.

The priest walks home from a wedding, is murdered and dismembered in the graveyard, and they don't have a bloody clue why or how. He felt his promotion slipping further and further away.

As Daisy handed the cups round, Simon tried to engage her in conversation.

'Have you worked here long, miss?'

'Oh, yes,' said Daisy, 'nearly twenty years now.'

'That's a long time,' said Howard, smiling at her. 'I don't suppose you saw anything unusual on the night the father was murdered that you think we should know about, did you?'

Daisy looked at Howard with some intensity, as was her way. This was different from any question the sister had asked her and one she had to think about. *Was there anything she thought they should know about?* Well, maybe there was. Maybe she had seen something and it was nothing to do with what happened inside the Priory and so she wouldn't be in any trouble if she mentioned it.

Would she? Should she?

While she pondered Daisy continued to stare at Howard, as though her eyes were boring into his very soul. He felt disconcerted and, with an embarrassed cough, sat up straight in the chair, struggling to balance his cup and saucer. He wasn't used to saucers. He wasn't used to a cup that had retained a handle.

'The girl is simple.' The bishop's voice sliced through the loaded silence. 'Very simple. Back to the kitchen now, please, girl.'

She would have to be, to work here, Howard thought,

looking around at the dreary room, slightly relieved that Daisy had stopped staring at him.

Within an hour, Howard and Simon had jumped back into the police car and were heading off down the gravel drive. As they turned left towards the four streets, Simon banged the dashboard.

'God, it's doing my fucking head in. I know there is summat we are missing, like it is just there, out of our reach, and yet we can't get a handle on any of it.'

Howard was silent, deep in thought. As he shifted up a gear, he turned back down the Dock Road into town and, looking into the rear-view mirror, he replied, 'We just keep shaking the tree, Simon, or, better still, let Molly Barrett do it for us. That nosy old woman is better than a dozen detectives on that street. If there is something to know, she will lead us to it, I promise you. We need to give her a little encouragement, sit back and wait.'

Annie O'Prey had finished brushing her step and wondered why Molly had been a no-show. Although their front doors were only two feet apart from each other, Annie turned back inside and walked through her house, out of the back door, putting her broom away in the outhouse, then walked through her back yard, into the entry and in thorough Molly's back gate.

The front door was never used for the purpose that it was intended.

Molly was in the kitchen, baking.

'The priest is dead, Molly. He won't be wanting those scones where he's gone,' said Annie in a superior tone, as she folded her arms and sniffed her disapproval of a woman trying to cheat the inevitable reckoning at the pearly gates.

Annie felt pleased with herself, having found a weakness and scored a point. Annie was on top.

Molly neither acknowledged Annie's presence, nor looked up from her task.

'I thought I would bake some for Daisy. I'm neither stupid nor senile, Annie,' she replied. 'I doubt a priest whose langer me cat brought home would be wanting a fresh scone.'

She mentally relished the put-down.

'I've always sent her a few in the batch I made for the priest. Daisy and I are good friends and now that a little time has passed, I thought I might as well pay her a visit, just to see how she is getting along. She has no friends as such and, God knows, it took her ten years before she even began to speak to me and I'm the easiest person in the world to get along with.'

Annie raised her eyebrows heavenwards. Only that morning, she had felt the need to discuss Molly's new-found self-importance with Frank, from the fish shop.

'God, that fat lump gets on me nerves something wicked, so she does. Thinks she's very important now that she's having cups of tea in the parlour with the bizzies. Such an interfering busybody she is herself an' all.'

'Don't listen to her, then,' said Frank. 'Leave the woman to her own devices.'

Both Frank and Annie knew that would never happen. Molly and Annie were best friends who complained about each other so often, it was as if they were sisters.

'There you go, Annie, that's a nice bit of fish,' said Frank, handing her the damp and neatly folded newspaper package. 'Give the skin to Molly's cat, keep him happy and away from my front door, for feck's sake. It's a jungle out there on your streets.'

Annie blessed Frank with smile as she left to impart to

Molly the gossip she had gathered from the fish-shop queue. All animosity towards her neighbour was forgotten in a flash of her naked gums.

Daisy looked out of the large sash window as she made the bishop's bed to see Alice walking with the pram down to the bottom of Nelson Street, and Molly walking up towards the church with a basket in her hand, covered with a tea towel. She hoped Molly would be heading to the Priory and, when she turned the corner into the drive, Daisy's heart skipped a beat.

She hadn't seen Molly since the Sunday before the priest died.

Daisy's head was hurting with all the things she had seen and heard, and now that the bishop was on his way back to Dublin, she hoped that Sister Evangelista would let her stay at the convent until the father's replacement arrived. Sister had told Daisy to call into the convent after she had cleaned the Priory, but for now she would stop and have a cup of tea with Molly.

Daisy had a visitor. At last, someone she could talk to about all the things burning in her brain.

Chapter Twelve

ALICE AND JOSEPH were on their way to Brigid and Sean's house.

Brigid was sitting in front of the range with her youngest lying across her lap, about to have her nappy changed.

'Hello, come in, come and sit down, and how's our baby Joseph this morning?' Brigid cheerfully greeted Alice. 'Has the tooth come through that was giving him hell yesterday?'

'Morning, Brigid, no, it hasn't and I really wish it would. He hardly slept last night and his cheeks are burning up like mad,' said Alice, lifting Joseph out of his pram.

'Have ye any Disprin?' Brigid asked Alice.

She didn't look up as she deftly removed the pink-topped nappy pin from the white towelling nappy worn by her scrap of a red-headed daughter. Brigid was house-proud. The whiteness of her nappies, as they blew in the breeze, was a source of joy to her. She had seen too many grey nappies blowing on lines around her and had vowed that hers would always be the whitest in the entry.

As soon as the dust from a load at the docks blew up and across the four streets, she was the only mother to dash straight outside to pull her nappies off the line and dry them indoors.

'No, I haven't used anything, to be honest. Kathleen usually deals with most of this. I am really not sure what to do.'

'Hang on, give me five minutes and I'll get him one, I've plenty. I will just change this little madam's nappy.'

Alice thought how much the red-headed baby reminded her of a skinned rabbit. The soaking wet nappy had filled the room with the heavy smell of ammonia.

To Alice's horror, Brigid now folded the nappy over and wiped it across her own face, rubbing down the side of her nose before holding her hair back to wipe her forehead and under her chin. Then she rubbed it across her cheeks and over her closed eyes.

'Oh, my giddy aunt,' squealed Alice. 'Why the hell did you just do that, with that stinking-wet nappy? The wee has been on that all night!'

Brigid laughed. 'Exactly, and it's all nicely concentrated. There's a reason why we Liverpool girls have the best complexions in England, Alice. A wipe-over with the first wet nappy of the morning is the only beauty regime we need.'

'What, you do that every morning?' Alice found it difficult to hide her revulsion.

'Alice, I have a brood of daughters and an endless supply of wet nappies. I have been doing it for years and so does every woman on the four streets and across the whole of Liverpool. Sean tells me the sailors all say the same thing, that there are no women in the world with skin as soft as that of Liverpool women. They say the sailors are so captivated by it, they sing sad songs about Liverpool girls as they leave port, so they do, and happy ones when they sail back in.'

Alice had to admit it. The women who never seemed to wash, and smelt none too pleasant, always had lovely complexions.

Many of the women on the four streets had lost most of their teeth and those they retained were black and crumbling, but their skin remained beautiful. You could even tell that Annie O'Prey had once had nice skin.

'Jeez, Alice, where have ye been living all of ye life?' said Brigid, laughing.

With expert deftness, she picked up the baby and handed her straight to Alice, who was so shocked she almost dropped her. How did she explain to Brigid that she had never even held baby Joseph until he was three months old?

But Brigid hadn't noticed and was still talking as she pulled back the curtain across her kitchen press to look for a Disprin.

Alice stood with the baby in her outstretched arms begging for her not to move or make a sound.

'Was there anything else ye needed?' said Brigid as she rooted around in her cupboard.

'No, nothing, I just thought I would pop in to say hello and to say that we would love to come again to the club with you and Sean, if you are ever going on a Saturday night again.'

Alice didn't take her eyes off the baby while she spoke.

'Wasn't it a grand night!'

'It was, yes, we loved it and Angela was great about minding Joseph. Jerry gave her sixpence when we got back.'

'God, I would have to pay someone a fortune to mind mine, so I would. We have so many, we have to wait until Sean's mammy is here, but she isn't going back for a few weeks so we can do it again. Will ye stay for a cuppa? Sure, go on, ye only have the one little fella to look after, ye have time.'

Alice was happy to stay for a while. She wanted to ask Brigid questions about Sean and their plans for America. Her golden opportunity came just as Sean's mammy walked in the back door.

'Oh, hello, Alice, how lovely to see ye. Are ye stopping for a cuppa?' Mrs McGuire said, before she had even taken her coat off.

Sean's mother was half the size of her son and a fine-looking woman. On her visit from her village just outside of Galway, she had adopted the Liverpool custom of leaving her curlers in underneath a hairnet. It was not something she did back at home, where they didn't bother with the curlers. A headscarf was good enough.

But now Mrs McGuire was looking worried.

'Brigid, Caoimhe does not like that school, I'm telling ye, she does not. I almost had to push her through the door. If ye ask me, the nuns in Liverpool are different altogether from the nuns in Ireland.'

Brigid said, 'I know, Mrs McGuire, but what can I do? The nuns say she will get used to it soon enough.'

Mrs McGuire was having none of it.

'Aye, she might that, but if you ask me, those nuns are too cruel. One of them slapped her across her little legs because she was crying for me. Dragged her in through the door by her arm, the sister did. She doesn't get that at home, Brigid, so why should she have to take it at school? Broke my heart, so it did, to leave her at the gate. Why won't the nuns let us into the yard to say goodbye? Cruel, so it is.'

Brigid was only half listening as she mixed a spoon of molasses into Joseph's bottle and handed it back to Alice, full of the dark liquid.

'Here, give that to Joseph,' she said, wiping the bottle with a tea towel.

'I will, thanks, but what on earth is in it?' asked Alice, as she smelt the teat of the bottle.

'It's a bit of molasses, nicked from one of the tankers,

mixed with a little warm water and a dissolved Disprin, mixed in with Joseph's milk to take the pain out of his teeth. He'll have a lovely morning nap after that.'

Alice nervously tipped the bottle and put it into Joseph's mouth. His eyes opened as wide as saucers when he took the first mouthful.

'See, they love it,' said Brigid. 'Kathleen will have a jar of molasses in the cupboard; just a spoon and he will be fine, but only a little. You can mix it in with the milk once a day, but be careful he doesn't get used to it now and want it all the time. The tankers don't come in every day and we have to take it in turns as to who gets the drippings from the loadings.'

'My God, that is the first time he has smiled in days,' said Alice, sitting down on the chair to nurse Joseph, who was sucking so furiously that she was afraid to break his stride.

She was also watching Sean's mammy, and waiting for an opportunity to talk to her about America. She leapt in almost straight away.

'So, do you get to visit your daughter in America, Mrs McGuire?'

'I do, Alice, and sure 'tis a wonderful place altogether. They pay for my fare to go and beg me to live there with them, but sure I can't, unless Sean and Brigid decide to go too. I can't leave them behind with all these babies to look after on their own, can I?'

Searching for the molasses had given Brigid an excuse to tidy out the press and wipe out the drawers. She gave Alice a sideways look as she emptied out the contents onto the kitchen table and wiped down the shelves. She had noticed Alice and Sean were in animated conversation about America on Saturday night. The conversation had made Brigid uncomfortable and she didn't want Alice starting to talk about it again to Sean's mammy.

'I have a mammy too, Alice,' said Brigid haughtily. 'And I have an opinion, and I'm afraid America is not for me and Mrs McGuire knows that. If the boot was on the other foot, you wouldn't want me to be dragging Sean away over to America and leaving ye all alone, now would ye, Mrs McGuire?'

The temperature in the room had noticeably dropped and Alice stood to take her leave. She was amazed by Brigid's lack of ambition and thought how much she wished she could change places with her. She would even have a dozen kids if it meant getting away from Liverpool and on a boat to America.

Later that evening, Sean won three matches in a row. It had been a good fight and he had pocketed seven pounds and ten shillings from each match. More than he took in a week's wages on the docks.

He was doing better than he had ever dared to hope and his savings were mounting up.

This was a relief. He had to train hard and, what with his job, it meant he was hardly ever at home. Boxing was a means to an end. He didn't enjoy working on the docks, but at least with the boxing he fought for the money and it was his. He wasn't lining the pockets of the thieving bastards over at the Mersey Dock Company.

As Sean walked home, it occurred to him that there were many things in his life he wasn't happy with, other than having to work every moment God sent.

One of them was Brigid's constant reluctance to talk about the day he was saving for, when they could pack up and leave for America, and join his family in Chicago. He wanted to work hard for himself and his family. To be in charge of his own destiny.

In America, he knew his efforts would be rewarded with a better life for them all.

In England, he struggled to save. Each week he made the dock company wealthier and had his head punched in every Friday night. Life had to be better than that.

His sister's letters were full of the most innocent yet enticing details.

His mother could not stop talking about the opportunies for those prepared to take a risk and put in the graft.

Already his sister and her husband were earning a small fortune, enough to buy their own home and pay for his mother to sail to America twice a year. This summer they had been to Florida for a holiday and had sent him a postcard. It made his stomach crunch to think how much easier and more prosperous life was for them.

Sean decided that he would talk to Brigid again when he got into bed. He would wake her up if he had to. Brigid had to stop this ridiculous, small-minded clinging onto what she knew and realize that emigrating to America was for the good of the family.

'Jeez, what is up with the woman?' he said out loud as he shook his head.

He loved home as much as the next Irishman, but even in Galway there was nothing for Sean other than poverty and then more poverty for his kids too. He punched the entry wall with his fist as he turned the top corner and, for the first time that night, his knuckles bled. Lucky that he had another week for the skin to heal over.

As Sean looked up he was shocked to see Alice standing by her back gate. He had enjoyed talking to her at the Irish centre. She had none of Brigid's reserve. They had spoken most of the night about America. Alice had told him she had kept all the brochures she had found that had been left by guests staying at the Grand before taking their passage across the Atlantic, and that sometimes she still read through them.

God, Jerry doesn't know how lucky he is, thought Sean. I wish I was married to someone who had a spirit like Alice.

'Everything all right, Alice?' Sean asked.

'Yes, everything is fine, Sean. I hope you don't mind me asking, but I want to know so much about how to get to America, and to try to persuade Jerry that it would be such a good idea. I wondered if we could talk again some time?'

Alice felt a thrill that came only when she was in her own secret world. Talking out her fantasies with Sean, without Jerry or anyone else being aware, was exciting. She wanted to know Sean better.

'Would you mind not telling Jerry or Brigid that I asked, though?'

'Aye, of course, and don't worry, I won't mention anything. If Jerry is as stubborn as Brigid, I know exactly what ye mean.'

Alice glanced up at the bedroom window, where Jerry had been sleeping for the last hour. As she looked back at Sean, her eyes gleamed in the moonlight. Sean noticed there was something different, unusual about her. Was she wearing lipstick? Unlike the other women, Alice never ever wore a hairnet and she had styled her hair in the fashion of the girls who worked in the offices in town.

Her deep fringe swept almost over her eyes, with the rest of her hair hanging loose on her shoulders.

Alice had experimented with changes every day for weeks. Sean had noted that she was always a little smarter than the other women on the four streets, in a very English kind of way. No one had seen much of her for years and yet suddenly it was as if she was everywhere.

This was the third time he had seen Alice in as many days.

Alice noticed the blood running down Sean's fingers. She reached out and took his hand in hers, examining it and dabbing his knuckles with her apron, making him flinch.

'Oh, my goodness, is that from your fight?' She looked up at him, holding both of his huge hands in hers, her eyes wide, and turned over the damaged hand to search for further signs of injury.

Alice now took her handkerchief out of her pocket and, wetting it with her saliva, began dabbing away at the open graze.

'No, Alice,' Sean laughed. He had knocked three men out cold tonight without a scratch. How could he tell her it was from punching the entry wall? 'I skimmed my hand on the wall as I walked past,' he said, pulling away.

The sensation of another woman holding his hands made him uncomfortable. Not because it was unpleasant, in fact it was just the opposite. It was a feeling he hadn't experienced for a long time.

He had enjoyed talking to Alice on Saturday night. He had noticed that she had become prettier as the months went by. Since Kathleen had moved into the four streets, Alice had filled out and was no longer the skinny wretch she had once been.

There was an air of aloofness, of reserve about her that Sean quite liked. She wasn't like the Irish girls at home who were apt to be overly friendly in their search for a husband. Alice had a detachment, which he now realized was quite exciting.

'It will be fine. I will run it under the tap when I get in.'

Sean gazed down. He could smell the warmth of her hair and was overcome by a sudden compulsion to bend down and kiss her.

The entry was asleep. Dark and deeply quiet.

'Sure, Alice, I am fine,' he said. 'It is no problem, really.'

Alice, resigned, pushed the handkerchief up her sleeve again and, drawing her cardigan across to keep out the night air, lifted her face to Sean.

'Sean, I think I said too much in front of your mother when I visited this morning and I really hope I haven't caused a problem. It's just that nothing pleases me more than talking about the prospect of living in America and Jerry won't even hear about it. I feel very lonely sometimes and would love to talk to someone who feels just as I do.'

Sean looked down at Alice's hand, which she had placed on his arm whilst she leant forward and whispered to him. She had made the same gesture when he had seen her outside of the shop. It was friendly and intimate. The sensation burnt through his coat sleeve. A warm hint of perfume wafted upwards and distracted him. He realized that never, in all the time he and Brigid had been together, had he smelt the feminine scent of perfume.

Alice was no longer the plain Protestant English girl. She was now almost pretty and, to Sean, in the midst of an assault on his senses, she was certainly very sexy.

Not because of what she wore, or how she looked, although that did play a part. But because of what she said.

She was talking his language and it was playing with his mind.

'I am working the graveyard shift tomorrow. Why don't you come down to the café on the Dock Road and we could have a chat, before I walk home?' Sean suggested.

'Great, that's fantastic, I would love to. I will see you there ten minutes after the klaxon then.'

Alice put her hand on the back gate and lifted the latch.

He smiled. She smiled. They lingered.

The moon glinted from the wet cobbled pavement whilst millions of stars shone and bore witness to the silent messages that flew from one pair of eyes to the other.

Nothing either of them could now do would erase those first few moments.

It had begun.

Sean had already had sex once that day.

Brigid was so scared of becoming pregnant yet again that she often slipped into the bedroom when Sean was washing after work and went down on her knees to satisfy her husband, in order to avoid full sex later.

She regarded it more as a daily task to be completed, rather than an expression of love or intimacy.

An act of efficiency. Two jobs in the time of one. Sean sorted. All finished and done in ten minutes.

The women talked openly and graphically about sex. Their jokes were as ribald as the men's. Each knew exactly who had sex and when. Every woman in the four streets often knew when another was pregnant, even before her own husband did.

Sex provided a reason to complain. An excuse to be ill.

The detail of conversations was always explicit and uninhibited.

Brigid was the only woman on the four streets who undertook this ungodly act and she was frequently besieged with questions from the others, appalled by what she did. Following the third child, they would never willingly volunteer to have sex of any description and went to imaginative lengths to avoid it, all except Maura.

Enthralled, they pressed Brigid for details each time they met in Maura's kitchen for a cuppa and a gossip.

'What does it taste like?' asked Maura, more curious than disgusted.

'It surely has to be a sin, Brigid. Do ye pray for forgiveness?' asked Sheila.

'Sure, I do. I never miss six o'clock mass, Sheila. I'm only a sinner for a few minutes. The father is fabulous and kind, so he is. He asks me for all the little details and I mean every one, to guarantee I am fully absolved, because, sure, we both know I will do it again,' said Brigid. 'He always asks me do I enjoy meself and I always answer, not at all, so that makes it all right, I reckon.

'Confessing to the father takes almost as long as keeping Sean happy. I spend longer on me knees praying for forgiveness and saying Hail Marys than I do with Sean's langer in me mouth. But I'd rather that than have another baby in me belly just now.'

All the women laughed at this, some with genuine mirth, others in utter amazement at Brigid's audacity.

'Ye can still get pregnant doing that disgusting thing, so ye can,' said Peggy when they had all calmed down. 'Ye might think ye is being clever, but ye will still end up with another babby. Do what I do. Just tell Sean to feck off and stop bothering ye.'

'Oh my God, has Sean tried it on with you too, Peggy? That's disgustin', the man is a fiend,' squealed Deirdre from Tipperary, who always got the wrong end of the stick.

'Jesus, no,' screamed Peggy. 'Sean may be the big man around here, but he'd know what a fist was, to be sure, if he tried anything on with meself.'

Brigid often wondered if she would ever one day tell them how she had discovered the way to keep Sean happy and to stop herself from becoming pregnant more often than she already was. Brigid knew she never could. It would be a betrayal and, besides, it was a sinful thing to do to speak in such a way of the dead. Bernadette and Brigid had shared many secrets and her special way to keep Sean happy had been one. Let the leaves of the sprawling oak tree, each one as big as a lady's hand, fan the summer breeze across her grave. Let her be in peace, with the daffodils, tulips and wild primroses in the spring. Red roses and lilac in the summer. Burnt-orange chrysanthemums in the autumn. All provided by the old woman, selling her flowers for sixpence a bunch, from a metal pail at the cemetery gate which Brigid placed in the old, discoloured jam jar at the foot of her headstone.

Often, when running back from six o'clock mass, Brigid would notice that the old flower woman had left for the day.

Having taken the remaining flowers from her pail and shaken the slimy water and strings of bright green moss free from the naked stalks, she would lay the tired blooms with drooping, sleepy heads against the gate railings, for the grave-diggers to collect and lay on some lonely and forgotten grave.

Brigid would pick up a few of the blooms (she never took them all) and then, running up the path, she would take the flowers to the friend she had not forgotten, Bernadette.

Brigid never confessed to the other women that, when they were all gathered in Maura's kitchen together, Bernadette was sitting at the table with them, too. She was sure of it.

Laughing and smiling with them.

When they banged their mops on the walls to summon each other to a powwow, they were also waking one of the dead.

They would think she was mad.

Maybe she was mad. Maybe it was her mind playing tricks. Over the last week Brigid had felt strongly as though Bernadette was trying to send her a message. It made Brigid uneasy, in a way she could not put into words, nor did she want to.

Maybe she hadn't seen her, but she was sure she had.

At first, Sean had enjoyed Brigid's routine.

An act, provided by his loving wife, thought to be in the domain of prostitutes alone, had been exciting. It had thrilled him. He knew he was lucky and that there were many men on the four streets who would die happy if their wives would do the same just once in their lifetime.

But now it had become robotic. He had his allotted few minutes, amongst her tightly choreographed domestic tasks, and it was the same every single day. His needs were just another item on her domestic checklist, slotted somewhere between dishes, mopping the floor and mass. He resented it.

But not tonight. Alice had stirred him.

Tonight he wanted full and proper sex. The kind that was normal between a man and wife. He would whisper to Brigid that he would jump off at Edge Hill and that she wouldn't become pregnant. He needed her closeness. To feel her in intimacy and warmth, like it used to be. He was desperate for reassurance that they were a team.

Like Jerry, Brigid had been asleep for over an hour when Sean slipped into bed, began kissing her neck and slowly lifting up her nightdress.

She was exhausted. Between teething toddlers and nursing babies, she had achieved only three hours' sleep the previous night.

'What are ye doing that for? Stop it now,' she whispered,

as she clambered up through the layers of sleep and looked at him with bleary eyes. She knocked his hand away. 'You've already been sorted today and ye will wake yer mammy, sleeping downstairs below us.'

Brigid rolled over and turned her back to him, pulling her nightdress in tightly behind her knees.

Sean was disappointed but, realizing there was no point in persisting, rolled onto his back and let his thoughts dwell on Alice.

The little Alice whose eyes lit up when she spoke about America.

He tried to sleep, constantly shifting his body weight on the mattress, searching for a limb on which to lay his weight on that wasn't bruised or tender.

His physical discomfort lessened as his thoughts wandered to the prospect of meeting Alice tomorrow. A woman who could talk about things other than babies and housework. A woman who was interesting. A woman who wanted more.

When sleep finally took Sean, he was already lost in the arms of Alice. And in a similar bed in an identical house further down the entry, Alice was lost in his.

Chapter Thirteen

KITTY AND NELLIE woke to Kathleen gently shaking them.

'Wake up, ye sleeping beauties,' she laughed. 'We have arrived.'

The first thing Kitty noticed was the smell. Without thinking, she put her hand over her mouth and nose and retched.

'Don't worry, Kitty love,' said Kathleen, 'ye will be used to it soon enough.'

'Aye, that's the smell of the proper earth, Kitty, so it is, and I'm glad to see, miss, that you have now become accustomed to it,' said Liam, gently poking Nellie in the ribs.

Even though Nellie was half asleep, she grinned.

'I'm so sorry,' said Kitty. 'I don't mean to be rude.'

'Not at all, child,' laughed Liam. 'If ye want rude, Miss Nellie can teach ye a thing or two. The first time I got her out of the van, on her first visit, she was as green as the turf, weren't you now, Nellie?'

Nellie looked sheepish. ''Tis true,' she replied, as from the tail of her eye she watched Liam imitating her throwing up and laughing to himself, making Nellie grin, reluctantly.

'Will ye pack it in, Liam,' said Kathleen. 'I am parched and want to move these girls inside to see Maeve and have a cuppa tea.'

Kitty was now standing outside the van, observing her new surroundings, as Liam lifted the bags out from under the tarpaulin. The deep-blue sky was broken by a full moon, illuminating the Ballymara road, a silver ribbon, all the way back to Bangornevin. Light also poured out from the open doorway of the farmhouse while the lamps in the windows beamed a warm orange glow.

Her surroundings could not have been less like the four streets.

To her right, she could make out the dark and forbidding hill that ran steeply up from the roadside and she could smell the tall rhododendron bushes which bordered the edge of the Ballymara road in a deep crimson fringe.

She could hear a gentle trickle of water and noticed an old stone sink standing in the middle of a stream at the bottom of the hill, directly opposite the pathway to the house.

To her left and out of sight, down past the farmhouse, she could hear the faster-running peaty-brown water of the Moorhaun river.

'That's what Nana Kathleen used for water when she was a little girl,' said Liam, nodding towards the stone sink. 'Ask her to tell ye the stories. Our own ancestors carved that and put it in place to collect and store the water from the stream. Come away in now and eat, plenty of time for exploring tomorrow.'

Kitty could smell so many things.

Water and peat. Crops and cattle. Iron and earth.

The smell was so rich, so natural, it stung the inside of her nostrils and caught the back of her throat, but she instinctively knew it was good air. Free from the smog, coal and stone dust that daily blew upwards from the docks and hovered over the four streets in a threatening cloud, coating the houses and windows with a thin layer of dust and grime.

The air here was free from the toxic yellow smoke spewed out by the chimneys of the houses that edged the Mersey and of the foundries set back from the Dock Road. Free from the fumes and chemicals churned out by the processing plants, which Maura was convinced were responsible for making Harry ill.

Kitty breathed in deeply and slowly. She had quickly acclimatized to the stinging purity and freshness of the air. Her lungs took their fill.

'Come away in and meet Maeve,' said Nellie, who was now fully awake and brimming with barely containable excitement. It was eleven o'clock and they were still up and dressed with no school tomorrow. She was bouncing up and down on the spot as she took Kitty's hand.

'You will love Maeve,' she said. 'She and Uncle Liam are so funny together, she gives out to him so badly and he just laughs at her, which makes her so mad. Come on now, away inside.'

Kitty was reluctant to leave the utterly peaceful quiet and the freshness of the night outdoors. If it hadn't been for the midges crashing into the van lights and swarming around her in clouds, she might have stood there for ever.

'Welcome to Ballymara,' said Maeve from the hallway, smiling as she bustled everyone indoors.

Nellie had explained, before they left, that Ballymara consisted of a road that ran from Bangornevin with two farms at the end.

'Bangornevin is a larger village altogether,' said Nellie.

Kitty was in for a shock. Larger meant it had just two hundred residents. She was expecting something the size of Liverpool. She had never been to a village in her life.

Kitty's first impression of Maeve was that she was stunningly beautiful. Her long auburn hair fell over her shoulders in big curls and her huge brown eyes poured out kindness like a tap. She had the bright rosy cheeks of a farmer's wife, and her figure was generous and comely. Kitty longed to fall into her arms and be hugged, but instead she held out her hand in the way Liam had in Dublin, just a few hours before.

Maeve, smiling, shook Kitty's hand. Kitty was taken aback by the coarseness and dryness of her skin. She had brought her new washbag of toiletries and was overcome by an impulsive urge to give her precious new hand cream to Maeve as a present.

'Come here,' said Maeve impulsively and threw her arms round Kitty. 'We don't do your English handshaking in Ballymara, miss.' And she led her towards the warm orange glow of the kitchen. Kitty grinned and looked over her shoulder towards Nellie, who winked and grinned back.

Kitty felt a weight slipping from her shoulders as she walked along beside Maeve. It was as though by leaving the four streets she had also left her problems behind her. She had been exhausted for so long by keeping a dark and draining secret and now she had been told she was pregnant. A baby. A bomb. An explosion of fact in the midst of what had once been her ordinary schoolgirl life.

She was totally unprepared for the next shock, when Maeve walked her straight into it.

Maeve's arm was still round her shoulders as they passed from the hallway into the kitchen. Kitty had only ever seen inside kitchens on the four streets and what greeted her made her mouth gape open in surprise.

The kitchen was huge. On the left a fireplace took up half

of the height and half the length of the wall. In front of it stood a square wooden table, crowded with more food than Kitty had ever seen in her life.

In the middle was a hot and freshly roasted whole leg of pork, on a bed of crackling. Next to the pork lay a wooden board with a large sliced loaf of warm white bread and a freshly churned pat of deep yellow butter. In a larger bowl, big enough to bath a baby in, was a steaming mountain of mashed potatoes, mixed with dark green cabbage with butter melting over the top like an ice cap. Whole roasted buttery carrots sat on a plate next to the potatoes. There were pots of home-made apple sauce and chutney, their lids under green gingham mob caps.

Then, as if that weren't enough, there was a Victoria sponge cake bigger than any Kitty had ever seen before and a bowl of thick cream.

'I made the filling today, with the fruit we bottled from last year,' Maeve told her.

Maeve moved to the fire, filled an enormous brown teapot with boiling water and lifted it onto the table.

Kitty couldn't even speak. Never in all her life, even on their new black-and-white television, had she ever seen a table so laden with food or smelling as good as this one did. For the first time in months, she was ravenous.

'How did ye know we would be arriving now and to have everything just ready?' Kitty asked.

'Well,' Maeve replied, 'JT, who lives above the post office in Bellgarett, was watching for ye passing through in the van and when he spotted ye, he ran down into the post office and telephoned Mrs O'Dwyer at the post office in Bangornevin. Mrs O'Dwyer went across the road to the pub that is at the back of Murphy's butcher's and of course she got a drink for her trouble, and wouldn't she just love that, would Mrs O'Dwyer, any excuse, I'd say, and then Mickey from the bar at the back of the butcher's ran down the road to John's house, who of course, ye know, is Nellie's daddy's cousin, to let him know ye had been spotted, and he came down the Ballymara road on his bike to tell me ye had passed through Bellgarett twenty minutes since. 'Twas easy enough.'

And they all laughed at the bewildered look on Kitty's face. Even Kitty.

Once they had all eaten and the table had been cleared, Maeve took Kitty and Nellie to their room. Kitty was feeling relaxed. She had joined in the banter round the table whilst they were eating and was even beginning to find Liam's jokes funny.

As Maeve opened the bedroom door, and Kitty laid eyes on the room for the first time, she gave a loud gasp. 'Is this for us?'

'No, it's just for ye bags,' replied Maeve playfully, 'ye can sleep in the barn.'

'Of course it's for us,' squealed Nellie. 'Didn't I tell you the bedroom was beautiful?'

'Aye, you did sure enough, but you never said we had our own beds!'

Kitty stepped into the room. When he had brought in the bags, Liam had switched on a lamp on a bedside table with a pink lampshade, which bathed the room in a warm and comforting glow.

On either side of the table stood two single beds with lace bedspreads and Kitty's new holdall sat on the one nearest the window. She touched it, as though checking it was real; all her precious new things contained inside.

Kitty noticed the walls were painted a beautiful, pale, duck-egg blue. Instead of nets, curtains of thick cream lace hung at the windows and the heavy over-curtains were the same duck-egg blue as the walls, with tiny sprigs of cream flowers.

The floor was covered with hand-made rag rugs in pink, pale blue and cream, and the doors and window frames were painted a buttery cream.

Next to the door stood a press, with a lace runner and a huge pink jug in a bowl patterned with blue, white and cream flowers.

Nellie had described the room to Kitty, but she hadn't told her how it smelt. How comfortable it was. How lush were the cream lace bedspreads, which Maeve had been threading herself since she was twelve years old, or how thick the rag rugs felt under your feet. She had never explained that there was a fireplace, which burnt something that looked like blocks of earth and smelt of heather.

Nellie had not told her that she would have her very own bed to sleep in and a beautiful polished press on which to lay out her new and lovely things.

Maeve then took them to the much prized indoor bathroom down the corridor where Kitty and Nellie cleaned their teeth together before they dressed in their nightclothes, ready for bed.

By the time they returned to the bedroom, Maeve had already hung up their clothes and stored their holdalls under the bed.

Nana Kathleen bustled into the room just as Kitty was very carefully emptying the contents of her washbag and laying them out on top of the press. She had never felt so proud or grown-up in her life, nor seen anything as beautiful as her box of talc and hand cream, neatly arranged on top of the lace runner. She stood admiring them until Kathleen spoke.

'Well, look at ye two, all ready for bed, eh?'

Nellie loved how happy her nana was when they came home to Ireland.

Kathleen turned back the bed covers, and Kitty marvelled at the creamy crispness of the thick Irish linen sheets as she slipped into the coolness, despite the fire in the room. She squealed as her feet bumped against something hot and made of stone.

Everyone laughed.

'It's the Irish version of a hot-water bottle, Kitty. To keep the bed from the river air and your feet warm for a good night's sleep. We have the river at the back and a stream at the bottom of the mountains at the front of the house, so it's a constant battle. Even in summer we need the bottles.'

Nana Kathleen kissed them both goodnight.

'We will be exploring and visiting tomorrow, girls, so sleep well tonight.'

As soon as the door closed behind her, Nellie whispered, 'Well, what do you think of Ireland, Kitty? Donchya just love it?'

'I do, Nellie,' Kitty whispered back. 'It's just the grandest place, I had no idea how grand. You told me what it was like, I know you did, but I had no idea it was anything like this and you had never told me how lovely Maeve is. Is this the room you slept in last time you came, Nellie?'

But Nellie was already fast asleep.

Kitty lay on her back, thinking and listening. She could hear the water running outside and the moths beating against the window-pane, trying to reach the light of the candle, which Maeve had left burning in a glass lantern on the press.

She could hear the distant, muffled chatter of Kathleen and her son and daughter-in-law, sitting round the kitchen fire.

Kitty couldn't help thinking how wonderful it would be if her family could live in a house like this. She was still in a state of dazed amazement at how much had happened in just a few short days.

Who would ever have believed this? she thought.

She smiled and rolled over onto her side, wriggled into the crisp sheets and breathed in the smell of freshly laundered Irish linen. Her feet nestled around the hot brick and she fell asleep thinking ... sure, aren't I the lucky one? Green with envy they will all be. And she imagined the expressions on her friends' faces when they heard she was taking a holiday.

When Kitty awoke from a deep sleep a few hours later, she had no idea where she was.

The candle on the press had burnt down and the only light in the room came from the thin shafts of moonlight slipping in through the gap in the curtains.

Kitty's heart began to race. She could feel it. She was used to it.

She had been woken in the middle of the night many times before.

She instinctively reached out her hand to feel for Angela and then it dawned on her where she was.

She strained to pick up what it was that had woken her and then she heard it, the sound of boots crunching on shifting pebbles and the deep muttering of men's voices.

Kitty had no idea what time it was but she knew it had been midnight before bed. She didn't dare to look out of the window but she could tell by the light that dawn wasn't far off.

The house was deadly silent. There were no longer any comforting sounds emanating from the kitchen. Everyone in the house was long ago in bed and asleep. The fire in the bedroom must have gone out because the air in the room carried the edge of a damp chill.

She heard footsteps move along the side of the house and then away into the distance, down the Ballymara road. But one pair seemed to be approaching closer to their bedroom window. She could make out the shadow of a man with a cap on his head, slightly stooped and silhouetted against the window. She heard a door open very gently and then click shut.

She guessed from the sounds of the boots on the pebbles that there were as many as five men walking away from the house down towards Bangornevin and maybe one in the opposite direction, to the other farmhouse at the end of the road. Yes, the footsteps had definitely split into three directions.

Kitty thought they must be burglars. But what would they steal? Even she could work out that you would need a car to carry anything of significance down the long Ballymara road.

Kitty lay, her heart beating loudly with fear.

She wondered should she wake Nellie or one of the adults.

She had no idea of the layout of the house, or where anyone else was sleeping, but she felt very strongly that she should leave her bed and find Liam.

Her hot-water bottle was barely warm as she stretched her legs and turned to look at Nellie.

'Nellie,' she whispered, 'Nellie, wake up.'

But there was not a flicker of response. Nellie was exhausted.

Right, there's nothing for it, thought Kitty to herself. I'm out of this bed.

She swung both of her feet out onto the rug and tripped over to Nellie's bed. Once again, she tried to wake her, but Nellie was having none of it. Kitty had been thrilled at having her own bed to sleep in, for the first time in her life, but now she realized she didn't like it that much after all.

She gently pushed Nellie over and slipped into bed beside her. They had slept together in hospital, except for that one night, which Kitty had never let herself think about since, not even once.

She whispered, 'Nellie,' twice more, but with no response, and before she had the chance to try again, exhaustion claimed her and she once again fell into a deep sleep.

Chapter Fourteen

'OI, WHAT ARE you doing in my bed, then,' were Nellie's first words when she opened her eyes the following morning.

'God, you would never believe it,' said Kitty as she rubbed her eyes and surfaced from sleep. 'There were men outside last night and I thought I heard one of them get into the house. I was right scared.'

Nellie burst out laughing

'That wasn't men, Kitty, that was a nightmare.'

'No, sure it wasn't, I definitely heard them on the pebbles outside and everything.'

Nellie looked at Kitty to see if she was serious. She was. Nellie was younger than Kitty, but recently Nellie had felt as if she was the eldest and that Kitty was vulnerable, but she had no idea why.

Kitty used to be full of fun, but then suddenly she wasn't any more. Nellie was as confused as Kitty about the pregnancy and she didn't want to talk about it. It was a bad thing for Kitty to be having a baby, Nellie knew that, she just didn't know how bad.

'Let's get up now,' said Nellie. 'Maeve's breakfasts are to die for, but before she does the breakfast, she milks the cow, come and see.'

Both girls dived out of bed and Kitty ran straight to the window. She felt alive and full of excitement about the day ahead.

Their bedroom was at the front of the house. A pathway led from the front door to the narrow road, on the other side of which was the stream Kitty had seen the night before, with a mountain rising straight up beyond, and Kitty saw the deep cerise rhododendron flowers she had smelt last night.

'Holy Mary,' she exclaimed.

'We will walk up it,' said Nellie, pointing at what was really just a very large hill. 'The trouble is that it is very wet and boggy below. You have to go quite a way up before it becomes dry.'

Kitty was lost for words. She was used to Liverpool, to concrete and bombsite rubble.

Kitty and Nellie went to the bathroom together but two seconds later they ran screaming down the hallway.

'Oh merciful God, help me,' Kitty yelled, holding onto Nellie's hand as they flew into the kitchen, knocking Kathleen to one side.

Maeve was bent over the fire, loading the second batch of peat onto the sticks in the fireplace. Liam was sitting at the table, drinking his morning tea.

'Oh my God, Uncle Liam, help us, a big fish has swum up the plughole into the bath,' screamed Nellie, as she hurtled through the door and flung herself at Liam.

'Oh my goodness,' gasped Maeve, 'ye have met the salmon then.'

The adults were helpless with laughter while Nellie and Kitty stared at each other.

'I caught it, ye eejits,' said Liam, 'but don't say that to anyone, or ye will have the Gardai knocking on the door and having me up before the magistrate, ye will.'

As Kathleen's glasses had steamed up, she took them off the bridge of her nose to wipe on her apron.

'Uncle Liam is the chairman of the angling club, which is very useful now as we know the gillie rota and when it's safe or not to fish. As the salmon swim up through the farm, we take a good catch for ourselves and, sure, 'tis our land they are on, so why shouldn't we? The angling club think they own the waters God put here. They make me sick.'

Kathleen and Joe had fought many a battle with the authorities over the fact that the best salmon river in the West of Ireland ran twenty yards from their own back door and across land their family had owned for generations. Kathleen wiped her eyes with the corner of her apron as she remembered her late husband Joe. He had worked so hard to make the farm what it was today and had poached many a huge salmon, sometimes with the help of his young sons, from a curragh, teaching them the way, just as his father had before him and his own before that.

'Oh dear!' exclaimed Kathleen. 'Never mind me, 'tis just the tiredness and the journey home, it always gets to me.'

Kitty asked Liam, 'Ah, was that your footsteps I heard in the night? Were there other men with ye?'

'Aye, five of us last night. John McMahon, his nephew Aengus and a few others,' Liam replied. 'Now, away with ye, girls, and get dressed.'

Once both girls were dressed they ran through the kitchen and out to the cowshed at the bottom of the path, where Maeve was now sitting on a stool, milking.

Kitty was nervous. She had never seen a real cow before, never mind stood so close to one, and she had certainly not smelt anything quite like this. She didn't say anything, but this was the first morning she hadn't wanted to be ill as soon as she opened her eyes.

'Shall we carry the bucket, Maeve?' asked Nellie.

It was a sunny morning and the midges swarmed round their heads, stuck inside their hair and flew down the collars of their blouses.

'God, don't they drive you mad,' said Kitty.

'They will be gone by the time breakfast is over,' said Maeve, 'and ye will be used to them by tomorrow. They sleep on the bog all day but, mind, they will be back out as the sun goes down for another bite at ye.'

The girls deposited the milk in the dairy, a concrete shed to the side of the back door where Maeve made her cream and butter. Kitty was amazed that the milk in the bucket was warm.

'Is this what we drank in our tea last night? It smells disgusting,' she whispered to Nellie. 'It smells like the cow.'

'I know, but you will get used to it and you won't know any different soon, I promise,' Nellie replied.

Kitty wasn't convinced and was dreading having to drink the milk at breakfast.

Uncle Liam was heaping bacon rashers from the griddle onto a plate as they walked back into the kitchen.

'Now, girls,' he shouted, 'we have a big day today, we have the harvest to come in. Kitty, I've assigned that job to ye and Nellie. We need the peat cut whilst it is dry and so we have left that one to ye.'

He looked at the girls. Yes, just as he thought, Kitty's expression was bewildered and serious. The harvest wouldn't be ready for a good few days and he was, as usual, fooling around.

He carried on. 'The two of youse can start work as soon as ye have eaten and we will just away down to the pub for the day now. Ye give us a shout when ye are all done. Is that all right there, Nellie? If ye puts yer back into it, ye should be finished by six tonight.'

Nellie playfully punched Liam in the arm.

'What's wrong?' said Liam, rubbing his arm. 'I thought that was why ye had come, to give Uncle Liam a rest. Mammy, I'm shocked. Ye have brought these wastrels here under false pretences.'

He took a sideways glance at Kitty, who was now laughing along with the rest. Getting that child to laugh is hard work, he thought.

'They have a busy day ahead, Liam, sure enough, without help from you,' said Kathleen. 'We are going to introduce Kitty to Bangornevin.'

'Ballymara will take only two minutes,' said Liam, 'so ye may as well or the girls will be driven crazy with the boredom by tonight and begging me to let them stack the hay, so they will.'

Pots of tea now appeared with piles of bacon and sausages cooked with sliced potatoes and heaps of bread. Kitty had never seen or tasted butter like it. It was a thick, creamy yellow and salty.

She thought about everyone at home, who at that very moment would be tucking into pobs. White, stale leftover bread from yesterday, soaked in milk with a sprinkling of sugar and warmed in the range. Or boxty, which was made with potatoes and flour, rolled round and flat, the size of a dinner plate. If there was butter to be had, Maura would scrape it on and then back off again and cut the boxty into quarters.

How could she ever eat that again and not think of this morning and this wonderful breakfast?

'Can you imagine what Angela would be like, if she could see me eating this breakfast?' she said to Nellie. 'If she knew what I was eating right now, Holy Mother, she would give out something wicked altogether. I can't understand why so many people leave here to go to America and England.'

'Well, Kitty,' said Kathleen, 'it's about work and money and being able to live. There is no work around for people and so they have to leave. Most farms can't support an entire family.'

'Aye, Mammy, but the wages in England, now, they are fantastic for working on the roads and the construction trade is roaring,' said Liam. 'That's why everyone is leaving. We have men here every month coming into Murphy's pub, looking for new men to sign up and take on.'

Liam's brother, Finn, who lived with his wife in Bangornevin, had joined them for breakfast. Now he looked irritated. 'Only the fools stay in Liverpool and work for the English. America is the country to be.'

Finn was as serious as Liam was funny.

The atmosphere round the table became tense and Kathleen leapt in.

'Hush yer mouth, Finn. Jerry has made a good life for himself and Nellie. You should be grateful there are jobs there for people to go to, because this farm would struggle to feed all of ye. What would ye be doing if Jerry and Bernadette had decided to return and work the farm, as was their right, him being the eldest, an' all? Jer went to England because he could and you were younger, to give ye a chance because he knew he could get work. Ye may not be in England, Finn, but ye are reaping the rewards because yer brother is.'

Finn looked sheepish. Nellie was surprised. This was the second time she had heard Bernadette's name mentioned openly. She was learning things she never knew before.

Maeve was already on her feet, choosing the moment to end the tension.

'Right, all of ye. I have a home to run, so will ye all away to whatever trouble ye want to make today and leave me to it.'

'Right, five minutes and we are off,' said Kathleen as the girls began to clear the table. 'We will be so busy today, we won't have the time to bless ourselves. The first thing we have to do is pop in and say hello to all the relatives, so they can see we are here, but first we have to use the phone in the post office and to let Maura know we have arrived safe and sound. And watch that nosy parker Mrs O'Dwyer doesn't earwig in. I will keep the nosy bat talking, whilst you girls call the Anchor and send a message home. God cannot have known what he was doing when he gave the nosiest woman on the planet control of the phone in Bangornevin. She doesn't even have to squeeze the information out of people now or eavesdrop in the shop, she just picks up the bleedin' phone.'

'Jump in the van,' shouted Liam from the hallway. 'I'm off to the village for feed from Carey's.'

Kitty again sat by the window in the van and, as they drove down the road, realized she was keen to reach Bangornevin and to explore Ballymara properly. She knew, without hardly having set foot in either, that she was falling in love with a place that a week ago she hadn't even known existed. Tommy had forewarned her.

'I don't know what it is, queen,' he said, 'but home, Ireland, it does this strange thing, it keeps hold of your heart and never lets you go. There is this feeling just here,' and he clenched his hand into a fist shape and gently punched himself in the gut. 'Some say it's grief for all we have loved and left behind. Others say it is the spirit of our ancestors pulling us back and holding onto us. For sure, I have worked with men from all countries on the docks and none have the same longing in their hearts that we Irish have for our home.

'But do you know what I think it is, eh, queen? I think it is the suffering. I think so many Irish hearts have suffered and died on our soil that the souls of those before have joined up into something powerful, which can keep a grip on ye. Ireland needs Irish hearts to keep her safe and to protect her and she feels it when we go. I believe she cries for the loss of those of us who desert her and is always trying to pull us back home. But I know this: I am glad of it, and I would rather have it and know where my heart truly belongs, than not have it at all and be an exile in doubt.'

Maybe it was in the blood, thought Kitty. If it was, it was only in her blood. Neither Angela nor the twins seemed the slightest bit interested. Maybe that was what God did. Maybe he just passed the ache on to the eldest child in each family, to ensure that one day they would return home to Ireland.

Bangornevin was built on a crossroads adjacent to the river. The spur road to Ballymara joined it once it crossed the Moorhaun and hugged the river down to the McMahons' farm, where the road became a dead end. No one had any reason to walk down the Ballymara road unless they were visiting one of the two farms or using the field just before the turning that had been set aside as a football pitch.

"Ah, Jesus, the lads in Bangornevin are mad about the football," Kathleen explained as they passed.

The Moorhaun river was rich with Atlantic salmon and at the crossroads to the village the torrent roared so loudly you could barely hear yourself speak.

The drive into Bangornevin took all of five minutes.

On one side of the crossroads was the grocer's, which sold everything from sweets to sheep-dip. Jerry and Liam's cousin owned the shop and on her last visit he had even allowed Nellie to serve the customers.

On either side of the road stood a row of very small white-washed houses. Directly across from the grocer's was the church. On the opposite side of the crossroads stood the village school, a tailor's shop, the tobacconist's, the post office, a hardware shop and a butcher's. The back half of the butcher's, which was divided off by a hessian curtain, was a pub. There was also a full-time pub in the village, but nothing sold there was as home-made or as strong as that sold at the back of the butcher's.

People made their own bread and what they didn't make was bought at the market on market day and stored in damp straw in the cold press.

Liam now turned left and pulled up outside the post office.

'Good luck,' he shouted as they all piled out of the van. 'Shall I call back for ye later, Mammy?'

'No thanks, Liam,' Kathleen shouted. 'We can walk back, or Pat will give us a lift.'

All three stood and waved as the van disappeared down the high street, Liam beeping the car horn and raising his hand to everyone he passed.

The post office was full of women gathered round the counter. As the bell over the door jangled and Kathleen and the girls walked in, every single person at the counter ceased talking and turned round.

Kathleen scanned the shop.

'Morning, Mrs O'Dwyer, morning, ladies,' she boomed.

In no time at all the women gathered round Kathleen and began asking questions.

'How much wages are they paying in Liverpool to work on the roads now, Kathleen? Is it true a man can earn a hundred pounds a month?'

'Are ye staying home for good now?'

'How is that crazy wife? Is she a patch on Bernadette?'

The questions came thick and fast, but Kathleen answered none of them.

Kitty was amazed that every person recognized Kathleen and Nellie, and that they even knew who she was too.

As the women kept Kathleen busy with what seemed like a hundred questions a minute, a very shabby-looking lady, dressed from head to toe in ragged black, much poorer than anyone Kitty had ever seen in her life, approached her.

'Ah, now, ye must be Kitty, come to keep Nellie company on her holiday, are ye?'

'Yes, I am.' Kitty smiled.

She noticed that the woman's shoes and clothes were in a terrible condition. What teeth she had were broken and nearly black.

'I know ye mammy's mammy, she's a Fahey from Killhooney, is she not, and her sister and all. I know her too.'

Kitty had heard her mother speak of Killhooney Bay but had never visited and had no idea that her nana's name had been Fahey.

'I'm not sure,' replied Kitty, smiling at the lady and feeling very sorry for her. She glanced nervously at Kathleen, not wanting to say the wrong thing or anything more than she should.

Kathleen was revving up to challenge Mrs O'Dwyer.

'We have come to use the phone, Mrs O'Dwyer,' said Kathleen with an authority in her voice Nellie had never heard before.

The truth was that not many people could walk into the post office and command any degree of respect. The doctor and his wife, who lived in the big house built especially for him and his family on the outskirts of the village, could speak in the same tone as Kathleen, when resisting the nosiness of Mrs O'Dwyer, but precious few managed it.

'Of course, Kathleen,' trilled Mrs O'Dwyer. 'Will it be the pub now in Liverpool ye'll be wanting?' She picked up the phone and began to dial.

'Aye, but not for me. Kitty here just needs to leave a message for her mammy, who will be waiting at ten o'clock for the call.'

Mrs O'Dwyer scared Kitty. She was staring and grinning in a fixed manner that was most disconcerting, all the more so because she had very few teeth. As Kitty moved towards the phone, she smiled slightly nervously back.

Mrs O'Dwyer beckoned Kitty behind the counter and handed her the phone. To Kitty's shock, Maura was on the other end.

'Mam,' she shouted, a little too loudly. She was excited beyond words to hear Maura's voice. She had already missed her mother more than she could say.

Kitty heard Kathleen talking very loudly in the post office and smiled to herself. Kathleen was distracting Mrs O'Dwyer.

Kitty turned to the wall to seek some privacy, as she heard Maura's voice travel down the line.

'Kitty, how are ye? Have ye been sick? Have ye eaten any-thing? Did ye sleep? Is Maeve being nice to ye? Have you put clean knickers on and given the dirty ones to Kathleen?'

Kitty laughed. 'Mammy, stop. I'm fine, everything is grand and Maeve is just the best woman ever, she's so nice.'

'Oh, heavenly mother, thank God. Your da and I, we hardly slept for worrying about ye.'

'Mammy, how is everyone at home? Is Malachi behaving and has the baby even noticed I'm gone?'

'Well, I would definitely say so now, we have all noticed, Kitty, none more than Da, we all miss ye. The place isn't the same, but the bedroom is tidy and that's a fact. If I hadn't stopped her last night, Angela would have put all your clothes in the twins' room and claimed the bedroom for herself. Yer da gave out something wicked when he caught her tiptoeing along the landing with all of your belongings piled up in her arms. I don't think she'll be trying that again now. She cried louder than the baby and said, "Da, it's only while she's on holiday," but your da didn't care, he was having none of it.'

Suddenly Kitty heard a beep beep beep in her ear.

'Mammy,' she shouted.

She heard, 'Bye, Kitty,' and then Maura was gone and Kitty, stunned, was left with a dead line.

They had had just two brief minutes.

'Was it the pips?' shouted Kathleen.

'It was timed on the two minutes, Kathleen,' said Mrs O'Dwyer officiously. Kathleen glared at her.

'Never mind. I told Maura before ye left that I would make sure ye wrote her a letter every other day and so now, Mrs O'Dwyer, we need airmail letters, please, if ye wouldn't mind.'

Although the call had been short and sweet, Kitty felt better for having heard Maura's voice.

Kitty looked round for Nellie and saw that she was outside the shop, talking to a girl who had rested her bike up against the post-office window. Kitty hurried outside to join them.

This, Kitty learnt, was Rita, who was Nellie's cousin, after a fashion, whose father owned the local grocer's.

Rita seemed very excited to see them.

'Do ye not have to go to school while ye are here? No? How lucky are ye? I would die not to go to school. Look what the witches did to me today.'

Rita held out her hands. Kitty and Nellie gasped in horror to see the red weals across her palms.

'That looks horrible. How did you get those?' asked Nellie.

'It was the dreaded catechisms this morning,' explained Rita. 'Oh God, I tried everything to stop Mammy sending me to school, but what can I do? The shop is across the road from the school. I have no chance. I knew we would be tested this morning and I knew I would get one wrong. I got the stick across my hand all right.

'I'm out now because I offered to run to the shop to get the Connemara donkey her cigs. I couldn't stand having me hands smacked with the stick again. She lifts it up so high and brings it down so hard, so she does.'

Kitty was horrified. They had the cane at her school but only the really bad lads got it and then just across their backsides with their trousers on. Never on bare skin.

'Who is it you call the Connemara donkey?' Kitty asked.

'Her name is Miss O'Shea, she's from Connemara and she looks like a donkey,' said Rita. 'Will ye get on Jacko, both of ye, and meet me in the village after we finish school one day? Everyone will be beside themselves when I tell them that ye are back, Nellie, so they will. I can't wait to tell them, now. Sure makes a nice change for me to be first in the class for once.' Rita roared with laughter.

Kitty already liked Rita. How could anyone have their hands caned and then laugh as much as Rita, only minutes later?

'You need to be ahead on more than village gossip to stop Miss O'Shea thwacking your hands,' said Nellie, looking worried.

Rita jumped on her bike, shouting, 'See you outside the gates soon, or come to the shop.' She cycled back across the road to the school, holding the handlebars very carefully.

Kitty and Nellie looked at each other. 'Well, I won't be complaining next time Sister Evangelista gives out to me,' said Kitty, 'and who is this poor Jacko we have to jump on?'

'He's the donkey,' laughed Nellie. 'I will make the introduction when I find him. Sometimes I have to run up the hill and look down at the farm. Usually, I can spot his ears, sticking up in the oat field. He is the naughtiest mule ever. He never does anything he is told. Sometimes he likes the walk to Bangornevin, but quite often he will just stand in the middle of the road and refuse to move. He really is the most stubborn animal.'

Kathleen walked out of the post office with the closest thing to steam coming out of her ears.

'Mary and Joseph, save me, that woman is the end. She asks so many nosy questions, I swear to God it must be against the law to have a woman so interfering running the post office.'

'Ah, sure, she's very funny,' Kitty replied, already regarding Bangornevin as though it were a fascinating tapestry.

But she knew this much, she was already in love.

The rushing sound of the river was both familiar and intoxicating, as though it called to her. Deep inside, she felt as though she belonged here, and yet she had only just arrived.

The Deane Farm
Ballymara
County Mayo

Dear Mammy and Daddy,

I am so sorry it was so quick on the phone. I had no idea those beeps were coming. We bought airmail paper in the post office so that I can write everything down so that you know what is happening.

I hope you are doing well at home. It feels like weeks already since I saw you. So much has happened that I am bursting to write and tell you all about it.

I am writing this sitting on my own bed, which has the most lovely lace bedspread you have ever seen, Mammy.

There is a press in the room and I have all my own drawers. I have a beautiful lamp next to my bed with the prettiest lampshade. On the top of the press I have laid out all of my new toiletries like ornaments. They look so nice, Mammy, and the new soap smells like flowers when it is wet. I cupped it in my hands and took it to Maeve to smell when I used it this morning and she said it was just the most beautiful soap she had ever smelt, just like fresh lavender.

I don't like to use the hand cream because I want to save it for special, but I took the pot into the kitchen and rubbed some into Maeve's hands. She works so hard, Mammy, her hands are so rough. She just loved it and she said, hang on now whilst I sit in the chair and enjoy this. Everyone laughed because she closed her eyes and put her head back and said, oh my God, aren't I just one of the fancy ladies now, I'll not be milking the cow any more, so I won't, and Uncle Liam said you will have Bella getting used to those soft hands now, Maeve, be careful or she won't want ye to be milking her any more when Kitty goes home and your hands go back to being as rough as a tinker's arse.

Everyone laughed so much. Everyone laughs all the time.

You would really like Maeve, Mammy.

No one seems to work here, Daddy. I mean they do, Uncle Liam works the fields, but they are his fields. There are no men knocking on in the morning and there doesn't seem to be anywhere anyone goes to work. I asked Maeve where the docks were and she said there weren't any and that everyone looks after the land and each other. That's what they do for work.

We are going to the market in Castlefeale where Uncle Liam will sell his calves and lambs, and Maeve is taking her jam from last summer. She says those who haven't made enough last year, because they were lazy, will be desperate to buy now because they will be running out.

Kathleen took us to visit her relatives today and every time we visited someone's house, we left with a present. We had to carry onions and all sorts of things home with us afterwards including a new yard brush called a scoodoo.

It made me laugh because it is made out of twigs, but I didn't laugh when I saw Maeve brushing the cow shed out because it really works.

All the relatives seem very nice and I met one of Nellie's cousins whose name is Rita. I would hate to be in school here because if you forget your catechisms, you get hit over the hand with a stick. Can you imagine that?

I hope everyone is being good at home and, Angela, you make sure you help Mammy with everything until I am back, which won't be long.

Mammy, my sickness is much better. I think I will be well enough to return home very soon indeed. If Nana Kathleen wants to stay with Nellie, I am sure Uncle Liam will take me to the boat in Dublin, if you or Da meet me. I know how the boat works now and wouldn't be afraid of travelling on my own.

It is just fabulous and because it is so, I can't wait to get back and tell you all about it.

The address at the top is all you will need to write back to me.

Nellie sends her love and asks can you let Jerry and Alice know that she does.

I will see you soon. Two weeks at the absolute most, I would imagine.

Don't be crying yourself to sleep at night, now, Angela, because you and the girls are missing me so much. Lads, be really good for Mammy and I will use the ten shillings Uncle Liam gave me to bring you all back a lovely present.

Lots of love,

Miss Kitty Bernadette Doherty

Kitty wrote her full name. It made her feel like a lady, not a child, and if she wasn't supposed to write the name Bernadette, why had she been given it as her middle name? As far as Kitty was concerned, everyone should use their middle name.

'What's your middle name, Nellie?' Kitty asked as she clicked the top back on the fountain pen Maeve had lent to her.

Nellie looked up out of her book as she spoke. 'Ethelburga, but don't tell anyone. I would hate anyone to know that. I don't know what Nana Kathleen thought she was doing at the time.'

That night, when the girls were preparing for bed, they noticed two ladies arrive at the front door. One was a cousin, Julia, but Nellie had no idea who the other woman was.

'I wonder what they have come to gossip about?' whispered Nellie to Kitty as they heard the earnest muttering of conversation and the kettle being placed on the fire.

'I don't know, but it sounds like a serious chinwag. The kind Peggy would be good at.'

They both laughed at the mention of gossip merchant Peggy.

Ten minutes later, the fresh air knocked them both flat out, and they were fast asleep.

'Thanks for driving out all this way to Ballymara,' said Kathleen to her visitor, Rosie O'Grady. Rosie was spending the night with Julia, Kathleen's sister, and was related by marriage to Julia's husband. She had travelled to Bangornevin following a telephone call from Julia to let her know her help was urgently needed.

No facts were forthcoming. None were needed and Rosie jumped into her car and travelled to Bangornevin as soon as she had finished work as the matron midwife at the hospital in Dublin.

Maeve knew all about Kitty's pregnancy and was helping Kathleen to find a solution. She also knew it was the priest's doing but she and Kathleen had made the decision no one else in Ireland would be told.

'Sure, we heard the news about the murder over here and it was in the paper. Such a scandal, it was. There are so many from Mayo in Liverpool, Kathleen, anything that happens there is news here, too. The only thing anyone has of any interest out here on the west coast is gossip.'

'Aye, Maeve, I know, but I had to tell ye. I have brought the child under your roof. Ye needed to know.'

'It is a problem for both of us now, Kathleen, we will find a way. The child has changed in just a day and it is a grand thing to see. Let's just leave her to enjoy what is left of her childhood whilst she can and not mention anything to her just yet, eh?'

'Aye, we won't. I couldn't agree more. As true as God, her mammy would never believe how much she has altered, so she wouldn't.'

*

Once they were sitting down with a cup of tea, Kathleen spoke. She was close to Rosie who had been through troubles of her own in the past.

Rosie had been born and brought up in Dublin, and had trained as a nurse before she married and settled in Roscommon, where her husband was a dairy farmer.

There were two types of farming men in Ireland.

Gentle family men, who did well at school, obtained the leaving certificate and put their brains to good use in developing their farms.

And there were those who ruled their homes and their farms with their fists.

The job of a woman who married a farmer was to ensure she chose the former.

Those who weren't so attractive and didn't quite have the freedom to choose in the way others did often ended up with the latter.

Rosie had used both her looks and her brains to make her match.

She was also the head of midwifery at the hospital in Dublin and sat on the midwifery council for Ireland.

'Has Julia explained everything to ye?' asked Kathleen to break the silence, once the pleasantries had been exchanged.

'Yes, she has,' said Rosie. 'Although, I have to ask, why has she been brought over here? Every day the boat is full of girls running from Dublin to Liverpool for just this reason. Why can't it be sorted out in Liverpool, for goodness' sake?'

Kathleen felt herself flaring up inside, but remained calm. She knew that she was on a shorter fuse than usual.

'Well, Rosie, I am afraid to say that the poor girl was taken advantage of by a man who should have known better. It is not her fault she is pregnant. She comes from a good Irish Catholic family. I have brought her here to try to save the family from the shame and the heartache.'

Rosie studied Kathleen over her glasses. It was obvious she didn't believe the story. Rosie might have been kindly, but she was no fool.

This was going to be harder than Kathleen had imagined. How could she tell Rosie, once Kitty began to show, that people would suspect Kitty's father of having murdered the priest? That a baby, growing in her belly, would provide a timeline straight back to the worst night of their lives. That police had never ceased asking questions every day since and were convinced the answer to the murder lay somewhere in the four streets. Like a dog with a bone, they just weren't letting go.

'How do ye know the child didn't lead him on?'

Rosie's words made Kathleen want to grab her by her scrawny neck and throw her out through the front door.

Instead, she curbed her exasperation.

'Because she is an innocent child and we know he took advantage when she was ill and in her hospital bed.'

As soon as Kathleen spoke the words, she wished she hadn't. She knew how incredible they sounded. Who would believe what had happened to Kitty, unless they had witnessed the priest going about his filthy work? She had seen him with her own eyes when she had walked into Kitty's bedroom at home and heard the girl pleading with him to stop.

Kathleen suddenly felt desperate. It appeared as though someone that she had hoped would provide guidance wasn't going to be much help at all.

'Look, Rosie,' said Julia, suddenly butting in, 'the reasons why and how the child got pregnant are none of our business now, are they? We were hoping you might have some useful suggestions, with you being so highly qualified and in the know, with regard to midwifery and all that. The problem is that no one in Liverpool, or here for that matter, must know the girl is pregnant. She has to have this child in deadly secret, Rosie, and we need your help.'

Maeve took the compacted straw plug from the top of the dark brown bottle and filled sherry glasses with the thick, deep purple damson wine that Kathleen and the girls had carried home earlier that day.

Rosie was a woman with a tough professional exterior but she was as soft as butter inside.

'I have no idea why this all has to be kept so quiet but it is not my business if the poor child has to be birthed in secret,' said Rosie, lifting up her glass.

'I am assuming this has something to do with the fact that you don't want to bring shame on this village or your own streets in Liverpool?

'I find that so sad, Kathleen. We have to change the way girls and women are regarded and treated in Ireland and if we keep hiding these girls away, nothing will ever alter. In Liverpool and across in America, women have it so much better than the poor girls here. I am assuming that what you are asking me to do is to place her into the mother and baby home in the Abbey near Galway?'

'I know it exists,' said Kathleen, 'but I have no notion how it works and to be sure, it had never crossed my mind that it would be possible.'

Rosie carefully placed her glass down on the table and twirled the stem around between her fingers. She remained silent as she thought. Something was obviously bothering her.

The peat logs on the fire slipped and sent a shower of

sparks flying into the room, distracting Rosie who then spoke directly to Kathleen.

'There is one attached to a laundry run by the holy sisters. She can have her baby in secret there. I can deliver it when her time is due and then the child could be adopted.'

Kathleen let out a huge sigh. There were answers. They were getting there.

Rosie wasn't just offering suggestions, as they had hoped, she was providing a solution.

'Who would adopt it?' asked Kathleen.

'Well, she wouldn't be the first Irish girl to be in this predicament, Kathleen, despite the numbers filling the boat to Liverpool. The children are adopted by American parents only, so that the child never makes contact with any of the mother's family in the future. The nuns who run the mother and baby home take over a thousand American dollars from the American parents and a hundred and fifty pounds from you, for her keep. Kitty will be placed in the home and work for the sisters until the baby is born and then, as soon as her confinement is over, you can collect her, once you pay the hundred and fifty pounds.'

'One thousand American dollars.' Kathleen almost choked on her damson wine. 'My God, the nuns are making a profit out of unwanted pregnancies. Holy Jesus, Mary and Joseph. I have heard it all now.'

'Do ye have a better plan?' asked Rosie, slightly offended that Kathleen wasn't more grateful. "Because if you do, I for one would prefer it. I have never delivered a girl in any of those homes and I have sworn, I never would. I couldn't be more against them and all they stand for. Call me a feminist or any other insulting term you may wish but I think a pregnancy is nothing to be ashamed of.'

Rosie was suspicious, knowing that there was more to this

girl's pregnancy than they were letting on. But that wasn't her business.

They had a distance to travel between here and what Rosie was proposing, but Kathleen could see it was an answer they had never considered. They just needed a hundred and fifty pounds and they would all be safe.

'How do we go about organizing this and having a look to see if it is the right thing to do, Rosie?' said Maeve, as she stood and refilled Rosie's glass.

'You will need a priest,' said Rosie.

We had a priest, thought Kathleen. It was a priest that was the problem.

'You can gain access to the home only if a priest either takes you, or sends a letter.'

'Can you not recommend her to the home, Rosie? You being a midwife and all?' said Julia. 'If ye have agreed to deliver the baby, surely they will accept a girl from ye?'

Rosie looked very uncomfortable and squirmed slightly in her seat.

She had never delivered a child in the Abbey and never wanted to. She was a hospital matron who was known for fighting the Irish authorities and their dated and repressive attitude towards women. By delivering a child in the Abbey, she was condoning the practice of humiliation and suppression. But how could she refuse what was in effect a request from Julia? God knew, Rosie had seen often enough how tough life could be for a single mother.

'I will write to the Reverend Mother and see what she replies,' said Rosie. 'When is the girl due?'

'Around Christmas and none of it is her fault,' said Kathleen, who was trying harder than she ever had in her life not to let her thoughts take the better of her tongue. 'Don't mention who she is yet, please, Rosie. Let us try and protect the girl's privacy for now, eh?'

'Aye, well, be that as it may, it is not my decision. When I hear from the Reverend Mother, I shall write to Julia, which will be a safer method of communication. This isn't something for Mrs O'Dwyer to eavesdrop in on.'

'Well,' said Maeve with a smile, as she emptied the last of the bottle into everyone's glass, 'that's something we can all agree on.'

As Maeve closed the front door after waving the two women down the path, she turned to Kathleen.

'I have heard of the Abbey, Kathleen, and I have been told it is very tough indeed. I am not sure if it is right for the child, but then I don't know what is.'

Kathleen's heart sank. She also knew of its existence, and others like it, but had no idea what they were like.

'God, what a mess,' she said. 'You go to bed, Maeve my lovely. I have a letter to write to Maura, which I need to have in the post in the morning. I don't think we have a lot of time. The child will be showing any day now.'

'Aye, but if we take this route, Kathleen, you have to remember the Abbey is only just outside Galway, so there will be girls in that home from hereabouts. You know how gossip travels like wildfire. Someone may have heard of Kitty being a visitor and know who she is. Visitors are so rare it will be known almost straight away and that Liverpool accent of hers doesn't help.'

'I know,' said Kathleen. 'We will have to hide her name. That is another bridge we will cross tomorrow.'

Once Maeve had taken herself to bed and Kathleen had washed up the glasses and cups, she sat down and, by the light of the dying embers of burning peat, wrote her letter to Maura.

The Deane farm
Ballymara
County Mayo

Dear Maura,

Well, my lovely, this is not a letter to read out to Tommy or anyone else, so I suggest if ye have opened this in front of anyone, tuck it away in your apron pocket, make an excuse and read it later.

Kitty is having a ball and has taken to the Irish countryside like a duck to water.

Ye have never seen anyone as excited as she is to be rising at five o'clock tomorrow morning for the market in Castlefeale.

John McMahon from the farm next door and Liam are taking two trucks for the cattle, so there will be plenty of room for them all. She will be back at lunchtime and full of it, please God.

Her and Nellie have taken on a list of jobs they would like to do whilst they are here, which includes milking the cow, would ye believe!

She hasn't been sick once since she arrived and I have watched her nerves return to nearly normal in just hours, which is a pleasure to behold, Maura.

Now, to our first problem.

We had a visit tonight from Rosie, who is the sister-in-law of Julia. Rosie's from Roscommon, and she is also the matron midwife at the hospital in Dublin. She has made a suggestion that Kitty remains here and is placed into a mother and baby home near Galway. She is writing tomorrow to the Reverend Mother who runs the home to see if she will accept her.

Kitty would have be moved fairly soon. I saw the first signs of her showing today. It won't be long before others notice too.

She would have the baby at the home and the sisters would place it with an American family for adoption. Hold onto the chair here, Maura. They sell the baby for one thousand dollars. Then we have to turn up with a hundred and fifty pounds and we can take Kitty home.

Now, the second problem. Kitty will be away from home for months not weeks, and there is no way on this God's earth Tommy will be happy about that and so ye will have to find a way of handling that one.

Before ye get carried away with any grand ideas that she can return home and ye can look after her, Maura, just bear this in mind. When she turns up back home with a belly, it will only be a matter of time before the penny drops with everyone. Even thick Peggy will work that one out.

Ye have to write back soon and let me know what ye think.

In the meantime, if the sisters are amenable, I will travel to see the home as soon as ye let me know. Rosie has agreed to deliver her baby in the Abbey and then we can take our Kitty out of there and back home to Liverpool.

I think it is our only choice, Maura. Maeve says not to worry about the money. We can all work the hundred and fifty pounds between us, so we can. We will all chip in.

Write back to me quickly, Maura. I need to move fast if the sisters are agreeable to taking Kitty in so early. There is one other thing, and that is that the events leading up to our holiday are common news around here. Everyone I have met in the village has asked me for the smallest detail.

I am beyond shame, Maura, but even I blushed when the spinster at Carey's corner asked me how big was the langer they found in the graveyard and God alone knows, she must be ninety.

We are going to have to be as secretive moving Kitty from here to Galway as we were bringing her here. Also, Maura, we shall have to hide her name and give her a new one, just to be on the safe side. You never know.

The home is run by the sisters themselves and until her confinement Kitty would need to work in a laundry they run at the Abbey. Kitty has never been idle and I am sure that if she is doing something useful, she will feel the days pass more quickly. The sisters are well used to pregnant women and will keep a good eye on her.

Anyway, Maura, Maeve, Liam and everyone here sends their love and best regards to Tommy and the children.

Let me know if everything is all right across the road. Brigid is keeping an eye on Alice for me. I will write to Alice next but you know what it is like, I am just a bit worried about her being on her own all day, with her not long being better. Call me a witch, if ye like, but I am not convinced that someone can alter so much so quickly and I am a bit worried that she may have a relapse.

Write back soon, Maura, love, please.

Lots of love,

Kathleen

Chapter Fifteen

MOLLY THOUGHT SHE would sleep on what Daisy had told her. After all, Molly had known Tommy and Maura since the day they arrived on the four streets, when Maura was six months' pregnant with Kitty. Molly had always admired Maura. She was a worker, that was for sure.

Molly was so shocked at Daisy's revelations, she inhaled a sultana from her fruit scone. What a palaver all that had been, thought Molly, as she pulled on her housecoat over her flannelette nightdress to walk downstairs.

It was four o'clock in the morning and, abandoning sleep, she decided to make a cup of tea as she placed the kettle onto the range and lit a candle. She didn't want to switch the main light on, in case Annie O'Prey woke and saw the light in the backyard. Molly nursed a mild disdain for Annie, who felt the need to tell Molly and anyone else who would listen all of her business.

'That woman leaks like a colander,' Molly had told her husband on a daily basis many years earlier, when he was still alive.

Molly maintained a level of one-upmanship, simply by withholding information from the inquisitive Annie.

Whilst Molly sat in her candlelit kitchen, in her hairnet and slippers, surrounded by a haze of blue smoke from her second Woodbine, burning in the ashtray next to her as she munched on a slice of fruit cake between puffs, she chuckled as she imagined the look on Annie's face if she had a notion of what Molly knew following her chat with Daisy..

Just at that moment, Tiger leapt in through the open kitchen window, making Molly jump with fright. He dropped a half-dead mouse at her feet. She never knew these days what the Siamese cat was going to bring in next.

In order to hold the squealing creature in place, he placed his paw on top of its tail and, as it wriggled and squeaked, he looked up at Molly, seeking her praise.

'Who's a clever boy now then,' she said.

The cat stretched his neck upwards in pleasure as Molly stroked his ears. He purred and arched his back, releasing his pressure on the mouse, which seized its chance and flew under the press.

Molly smiled. She had a new-found affection for the cat. Since the day he had walked in and dropped the priest's langer on the mat half an hour after the murder became news, Molly had become a minor celebrity on the four streets. It had all begun when she had bent down with a bit of newspaper to pick up the bloody bit of flesh from the kitchen floor. She might have been a widow for a good few years but she wasn't senile, she knew exactly what the cat had brought home.

There hadn't been a day since when someone or other hadn't begged her to relay every gory detail of the whole sorry event.

Molly secretly enjoyed the attention, but what she enjoyed most was Annie's jealousy at Molly's new-found celebrity status.

'I have to hurry along now, Tiger, lots to do today,' said Molly, as the cat brushed up against her legs, stretching his head to fit snugly inside her cupped hand.

She had made her decision. It wasn't yet five, but she would need to do a bit of baking and start her polishing early. Molly was expecting important visitors. It would be a very busy day indeed.

It was Harry who took the letters to Maura in the kitchen.

Gentle, kind Harry. He was so excited that he almost opened them himself.

Kitty and Nellie had been away for just over a week and Harry missed them both every day.

Kitty was more like a mammy to Harry than a sister but as the eldest boy, of both sets of twins, he also felt like a big brother to Kitty. He felt that it was his job to look after her, especially since she had come out of hospital following the awful car accident when she and Nellie had been run down by Callum's car. Callum had tried to blame the fact that Liverpool was still covered in snow in March.

They all knew it was because Callum couldn't drive and the car was stolen.

Harry was growing up rapidly. A serious little man, he knew well the meaning of responsibility and manners. Tommy had taught him almost every day, just by being Tommy.

Each Sunday, as they attended mass together, Tommy would walk on the outside of the pavement and encourage the four boys to do the same, ensuring that Maura and the girls were on their inside.

'Manners maketh man, Harry, or that's what they say and I don't think it can be far wrong.'

'Why do we have to be on the outside, Da?' asked Harry.

'Well, son, it's so that when a horse and carriage come along and send up a wave of dirty water, it hits us and not your mammy or the girls, so it doesn't.'

'But, Da, the only horse and carriage is the rag-and-bone man and he doesn't work on a Sunday.' Harry liked to be precise.

'Yes, son, but it's manners and so we just do it.'

'But why, Da, if there's no horses and carriages? I don't get it.'

'Harry, ye will get a lashing from yer mam's tongue soon if ye don't stop talking.'

Harry was good at his manners. At school he would knock over chairs and children in his rush to open the classroom door for the sisters and the teachers, and he always carried a school bag home for one of the girls.

He also knew the meaning of chivalry. Harry was a reader. He couldn't devour enough books from the school library. It was in his nature to worry about Kitty and Nellie being so far away. Although neither Maura nor Tommy would answer his questions, he knew the trip had something to do with whatever it was that had happened. They all knew something was wrong.

And Nellie, well, Harry just loved Nellie and had done since she was a baby. He had always felt that it was his job to look out for Nellie on the four streets. Harry missed Nellie a lot.

The day that Callum's car had hit both of the girls at the top of Nelson Street, Harry had been one of the first at the scene and he had truly felt as though he would die with worry when they were taken to hospital.

And now here they both were, off in Ireland, and he found himself wondering every day, were they both all right?

'The post has come, Mammy, shall I open them for ye?' said Harry expectantly now.

Maura smiled and kissed her serious prince on the top of his head.

'If ye don't mind, Harry, I will read them when ye have all gone to school and then tonight, when we aren't so rushed and yer da is home from the docks, we will all sit down and read them together. What do ye think about that?'

Harry had known it was worth a chance, but he hadn't for a moment thought he would have any luck.

He laughed. 'Aw, rubbish,' he said, as Maura rubbed his hair.

'Go on, ye cheeky scoundrel,' she said. 'More like an old man than a boy in yer ways, going on a hundred, ye are. How many books is it ye have read this week then, eh?'

Angela burst through the door at the bottom of the stairs. 'Letters, letters, let me see, let me see,' she squealed, running over to Maura and trying to grab them out of her hand.

'Get away with ye, ye cheeky article. I'll give ye a slap on the legs if ye so much as touch those envelopes without my say-so.'

Maura snatched the letters back from Angela and tucked them into her apron pocket. She missed Kitty so much. Angela was more of a handful and a hindrance than she was a help.

Tommy had left for work half an hour since. He had helped her to get the boys up and organized before the men had called for him and he had the fire lit in the range at six o'clock.

'I don't know how I would manage if ye weren't such a good man, Tommy Doherty,' Maura had said, as she kissed him goodbye that morning.

Tommy slapped her backside. 'Good in many ways, eh?' he roared. He grabbed Maura's hand and pulled her in to him for a hug. The children had yet to charge down the stairs. 'An early night for us, eh, queen?' he whispered cheekily, as his hands roamed across her backside.

Maura pulled away. 'God, what are ye like? Do ye think of

nothin' else? I swear to God, ye cannot be pulling your weight down on the docks, ye have far too much energy left!'

Despite her protestations, Maura was smiling. Not as much as Tommy, however, who would make a point of letting the fellas know, when they knocked on, that he was on a promise for the night.

It singled him out, made him different from those who had to plead for sex. Tommy loved to make the others jealous by bragging about his good fortune, in having a willing wife even though that was something she would never in a million years disclose to any other woman on the streets. There was no credibility to be gained in not making your man beg.

Things were slowly returning to normal. The shock of Kitty's absence had diminished slightly, now that the parting was over. Tommy thought about his princess all the time, but his memory conjured up images and memories of his Kitty before, his happy Kitty. Not Kitty as she was today.

Once the children had left for school, Maura hurried through the morning chores, wasting no time. Her desire to carve herself a peaceful hour to read and digest the letters slowly was uppermost in her mind. They were burning a hole, calling to her from the depths of her pocket, the unfamiliar sound of the flimsy, pale blue paper crinkling as she worked.

She found herself extra chores, as though to punish herself and make herself wait, unsure whether she should be excited or nervous about the contents. She cleaned the splashes from the kitchen window and wiped over the skirting boards with the floor cloth. She mopped the floor, scrubbed the table and changed the bedding on the cot.

Maura regarded the arrival of the letters in the same way she would a visitor to the house.

The hour she stole to read them was her guilty pleasure and it must be deserved. She had to have earned it. The kitchen must be spick and span.

Once the chores were finished, she put the baby down for her mid-morning nap, stoked up the fire, made herself a pot of tea for a cuppa and sat in the comfy chair. Still, teasing herself, she looked around and surveyed her handiwork, delaying the opening by a further tantalizing minute. Then, satisfied that she had truly earned her break, she opened both of her letters.

Maura turned to Kitty's first. When she read the last few lines, where Kitty said she was desperate for home, her heart leapt.

Maura wanted her back, too. The fact that Kitty felt she might be back in just two weeks was wonderful indeed. As Maura folded the letter again and painstakingly slid it back inside its pale blue envelope, she crossed herself and looked up at her statue of the Virgin Mary on the mantel-shelf above the range.

'Please, let it be,' she whispered.

Maura then opened Kathleen's letter, slipping the knife under the gummed flap, and realized she was holding her breath. She knew that if Kathleen had written, she would have significant news.

As soon as she had finished reading the letter, she cried.

It held nothing but bad news. Months not weeks without her daughter. The need to find a hundred and fifty pounds, and the impending moment when she would have to tell Tommy that Kitty wouldn't be coming back any time soon.

A desperate sadness washed over Maura.

There was Kitty, looking forward to returning home with all her tales and presents, and Kathleen pointing out that there was no possible way, for all their sakes, that she could before her baby was born.

Maura knew, if the police knocked on the door and someone cracked, Tommy would end up swinging from the gallows. The thought sent the fear of God through her. God alone knew what would happen to them all. And what of their friends who had helped them? Jerry and Kathleen, Brigid and Sean?

She had dreamt of Bernadette last night and although she could not remember the details, she had woken with a feeling of cold dread in the pit of her stomach. Tommy's morning playfulness had banished the fear left behind by the dream, but now that she had stopped working and rested, it washed over her once again.

She had prayed that Kathleen's letter would tell her the Epsom salts and the gin had worked, and that Kitty had started, once she reached Ireland. God knows, she had given her enough. Girls that age were sensitive. It was easy to lose a baby at such a young age, surely? These were the desperate thoughts Maura had harboured all day, every day, whilst she waited for a letter from Kathleen.

Maura's back door opened suddenly and in scuttled Peggy.

There was no privacy on the four streets. No one ever closed their doors and no one ever knocked, either.

'Oh, queen, what's up?' said Peggy, flopping down into the chair opposite Maura.

It was known as the 'not so comfy' chair, because some of the springs under the cushion were broken, and others had been unhooked and stretched to fill in the gaps. It was the chair Maura often sat in, being lighter than Tommy.

There was a strong possibility that Peggy would sink between the springs and struggle to rise again. She could be in for the day.

Peggy reached over, which, given the size of her belly, was an impressive act in itself, to take one of Maura's hands in her own, while eyeing up the pot of tea and the brack, cooling on the wooden draining board.

'Come on, queen, tell me, so. What on God's earth is wrong with ye?'

Peggy had only popped in for a cuppa. She had just enough coal left for two nights, until Paddy was paid on Friday and was, as needs must, economical with the range.

Maura had given up trying to tell her how to manage.

Peggy felt it was her right that she and Paddy each smoked twenty a day and had one or two extra drinks in the club on a Saturday night. Maura had told her so often that she needed to save for a rainy day and how to cope on the family budget.

Peggy was the last person Maura wanted to see, but she would never make her unwelcome. Neighbours on the streets were all as close as family. You couldn't choose your family and when you were an Irish immigrant, your friends and neighbours either. You got on with it and mostly loved them anyway.

Maura wondered if the chair cushion would smell when Peggy left.

She knew it would.

As Peggy leant over towards Maura, an unpleasant odour wafted across from the top of her apron. Maura was used to this. It didn't make her baulk. Back home, baths were looked on as a treat but Maura was very aware that in Liverpool her countrymen were called the dirty Irish.

If anything, her irritation with Peggy was not because of her smell, or her dirty habits, or her lack of housekeeping. It was the fact that every time the welfare officer, the school nurse or the Prudential man knocked on Peggy's door, she reinforced this prejudice and that annoyed the hell out of Maura. Now she could see that the dull, dark hair wound round Peggy's curlers was covered in the telling white flecks of lice eggs.

As soon as she had heard the latch lift on the back gate, Maura had shoved both letters deep into her apron pocket and out of sight.

'Oh, nothing really, Peggy,' she replied now with more chirpiness than she felt. 'I had a letter from Kitty on her holiday with Kathleen and, you know, I just miss her.'

Peggy sympathized. 'Who can ye trust to run a message now? Boys are useless, and she was grand with the washing and cleaning and looking after the babies. I would miss her too.'

Maura almost laughed out loud at Peggy's ability to talk the talk, as if she ever cleaned. Maura's missing Kitty had nothing to do with what she did in the house or how she helped with the kids.

It was the fact that she couldn't reach out and wrap her arms round her. She missed Kitty's gentle little voice and for so long she had missed her laughter.

'I thought she might be so taken with the farm, she would look down on us lot and not want to return home.'

'Of course she wants to come home,' said Peggy. 'You and Tommy are her mammy and daddy, so ye are, that's where every girl wants to be. The farm might be fabulous, but there's no place like ye own bed, no matter how many kids and bugs ye share it with.'

Maura shuddered. There were no bugs in any of her beds.

She put the kettle on to freshen up the mash of tea.

She was regretting letting Peggy think that Kitty was looking forward to coming home. How would she explain it if she had to stay?

God, she thought, why is everything so difficult and secretive?

As soon as Peggy left, Maura decided to share her news with the only person she could. She put on her coat and ran down the entry.

Maura sat herself down in the chair by the fire in Jerry's house and picked Joseph up.

Alice made them both a cuppa, then sat down with a cup and saucer of her own in her hand. Maura silently leaned forward and handed over the envelope.

Alice put her cup and saucer on the floor, tucked it just under the chair, so as not to knock it with her foot, and took the letter out. Whilst she read, Maura sang to Joseph and played a hand-clapping game. Joseph giggled and bounced up and down on Maura's knee.

For a few seconds, Alice stopped reading, looked up and smiled. She knew she could never be as natural with children as Maura was and it made her sad.

She did feel sadness. It was a new experience, but she felt it.

When she had finished reading, she folded the paper and, without a word, put it back into the envelope, handed it straight back to Maura, then reached out to take Joseph.

Alice stood Joseph up on her lap to pull up his knitted leggings. His clothes had become dishevelled during his clapping game with Maura. And then, sitting him back down on her knee and pulling down his pullover over the top of his leggings she finally spoke.

'Phew, I never expected that. I half thought they would have sorted her out in a different way over there. Thought they might have had a few remedies we don't have here.'

Maura's face burnt and the all-too-familiar tears pricked her eyes.

'Well, she is being sorted out in a way, just not the way you thought, Alice. I am going to have to tell Tommy tonight and then I will need to leave for Ireland, although God knows how I am going to manage that, with no Kitty to watch the kids. Tommy cannot miss a day's work or someone else may take his place on the gang.'

'I will help out,' said Alice, 'don't worry about that. Between all of us, we will manage.'

Alice's kindness took Maura by surprise. This time the tears won and Maura cried. Again.

Alice looked hard at Maura, but could not feel pity. It never happened.

It was close. Very close. Pity teased her from the borders of her emotional awareness. Running in and running out again.

Elusive.

Alice decided to take advantage of Maura's weakness.

'Maura, you do know that lots of women have abortions now, don't you? It could even be legal soon, so the talk on the news says.'

Maura looked up from wiping her eyes, but before she could respond, Alice ploughed on.

'Before Kitty left, I made enquiries. It would cost fifty pounds, that's all, and then it would all be over and done with in just a few hours.'

Maura jumped to her feet and screamed, 'Holy Mary and Joseph, I hope to God you didn't tell anyone it was for my Kitty? Did ye, Alice? Did ye? Tell me, for God's sake.'

'God, no, of course I didn't, Maura. Calm down. I said it was for me.'

Maura had knocked the teacup and saucer onto the floor with a clatter. She squatted down to clear up the mess and Alice once again ploughed on.

'I asked the abortion midwife, Mrs Savage, what she did and it all sounded simple and easy to me, and not a coat-hanger in sight. Maura, there never has been, not for a hundred years. The house is in Bootle, it's clean. There were two women who left her house together as I arrived and they both looked happy enough. Mrs Savage explained everything to me carefully and it is so easy.'

Maura was wiping up the spilt tea off the floor.

'*Maura!*' Alice shouted. 'Will you leave the bloody cup and just sit down and listen to me, please.'

Maura was agitated. She couldn't understand how Alice could speak of a mortal sin and the taking of a life so calmly.

Her hands flitted like birds in front of her as she waved away Alice's words.

'I have never had or heard such a conversation, Alice. There are no Mrs Savages in Ireland and there is nothing your Mrs Savage can do that I couldn't do for my own daughter.'

'Yes, there is, Maura.' Alice was almost shouting. 'There bloody is something that can be done but your eyes are so shut with your stupid, pious, left-footing, Catholic ways, you won't even listen. You are being ridiculous, Maura, and obsti-nate. We have all got into a mess over this. The least you could do is show an interest in what I have taken the trouble to find out. I'm not the one who is pregnant. I didn't drag Joseph all the way to Bootle on the bus for myself, you know. You owe it to us all to hear me out.'

Maura collapsed back down into the chair. Alice had pricked her conscience. She thought again, as she did once every few minutes, that this was all her fault for having believed in the priest. Alice had just said, 'You owe it to us all.'

No one else had said it. No one had pointed a finger at her, but often she could hear Tommy think it, and today Alice had uttered the truth, yet to be acknowledged. The truth everyone knew.

That dirty, stupid truth. It was all Maura's fault.

She didn't look at Alice. She turned her head and stared deep into the coals burning in the fire. She could smell the cake Alice had made, slowly rising in the oven.

Joseph was trying to stand up on his own feet, pushing against Alice, stretching his arms out to Maura. She noticed him out of the tail of her eye and smiled a thin, tired smile, taking him from Alice. Joseph snuggled into her chest as he sucked his thumb and peeped out at his mother from Maura's arms.

Maura was again lost in thought.

For a fleeting second, she went back to better days.

She imagined a wet afternoon in front of the same fire, in the same room, but with Bernadette sitting opposite her, not Alice. She saw again the glass of long-stemmed, deep-yellow buttercups mixed with fireweed that Bernadette had placed on the windowsill to brighten up the kitchen.

Bernadette, the only woman on the four streets who thought weeds were worth picking. And she had been right.

She used to laugh and say that she picked the weeds because they reminded her of the heather and the peat flowers from home. The wild rhododendrons, the blue-eyed grass and the lady's tresses.

Maura missed the flowers too. She missed her daughter. She missed Bernadette.

'I used to sit in front of this fire with Bernadette,' said Maura quietly. 'We used to laugh and chatter and listen to the heartbeat of Kitty who was growing in my belly at the time, with an upturned glass that we had Tommy file the base off.'

Maura had broken the taboo. She had mentioned Bernadette. Without even realizing, she had taken her revenge.

Maura had reached a depth of despair she had never plumbed before. She almost cried again, this time for the hours she had spent in this very chair, laughing with the friend she had loved as a sister.

But the comparison with Bernadette had not wounded Alice. It had taken her by surprise for just a second, but nothing more.

She could see Maura's desolation and took advantage of her tears.

'Mrs Savage is a properly trained midwife and knows what she is doing, Maura. She would place some dried seaweed sticks into the neck of Kitty's womb. It does hurt a bit, but Mrs Savage will sell us some opium to help with the pain. The seaweed sticks absorb the fluid from around the womb and then the sticks swell and they push open the neck of the womb. Kitty would have a miscarriage and, honestly, it's just like her having a late monthly and no different from what you have been doing with the hot baths, the Epsom salts and the gin. But it has to be done as early as possible, as you well know. Bring her home from Ireland, Maura, and let's take her. It'll cost us fifty pounds, not a hundred and fifty.'

Maura looked at Alice with steely eyes. She didn't like the fact that Alice had spoken aloud about the gin. Alice had exposed Maura's hypocrisy in all its nakedness.

Maura stood up, placed the pieces of broken china on the draining board and with her back to Alice spoke very calmly. Her words were measured, devoid of emotion and bordering on coldness.

'I know what I have tried to do, Alice, but I was wrong and wicked to have even attempted it. I will not take her to any backstreet abortionist. Kathleen is right. Your mother-in-law is a holier woman than all of us put together. I will travel to Ireland and see Kitty into this home. It is the right thing to do.'

She turned round and glanced at Alice with torment on her face.

'Look, I'm sorry. I didn't want to offend you,' said Alice. 'I was just thinking of what's best for Kitty.'

Maura looked Alice squarely in the eye. Reflecting on the times she had spent with Bernadette in this same kitchen had made her feel stronger.

'And ye think I don't, Alice? Ye think I don't know what's best for the child I failed to protect from that wicked man?'

Alice stood at the back door and stared as Maura walked down the yard path towards the gate.

She lifted the latch, then turned and, with a furrowed brow, asked, 'What kind of midwife is it that kills babies?'

And before Alice could say a word in reply, she was gone.

19 Nelson Street
Liverpool
Lancashire

Dear Kathleen,
I am grateful to ye, so I am, for writing to me so quick like, to tell me that Kitty and Nellie are having such a grand time, thanks be to God.

It was a joy to open Kitty's own letter, Kathleen, and to

be honest, when I read yours, it was a bit hard on my emotions, but not too bad now, Kathleen. I'm used to the idea of a home for Kitty and, God willing, I will stay that way so that I can be strong for her and help her through.

I feel overwhelmed altogether by what we have to do.

God alone knows why the Epsom salts and gin didn't work, at her age too, Kathleen. I was sure it would all be over by now and that we would be back to normal.

Ye know I trust all ye say and if ye think this is the way it has to be, then so be it.

I feel bad about putting on Maeve with all of this and, sure, isn't she an angel herself to help us out, so she is. I would like to come over and see the home for myself, but first I have to tell Tommy that Kitty is to be away for longer than he thought, although to be fair, Kathleen, I don't think either of us are thinking straight. Tommy says the answer is to just keep moving.

I never knew Tommy to say boo to a goose before, but he's a different man now so he is.

We have thirty-two pounds saved in the bread bin and I will need four to come to Ireland. It has taken us fifteen years to save that money, so I have no notion where we will get the hundred from.

I know ye are right about Kitty. If she returns home and has a baby after all that occurred, then it is sure that everyone will make the connection.

Also if Kitty were here, she is so sensitive that she would never recover from the way people would treat her either. The lamb has no idea.

Sometimes I wonder, Kathleen, if we should have been as cruel as some others are. If Tommy had taken his belt to the kids, or if I had slammed them up the

stairs with no food in their insides, would they have
been harder altogether and more able to fend for
themselves?

Would they not have been as sensitive and would
Kitty have spoken out to us about how that man had
been doing his bad things to her and what was happening in her own bed while we were just downstairs, only
feet away from her?

Kitty has no idea how hard it would be if she were
here and people knew she were pregnant.

Those she calls her friends today will become her
enemies tomorrow and God knows what the sisters
would say or do. If there was a hint of suspicion, all my
kids would be thrown out of the school at the very least.
I would fear for us all, Kathleen.

It is what we have to do and the more I have thought
about it all day, the more sure I am.

As long as the sisters are from a good and kind order
and look after her, that's what is important.

Adoption is the right path and that is why I want to
visit Ireland to see her, Kathleen. I know my own baby
girl and all that she is, a baby still herself. This will
upset her, as she has loved every baby I have given birth
to as though it were her own. But, sure, I don't need to
tell you that.

I need to talk to her about this and explain what is
happening.

If ye do it on your own, Kathleen, she will be looking
for me and wondering why I'm not there. I want to be the
one to explain to her why we have to hide her name and
choose a new name with her. I think Cissy would be good.
That way, if someone forgets, Cissy sounds so much like

Kitty, it could be passed off with no trouble at all.

Everything here is good. We went to the club on Saturday night for the first time since everything kicked off. It was a delight to see Jerry and Alice there too.

Alice is doing fine. I have seen her tripping up and down the street with Joseph in his pram and popping in and out of Brigid's house, and on Saturday night we all sat together at the club.

Alice didn't dance, but she had a grand natter to Sean whilst Brigid danced with Jer.

She is a credit to ye, Kathleen. She looked fabulous and had made a big effort. She gives me hope in my own despair. Who would have thought, a year ago, that we would see Alice pushing a baby round in a pram and tripping up to the Grafton rooms with the rest of us. She had done her hair and looked lovely, so she did.

God has brought her here to show the rest of us that no matter how desperate things appear, there is always hope. I am sure of that now and ashamed of how I treated her in these past years. I loved Bernadette like my sister, but she has gone and if I have learnt anything now, it is that life is short and you never know what is going to happen next.

I will book my ticket and phone the post office to let you know when I will be arriving. I cannot wait to see my girl, so.

See you very soon, God willing.

Your dearest friend,

Maura

Maura had wanted to write chapter and verse on how full of herself indeed Alice was, but sure, hadn't she offered to help, so that Maura herself could visit Ireland and settle Kitty into the convent. And, anyway, there was no benefit to be had in worrying Kathleen. She had enough on her plate, and they all had more important things to do than fret about Alice.

Tommy had turned a corner.

The night in the Grafton rooms on Saturday had been hugely enjoyable. There had been a singer doing a turn and they had all had a laugh and a dance. Things were calming down at home and as time went by the horror of the past receded. He desperately missed Kitty, but she would be home shortly, he was sure of that.

'I'm home,' Tommy shouted an octave too loudly as he walked in through the door, even though all the children could see him. 'Whose the first with a kiss for yer da?' The best part of every day for Tommy was just this, walking into his warm kitchen and the bosom of his family.

The boys and Angela elbowed each other out of the way, pushing forward to be the first picked up by Tommy. Even the baby sitting in her box began to squeal and wave her arms with excitement as she bounced up and down on her nappy and spat her dummy halfway across the room to attract his attention.

Maura was stirring a pot of stew at the range. She turned round and smiled.

With the baby in his arms, Tommy walked over to the range and pulled the ties undone on the back of Maura's apron so that it fell open. Facing towards the children, he placed one arm across his belly and gave an exaggerated laugh.

'For goodness' sake, will ye stop it!' Maura shouted as the shoulder strap fell from her apron and slid down to her waist. She playfully smacked Tommy with the wooden spoon. The children burst into squeals of laughter at her protests. Inside, her stomach churned at the thought of the news she must tell him later.

The light was fading as Maura scurried along the street to the postbox and then on to mass, glancing down the cobbled entry as she walked. Cowed by guilt. Alice had spoken aloud the thought she had kept hidden and now it wouldn't leave her mind. A nagging, constant thought. It was all her fault.

As she pulled up her coat collar to keep out the breeze, she looked up at the top of the street and yet again saw the blue and white panda car pass by, slowly and menacingly. Her heart beat faster. The only thing standing between that car and the hangman was a deadly secret.

As she stepped off the kerb she saw another police car parked, yet again, outside Molly Barrett's front door. It had been there earlier in the afternoon and she had noticed Annie O'Prey, on her hands and knees, scrubbing Molly's step, with what looked like her ear stuck to Molly's front door.

'God, will Molly ever give up feeding them for company and just let them go?' she whispered to herself, as she ran towards the post box.

Alice was settling Joseph down when she looked out of the bedroom window and saw Maura once again running down the road from the pillar box towards the church for mass. The priests from St Oswald's had been covering at St Mary's since the murder and Kathleen had warned Maura not to miss a mass. If she did, it would be a change from her normal pattern that might be noticed.

Running scared. Chased by the bells. Propelled by her guilt. Fleeing from the shadows. Terrified of missing mass.

Fearful of incurring the wrath of the priest for not making God her priority and showing him the devotional respect he deserved, of not taking the half-confession in case she should meet her end that night.

'What difference will it make if she can't confess the worst sin of all? They never learn, do they?' Alice whispered into the side of her baby's face. 'What does a priest have to do to turn them away from his Church, eh, Joseph? How wicked does he have to be?'

Howard had felt his heart begin to race as Molly told him her story. He knew they now had to tread very carefully, or they could lose their murderer and their case.

Howard couldn't help himself. As Molly spoke, he imagined promotion. He could see the silver epaulettes upon his shoulder. A vision popped into his head of being introduced to the young Queen and her husband when they visited Liverpool. He saw his and Simon's photograph on the front page of the *Liverpool Echo* and his name in the headline.

'This is it. All we have to do is charm the old woman, make her feel important and she will help to deliver those goods in a court of law, eh, Simon. We have scored, mate.'

'Do you really think so?' Simon asked. 'You think all it will take is for Molly to persuade Daisy to talk in court? I thought Daisy was supposed to be simple?'

'Well, she is, but if Molly can testify to her character and to be honest, who says the girl is simple, eh? She doesn't seem that bad to me. No, Simon, never fear, Molly Barrett is the step we need to our promotion, mate. She is a canny woman, that one. What judge wouldn't believe her, eh?'

Chapter Sixteen

ALICE ASKED HERSELF, was it wrong meeting Brigid's husband, Sean, to just talk to him? She instantly decided it wasn't. Alice knew neither pity nor guilt.

Alice and Sean had already met twice in the pub in the Dingle tucked into the corner in the snug, beside the fire, away from the noisy bar where the men gathered to drink when they knocked off work.

Sean ordered a Guinness for himself and a Babycham for Alice, served in a flat champagne glass, with a gold rim and a leaping Bambi on the side.

Alice nursed the glass and twizzled the stem. Just holding it made her feel special. She watched the small, soft bubbles float to the surface. She giggled when they gently popped against her nose as she lifted the glass to her lips.

Alice had never drunk Babycham before. It would have been considered a hideous expense. Guinness was deemed good enough for everyone on the streets, including pregnant and nursing mothers.

The last time they met, Sean had shared with her one of Mary's letters from America and had watched Alice's face light up as she read it, enthralled by her description of Chicago, her everyday existence and the possibility of a different life for Sean.

Mary had written that the previous night, they had been to a drive-through cinema and watched a movie, *West Side Story*.

Alice could not even imagine what a drive-through looked like.

Mary also wrote about how she, her husband and Sean's brother, Eddie, were trying to persuade their old school friends to travel to America and join them, because they so desperately needed men. It broke their hearts to think of how many from home were still struggling, when they had so much to offer in America.

They had been awarded a construction contract to build a high school in Chicago. Mary had written,

I cannot begin to tell you the work opportunity out here.
We work hard and are honest and have a good name.
We are turning down well-paid contracts every day
because we cannot cope with the amount of work we are
being asked to quote for.
If it is the fare ye are concerned about, just tell me.
We can and will pay for the whole family to travel out. It
won't even be us paying, Sean, it will be accounted as a
business expense.

'Can you imagine that?' said Sean to Alice. 'It won't even be them paying, with the business being so big. I don't understand why I am working my guts out day and night when a new world is waiting for us all, yet Brigid won't hear of it or even talk about us going, unless we pay for ourselves. Brigid knows that will take another two years of my having to beat some poor sod's head in every Friday night.'

Sean's voice began to rise in frustration but Alice didn't

try to stop him. It gave her pleasure to know that he was venting his anger and frustration with Brigid. That behind Brigid's perfect facade of calm and organization, things were far from well.

They had arranged a further illicit meeting. The unspoken knowledge that they both shared the same dream drew them together. Neither questioned what they were doing but, for the first time, Alice felt a thrill of excitement as she looked at the kitchen clock and realized that, in just six hours, she would be sitting opposite Sean again. Whilst she supped with Sean, Brigid would be minding Joseph. The delicious, double treachery made Alice's eyes shine brightly with betrayal.

Earlier in the day, Alice had pushed open Brigid's back door with one hand, as she parked the navy-blue Silver Cross pram under the kitchen window and shouted through the door, 'Are you sure you don't mind having him?'

Brigid stood on her tiptoes and leant forward to look out of the kitchen window at Joseph in his Silver Cross, the Rolls-Royce of all prams.

'Holy Mary, is he asleep? Is that lucky, or what? Of course I don't mind having him, especially if he's asleep now,' she shouted, as she stacked the baby bottles she had been washing on the draining board and took a tea towel from the hook underneath the sink to wipe her hands dry.

Alice pushed the pram brake down to lock it and stepped into Brigid's kitchen, tucking her always errant wisps of carefully styled hair back into her criss-crossed hairgrips.

Anyone else would have thought twice about leaving an extra baby with Brigid this particular afternoon.

Brigid's youngest was teething. Brigid herself was

exhausted, pale from lack of sleep, and the black bags under her eyes made her appear much older than she was.

'Mrs McGuire is at the shop and she will be back to help in a minute. We will be fine. Is he fed?'

'Yes, and he has only just dropped off in the pram on the way over,' said Alice, as she turned to face the mirror to catch a glimpse of herself. She took out some of the hair-grips and then slipped them back in again. 'God, I wish I had worn a hat today. The rain will pour any minute, I can tell.'

When Alice had first asked Brigid to look after Joseph, she had said she was visiting a sick friend whom she had once worked with at the hotel and that she would be gone for just a few hours.

It had been a simple and easy deceit, as long as she wasn't asked too many questions.

'Have ye time for a cuppa, Alice, before ye go? I'm desperate now, so I am. I haven't stopped all day. Shall I put the kettle on?'

Brigid was keen for Alice to stop and talk.

Mrs McGuire was as bad as Sean and had never stopped harping on about America.

Although Brigid would never mention it, she was upset that they never considered her own mammy and daddy in Cork. She missed them every day and the thought of travelling all the way to America, putting so many more miles between them, was more than she could bear to contemplate. Yet Sean and Mrs McGuire kept pushing and pushing.

The previous Sunday, there had been a mass at the cemetery in Cork for Brigid's brother who had died young in a tragic accident, fifteen years before. Brigid had been the only sibling not in attendance and she felt that guilt keenly.

Now Sean and his mammy wanted to take her further across the sea, miles away from all that she ached for, and she couldn't bear it.

Rather than moving away from Ireland, she yearned to return, to be again with everyone they knew and had grown up with. She wanted their daughters to love their country as she did and yet each year went by without a visit. The same excuse was always given.

The need to save money.

Mrs McGuire came to them to visit, so why would they struggle with all those children and the travelling?

Bloody Mrs McGuire.

Brigid thought she had everything under control and she did, most of the time. But when his mammy came to visit, her ability to keep their domestic routine, as well as Sean's levels of expectation, continuing as normal was stretched to the limit.

Alice said, 'I haven't time, sorry, Brigid, but I will later. I shan't be long and thanks again. I really appreciate it.'

Brigid stared at Alice's departing back and suddenly felt close to tears. She was not one for self-pity, which she regarded as a sign of over-indulgence, but she had been looking forward all day long to Alice calling in.

Just to talk about the things that kept every day ticking along in the rhythm of the four streets. Anything that was outside of her own four walls and ten children.

Alice was flying to the bus stop at the top of the road when she almost collided with Mrs McGuire and Peggy. The children followed them like a row of ducklings, bobbing along in their wake.

Peggy instantly sensed that all was not quite right.

'Well, hello, Alice, ye look grand indeed. Where are ye off to, then?'

There was no such thing as a secret in the four streets and what Peggy didn't know about everyone wasn't worth knowing. There was no way she would allow Alice to scuttle past as she was obviously trying to do, without a full explanation.

'I'm off back to the hotel to visit the housekeeper. She's a bit poorly. I trained her before I left and I knew her even before then. She has asked especially for me to visit and I thought it would be a bit peevish not to pop back to see her, seeing as how it's my fault she ended up with the job ...'

Alice was gabbling.

Peggy and Mrs McGuire stared and for a few seconds neither spoke as they digested Alice's words.

Alice realized she was gabbling. They realized she was gabbling.

She thought they could probably tell, just by looking at her, what she was up to.

Mrs McGuire stared at Alice with naked curiosity.

'Where is Joseph?' said Peggy. 'Has Kathleen come back home?'

'Brigid has him and I shan't be very long. I'll be back before he wakes.' And, with that, before they could answer, just as the Crosville bus came into sight, Alice shouted, just a little too loudly, 'I have to go, I don't want to miss the bus,' and then she was off round the corner, onto the bus and disappeared in a flash.

'Sick housekeeper, my eye,' said Peggy, as she and Mrs McGuire turned round and began walking again. 'Wearing stockings and lipstick at four o'clock? She must think we are stupid. That one's off for a job interview, I'll bet.'

'Either that, or she has a fancy man,' said Mrs McGuire, spitting on her handkerchief to wipe the cinder toffee from around her granddaughter's mouth.

Brigid's daughter squealed at her grandmother's saliva being wiped across her sticky face.

'Now shush, don't tell Mammy I bought ye sweets,' Mrs McGuire said to her earnestly. 'What yer mammy doesn't know won't hurt her, now, will it?'

Sean had run up the steps as soon as his shift finished and arrived at their pub in plenty of time. He was already sitting, waiting for Alice, on the studded burgundy-leather seats in the corner of the snug behind a dark-oak partition.

He had bought the usual Guinness for himself and a Babycham for Alice. Sean didn't want to touch his drink until she arrived. He lit a cigarette and, taking another out of the packet for Alice, propped it up against the ashtray, waiting.

It had begun to rain heavily and he wondered if she would still come or if the downpour of rain would make her think twice.

It would be the third time they had met and Sean knew it was now risky. However, it made no difference. The thrill he felt at the prospect of spending more time with Alice was greater than what he felt when the bell rang at the end of a bout to announce that he was the winner.

This was potentially far more dangerous.

He turned his gaze towards the half-frosted snug windows and felt grateful they were hidden. No one came in here before seven in the evening. They would be safe.

Noisy chatter from the bar had spilt over into the snug. Men were arriving in small groups, heading for the first drink of the day, followed by the women from Upper Parliament Street, looking for their first early trick of the night.

The air in the pub was a deep hazy blue from the smoke of Woodbines and Players, which mingled with the smell of yesterday's stale alcohol, soaked into the dark wooden floor. The fire provided enough heat and the apple-wood logs helped to transform smells that were odious in the cold light of morning into the more pleasant aroma of freshly roasted hops and warm beer by dusk.

Sean lit his cigarette and as he threw the match into the fire, he saw Alice run past the half-frosted window. He took a deep breath and tried to calm the knot in his stomach.

He had thought about nothing but meeting her again since the last time. She had filled his thoughts and his mind.

At work he had been unable to look Jerry in the eye and, without realizing, had fallen into a subdued mood, which made the other men on the docks wonder what was the matter with the big man. But a man's thoughts were his alone, so no one pried. Unlike the women.

Alice dashed into the snug, breathless and soaked. She had reasoned that if she ran fast from the bus stop to the pub, fewer raindrops would wreck the hairdo she had spent hours teasing into place.

She was wrong. Her fringe had long escaped her hairgrips and was plastered to her forehead. Drips ran down into her eyes, smudging the eyeliner and mascara she had applied with such precision.

She didn't care. As she ran into the snug, her heart melted. Sean instantly shot to his feet and removed his cap in honour of her presence. He was the only man ever to have done that for Alice and suddenly she felt like the woman she knew she always should have been.

Not like the one who had tricked Jerry into having sex with her to make him propose.

Alice removed her coat and Sean reached out his hand.

'Here, give it to me. I will hang it by the fire to dry. Make sure you don't forget it before ye leave.'

Alice relaxed and began to laugh. It was amazing to her how easily laughter came when she was with Sean.

'Sean, in this weather, only an idiot would forget a coat. Have you seen how heavy the rain is?'

Sean began to laugh with her as he poured her drink and then, both turning to face the fire, drinks in hands, they picked up the conversation where they had last left off and talked and talked.

Sean had never spoken so many words to Brigid in one day, ever.

Alice had never spoken so many words to anyone in her entire life, ever.

For the first time, Alice talked about her childhood.

She told Sean of her panic and need to flee the hotel and how scared she had been of ending her days alone, in a bedsit as the previous housekeeper had. She skimmed over how she had tricked Jerry into marrying her but praised how Kathleen had nursed her back into sanity. She talked of the tablets, the breakdown and her isolation and feeling like an outsider in the four streets. When she had finished, Sean leant across the table and took both of her hands in his.

Neither spoke. Alice stared down at her small hands enfolded in Sean's huge fingers. He rubbed the back of her hand with his thumb, then brought it up to his lips and placed one deeply tender kiss on the palm.

Alice's first instinct was to pull her hand away and she almost did. But Sean held on firmly.

'Don't,' he whispered. 'Enjoy this, you deserve it. You deserve this and more.'

Alice had never cried. She had never felt sad enough to cry. She lived somewhere in a half-world and had looked curiously at others who could.

She had stared at the tears that ran down Maura's cheeks, as they so often did these days, in slight wonderment. She had seen tears brim in Jerry's eyes, on the night Father James had been caught in Kitty's room. It seemed, at one point, as though everyone was shedding tears of one sort or another.

Everyone except for Alice, who hid in her bedroom and listened from a distance.

Now Alice felt her face flush. It was as though a torrent of emotion had escaped from somewhere inside and now swam through her veins, prickling the surface of her skin and forcing the tears into her eyes. She quickly blinked them back.

'God, what is happening, Sean?' she whispered, although they were the only two people in the snug.

Sean smiled. 'I haven't a clue, but I know I have to see you again and soon.'

Alice wrenched her hand away and jumped out of her seat with a yelp. It was dark outside. They had been talking for three hours.

The bubble of warmth burst in a second and was replaced with dread.

'What am I to do? Oh my God, Sean, it's dark. Brigid will think I have deserted her and left her with the children, and Jerry will be sending out a search party.'

Sean had already reached for her coat and was helping Alice into it. He looked at the clock on the snug wall.

'The bus will be here in five minutes, let's run.'

'What, together, are you sure?'

'Aye, no one will see us. It's dark now. Brigid thinks I have been at the boxing club.'

Alice picked up her bag and they both flew out of the pub swing doors and ran down the road, Sean holding tightly onto Alice's hand as they did so.

It was a Friday, which was fish day, and Mrs McGuire had decided Brigid needed a break and to treat the family to a fish and chip supper. She was cross that Alice had left Brigid with Joseph to look after and had let her daughter-in-law know exactly how she felt.

'I don't ever see anyone giving ye a break, Brigid. Seems to me like you're always being put upon by others.'

'I have you here, Mrs McGuire. You give me a break,' said Brigid, who was feeling a little sorry for herself.

Lifting Brigid's wicker basket down from the peg and placing in it a pudding basin still warm from the range, covered by a pan lid, Mrs McGuire tied a headscarf around the curlers Peggy had put into her hair earlier in the day, before heading off to the chip shop.

It was the first time ever she had worn curlers outdoors and she felt as though she looked very conspicuous.

'When Sean sees me in these, he'll be asking me what radio station I can pick up,' she laughed as she tied the scarf under her chin. 'Ye would never see our Mary in these. She visits to a salon every week now, so she does. It is different altogether over there in America, Brigid.'

And with that, much to Brigid's relief, she was gone.

Mrs McGuire loved the chippy. If she was honest, she loved the chippy more than she did Brigid.

There was no chippy back home, although there had been talk of one for some time.

The prospect of a chippy in the village was partly inspired by the envy of Mrs McGuire's neighbours, whom she loved to regale with stories of the rare delicacies to be found at Mr Chan's.

Saveloys. Oh, how she loved the way that word rolled off the tongue.

Was there ever a more exotic word?

'In Liverpool, I often pop to the chippy for saveloys,' she would say to her neighbours.

'God in heaven, s-a-v-e-l-o-y-s. What would they be?' her neighbours would demand to know.

As it was a Friday night, the chip shop was busy and Mrs McGuire felt mildly irritated as she noticed that the queue was almost to the shop door. Taking her place at the end, she stepped into the brightly lit shop full of hot steam and chatter and untied her headscarf to shake away the surface water. As she fixed it back into place with a knot under her chin, she keenly looked around her to see who else could afford to be in the queue.

Some of the women whose families she knew from back home shouted out greetings.

'Is Sean fighting again tonight, Mrs McGuire? He's on a winning streak, so he is, we will all be putting money on him soon.'

The fish and chip shop was a luxury and Mrs McGuire was surprised to see so many people there. Some of these women have more money than sense, she thought to herself.

'No, not tonight,' she replied. 'He's running short of lads willing to take him on. It's a practice night tonight, so don't waste ye money, he will definitely beat himself.'

She wiped a circle in the steam on the window so she could peer out into the street. The sulphur-yellow street lights had transformed the dirty wet black pavements to the colour of golden marmalade.

She heard the familiar ding-ding of the bell on the bus across the street and her inbred nosiness made her squint to see if she knew anyone alighting.

She recognized Sean instantly. Of course she did. She was his mother and there were very few men in Liverpool as tall or as well built as Sean.

She watched his athletic leap from the platform of the still-moving bus and thought, typical Sean, always in a hurry. As he swung down from the pole and landed on the pavement, he reached up to help someone else down. It looked like a woman, but Mrs McGuire couldn't really see. She leant forward, with her face almost pressed against the window, and wiped furiously at the greasy glass until it squeaked.

'What you want, lady?' Johnny Chan shouted. It was the third time he had asked for her order.

Flustered, Mrs McGuire reached into the basket and handed him the pudding basin with the enamel pan lid for the peas. 'Three fried fish, three saveloys, five peas and five chips, please, Johnny.'

She stepped back over to the window to see the back of the bus disappear down the road, but there was no sign of her son.

With the parcel of fish and chips safely wrapped up in newspaper, and resting on top of her pudding basin, she hurried back towards Nelson Street.

As she neared the top of the entry, Little Paddy flew out of the newsagent's, with his da's ciggies in his hands, and crashed straight into Mrs McGuire, almost knocking the basket straight out of her hand.

'Sorry, Mrs McGuire,' Little Paddy apologized, as he ran past.

'Gosh, Paddy, ye are in a dreadful hurry,' she shouted. 'Look where ye are going! Ye nearly knocked me off my feet.'

If Little Paddy looked where he was going, his da would accuse him of dawdling and give him a belt. He hated it if there were lots of people in the shop. It made his breath short with anxiety and then he couldn't run as fast as he wanted.

Only yards away, Sean and Alice stood in the middle of the entry, each fully aware they were playing with fire. The knowledge thrilled them. All around they could hear the familiar sounds of domestic street life: dogs barking, babies crying, mothers shouting, outhouse toilets flushing.

The only illumination was from the moon and stars, plus the reflections on the pavements of light tumbling from kitchens or bedroom windows, across backyards and over the entry wall.

Occasionally a child ran across the entry, like a river rat darting from one backyard to the next, sent from a house without, to borrow from a house that had.

Light to dark. Yard to yard.

The same sounds repeated daily as they had been for generations.

Different children. Different dogs. Same cacophony of life.

Sean and Alice were startled as suddenly, out of the darkness, a young voice shouted, 'Hiya, Sean, hiya, Alice,' making them both jump out of their skins.

They stepped aside as Little Paddy rushed past and they stared aghast at his departing back. Alice came back to reality with a thud.

'I have to leave now. Wait until you see me leave your house before you go in,' she said, beginning to move away.

'Monday,' whispered Sean urgently, taking hold of her hand

and pulling her back. 'Say you will come again on Monday.' He brushed the damp hair back from her face with his free hand.

'I don't know if I can. I can't ask Brigid to look after Joseph again, can I?'

She looked down at her wet leather boot and kicked the cobblestones.

Scamp, Little Paddy's skinny, shaggy-haired grey dog, ran past. He had been waiting loyally outside the newsagent's for Little Paddy and had hung around, sniffing Mrs McGuire's basket, until he realized no chips were flying his way.

Wherever Little Paddy went, Scamp went too.

Alice and Sean, searching for a reason to delay their parting, watched the departing dog until he was swallowed by the night.

Alice had made up her mind. 'If Kathleen is back, then yes, I will,' she whispered, looking into his eyes.

Sean pulled her in to him, gave her one deep, long kiss and then, shocked by his own boldness, stepped quickly back.

Alice lost her breath and thought she might faint. She had been kissed. Without trickery or plotting or devious manipulation. And, swaying, she laid a hand on Sean's arm to steady herself.

Turning quickly, with her hands thrust deeply into her pockets, Alice walked away, looking back once at his grinning face. It was as though he now knew something he hadn't before and whatever that knowledge was, it had made him very happy.

She couldn't keep the grin from her own face and as she smiled back, she felt a heat slowly rise inside her, threatening to erupt into joyous and uncontrollable laughter.

And then, as the terrible fear of being caught once more took hold, she ran like the wind, in through Brigid's back gate.

To Brigid. Sean's wife. To collect her son.

Sean waited and watched. Suddenly, he wanted to tell everyone. He had fallen in love, with Alice.

The thought that she was running to his house to collect her baby from his wife did not make him feel in the least bit guilty.

Guilt and honour had been tackled and beaten by exhilaration and desire. The sense of peril made him feel alive and euphoric, just as he did in the seconds before he was about to step into the ring.

Now the thought that he would not see Alice until Monday made him groan.

How could he wait a whole forty-eight hours to talk to the woman whose passion for life matched his own?

It seemed like an eternity.

As she turned the corner into Sean's backyard, Alice momentarily held onto the latch before she clicked the gate shut.

'Oh my God, this is madness, you crazy woman,' she whispered, leaning her forehead against the wet, cold, splintered wood.

She turned round to look in through the kitchen window and saw Brigid's outline sway as she rocked Joseph in her arms. It was a touching scene. But all Alice could think of was how long it would be until Monday when she could see Brigid's husband again.

Over at the Priory, Sister Evangelista had pulled her car right up to the front door. Switching off the engine, she took the crisp white linen handkerchief which lay on the passenger seat and blew her nose. Through the windscreen, she surveyed the Priory garden well lit by the almost full moon.

Her gaze wandered over the low wall towards the towering monuments and effigies standing in the graveyard. Unable to help herself, she took a moment and fixed her gaze upon the spot where Father James had been found. Fog clung to the gravestone, creating an eerie scene.

The bishop had become concerned by the number of people calling at the Priory to speak to Daisy and had dispatched Sister Evangelista, at this ungodly time of night, to move her across the road into the convent.

The police had said that they would be at the Priory tomorrow morning to interview Daisy.

The bishop had wanted to know why.

'I cannot be sure, Father,' Sister Evangelista told him, 'but I am almost certain it has something to do with Molly Barrett. She's been spending a great deal of time at the Priory. It cannot be a coincidence, surely?'

'What did the stupid fecking girl tell the woman?' he roared. His temper terrified Sister Evangelista.

She didn't like the way the bishop was speaking to her. They were co-conspirators, both doing their best to cover up the evil work Father James had been engaged in under their very noses. Did the bishop not know that Sister Evangelista was in turmoil? She had loved Father James, whom she thought the most perfect of men. She was struggling, finding it all so difficult. When she wasn't dealing with this mess, she was deep in prayer, asking the Lord to give her the strength she needed to cope. The bishop's bad temper was the last straw.

She had cause to spend a great deal of time on the phone to him recently. Her conscience would not let her stray too far into the reaches of fantasy, but of this she was certain: Kitty Doherty had disappeared, allegedly for a holiday. In all her years, the furthest she had ever known a Doherty to venture from the four streets had been to the Formby pine dunes on the church charabanc, to celebrate the Coronation.

She was also certain the girl was pregnant and there was a murdered priest, with the devil's own work hiding in his desk and cupboards, who had been in and out of the Doherty house like a demon's whisper.

All of this, she had discussed with the bishop.

'I have prayed long and hard, Father, and I am very sure that all of this information would help the police. The Lord knows, it is weighing me down badly.'

The bishop was none too happy with this suggestion.

'Sister, we had a bad man as our priest in your church. Do ye know how much damage would be done to the authority of the churches across Liverpool, if not the whole British Isles, should this information become public knowledge? At the very least, the church would be boarded up, and the convent and the school closed. Is that what we want to happen? And as for what Rome might decide to do to us personally ...'

'But what about Kitty Doherty, Bishop?'

'What about her, Sister? A sick child has been sent back home to Ireland for a holiday and a rest. God willing, she will return cured. Sister, ye will keep all of these fanciful notions inside your own head and ye and I, we will give thanks to God that he sent us, people he knows he can trust, to do the right thing. We have made the right decision to put our responsibilities first. Let the police do their job, we shall do ours.'

Sister Evangelista wasn't at all sure that they were doing the right thing. Her heart was in conflict but, as usual, she replied obediently, 'Yes, Father.'

The driveway flooded with light as the Priory door opened.

There, framed in the doorway, was Daisy, with her bag, waiting to leave.

Daisy was happy that she would be sleeping at the convent and leaving the huge empty Priory, with its damp, black bricks, hugged by lichen and creeping ivy. The elusive whispers, which began as night fell, had always unsettled her and now Sister Evangelista would save her from it all.

The demons outside and in.

He had been told to ask for telephone extension twenty-four, which was the mortuary, and to say that he needed to speak to the technician about an inquest hearing in the morning.

The time and the place were always the same when one or other of the tight-knit circle needed to make contact with Austin.

Austin stood by the phone and waited for the call. This was the only place in the hospital where he was unlikely to be disturbed. The technician, always keen to leave before he should, at six-thirty, had no objection when Austin told him he would cover for him.

Stanley was in the porters' lodge. He and Austin were both on the late shift and working until ten. Stanley worried Austin. He seemed unable to act as though nothing had occurred.

To carry on as normal.

'Pull yerself together, man,' Austin had told him only yesterday. 'Have the bizzies been? Has anyone contacted us? Have we heard a thing? No, we haven't, now shut yer gob and behave. Nothing has happened other than you looking and behaving as guilty as hell.'

Stanley was no fool and shot back at him, 'Are you fucking joking? One of our own has been murdered in a graveyard, had his dick hacked off and fed to a cat. We have no idea who did it, he's in our group and you say nothing has happened! How do we know that the person who murdered him isn't coming for us? How do we know that the police won't be led to us, when they are looking for whoever murdered the priest? How do we know that the priest didn't keep all our photos in his stupid fucking Priory? Austin, you are fucking mental. We are in deep shit, mate, and you had better find out what the hell is going on or I'm off.'

But Austin was quite sure that the father wouldn't have kept the photographs in the Priory. None of them kept anything at home. All their photographs were in the hospital, in a locker under the name John Smith. No one asked who John Smith was. No one ever needed to know.

The shrill ring of the phone bounced back off the cold mortuary tiles, filling the room and sounding much louder than it actually was.

The voice on the other end sounded troubled.

'Is that ye, Austin? Are ye alone?'

'Yes, I am,' Austin replied.

'The police are questioning the girl, Daisy, tomorrow.'

'Are you fucking joking? Why?'

It was Daisy who let them into the Priory when members of the circle visited to drop off films or pictures, and the priest had even let Austin visit Daisy when she first arrived in Liverpool. Stanley only liked boys and Daisy had been almost too old for Austin, but he had used her for a year or so.

The Priory had been the best cover for them all. No one would have suspected a priest, or so they had thought.

Although he didn't need to, he dropped his voice to a whisper.

'Do the police have the pictures? Can we be identified? Do

they know we let the priest into the hospital? Are you running?' His questions chased one another down the line.

'Don't be stupid,' the bishop replied. 'How can I run? Do I not need to find out what is going on? They don't have the pictures. I put them meself into the incinerator at the convent, with the help of the sister.'

Austin breathed a sigh of relief. They were safe.

'In that case, why do the police want to interview the housekeeper?'

'She apparently had a long chat to one of the neighbours, a Molly Barrett, from Nelson Street. The next day, the police were at her house for most of the day.'

'Look, we didn't murder the priest, I keep telling Stanley. That is what the police are looking for. A murderer. Not us.'

The mortuary door clicked open. Austin almost jumped out of his skin as Stanley stepped in.

'Aye, but we don't know who killed him. The sister has a notion the Doherty house is connected and the Kitty girl is pregnant. We don't know if any of that is true. My worry is that their enquiries will lead them to us and the group.'

There was silence for a moment as Austin accepted a cigarette from Stanley and bent his head to take a light.

'Well, you keep finding out what is happening and we will do our bit here. We need to make sure that we shut down any clues that may lead them to us, don't we, Bishop?'

'True enough,' the bishop replied. 'Now I have a plan to move the girl back to Dublin, out of the way as soon as possible and I need your help.'

As Sister Evangelista helped Daisy load her bags into the car, she chatted to her about the police request to interview her.

'Have ye any idea why, Daisy?'

'I haven't, Sister.'

'Did ye say anything to Molly, when she visited, that might give ye a clue?'

But Daisy just stared vacantly out of the window and didn't reply.

Alice saw Jerry first, before he saw her. He was sitting at Brigid's table, tucking into a plate of food. He looked so natural, chatting to Brigid as she washed up at the sink, that a stranger looking in would have thought it was something Jerry did every night of his life. Joseph was now perched on his knee, trying to grab the fork before it reached Jerry's mouth.

'Oh Lordy, what are you doing here?' Alice exclaimed, in a voice far too high-pitched. 'I left a stew in the oven at home.'

Before Jerry could answer, she reached out for Joseph and turned to speak to Brigid. 'Has he been good?' she asked.

'He's been grand, no trouble at all,' said Brigid, moving over to wipe the hands of her own tribe, who sat round the table.

'Thank you, Brigid, you have been fantastic.'

'I had baked a pie, but Mrs McGuire went off to the fish and chip shop. Jerry didn't know if you had left anything for him, so I gave him the pie. Sean will no doubt have that as well as the fish and chips when he finally arrives home, being the greedy pig that he is now.' Brigid was grinning. Jerry was still tucking into the pie.

Joseph was nestled against Alice's chest, half asleep.

Two of Brigid's babies were asleep in the pram, which was where they would stay until their elder sister was old enough to be transferred from her cot to a bed.

Everything is so normal, thought Alice, and yet only feet away I have just kissed your husband.

She wanted to laugh out loud.

'How was the housekeeper?' asked Jerry, who was genuinely interested.

'Oh, well, not that great, I'm afraid. I would like to call again but we will see. It's having the time. Not that easy at the moment.'

'Not at all,' said Brigid, generously rushing in. 'I will have Joseph any time, so I will. It's not a problem at all for me.'

Alice began to fake her protest but Brigid cut her off. Brigid was playing into Alice's hands, beautifully.

'I won't hear a word, now shush. If ye need to go again, just bring him over to Auntie Brigid.'

Alice didn't feel a shred of guilt. Not a flicker of remorse.

What she did feel was jealousy. It had been brewing since the first time she had met Sean alone. And now, at this moment, in Brigid's kitchen of perfect pastry and well-behaved children, it was stronger than ever. Alice was jealous of the Brigid who in just a few moments would fuss round Sean as soon as he walked in and slipped into their ordered and happy family life.

A realization dawned upon Alice. Sean was two different men. There was the man she had come to know, who had sat in the pub with her, and the man he would become when he walked into his own home and sat at his own hearth.

She didn't want to be there when that happened.

Claiming Sean as her own would be easy. Removing him from the grip of his wife, daughters, mother and his comfortable domestic routine would be much more difficult.

'Jerry, I am taking Joseph over to bed, he is almost asleep,' she said, pulling back the pram quilt and laying Joseph down.

As Alice fastened the studs on the side of the pram hood, Jerry spoke while he was still eating. 'I'm coming, I'm coming,' he spluttered, shovelling the last forkful down, and thinking that whatever Alice had prepared for supper would not be a patch on Brigid's pastry.

'Would ye like some on a plate to take home, Jer?' asked Brigid innocently, not realizing that Alice would perceive the offer as a direct attack upon her competence as a wife.

Jerry, desperate to say yes, looked to Alice for approval.

'No thanks, Brigid. He has to eat the food I prepared at home yet.'

Alice locked eyes with Brigid and smiled as she spoke. A thin smile. Her mind elsewhere.

Thinking. Brooding. Plotting.

'Ah, 'tis the only way to a man's heart, making him good food, I can guarantee that, so I can,' said Brigid as she stood with one hand on the back door and the other in her apron front pocket. She cut a lonely silhouette framed in the light, watching them both walk down the path together. ''Tis how I caught my Sean. Once he had tasted my pastry, he didn't stand a chance,' Brigid chuckled.

'Really?' Alice threw the reply over her shoulder, laced with more than a hint of sarcasm. 'I'll have to remember that one for the future.'

Mrs McGuire walked down the entry and stopped as Sean loomed into sight. 'Sean,' she called out. 'What are ye doing, stood there?'

Sean looked at his mother and was speechless.

How could he say, 'I'm waiting for Alice to leave my house so that I can go home'? His mouth flapped open and closed again while he desperately tried to form a sensible sentence. They both heard the back gate click shut and turned together to see Alice and Jerry walking towards them.

'Hello, Alice, Jerry,' shouted Sean. He was playing for time while he thought what to say to his mother.

'Hello, Sean. Hello, Mrs McGuire,' said Jerry. 'Jesus, Sean, ye have the best pie waiting for ye in your house. I almost stuffed the lot down and left ye nowt.'

'Kathleen will be delighted to hear that the best pie you have ever tasted was made by Brigid,' whispered Alice sharply under her breath to Jerry, just as both men roared with laughter.

Without realizing it, Sean's eyes were fixed on Alice.

Hers gave nothing away. Mrs McGuire forgot to ask again why she had found her son standing alone, kicking the entry wall, rather than in his own home.

Little Paddy ran in through the back door, shouting, 'Mammy, Da, I have the ciggies.'

'What took ye so feckin' long, ye lazy article?' grumbled Paddy, as he took the fags. 'I bet ye fecking dawdled all the way, didn't ye?'

'I did not, Da, I ran all the way.'

'Ran, my arse, ye bleeding liar.'

'Da, I did, I ran.'

Big Paddy cuffed Little Paddy across the ear with one hand whilst he snatched the ciggies from him with the other.

He had run out of cigarettes an hour earlier and had been pacing the floor, glancing at the back door every thirty seconds, waiting for Little Paddy to return.

The dog lay on the floor, with his tail tucked in and his ears down, as close to Little Paddy as he could possibly be.

Little Paddy began to whimper.

'Stop crying like a babby, Paddy,' said Peggy as she walked into the room.

'I can't help it. Da just hit me over the ear and called me a liar. He said I didn't run home with his cigs, an' I did.'

'If yer da says ye didn't, ye didn't and don't cheek him.'

'I did, I'm not a liar, Mammy, an' Alice and Sean can prove it, so they can.'

'Alice and Sean?' said Peggy. 'How can Alice and Sean prove it?'

Big Paddy was taking out a ciggie and putting a second one behind his ear, ready to go before the first one burnt out.

'Because they both saw me in the entry and I spoke to them. They saw me running, so they did.'

'Alice and Sean?' said Peggy for the second time. 'What were they doing in the entry then?'

Peggy had begun washing the dishes and was rinsing a dinner plate under the running tap.

'They was kissing,' whimpered Little Paddy.

Peggy had leant over to lay the plate onto the draining board. Paddy had struck a match to light his ciggie. Both looked at each other in shock as the plate slipped from her hand and smashed into pieces all over the kitchen floor.

Chapter Seventeen

KITTY AND NELLIE stood anxiously waiting, just inside the open front door, excited and holding hands, sheltering from the midges. The light was fading fast when they spotted the lights of the farm van trundling down the Ballymara road.

As it passed, it illuminated the rhododendrons on the opposite side of the road. Kitty wondered if her mother would be as taken with their size and wildness as she had been.

Liam's younger brother, Patrick, who was driving, teased both girls, slowing down just outside the front gate, then grinning and waving through the window, before speeding onwards towards the McMahons' farm to turn the van round.

Kitty ran to wait at the gate. Patrick and Kathleen had been to Dublin to collect Maura and had left long before the girls had woken.

Kitty could scarcely contain her excitement. Now she and Maura hugged and held onto each other tightly, before walking down the path and in through the front door.

The fire had been stacked high and the flames made the kitchen brighter and warmer than usual. The smells of burning peat and freshly baked bread competed with each other. Maeve, who was moving the dishes of food around the table to make space for the salmon, quickly removed her apron. Glancing in the mirror hanging above the sink, she pushed the stray strands of auburn hair behind her ears and, licking the top of both index fingers, ran them quickly across her wayward eyebrows.

Both of the dogs were fast asleep, stretched out on their sides in front of the fire, paws covered in the softly drifting peat ash. Their legs were twitching in a dream world, chasing rabbits.

'At last,' beamed Maeve, scooping Maura into a hug.

Maeve would never betray the fact that she had been more than a little worried about Maura's arrival. For Maura lived in Liverpool. A city of sophistication. With bright lights and modern ways. With music and culture and fancy clothes. Liverpool had everything Mayo didn't. Maeve had heard there was a clothes store called C&A, stocking every fashion you could find in the magazines, and a Woolworth's bigger than any building Maeve had ever seen. The doctor's wife also came from Liverpool and she had proudly shown Maeve the china she had bought in a store called Lewis's.

But one look at Maura told Maeve she had nothing to fear.

'Bernadette's lovely friend. I have heard so much about ye,' said Maeve, linking her arm through Maura's.

A look of sadness crossed Nellie's face. Then came that familiar ache in her diaphragm. The deep loneliness she could never explain. The longing for a mother she never knew. She wanted to plead with Maeve, *Say her name again. Please, say it like you used to say it to her.*

'The child has been pacing around all the day, looking up the road waiting for ye, so she has.'

Maeve grinned at Kitty, who nuzzled in and tightened her

arms round her mother's waist, sheepishly burying her face in Maura's shoulder.

Kitty inhaled deeply the scent of her mother, the familiar mixture of Nelson Street and cigarette smoke. She was calmed. Everything was better than it had been and it would be even better, now that Maura was here.

Nellie watched Kitty hugging her mother.

She had Alice, but Alice had never hugged Nellie.

She looked at the expression on Kitty's face. Nellie knew she had never felt whatever it was Kitty was feeling right now.

Nana Kathleen had been watching too and now she put an arm gently round Nellie's shoulder, kissed the top of her head and asked, 'Are ye glad to see me home, or what, young lady? And where's me kiss, for goodness' sake?'

Almost as soon as Maura walked into the house, Liam's brother, Finn, arrived with his wife Colleen, as did the McMahons from the farm next door. Each had seen Patrick's van pass by or turn at their door. Julia, Nana Kathleen's sister, and her husband Tom, also pulled up in their van outside.

The noise in the kitchen was deafening, as everyone made Maura feel welcome.

Kitty was keen to hear the news from home.

'Has Sister Evangelista said anything about my being away?' she asked nervously.

'Not at all,' Maura replied gently. 'The sister has her hands full, mind. They have Daisy from the Priory in the sick bed at the convent and she has been there for days. No one knows what is up with her, but she has taken to her bed, so she has, and they all seem in much of a dither.'

Maura didn't add that the police had been at the convent every day, wanting to interview Daisy, and were being given short shrift by Sister Evangelista. This news gave Maura some comfort. What on earth could she possibly say to the police that would present any danger to them?

In honour of their guest, Liam had opened the bottle of whiskey, usually kept until after the harvest. The weather had been so good of late that the village was preparing for the harvest to begin the next day.

As usual, Kitty woke not long after falling asleep.

She wondered if the night would ever come when she slept all the way through. Now she strained to hear if anyone else was awake.

Maeve, Kathleen and Maura were still in the kitchen, peeling potatoes and placing them in a pan big enough to bathe an average toddler. Their voices were muffled but comforting enough to send Kitty straight back to sleep.

'It was very plush,' said Kathleen, as she plopped another peeled potato into the cold water in the pan. 'I have never been inside anything like it. Polished wooden floors, a big oak press and very smart rugs and curtains. I wasn't allowed to see the bedrooms. The Reverend Mother said no one is allowed to, but she assured me that the beds were very comfortable. If the bedrooms are anything like the morning room and the hall and stairs, it'll be the poshest room Kitty will ever have slept in.'

'Did they seem kind enough, though, Kathleen? I don't care about posh. God, the child is used to nothing like posh, it's kindness she needs.'

Maura sat down, wiping her hands on the clean apron Maeve had loaned her.

'She was the Reverend Mother, Maura, more businesslike, I would say, but the young novices, they seemed lovely, now, and I'm sure they will be the ones Kitty has more contact with.'

'And what is this Rosie O'Grady like, then, who will be delivering the baby? I know she is your sister-in-law, Kathleen, but is she a good woman?'

'She's Julia's sister-in-law, not mine, and a very well-qualified midwife. What is more, she will keep her trap shut.' Kathleen rubbed the top of Maura's arm comfortingly as she said this. 'I wish the boat had come in earlier and ye could have come to see the Abbey with me, Maura, but this morning was the only time the Reverend Mother had free and time is short.'

Maeve looked at both women. Her heart was heavy and she hated the conversation. With no children of her own, she would love to have adopted Kitty's baby but Liam wouldn't hear of it. He was still hoping, even though Maeve was approaching forty, that one day soon they would be blessed with their own son.

'Let Kitty have tomorrow, before ye tell her,' Maeve said. 'Kitty and Nellie have looked forward to the harvest so much and they will have great fun. If ye ask me, I think one or two of the village lads may have their eyes on our little ladies.'

Kathleen poured away the cold water from the two big hunks of bacon in which they had been soaking all day, and put the pan under the tap to refill the pan.

'Aye, well, they may do, but Kitty is just beginning to show. We can't wait too long before she is taken to the convent. She can have the harvest and then I think we have to take her. But we will let her have her last day here without worrying about what the next will bring. She doesn't need to know yet.'

'We can all drink to that,' said Maeve, with a wink, emptying out the remainder of the whiskey into the glasses.

They sat on the settle in front of the fire. Maeve kicked an ember out of the fire, then jabbing the poker into the flaming peat, she lifted it up to light her last cigarette of the day. The heat from the embers almost singed her eyelashes and tears sprang to her eyes. Wiping her face with her apron, she passed her cigarette along to the other two so that they could light their own.

Picking up her glass, Maeve said in a quiet voice, 'Who says it's a man's life, eh?'

In unison, all three lifted their glasses, took a sip of the whiskey from one hand and a large pull on their cigarette from the other.

'I hope bloody Liam is asleep when I get into bed and isn't going to give me a hard time, looking for his wicked way before the morning. I could do without it tonight,' said Maeve as she exhaled a long blue thread of smoke.

'He's his father's son, Maeve, so ye have no chance,' said Kathleen. 'Be prepared.'

All three laughed, took another drink, and stared into the fire.

Maura wanted to tell them that she had seen Bernadette standing at the farmhouse door when she had arrived. That she had felt a cold hand slip into hers as she walked from the van to the front door. Would they think she was mad if she did?

Bernadette, thought Maura, our lovely Bernadette.

In the comforting silence between the three women, Maura felt cold air pass in front of her and rest right next to her. She knew that, joining them, sitting with them, in their motherly, loving silence, was the friend, sister and daughter-in-law they had all loved best of all.

*

The flaming red sky of the previous evening kept its promise and the sun rose early, burning away the river mist, ensuring that there would not be one drop of soft, west coast rain to spoil the harvest.

Kitty stood at the back door to the farmhouse, the milking pail in one hand, the other shading her eyes, as she strained to look up the hill. This morning's weather would put everyone in high spirits.

Maeve appeared in the passageway and bent to take the pail handle and helped Kitty carry the milk into the dairy shed.

'People will start arriving soon so get your breakfast now, quick, young lady. There will be no chance at all to stop this morning once the cutting gets under way.'

Maeve had been up since five, preparing breakfast early, and had kept it warm on large enamel plates on the range shelf next to the fire, where the big pan of potatoes began to simmer.

'It will take at least an hour for the potatoes to come to the boil,' said Maeve when she saw Kitty looking at the huge pan. 'And still we have the cabbages to cook.'

Maeve was red-cheeked and flustered, but it was all a dramatic effect. She had everything beautifully under control.

The two big hunks of bacon had been simmering on the fire overnight. It had taken all Colleen and Maeve's strength to lift the pan together and heave out the bacon haunches, which were now cooling on the huge wooden table, ready to be carved up for the lunch.

'That bacon looks grand, Maeve,' said Liam, trying to pull a slice off as Maeve walked past.

'Keep yer hands off, ye thieving bugger,' said Maeve, slapping him on his cap.

Liam and the men were tucking into large plates of eggs, sausage and fried potatoes. Kitty's morning sickness had well and truly passed, but she still couldn't eat the sausages.

'God, they smell just like the pig stall. I'll be sick if I eat them,' she said to Nellie.

Now they heard a strange noise coming from outside.

Nellie ran to the door. 'It's the thresher, the horses are pulling the thresher.'

Kitty was amazed by the sight that greeted her.

Men, women and children were walking across the peat, carrying their pitchforks and scythes, following a horse-drawn contraption in the form of a square wooden box on wheels.

Everyone from indoors moved into the fields to greet those who had arrived and, within what seemed like minutes, they were all at work. The cutter moved slowly as others began on the outside edges with scythes. The oats were put through the thresher to separate the grain, then the stalks were gathered up with pitchforks and stacked six feet high.

The women remained in the kitchen, preparing the food to be carried out to the barn at midday.

'Run and put these cloths on the hay bales in the barn now, please, girls,' said Maeve. 'Nellie, you remember what we did last time you were here, don't you?'

The girls ran into the barn and shifted around the bales Patrick had pulled down for them earlier, arranging them into seats, with eight bales in the middle to serve as a table.

'Can we go to the field now, Maeve?' the girls shouted through the back door when they had finished.

'Aye, off you go and help Uncle Liam and the others and,

mind, keep yer hands off them lads,' said Maeve with a wink at Nellie, who blushed bright red.

And off they ran to catch up with Patrick who was supervising the building of the straw stacks.

'Can we help, Patrick?' said Nellie.

'Not with this. I have enough lads. I have to round off the tops so that the rain runs off and doesn't wet the straw.'

'What shall we do then?' Nellie was jumping up and down by now, almost taking his pitchfork out of his hand.

'Aye, go on, then,' he said, handing Nellie the fork. 'Gather up the straw from the thresher and pile it up onto the cart Jacko is harnessed up to. The cart will be moving over here in a few minutes. I see yer man, Aengus, is talking to Kitty, then?'

Nellie looked over and saw the McMahons' nephew had stopped work and was chatting to Kitty.

Aengus had spotted Kitty as she ran into the field. He rested on his pitchfork and thought that he had never seen a young girl look so happy.

'Morning, miss,' said Aengus, raising his cap as soon as he was within earshot of Kitty.

While Nellie had run on ahead to talk to Patrick, Kitty had stopped to tie her bootlace and was squatting down amid the freshly cut stalks.

'So, how do ye like Bangor then?'

Kitty straightened and squinted in the sunlight, her hair loose and hanging about her shoulders. His accent was so strong that she could hardly understand a word he said.

''Scuse me,' said Kitty. 'I'm sorry, I'm not from round here.'

'I know,' said Aengus. 'That's why I'm asking, how do ye like it in Bangor?'

'Oh, I'm sorry,' said Kitty, laughing sheepishly, 'you mean Bangornevin?'

'Aye, I do, but no one ever says the Nevin. Unless ye are visiting from Liverpool, of course, and then ye would be daft enough to say it.'

He was teasing Kitty and grinned as he spoke.

Kitty half grinned back and looked down, as though studying the freshly cut field. The smell of the fresh straw made her nostrils flare. The grain dust shone like gold splinters in the shimmering sunlight and, once again, she had need to shield her eyes as her fingers intertwined into an arch above her brow.

'What's ye name then?' he asked.

He had replaced his cap and was leaning forward with both hands on the top of his pitchfork. He swayed gently from side to side as he studied her face, waiting for a response.

She saw that his eyes were as blue as his hair was red and the contrast was startling. His complexion was pale and freckled. Kitty noticed a matt sheen on his skin where the grain dust had stuck to his sweat.

A brown cravat was tied in a neat knot at his throat and his white shirt fell open at the neck, billowing against his braces as the wind pulled it free from his ragged-bottomed trousers. Even after a short time, Kitty was aware that a neat trouser hem was a rare thing in Bangornevin and yet she had seen Maeve, night after night, sewing them up by the light of the lamp when everyone was in bed.

Kitty averted her eyes, aware that she had been staring.

'Well?' he asked again and Kitty noticed he was grinning from ear to ear.

'My name's Kitty.'

'Kitty. That's a nice, normal name. Mine's Aengus.'

Kitty laughed. 'Well, Aengus is normal enough. Aengus.' She let it slowly roll off her tongue. 'We have just learnt a poem in school called "A Song of Wandering Aengus",' said Kitty.

She looked thoughtful as she scampered around inside her own memory in search of the poem, and, unable to find it, instead spoke his name out loud.

Again.

'Aengus. 'Tis a nice name.'

He began to speak in a slower, softer voice:

'But something rustled on the floor
And someone called me by my name:
It had become a glimmering girl
With apple blossom in her hair.'

He looked at Kitty and smiled. She felt her stomach flip.

'If ye go to school in Mayo, Yeats is pushed down your throat, or ye can't pass the leaving cert,' he explained.

'Leaving cert? What on earth is that?'

'It's hard work, that's what it is.'

Nellie ran up alongside and took hold of Kitty's hand.

'Time to start putting the food out,' she said.

Kitty was reluctant to move away.

She liked this boy. She wanted to speak with him for longer. Kitty had never talked to a boy. Boys were like another species at school. She never imagined one would specially talk to her. Why would he do that?

'Ah, food. Well, we will need that soon, to be sure. I will see ye at the barn then, ladies.' Aengus raised his cap and walked away.

As soon as he was out of earshot Kitty said, 'Oh God, was

he gorgeous or not? Tell me, Nellie, look back, is he watching me walk away? Go ahead, look.'

Aengus was whacking the boys, who were mercilessly teasing him, with his tweed cap. As he looked up, he saw Nellie looking and lifted his cap high in the air in salute.

Nellie turned back sharply. 'Oh God, Kitty, he's looking straight at us.'

Both the girls giggled and, with an audacity she didn't even know she possessed, Kitty turned round and waved back at Aengus.

'Oh my God, oh my God, am I mad or what?' said Kitty as she giggled. With shining eyes and long hair flowing, they ran to the barn, burning onto the skyline an imprint of youth, as they faded through the brimming air.

Within half an hour, the barn was full with villagers. Maeve and Kathleen gave each helper a heaped plate of food.

'No half-measures at Ballymara farm,' shouted Maeve as she dished up the meal.

The fiddler had shown up and began to play for his lunch. Over in the corner of the barn, some of the women were already swishing their tea round in their cups before they tipped them up and handed the leaves to Nana Kathleen to read.

'One, two, three. There must be enough tea left for the leaves to be swilled round a full three times or the luck doesn't come,' said Kathleen to the circle of women gathering round her.

The first young woman to hand over her cup was shaking like a leaf.

'Aha,' said Kathleen. She had already noted that the young woman's breasts were bigger than they had ever been before. She had also known her mother, who was as flat as a pancake.

'I think that maybe a babby will be on its way very soon,' grinned Kathleen, looking up from the teacup.

'It is, Kathleen,' the girl whispered, leaning in conspiratorially. 'We haven't told Mammy yet, because she's not so well but we will do, this Sunday, after mass.'

Kathleen continued, 'I think there is a move coming soon, I can see open land and a river.'

'Oh, Kathleen, that is just so fantastic. We are moving to Mulingar and have our own farm from his daddy, right down on the river, with fishing too.'

Kathleen had heard that in the post office from Mrs O'Dwyer.

She smiled. 'Well, I never. Ye know, the tea leaves, they never lie, ye can keep nothing from them at all, so ye can't.'

Aengus had studied Kitty all through the lunch. She had been busy helping to serve the food and as she walked up to the house, carrying the empty tin trenchers, Aengus caught up with her.

He fixed her once again with his magical grin and, with his bright blue eyes smiling, asked her, 'Will ye be away to the Castlefeale dance next Saturday?'

'I may be,' said Kitty.

'And if ye are, would I be able to walk with ye?'

'Ye may be,' said Kitty, smiling back at him. 'I'll have to ask my mammy.'

And with that, afraid of making herself look foolish, she ran up the path to the kitchen door to help the others with the dishes.

Aengus, watching Kitty's back, whispered to himself:

'With apple blossom in her hair
Who called me by my name and ran.'

Inside the kitchen, Maeve was loading the trenchers into a straw donkey basket.

'Girls, would ye take these over to the stream and give them a rinse for me and then bring them back.'

'And come here and give your mother a hug, miss.' Maura grabbed Kitty from behind and hugged her so tightly, she squeaked in protest.

'Mammy, I can't breathe.'

Maeve looked on fondly and laughed.

Maura spun Kitty round and placed a big kiss on the top of her head. For a small second, mother and daughter savoured the moment whilst Maura silently prayed.

Tomorrow would be a very different day.

The girls each grabbed a handle on the basket and skipped outside. Kitty didn't know if it was the music playing that had created an atmosphere of high gaiety, or the gorgeous boy who wanted to talk to her, or the happiness and love she felt whilst she was staying in the farmhouse. She knew only that she felt so happy, she desperately wanted to cry, and as her eyes welled up, she could barely stop herself.

Being pregnant was something she had entirely forgotten until this moment.

They stopped at the stone sink perched on the stream. Kitty knelt down and, for a moment, put her head in her hands. It was the only place she could be alone.

'What's up, Kitty?' said Nellie.

'I don't know. It is just all so much. Everyone is so wonderful and I have never felt this happy, I don't think, ever in me whole life.'

Chapter Eighteen

Angela hated having to wait for the boys to catch up when they walked to school. The only one who could concentrate on an instruction for more than five seconds was Harry. The rest wouldn't listen to a word she said.

'Ye aren't our Kitty or Mammy, ye know,' shouted Malachi. 'Ye can't tell us what to do.'

He stuck out his tongue at Angela and grabbed the school bag out of her hand so that it fell to the floor. Picking up the bag, Angela swung it round full circle until it walloped him between the shoulder blades with a thud so hard that Malachi fell forward and hit the pavement with a smack.

His screams pierced the morning air and brought neighbours to their windows to see what was happening.

'Don't do that, our Angela,' shouted Declan, bending down to help Malachi up.

Declan had crusty hair and dried pobs in his ears.

Earlier in the morning he had dared to answer Angela back, who had responded by picking up his bowl of pobs and upending it on his head. The warm milk and bread had run down the sides of his face and into his ears.

'I'm sick to death of all of youse,' shouted Angela. 'None of ye does as ye is told. I'm leaving and going to school on me own now.'

She stormed off ahead, just as Little Paddy caught up with them all. Harry had pushed the baby in her pram round to Alice's house before setting off to school. He met up with Little Paddy as he ran out of his back gate.

'Sure, ye look mighty fed up, Paddy,' said Harry. 'Why haven't ye been out on the green playing all weekend?'

'I got a belt from me da, an' I wasn't allowed,' Little Paddy replied, looking very miserable and downbeat. 'He said I told another lie, but I didn't, I know what I saw, but I 'ave to keep me gob shut. I hate feckin' grown-ups, I do. I'm going to run away to sea on a ship, as soon as I'm old enough.'

Harry nodded sympathetically. He wasn't that keen on grown-ups himself. He thought they were very chaotic and disorganized.

'Ye can tell me, Paddy. I won't say a word to no one, I promise.'

'I can't tell ye. I still can't sit down yet, my backside is so sore. I'm not risking it again, but I will tell ye this, Harry, next time I see something, I'm comin' for ye to see it with me. Everyone believes you and no one believes me, so they don't, an' I hate being called a liar, because I have never told a lie to anyone – I haven't.'

For a reassuring moment, Harry put his arm round Little Paddy's shoulders.

Little Paddy flinched. 'Can ye feel the pain?' he asked. Little Paddy's shoulders hurt too.

'Yes, I can, Paddy, it's terrible,' said Harry, and he meant it. He could feel his friend's pain.

The only noise, as they shuffled along, came from Little Paddy's shoes, which were three sizes too big.

Harry had watched Angela as she stormed away. Now he picked out a soggy lump of pobs from Declan's hair.

He hoped his mammy would be home soon. He hadn't known she was leaving for Ireland and the news had been met with an outpouring of tears from the girls and stunned silence from the boys. Tommy seemed flustered and promised them all she would be back in a few days, but not with Kitty. Kitty would be staying in Ireland a little longer.

Harry was thoughtful as he walked. Alice hadn't seemed that happy to look after the baby and it already felt as if the house was falling apart without Maura.

As they passed by Molly Barrett's, her door suddenly swung open and there she stood with a plate in her hand.

'Biscuit, boys?' she said, nodding at her plate. Little Paddy and Harry looked at each other.

'Yes, please,' said Little Paddy, with enthusiasm. Peggy only ever baked on Sundays.

Harry was frightened of Mrs Barrett but he didn't know why.

Tiger pushed past Molly's ankles and with its eyes fixed on the boys, pushed itself up against Molly's legs. The cat hissed softly as it regarded the boys and both little Paddy and Harry involuntarily placed their hands across the front of their shorts.

Molly wasted no time in quizzing Harry, who couldn't take his eyes off the cat. 'I saw yer mammy leaving the house when I was letting Tiger in, Harry,' she said, with a fake smile, which didn't quite reach her eyes. 'She had a big bag with her, she did. Gone away, has she?'

Little Paddy turned round and looked at Harry with an expression of complete amazement. 'Yer mammy's gone away, where?' he almost shouted. 'Mammy said you is coming to our house for yer tea tonight. Is that why?'

Harry had no idea what to do or say without appearing

rude. He decided that honesty was the best policy. He couldn't lie, Tommy hadn't told them to lie and that was a big sin anyway.

'She's gone to see Kitty in Ireland, but she will be back soon, Mrs Barrett.'

'Will Kitty be with her?'

Mrs Barrett wasn't giving up and Harry wished Paddy would stop accepting biscuits from the plate.

Harry was no fool, he had told her all a nosy neighbour needed to know. 'I don't know, she might be,' he replied, then, 'Paddy, we will be late, we have to go. Bye, Mrs Barrett.'

It had become apparent to Angela that their mother must have been on the go constantly when she was at home. Angela was exhausted and yet her only job was to supervise breakfast and see everyone safely through the school gates.

'It's a catastrophe in our kitchen, so it is,' she wearily told her friend, as she walked into her classroom that morning. 'Everything falls on my shoulders, now that Kitty and Mammy have taken a holiday. It is truly shocking, so it is, to put on me so.'

In assembly prayers that morning, Harry prayed, 'Please God, bring Mammy and Kitty home this afternoon, because I'm not looking forward to Peggy's tea tonight. Amen.'

Alice had Maura's baby on her knee, ready to feed her a bottle, and was surprised to see Peggy march in through the back door.

'Morning, queen,' said Peggy breezily. 'How are the little ones?'

'They are both fine, thank you, Peggy.' There was a note of query in Alice's voice.

The unasked question. What the hell are you doing in my kitchen?

Alice was instantly on her guard. Peggy was the biggest gossip in the street.

'Brigid tells me ye are away out today. Can I do anything to help?'

Peggy hovered over Alice, grinning and peering. The thought that Peggy looked just like an old crone fleetingly crossed Alice's mind.

'No, thanks, Peggy. I have everything under control and besides, I am only popping into town for a couple of hours. I won't be long.'

'Ah, town is it, then? And what would ye be getting in town?'

Peggy had sat herself down in the armchair and made herself very comfortable. She looked as though she was settling in for the morning. Alice felt herself seething inside. Peggy smelt especially high, which did not help.

'Well, I'm off to see a friend and then I thought I would call into the meat market on my way back,' she said.

'There's good meat in Murphy's. Ye won't get any better in town.' Peggy sniffed.

Alice felt as if she wanted to scream. How could she rid herself of this stupid woman?

'Well, Peggy, I fancy a change, thanking you all the same, and now if you don't mind, I would like to get on.'

Peggy looked shocked. 'Are ye taking both babies with ye?'

'Heavens, no. Brigid is looking after them for me, until I get back. I have enough trouble looking after one, never mind two.'

'Aye, well, Maura will be back before ye know it. She has only taken Kitty to visit her granny,' said Peggy.

Peggy now knew for sure that Little Paddy had been lying and deserved the beating he had got from his da.

Alice was as cool as a cucumber and, sure, wasn't Brigid looking after Alice's kids, whilst she went into town?

No, not even Alice could kiss someone else's husband and then act this calmly under Peggy's laser scrutiny.

Yes, she was sure. Little Paddy had been lying again.

'Oh, well then, I didn't realize ye was leaving so early, I'm sure,' said Peggy, aware that she was not as welcome in this kitchen when Kathleen was away with Alice presiding.

Hurt and wounded that she hadn't been offered a cuppa, she heaved her huge frame out of the chair on the third attempt and then waddled down the road, to scrounge her morning tea and as many biscuits as she could lay her hands on at Mrs Keating's.

Alice met Sean outside the Railwayman pub, where she slipped a key into his hand.

'What's this?' said Sean, looking down at it in astonishment.

'It's for room twenty-one in the Grand. It is the room kept for overbooking and that never happens on a Monday. I kept it by accident in my coat pocket when I left.'

Alice was whispering and yet they were the only people on the street, or near the pub, as it had yet to open for business.

'The locks haven't been changed and the room will be empty. We can talk without being interrupted. Meet me there in half an hour.'

And with that she was gone.

Sean slipped up the staircase of the hotel unnoticed.

Maids and bellboys bustled about and the reception desk was far enough away from the staircase that entering the room was far easier than he had imagined. He had only been inside for five minutes when there came a gentle tap on the door. He opened it quickly.

Alice had been leaning her weight against the door so heavily that she almost fell in.

Neither spoke. Both were profoundly relieved to be alone together, at last.

'Did you get the bus after mine?' asked Sean, breaking the silence and grasping for something to say.

Alice nodded. They looked at each other. There was no need for words. There was only need.

The room, which was the size of a small school hall, felt cavernous and cold, even though it was full of spare chairs and tables, being stored for use in any one of the meeting rooms.

The Georgian panelling was painted in a dove grey and edged in a white ornate border, which made it feel cooler. The curtains at the tall windows, a faded pale-grey velvet with swathes and tails, dusty.

There was no warmth. No soul. No heart.

But they neither noticed nor cared. They could have been in a cave for all that they were aware of their surroundings.

Once Sean had reached out and pulled Alice into his arms, it took only seconds for them both to move from the door to the bed.

Within half an hour it was all over and, as they lay on their backs, they both lit a cigarette. For the first time in her life, Alice felt alive and liberated.

She stared at the ornate white coving that encircled the gilt light fitting, in the centre of the smoke-stained ceiling. As she exhaled she turned her head to look at Sean and said, 'God, Sean, I'm normal.' And her laughter danced, all over the bed.

Sean leant on his elbow and looked down at her, smiling. 'Alice, adultery is a sin. It is definitely not normal.'

She lifted her slim frame off the bed slightly and stubbed her cigarette out in the ashtray on the bedside table. As she did so, she thought of the number of times she had emptied the same ashtray in this very room.

'It is, if you are me,' she said. Then she took the cigarette out of Sean's hand, stubbed it out into the ashtray and set about committing adultery for a second time.

Daisy felt fine. It was Sister Evangelista who had told her she was ill. Daisy had been keen to stay at the convent but she did not want to be confined to the sick bay.

One of the novice nuns, who was also a nurse at the Northern, brought Daisy her meals and spoke to her as though she were very poorly indeed.

She had been told so many times she was ill that she was beginning to feel as though she really was sick and this morning she hadn't wanted to leave her bed.

What was there to get up for? She was only permitted to sit in the chair at the side of the bed and soon got pretty cold doing that.

She had been told she wasn't allowed to look out of the window, or to step outside.

One of the sisters brought her some books and there was a bible to read, but Daisy could hardly read anything more than a shopping list. Books were no use to her and she couldn't understand them anyway, even when someone else read to her.

Daisy didn't feel like her food today, either. Something was wrong. Things were changing, people were whispering and she didn't like it.

It was evening and they had switched Daisy's light off an hour ago. Daisy began to cry. She wanted to return to the convent in Dublin, where she had lived before she came to Liverpool. It was the only home Daisy had ever known and she desperately wanted to return. Daisy hadn't cried for a very long time. From a very young age, she had learnt the lesson that crying made no difference.

No one heard. No one cared. Nothing changed.

Sister Evangelista burst into the room without knocking, her arms full of what appeared to be freshly pressed undergarments. She placed them on the bed next to Daisy's feet and began peeling clothes from the top of the pile.

'Daisy, get up, get up,' she hissed. 'You have to get dressed.'

Daisy sat upright in bed. 'But it's night-time, Sister.'

'I know Daisy, I know. You have to get dressed. Come on, girl. Quickly, I have news from the bishop. Ye are going back to the convent in Dublin, but you have to go now and catch the night ferry with the bishop.'

'The bishop is here?' Daisy was confused. If the bishop was here, he would be at the Priory and so should she be.

'Not here exactly, not at the convent. Look, please, Daisy, just do as I ask, would you.'

Sister Evangelista had brought with her a case, packed with smart clothes Daisy had never seen before, and in no time she was creeping down the back stairs, with the sister urging her to be quiet.

Sister Evangelista opened a large wooden door that led to the convent garden. In a dim pool of light, on the other side of the tall wrought-iron gate at the garden entrance, were two men, huddled together against the cold air, waiting. Daisy noticed a parked car. She squinted into the darkness to see if there was anyone sitting inside.

Sister Evangelista took Daisy by the arm and hurried her along the garden path.

'These two gentlemen are friends of the bishop, Daisy. They are going to take you to meet him. He is waiting. They will take you across to Ireland on the ferry and then return you to the convent. You will be happy there, won't you, Daisy?'

Sister Evangelista handed the case to Austin. Now she grabbed Daisy by the hand and looked into her eyes. She had been perturbed that the two men had not wanted to tell her their names and had been less than friendly when they arrived,

Daisy shook her head and began to cry for the second time that day. She knew the two men. She didn't want to go anywhere with them. Not even to the ferry.

'No, Sister,' she whispered. 'I don't want to go, please don't make me, I just want to stay here.'

'Daisy, I have been instructed by the bishop and he is very definite in what he says. You may not know that your family pay for us to look after you. The convent in Ireland, where you were brought up, well, that's the best place for you now that Father James has gone. You deserve that for looking after the Priory for all this time. Time for someone else to take over all that hard work now, Daisy.'

Daisy's tears had turned to sobs. Sister Evangelista looked towards the men the bishop had sent to collect Daisy, and, with a shock, realized they had disappeared, as had the case. At that very moment, Miss Devlin, who had stopped late at the convent for supper and prayers, walked down the back steps towards them with the police officer, Howard, at her side.

Sister Evangelista thought they were too familiar altogether.

'Here ye are. I thought Daisy was up and taking a bit of fresh air, didn't I say she would be, now?' said Miss Devlin.

She grinned from ear to ear, flushed with the attention Howard had paid her. He had called back at the convent on the off chance, knowing she would be there this evening, and had offered her a lift home in the panda. And as luck would have it they had spotted Daisy in the garden. Before Miss Devlin knew it, Howard was out of the back door and down the steps. She had to run to keep up with him.

Sister Evangelista forced a smile.

The bishop would be furious.

She had hardly agreed with a word the bishop had said since the father had died. She was now coming to the conclusion that the best way to have dealt with this would have been to tell the police everything, hand them all the photographs and pictures. It was as obvious to her as the nose on her face that it was a parent who had killed the priest. Any parent who discovered what that evil disciple of the devil had done to their child would surely be seized with a rage so strong they would kill, without even knowing what they were doing.

Now she was an accomplice. She had helped to burn the photographs and destroy all the incriminating evidence.

'Tell the police Daisy has run away,' the bishop had said, when he issued the latest instructions. 'We need to sneak her out and return her back to the convent in Ireland, where she will be safe.'

Sister Evangelista's heart had sunk. Everything was moving too fast. She was sure there were things the bishop knew and she didn't. Who on earth were those two men, for example? One of them had looked very familiar, but she had no idea why.

Had she seen him in the Priory ever?

God, this was a mess. What did the bishop propose to do about Molly? He couldn't send a couple of men to carry her off to a convent and God alone knew what Daisy had told her.

Sister Evangelista turned to face Howard. From the corner of her eye, she saw that the car the two men had arrived in slipped slowly and silently down the hill away from the back gate of the convent garden.

They knew, she thought. They knew. They must have seen Miss Devlin switch on the cloakroom light and open the back door with Howard behind her, and they had vanished, taking the case with them, so that it didn't look as though they had planned to sneak Daisy away. She remembered where she had seen the familiar one and felt faint and sick. He had appeared in one of the photographs. But the bishop had sent him?

Her mind was screaming, her heart was racing and pounding against her ribs. As she opened her mouth, she felt sure her voice would wobble and crack, and yet out it came, each word dripping in falsehood, succeeding in concealing her inner turmoil and panic.

'Hello, Officer. Daisy has been a little upset. Her nerves are very bad, and we thought a bit of night air would do her good and calm her down.'

Howard looked at Daisy's face. It was blotched and streaked with tears.

'Hello, Daisy,' he said gently. 'Listen, I'm sorry, queen, if yer nerves are bad, like, but do you know, I think the sooner we get this interview over, the better things will be, don't you agree, Miss Devlin?'

Miss Devlin was keen to impress Howard.

'Oh, I do indeed,' she trilled.

Howard thought that if Miss Devlin or Sister Evangelista knew what Molly had told him and Simon, they would be very keen for Daisy to be interviewed too.

'Well, I am sure the morning will be fine, won't it, Daisy?' said Sister Evangelista. 'But if you don't mind, I shall put her back to bed now, especially if you are coming back in the morning. I know how keen you two are, I imagine ye will be here for breakfast.'

Sister Evangelista managed a laugh. It was hard, but she managed.

Not her usual laugh. You would normally have to look at her to know she was laughing or catch her shoulders shaking. Her entire life in a convent, from when she had arrived as an orphan, had trained her to practise a special, silent laugh, cultivated over years so as not to disturb the peace. Tonight it was more like a pebble rolling around in a tin can. But a laugh it was.

As she put Daisy back to bed, a novice joined them with a depressing but expected message.

'The bishop is on the phone, Reverend Mother, and he said he needs to speak to you without delay.'

Sister Evangelista knew that he would be very unhappy indeed to hear Daisy was to be interviewed by the police in the morning. She had done all she could, including convincing everyone that she was ill, to prevent the interview from taking place. It was out of her hands.

The girl was simple. Surely they could see that? As the sister pulled the cover over her, Daisy smiled in gratitude, a woman who still looked exactly like a child.

Sister Evangelista sighed as she left the room. It was all in God's hands now. She had resigned herself to the fact that she had lifted the entire situation up to the Lord and felt a huge sense of relief as a result.

As she moved towards her office to speak to the bishop, she knew she would not, could not, challenge him. She could not be sure that the man he had sent was in the photograph, but curiously she felt bolder. She would be keeping a very careful eye out from now on and would be more forceful with her own opinions.

As was her custom, Molly sat and watched the ten o'clock news whilst eating a slice of warm millionaires' shortbread.

She had made a fresh batch for the police officers tomorrow.

Molly knew they must interview Daisy and hear her words for themselves, but that would happen soon enough. They had told Molly that she would need to be a witness in court and that her evidence would be crucial to the case.

Molly liked that. Nothing she had ever done in her entire life before could ever have been described as *crucial*.

This was an occasion. Tomorrow, she would take out her curlers, put in her teeth and tell the police that Maura Doherty vanished in the middle of the night. No one in that family had ever spent a night away from Nelson Street and now, suddenly, two of them had disappeared.

This was news. Possibly, even *crucial* news.

It infused her with a feeling of self-importance that she was the only person her friend Daisy had told about witnessing the murder. Molly had told the police and no one else.

The police couldn't rush Daisy. Molly had told them that and they agreed. They had already met her, they knew they would have to coax the information from her gently. That was why they were waiting for her to leave the sick bay at the convent.

Molly smiled as she heaved herself out of the chair and bent down to switch off the television. Annie O'Prey will have seven kinds of a fit when she knows what I have been keeping from her, she thought to herself, carrying her cup and plate over to the kitchen sink.

Tiger let out one of his piercing howls from the yard and Molly heard the tin bin lid slip onto the yard floor and clatter across the cobbles.

'That bloody cat,' she said to herself, as she opened the back door. 'The bin will be full of river rats in the morning. Tiger,' she hissed. 'Tiger, come here, here, you naughty boy.'

It was pitch-black outside. The night had settled down and the street slept. There was not a shaft of dawdling light to ease her way to help her find the cat.

Molly heard another noise, this time from the outhouse.

'Tiger, is that you? Here, you daft cat,' she said.

There was no response. All was quiet.

'Ah sure, well, I need to go to the lavvy anyway,' she muttered as she shuffled across the yard and opened the outhouse door.

Molly kept a candle and a box of matches on the ledge and knew exactly where to put her hand. Plagued by a weak bladder, she could have the candle lit within seconds. As she struck the match, she shuffled round to negotiate her way down onto the lavvy seat.

That was when Molly saw him, waiting for her, behind the outhouse door.

The wooden mallet hit her so hard on the side of her temple that it carried her across the outhouse and into the wall. As her skull shattered, the last thing she saw was Tiger, with claws extended, leaping onto her attacker, but he was too late.

Molly was dead before she hit the floor.

Chapter Nineteen

THE STRAW BALES had been restacked, cloths folded and dishes put away. The bales almost reached the roof of the barn. Nellie and Kitty lay on the top, chins in hands, and gazed out over the harvested fields.

The barn retained the heat of the day and their nostrils were filled with the thick scent of straw and hay, mingled with freshly cut oats. The smell from the midden entered inwards as the breeze altered direction and, unwelcome, rested with them awhile.

Oat sheaves, which yesterday had stood five feet tall and swayed in the breeze, were now stacked into rounded mounds, dotted casually across the fields.

The girls could hear the river running in the distance.

The surface of the fields shimmered a platinum harvest gold in the last rays of the red sun as it slowly dipped behind the emerald mountain that rose from the foot of the furthest field.

'That must have been the best day of me life,' said Kitty wistfully, squinting into the middle distance to watch Jacko as he began to lumber slowly across the stones on the edge of the riverbank.

'Aye, mine too,' said Nellie.

Nellie sat up cross-legged and studied her white socks intently. Tiny, bright-red straw bugs were weaving their way in and out of the white threads. Distracted, she attempted to pick them out, one at a time, with her nails.

Giving up, she nudged Kitty.

'What about the glorious Aengus, then, eh? He took a right shine to you, so he did.'

'Oh sure, he did not.' Kitty blushed.

'Oh my God, he so did and ye to him. Ye should have seen your face.' Nellie began to imitate Kitty. 'Oh, I'm so terribly sorry, Aengus, I'll just have to ask my mammy. Now hang on a moment, er, yes, she said yes, a yes, that is. Not that I'm keen now, but, yes.'

Kitty extended her leg and with her foot ejected Nellie straight off the top layer of straw and she landed on the half-layer below. Both girls were laughing as Maura appeared at the front opening of the barn and called to them.

'Come on now, girls,' she shouted up. 'Time to come indoors. Kitty, ye need to have a bath.'

'Why in the name of God do I need a bath?' asked Kitty indignantly. 'I had one on Sunday.'

'Just do as I ask, please.' There was an element of tension in Maura's voice and Kitty picked up on it straight away.

'What's wrong, Mammy?'

Maura immediately reverted to a mask of gaiety. Kitty's last night had to be a nice one. That was all that mattered.

While Maura and Kitty stepped inside and Kitty took her bath, Nellie sat on the edge of the stone sink and watched the back of the truck loaded with oats disappear down the Ballymara road.

A dark cloud had gathered in the sky above the farmhouse and the air was becoming oppressive. Nellie could hear thunder in the distance but as yet there was not a drop of rain falling on Ballymara.

'Eat fast now, Jacko,' she shouted. 'It'll be all wet soon.'

A rumble grew louder in the distance and Nellie took herself inside. She wanted to speak to Nana Kathleen. Something was occurring. She could sense that Maura was tense and a feeling she didn't much like had slipped into her gut.

As Kitty lay in the bath, she guessed people were talking about her, because she heard her name mentioned more than once. Maura had told her to wash her hair, even though it had been washed only two days ago.

She looked down at the peaty-brown bathwater, which was the colour of weak tea. She still couldn't get used to it and marvelled at the colour each time she filled the sink.

'Is this water safe?' she had asked Maeve on her first night.

'Well, at least five generations have been drinking it here in this house and no one dies before their fourscore years and ten, so I reckon it must be so,' Maeve had said.

Kitty looked down at her belly. The mound was now breaking the surface of the warm brown water. She hadn't noticed that a few days ago. She slowly ran her hand over the firm swelling. She pressed gently to see if she could feel anything. It's a baby in there, she thought to herself, a baby girl or a baby boy. In there.

It felt alien and unreal.

She sat up, rubbed herself down with soap, rinsed it away and then quickly stepped out of the bath. She did not want to look at the visible manifestation of that awful night.

When Kitty arrived back in the kitchen, Maeve and Maura had set the tea out on the table and Nellie was sitting in the big chair by the fire.

'Now then,' said Maura, in a breezy tone. 'Come and sit down, we need to have a chat.'

'Oh no,' said Kitty, 'not another chat, Mammy.'

Her heart sank. Last time Maura wanted a chat it was to tell her she was pregnant. She never wanted to chat again.

'Is our holiday over now, is that it? Do we have to go home? Nellie, are you coming with us or are ye staying longer? Oh, Maeve, I will miss ye so much.'

Kitty had jumped to conclusions and also to her feet to hug Maeve, who, with her arms wrapped round Kitty, moved her back over to the fireplace and sat down with her on the wooden settle, winking above her head at Maura.

Nana Kathleen walked into the room, having just closed the front door.

She had met Liam outside and waved the truck down as he drove past to turn round at the McMahons' farm.

'Go back to the village and stay at Colleen and Brian's for ye tea. Don't come back now until as late as ye can. Give little Kitty a bit of space while we tell her what is happening, will ye now?'

Liam's face was covered in grain dust from the thresher and, as he frowned, specks of it fell from his eyelashes. He lifted his cap and wiped the back of his hand across his eyes.

'Jesus, the poor feckin' girl,' he said as he put the cap back on. 'I'll be off then.' And he rammed the gearstick back into first, put his foot down on the accelerator and drove the truck as fast as it would speed back down the Ballymara road. As Kathleen reached the door she looked back and saw Liam had one hand lifted in a wave to her as he passed.

Just the way his father, Joe, had always done before him.

Kathleen smiled and, at the same time, she felt the familiar pain of loss somewhere deep in her heart.

'Shift up now, missus,' she said to Nellie as she tapped her knees with her hand, indicating that Nellie should move over.

Nellie jumped out of her seat and then as Nana Kathleen sat, she plonked herself back down on Kathleen's knee, a more cushioned resting place than the chair itself.

Nellie was quiet. Studying Kitty and Maura, she had placed her thumb in her mouth and, leaning her head back on Nana Kathleen, began to suck it for the first time in years. She was exhausted. The heat of the day and the glow from the fire were forcing sleep upon her. She adored the smell of the burning peat in the huge fireplace. The brown bricks, hewn from the earth and pulled on a cart by Jacko, were a novelty after the coal and coke back home.

Nellie had spent each evening she had been at the farm-house on the same chair as her nana, lost in her thoughts as she watched the flames flicker. She blinked furiously and fought to keep her eyes open but she lasted only moments as, enveloped in the familiar smell of hearth and home, and on her nana's bosom, she fell into a deep sleep.

Maura was much more confident than when she had told Kitty she was pregnant and she wasted no time in getting straight to the point.

'We have found somewhere for you to have the baby, Kitty.'

Maura didn't wait for a reaction. She wanted this to be over and done with as fast as possible.

'Rosie, who is the sister-in-law of Nana Kathleen's sister, Julia, she will be the midwife.'

Kitty didn't speak but turned round on the settle to face Maura full on. She looked to Nellie for support but she was in what Tommy called 'the land of nod'. As she relaxed into sleep, her thumb had slipped out of her mouth and rested on her chin in the midst of dribble. At any other time Kitty would have laughed, but she knew this was not the moment.

'It is a home near Galway, run by the nuns, but there is a small problem. We will have to leave very soon as ye are beginning to show now. Only those of us who know have noticed, mind, but ye are. When ye have the baby, I will be straight back to get ye out, but we will leave the baby behind. It will be adopted by an American family and, please God, they will never know who its father was.'

Maura stopped talking and looked at her daughter who in the last few weeks had moved from childhood and transformed into a young woman. Her face had altered. She had definitely put weight on from being at the farm, apart from as a result of her condition, and it had filled out her features beautifully.

If I took her home today they would all see such a difference in her, Maura thought to herself.

She took a breath.

'And there is another thing, they think your name is Cissy.'

'Why do they think my name is Cissy?' squealed Kitty in a high-pitched voice.

'It's the best way to protect you and make sure the whole thing is kept secret, and then when it is all over, you can move on with your life. Our life. There will never be a record of anyone called Kitty ever having been there.'

Kitty knew that there was no point arguing about the name. It had obviously been discussed and decided long before she was told. She studied Nellie and looked distracted as she spoke.

'Can I come home to Liverpool first?' she asked.

Maura took a deep breath. 'Everyone in Ireland knows someone in Liverpool and the other way round too, Kitty, so if we really want to keep this secret, it would be best that you don't. We cannot risk one person guessing. Once someone knows, there is no way of unknowing it.'

She saw no need to explain that, under normal circumstances, this would be a good enough reason, but for them it was imperative that no one ever found out and connected the extraordinary coincidence of a child pregnancy in the same parish as a dead priest with his langer chopped off.

'Cissy is an obvious choice of name as it is so close to Kitty,' Maura whispered to her gently as she took Kitty's hand.

Kitty rewarded her with a faint if sad smile.

'We have to leave tomorrow. I have already packed your bag whilst ye was in the bath. We will leave after breakfast. Liam is taking us there in the truck and then Kathleen, Nellie and I are travelling on to Dublin and returning to Liverpool. As soon as ye have had the baby, I will be back with the money to collect ye.'

Maura still hadn't worked out how in God's name they were going to raise that amount of money, but she had put her faith in God and expected him to deliver. He owed her, big time.

'With the money?' said Kitty. 'Will ye have to buy me back?'

'No, not at all. It's just the money to cover ye board and lodgings and the adoption papers. I haven't seen the home but Kathleen tells me it's very grand. The thing is, Kitty, they have a laundry attached to the mother and baby home and ye may have to work to help out. They don't normally take in women until much later than ye but this is an exception and so, early on, ye will have to do a bit of work to help towards your keep. I am going to ask tomorrow if ye can be excused from that. I don't mind paying more for ye if that's so.'

Kathleen remained quiet. She hadn't told Maura that she had asked the Reverend Mother if Kitty could be excused from working in the laundry. The reply had been withering.

'Mrs Deane, this is a working abbey, not an hotel.' The conversation had ended there and then.

Like every child in Ballymara, then and now, Kathleen had been educated by the nuns and was still to this day too scared to answer back.

Once again, Kitty was in shock. She was out of control of everything. Where she lived. Who she lived with. And her name, she was no longer even allowed her name. She was hidden. Her name was hidden. She felt as though she were slipping over the edge of – what, she did not know.

Maeve picked up Kitty's hand.

'The thing to remember, Kitty, is that we aren't far away and this may seem like a long time to ye at the moment but ye will soon be out and life will return to normal.'

Kitty looked from Maeve to Maura. 'Mammy, can I not do my schoolwork while I'm there? Why do I have to work in a laundry? That sounds shocking.'

'It's not, my love. It's just something that has to be done to take us to the other side of this mountain. I will tell everyone in Liverpool that my sister is having another baby and that she needs help and ye are staying with her until after her delivery to help out. Everyone at home will believe that because they all know what a grand little helper ye are to me.'

Kitty was in a daze. She knew she had a million questions to ask and yet she had none. Sleep, having claimed Nellie and now looking for a fresh conquest, had passed over to Kitty, threatening to own her too.

She wearily stood up. 'Did ye pack my washbag?' she asked with an element of panic in her voice.

'Don't worry.' Maeve smiled at her. 'I've left all ye lovely things next to the bag for the morning.'

Kitty wanted her bed and to be alone. What had been a lovely day was over. The sky had darkened and the first drops of rain began to fall.

There was nothing left to say.

In a state of growing numbness, she kissed Maeve and Nana Kathleen and took herself to bed. Nana Kathleen rose from the chair, letting Nellie flop into the big cushion and take it for herself. She pulled a knitted shawl down from the back of the chair and placed it over Nellie as she followed Maura and Kitty to the bedroom. Nellie remained oblivious.

The two women fussed over Kitty, chatting about how quickly the time would pass and how much they would miss her. They wittered on about writing and the children writing and making sure Angela didn't claim the bedroom for their own. It all flew straight over Kitty's head. She was too numb to respond.

Eventually, they stopped their fussing and left.

Maura, with anxious looks and damp eyes, a shadow of her former self, kissed her daughter goodnight. Distress was slowly creeping into her voice, at having to leave her daughter in a strange place with unknown people.

Kathleen led Maura away and the door clicked gently shut.

Kitty lay and listened to their footsteps fade away down the corridor, Maura's light and gentle, her delicate weight barely making an impression upon the stone floor.

Unsure. Unhappy. Miserable, little steps, tripping along-side Kathleen's, which were slow. Solid. Heavy. Assured.

Once alone, Kitty let her tears flow. She was more resigned than afraid. She had known that something had to be done. She hadn't realized she would have to do it alone. Nor that for such a long time she wouldn't see her brothers and sisters or be allowed back home to Liverpool. It felt like never. What she would give now to hear the moaning, complaining Angela kicking off and giving out. She swore to herself she would never again feel resentment towards her siblings.

Kitty placed her hands on her belly and let them softly travel over the mound, which, to her astonishment, was still there when she lay flat on her back. She could feel a firm ridge, just below her belly button. She cradled her tiny belly in both of her hands. A baby. Her very own baby. Her flesh. Adopted.

It was now dark with rain falling heavily. A streak of lightning rent the sky apart and flooded her room with a bright light.

She remembered Aengus's face and his offer to walk with her at the Castlefeale fair.

She saw his blue eyes, his red hair and his cheeky smile, and just the memory of their meeting made her feel desperately alone.

She would never see him again and yet he had made her heart somersault and sing, all at the same time, just by the way he looked at her.

She rolled onto her side, pulled her knees up to her chest and hugged them.

The thunder roared and gave cover to her sobs, which were so loud and strong that her body heaved and shook as they went on and on, barely allowing her time to draw breath.

She wanted to scream at her inescapable loneliness, at the pain of there being no comfort to be found anywhere, to scream and never stop, but she knew she couldn't. It was hopeless. It didn't matter how much she screamed, it would change nothing. No matter how much she wished or prayed or asked people for help, nothing would alter. No one could help her.

Maura was returning home without her, tomorrow. Kitty would leave the warmth and welcome she had felt in the farmhouse.

She would be left at an abbey to live with nuns and strangers and to work in a laundry. She would have no family or friends around her and would have no one who loved or cared for her anywhere near throughout the pregnancy or the birth.

This was it.

Her new life.

This was the awful it.

Aengus had taken supper at the McMahon farm before he returned home.

He had arrived to help his Uncle John with the harvest as he had every year since he could remember.

John jumped into his van and offered Aengus a lift back to Bangornevin, stopping on the way at the Deane farm to drop a basket off for Maeve that his wife had made him take with him.

'Are ye bloody mad? It's pouring down, woman,' he had said to his wife.

'Do stop complaining now. Maeve gave all her eggs away today and she needs more for the morning. Do as I say. Go on, away with ye.'

And with that and brooking no nonsense, she had closed the door.

As John ran through the rain towards the Deanes' front door, Aengus left the van and walked down the path with the oilskin to cover John who was already almost soaked through.

When his aunt had asked John to take the eggs, Aengus's heart had skipped a beat. He was glad of the rain and an excuse to leave the van. He stood a few steps behind his uncle in the remains of the firelight radiating out through the front door.

To his disappointment, his uncle refused the invitation from Maeve to step inside as he handed over the basket. The thunder eased and, in the silence that followed, Aengus heard an unfamiliar noise. He looked towards the bedroom window just feet away from where he stood.

His ears pricked as he heard the sound of a wounded animal, which pulled on his heart as if dragging it down deep into his chest. He stared at the window, looking for a light or a flicker of the curtains, anything to show him where the noise had sprung from.

It stopped suddenly, but Aengus was glued to the spot. While Maeve and his uncle were chatting about the success of the day, he strained to hear the sound again.

But there was nothing.

Kitty's heart had already broken.

There was no sound left to be made.

The Abbey and the laundry lay at the bottom of a shallow valley and were approached via a long gravel driveway.

The drive would have been easy to miss if it hadn't been for the two red-brick pillars, standing proud like two lone effigies, supporting the high wooden dark-green fence that surrounded the Abbey. A thick belt of tall fruit trees grew directly behind as though providing an additional barrier to entry. Torpid branches reclined along the fence top, slipping down exhausted from carrying their weight of green apples.

'The kids from the village will have them apples before they are ripe,' said Liam as they drove through the black wrought-iron gates, which were opened wide.

Nellie was sat on Kathleen's knee, Kitty on Maura's, crammed into the front of the truck. They had left the last village ten minutes since and Nellie was now desperate for the toilet and had been for over half an hour.

'They would have to be brave kids,' answered Kathleen.

Liam nodded. The unspoken truth, suspended in the air of the small cab.

The truth everyone knew.

The nuns were the sisters of no mercy. If you stole from a convent, no matter how poor or how hungry your family, the Gardai would be summoned. Forgiveness was a valuable commodity, the currency of redemption. Not to be wasted on poor, hungry children.

Kitty hadn't spoken a word since they passed through Castlefeale.

She had clung to Maeve when they left her, early in the morning.

Maeve had slowly unhooked Kitty's hands that were clasped round her back. Holding both of them in her own, she looked into her eyes and said, 'Kitty, promise me this, that ye will come back very, very soon. Promise me now. I want ye to know that if you need somewhere or someone, I am here with no need of warning.'

Kitty found it hard to reply. Her throat was tight and the effort required to answer had all but deserted her. She had been morose over breakfast and lost in her own thoughts, her hand never far from Maura's.

She felt herself drag the words up from somewhere deep inside as she answered, 'I will, Maeve, I promise I will.'

Maeve had wanted to give her something to take with her and to hold onto: the knowledge that she was welcome, indeed, wanted, back.

Maeve put her hand into her apron pocket and brought out something gold and glistening. She slipped it over Kitty's wrist.

Kitty was speechless. It was a bracelet, hung with exquisite and beautiful charms.

With her mouth open in amazement, she lifted the charms one by one. A thatched cottage, a milk churn, a lady's boot, a fish, a tiny bird and a teapot.

Kitty felt guilty. She looked from Nellie to Maeve. Nellie was directly related to Maeve, so surely this was Nellie's.

'Sure, now don't you be worrying about that, little miss,' said Maeve, grinning. 'She has me whole jewellery box marked out as her own, that one does.'

Nellie and Maeve both laughed as Nellie came and joined them both in the hug. Nellie's sweet nature would not for one moment allow her to show a pang of regret that Maeve was giving the charm bracelet to Kitty. Nellie instantly felt guilty. She had so much compared to Kitty.

Maeve hugged them both together.

'Well, that's grand, then, and I will be waiting to see ye, so I will. I expect ye back here next year with our Nellie and Kathleen because I have no idea how I will manage another harvest without ye help. I would have given up and sent everyone home if it hadn't been for ye, Kitty.'

Kitty smiled. She almost laughed, for the first and last time that day.

As they drove off down the Ballymara road, Kitty and Nellie turned round to face the small window in the back of the cab and waved.

Maeve walked across to the other side of the road and stood by the stream so that she could remain for longer in their view.

The rain was falling in the Irish way, soft and misty, but Maeve didn't notice. She wanted to do more for Kitty and if all she had left to offer was to show her she cared by standing in the rain, then that was what she would do.

Kitty and Nellie sat forward together as the van tyres crunched across the gravel drive, creating a noise loud enough to announce their arrival. An imposing white building loomed into sight with a short flight of steps leading up to the front door.

Both girls placed their hands on the dashboard and leant closer to the windscreen for a better view.

A smaller building stood a short walk away from the convent with a long windowed corridor linking the two. Manicured lawns bordered the drive.

'The grass looks like it's been shaved,' said Nellie as they pulled up outside the first white building.

As they piled out of the van, the large wooden door opened and a nun stood with her hand on the big brass doorknob.

She didn't speak. She barely moved. She watched, without a flicker of expression. Maura felt uncomfortable.

'Jesus, would a smile hurt? A kind word never broke anyone's mouth, now did it,' she whispered to Kathleen as they lifted Kitty's bag out of the back.

A feeling of cold dread had already lodged itself in Maura's gut and it was going nowhere.

They felt conspicuous under the nun's gaze. Liam lost his usual light-hearted manner and felt as though he was walking awkwardly.

'Feck, does she have to stare like that?' he whispered under his breath as he pulled back the tarpaulin on the back of the van.

'Shush, Liam,' whispered Kathleen. 'She will turn ye into stone with that look. Come inside with us. I forgot to mention, you're Kitty's father. Maura knows, so she does. Just let me do the talking and don't forget, Kitty, yer name is Cissy.'

Liam looked as if he was about to faint. He had been taught by the nuns and still, as a grown man, he trembled in their presence. He hadn't wanted to step foot inside the convent and had hoped he could wait in the van.

They walked slowly towards the nun, who appraised each one individually as they approached. No smiles or words of welcome came their way.

Maura felt as though they were trespassing.

Had they come to the wrong place? Was someone about to turn them away?

Suddenly, from behind the door appeared an older nun, the Reverend Mother, Sister Assumpta, who glided beneath her habit like a butterball on wheels. Maura had never in her life seen nor met such a rotund woman. There was no wobble, no lurching gait.

'Good morning, Mrs Deane.' She looked directly at Kathleen.

Sister Assumpta's small, bright blue eyes were almost totally occluded by her plump red cheeks. Nellie was stunned by her likeness to the butcher back home in Liverpool.

'Come along inside.' Her voice was well suited to her size and sounded masculine, far from the kindly, maternal voice Maura had imagined.

She moved towards a white panelled door on the left and turned yet another large and shining brass knob. She swung the door open and with a wave of her hand ushered them inside.

'Who in God's name cleans all this brass?' whispered

Maura to Kitty as they walked hesitantly into the room.

The dark shining wooden floorboards were covered with beautiful rugs and the windowsills were lined with silver ornaments that shone brightly, even though it was a dull day.

'Who cleans all this silver?' whispered Kathleen to Nellie.

'Please, do sit,' said Sister Assumpta as she moved behind her desk and sat herself in an ornate chair of carved wood and leather.

They all did as instructed and sat in chairs assembled round the desk. There were not enough so Liam withdrew into the background and stood against the wall. He ignored the look Kathleen had thrown his way. Still, no one spoke.

Although there was no sun, bright daylight poured in through the tall window behind the desk, transforming Sister Assumpta into a faceless black shadow.

Sister Celia, the nun who had watched them arrive, walked into the room carrying a tray of tea, which she placed on Sister Assumpta's desk and then without speaking a single word, left the room.

'You must all have a thirst after a long journey,' Sister Assumpta said with a false brightness. 'Mrs Deane, would you like to pour?'

Kathleen jumped to her feet as Sister Assumpta smiled at her. It was a brittle and fixed smile, exuding no warmth.

'Thank ye, Reverend Mother,' said Kathleen.

As she stood, Nellie pulled on the back of her coat. Kathleen turned round and knew the look on Nellie's face.

'Mother, could Nellie here please use the bathroom? She has been desperate for some time now, haven't ye, Nellie?'

A look of displeasure crossed Sister Assumpta's face.

Oh God, please don't say no, thought Nellie, who was sure that if she had to wait much longer, she might wet herself.

Maeve had plied her with tea in the morning and now she regretted it.

Sister Assumpta rang a bell on her desk and then put it straight back down again.

'Sister Celia will have returned to the kitchen by now. Come with me,' she said brusquely to Nellie as she rose and opened the door. 'See, down at the end of the floor runner,' she pointed, 'there is a corridor to the right.'

Nellie nodded.

'Turn right there, it is a short corridor and the washrooms are at the end. Be quick now and do not talk to anyone, that is forbidden, do you understand?'

She had pulled the door almost shut behind them and stood with her hand on the brass knob. Nellie instinctively knew she was making sure the others couldn't hear. Her manner was now far from friendly and her look was cold.

'Walk on the floor, not the runner,' she hissed under her breath.

'Thank you, Reverend Mother,' said Nellie and she began to quickly walk down the corridor. As she looked back over her shoulder, she saw the last of the nun's habit sweeping across the wooden floor as she glided back into the room.

There was no one in the corridor and not a sound other than that made by Nellie's shoes on the floor as she walked alongside the Persian runner.

As she turned into the corridor on the right, the opulence of the main corridor instantly disappeared. The walls were painted an aquamarine blue and the only ornamentation was that of grottos to the Holy Mother, placed at regular intervals, and pictures of Our Lord, carrying his cross on the final stations.

Ahead was an opening leading on to a brown-tiled floor.

Nellie tentatively stepped inside and looked around. She saw washbasins to her left and cubicle doors to her right.

Nellie felt as though she were not alone and yet she could see no one else. All the cubicle doors were closed. She bent slightly to look underneath, but there were no feet on the other side of any of them. Nellie cautiously opened the first cubicle door and jumped in alarm as she let out a startled yelp. Behind the door, crouched on top of the toilet seat, was a young girl with her fingers to her mouth.

She whispered, 'Sh, please God, please don't make a noise. I need ye to help me, please.'

Nellie, already older than her years, let out a deep breath as she looked at the girl. She instantly noticed her unusual dark hair, which was roughly cut and very short, like that of a boy. Her brown eyes were huge as she stared at Nellie, all but begging her as they threatened to overspill with tears.

Nellie whispered, 'All right then, please don't cry,' as she stepped inside and, with great seriousness, slid the bolt across on the cubicle door behind her.

As she did so, she stared at the toilet door for just a second before turning round.

Nellie knew she was special. She had known for a long time. It wasn't just that she didn't know anyone else whose mother had died in childbirth, or even that from time to time she saw her ghostly mother. It was simply her life. She was different. Things happened to Nellie.

'Can ye help me, please?' the girl pleaded.

Nellie turned round to face her.

'What can I do? What's wrong?' said Nellie.

'I came here to have my babby five years ago. My daddy died while I was in here and my mammy can't pay to get me out. She knocks at the door every day and they don't even let her in. They just send her away. I see her from the window and for months I didn't even know she was trying, I thought she had forgotten about me. I have to get to Dublin. Can ye please help?'

'How did you know we were here?' said Nellie.

The girl was whispering hurriedly as she wiped away her tears with the back of her hand.

'I was cleaning the floor in the hall when the lady with the silver hair came to visit. I heard her say she was coming back today and so I thought I would clean the toilets and hide in a cubicle in case anyone came. If they find me, I will be punished so bad.'

Her panic mounted as she spoke the last few words and she began to cry again in a way that was so heartbroken it grabbed Nellie's heart.

'We are travelling to Dublin straight from here, but I don't know how we would get ye away.'

And then suddenly, the tarpaulin came into Nellie's mind.

'If ye can get to the front, can ye get under the tarpaulin on the truck?'

The girl began to laugh and cry at the same time.

'I can, oh God, thank ye. The last time I got away, I waved down a car on the road and it was the priest who stopped and brought me back. I was so desperate. I will go round the back and I will crawl out from behind the bin in front of the truck, if ye can help me.'

'I can and I will,' said Nellie. 'But before I do, what is your name?'

'It's Besmina.' Besmina grinned at Nellie.

'Before I go, Besmina, I have to use that toilet.'

*

Kathleen had poured the tea and handed a cup to Liam, Kitty and Maura. Kitty noticed how Sister Assumpta looked straight at her with an expression of astonishment when Kathleen handed Kitty the tea. Maybe Kitty wasn't supposed to have any tea. Maybe the tea was just for the adults. For an awkward moment the atmosphere froze, as Kathleen and Maura had exactly the same thought.

'So, Cissy.'

Kitty stared at her tea.

'Cissy,' the voice boomed.

Kitty's head shot up. 'Yes, Reverend Mother.'

'You will be sharing a room with eleven other girls and working in the laundry until the day of your confinement. You will rise at five in the summer and five-thirty in the winter. First mass is at six and then we take breakfast each day, during which one girl takes the readings. Can you read, Cissy?'

Maura and Kathleen tried not to look shocked.

'Yes, I do, Reverend Mother,' said Kitty quietly.

'She reads very well, in fact,' said Maura, feeling her hackles rise. 'As soon as she comes home, she will be continuing with her education.'

Sister Assumpta gave a small, almost imperceptible snort.

'I'm quite certain she will, Mrs Doherty. It's a shame her education ever had to be broken, some would say.'

Sister Assumpta was now wearing her small reading glasses and shuffling papers around on her desk.

'However, we are where we are. Many girls who end up here can neither read nor write.'

As she spoke, she peered over the top of her glasses at Maura. Her look was almost provocative. Tempting Maura to talk more. Testing her.

Kathleen jumped in quickly before Maura could. 'Will it be possible to speak on the telephone on occasion, Reverend Mother?'

There was no time wasted in the delivery of a response.

'No, it will not. We run an abbey and a workplace here, Mrs Deane. We reject, wherever possible, interference from the outside world. We seek peace and quiet in which to worship Our Lord and honour our total obedience. Telephones are a distraction from prayer.'

As she spoke, both Maura and Kathleen stared at the black Bakelite phone on her desk.

Sister Assumpta continued. 'The girls have three meals per day and two hours off after lunch each afternoon, for the nursery, recreation and devotion. Bedtime is at nine o'clock. Do you have any other questions?'

The words 'if you dare' hovered in the air.

Kathleen and Maura were silent.

Sister Assumpta looked over her glasses at them both. They could only just define her facial features against the bright light.

When neither replied, she lifted up a paperweight from the desk.

'I have the adoption papers here for you to sign, Mrs Deane. We usually keep the babies until they are three years of age. However, in this case, upon the request of such an eminent midwife, we have agreed to arrange for the baby to be adopted almost immediately. We have many American couples desperate to provide a child with a good Catholic upbringing along with letters of recommendation from our priest, Father Michael, from the church of the Blessed Sacrament in Chicago. He arranges everything at the American end. This way, Mrs Deane, ye can be sure that the paths of the child and yourself never cross.'

Sister Assumpta barely acknowledged or addressed Kitty. It was as though it were Maura having the baby.

'As soon as she begins her labour, we will inform the midwife, by telephone, and she will contact yourself in good time.'

She stopped in mid-flow and peered over her glasses at them yet again, as if expecting there to be an objection.

But both Maura and Kathleen were too dumbstruck by the nun's cool and authoritative manner to utter a word.

'The midwife has told me that you wish to remove the mother from here almost immediately. Is this correct?'

Again, the look.

'Yes, that is quite right.' Maura now spoke in a voice that was little more than a squeak.

'In that case, we will require another thirty punts, making a total of one hundred and eighty punts. Is that acceptable?'

Maura felt as though the floor was opening up under her. Why had Kathleen brought her here? How in God's name would she ever find that kind of money? It was impossible. She would end up in a debtors' prison if she carried on with this. They would have to find some other way. God knew what, but they would.

Suddenly Liam's voice boomed out from what appeared to be nowhere.

'Here is a hundred punts, Mother, and we shall bring the rest when we collect, er ... Cissy here.'

Maura and Kitty stared at Liam as though he had gone mad, but Kathleen looked down at her teacup. Maura realized that Kathleen had known about this all along.

Liam walked over and, peeling off fifty pounds from a

large wad of notes, placed the money down on Sister Assumpta's desk, then took his cap back out of his pocket and wringing it in his hands returned to the shadows once again.

Kathleen broke the silence.

'May we take Cissy to her room now, please, Sister, and help her unpack?'

She wanted to leave the study as soon as possible. This interview was far more difficult than the one she had previously undertaken. It was as though the shame of Kitty's pregnancy were heavy in the room and hung around them like a smell.

Sister Assumpta rose from her desk and glided to a dark-oak chest of drawers, from which she removed a heavy metal money-box. She selected a key from a cord around her waist and opened it, placed Liam's notes inside and slid it back into the drawer.

'No, I am afraid not,' she replied, closing the drawer and turning the key.

There was not even a note of regret nor a hint of an apology in her voice.

Sister Celia had baked a delicious fruit bread that morning and Sister Assumpta was keen to try a buttered slice whilst it was still warm from the oven. It was almost two hours since she had eaten.

She glided towards a thick golden cord hanging by the side of the fireplace and pulled it twice. In the distance they could all hear the gentle tinkling of a bell.

'I think it is time now for the girl to settle in and begin her first day. She cannot do that whilst you are still here. God has no patience with idle hands. It is time for you to leave her.'

She smiled yet again, a false and brittle smile. Her rapidly blinking eyes delivered her words as though they were flying steel tacks, pinning Maura to the chair.

Time to leave her.

Kathleen sprang up as though touched by lightning.

The moment was here. It could not be delayed. They could not invent excuses to hold onto Kitty.

'Get up, Maura,' hissed Kathleen.

Maura wanted to scream at the nun: her name is Kitty, not Cissy or 'the girl'. She is a person, she has a name, she is my daughter. Maura stood and reached out to take hold of Kitty's hand. Kitty was cold and rigid with a look of terror on her face.

'Mammy, please don't go.' She stared into Maura's eyes imploringly. 'Mammy, please, please don't go and leave me, please.'

But suddenly, from nowhere, two nuns silently entered the room and, before Maura could intercept, each took hold of one of Kitty's arms and almost lifted her, crying, from the room. Kathleen grabbed hold of Maura's arm and pulled her back, as she moved to run after Kitty. She had known it would be bad. Her sister, Julia, had warned her. She just hadn't thought it would be this bad. Kitty's screams of, 'No, Mammy, Nana Kathleen, please,' echoed down the hall. The pain in Kathleen's heart was bad. God knows what it must be like for Maura, she thought to herself.

Kitty's screams for help became fainter as she receded into the distance. Maura sobbed into Kathleen's chest and Kathleen held her tightly, in case she should make a break for it and run after Kitty. Liam, not knowing what to do, placed his hand on Maura's back. A gentle reminder that there was someone else who would prevent her from reaching Kitty.

Sister Assumpta stood with her hand on the door, waiting for them to leave, her body language all but ejecting them from the room, when Liam suddenly spoke. 'Where's our Nellie?'

He eventually found her standing at the side of the truck.

'Where did ye get to? All hell's broken loose in there altogether. Did ye not want to say goodbye to Kitty?' Liam said.

He was talking for the sake of it, upset and agitated by Kitty's distress. Yesterday, he had watched as she and Aengus had flirted and laughed together. From the top field, he had seen Aengus raise his cap and smile as the girls ran. Was that only yesterday?

Kathleen walked down the steps with Maura, virtually holding her up.

'Jeez, she's torn with the grief, so she is,' said Liam to Nellie.

Sister Assumpta had closed the convent door before they were even on the second step.

No wave. No smile. No goodbye.

'That nun is one fuckin' scold of a woman,' Liam whispered to Kathleen. 'God help Kitty in that place, because she won't.'

As they drove through the convent gates, Nellie turned to gaze out of the back window. The cab was silent apart from Maura, who was quietly sobbing.

Nellie checked the tarpaulin and saw the girl shift slightly underneath. She hoped she would be safe in there until they reached Dublin. Nellie realized this was the worst of days. She had lost Kitty and in her place, lying under the tarpaulin, she was smuggling her new friend, Besmina, out of the convent.

'Have ye ants in the pants?' said Kathleen to Nellie, exasperated. 'Ye haven't sat still since we left. What in God's name is up with ye?'

'Nothing, Nana, are we nearly there yet?'

'Aye, ten minutes more,' said Liam.

No one had spoken very much at all since leaving the

convent, each imagining a different version of what life there would be like for Kitty.

In Maura's thoughts, Kitty was sitting in a dorm with girls similar to herself. They were laughing and joking, and kind novices were laughing with them. She had eaten a good supper and was laying out her belongings on a press, as she liked to do. She imagined Kitty placing her freshly ironed nightdresses in a drawer. Maura knew Kitty would feel lonely but at least she would have other girls her own age around her and, surely, they would have a bit of fun and get to visit the village in the afternoons when the laundry was done.

She tried counting the days until she saw Kitty again.

'I will make a chart on the wall at home, to mark off the days till she comes home.' Maura hadn't really meant to say this out loud but once she had done so it made her feel much better.

'That's a fantastic idea, Auntie Maura,' said Nellie. 'I will too, an' I will draw a picture every day of things that happen. Can we write to her?'

'God, I hope so,' said Maura. 'It's not a prison. Liam, I need to talk to ye about what ye did.'

Maura thought it would be better to tackle Liam than Kathleen about the money. She had made the decision not to approach her own family whilst in Ireland. There was too much to explain. They had even less than she and Tommy. Too much to keep secret.

'Maura, we don't need to talk. There are times people need to look after each other. Don't worry about us and, anyway, it's been a good harvest, we are fine.'

'That's kind, Liam, but we will find a way, one day. We will pay ye back.'

'Ye already have, Maura, ye paid us in advance. Ye picked

Jerry up off the floor, when Bernadette died, and Mammy says she doesn't know how Jerry would have survived without ye and Tommy. Ye have already paid, Maura. It's time for us to pay ye back.'

Silence fell once again in the cab. Nellie knew this wasn't a conversation she should be involved in. She knew her place.

The light was beginning to fade as Liam decided to pull up outside a café. 'There's two hours until the ferry. Time to fill up on some grub before ye leave, girls.' He jumped out and, as he went to lock the door, noticed one of the ropes on the tarpaulin was loose.

'Bloody hell, this could have blown off if there had been a wind. Mammy, I need a pee. Will ye tighten this rope?' said Liam.

'I'll do it, please, I can,' said Nellie.

Kathleen laughed. 'Go on then, madam. I'll go and get ye some food. Will egg and chips be all right now?'

'Aye, that'll be grand, thanks,' said Nellie, as she pretended to tighten the rope.

Nellie heard the café door close, quickly undid the knot and lifted the corner of the tarpaulin.

'Quickly, get out now,' she whispered.

The tarpaulin shuffled and shifted; Nellie saw a crop of dark hair as Besmina appeared. Grabbing Besmina's arms, Nellie helped to drag her out from underneath the tarpaulin. As soon as Besmina's feet hit the pavement, Nellie was already tightening the ropes.

'Oh God, I cannot believe I am free,' said Besmina, looking around her. She began to laugh and cry at the same time. 'What street am I on? Which street is this? Where is the river?' She was talking fast as she spun round, trying to take her bearings. 'My nanny lives on Faulkner Street, I have to get to her first. My mammy's moved and I don't know where she has gone to.'

'How do you know your mammy has moved?' asked Nellie.

'I got the laundry van driver to post a letter for me, with his address on for the reply. He told me the letter came back saying, "No longer at this address," so I need to get to Nanny to find out where Mammy is.' Besmina was still looking around her, trying to see the street sign.

'How do you know your nanny is still in Faulkner Street? She might have moved too.'

'No, she will not have moved, I was born in her bed and she was born in that house, as was my mammy. She will still be there.'

'Why couldn't ye get away?' asked Nellie. 'Please tell me, it's just that we have left Kitty there. Will she be OK?'

'Will she be OK? Are ye fucking mad? It's worse than a prison. It is worse than hell. Will she be OK?' Besmina began to laugh incredulously.

The café door opened and Kathleen put her head out. 'Come on, Nellie, your meal is ready. What are ye doing?' Kathleen looked at Besmina curiously.

'Nana, do ye know where Faulkner Street is near the river?' asked Nellie. 'This lady is lost.'

'Ye couldn't be closer, love.' Kathleen laughed. 'Go to the end of this street and it's there, right in front of ye on the other side.'

'Thanking ye, missus,' Besmina shouted back. She looked at Nellie. 'Ye saved my life, Nellie. I might have grown old and died in that hell if ye hadn't been brave. Some get transferred to the asylum when they go mad with the frustration of being locked up. If ye have left your Kitty in there, for God's sake make sure ye go back and get her out, will ye. Don't leave her there, thinking them nuns is nice and kind. They become the devil himself in that place.'

And with that, Besmina turned round and ran up the road in the direction Kathleen had indicated.

Nellie stared after her as she watched her disappear into the dusk, feeling sick and heavy-hearted. How could she walk into the café and tell them what she knew? She had helped to smuggle a girl out. She might have got Nana and Maura into trouble. Nellie didn't feel afraid. She knew she had done the right thing. But she also knew it was a secret she would have to carry alone.

Chapter Twenty

ALICE WAS BATHING Joseph in the kitchen sink, whilst Jerry sat in his armchair, reading the paper, when Tommy walked into the kitchen.

As the back door opened, Joseph's expression altered to one of wonderment. He put both of his hands onto the front of the sink and leant forward to see who had arrived, expecting Kathleen.

'Evening, Alice, Jer,' Tommy shouted as Joseph yelled and kicked his legs frantically in order to attract Tommy's attention.

'What ya doin', little fella, eh?' laughed Tommy as he stepped over to the sink and playfully splashed small waves of water over Joseph. 'Would ye look at him now, growing bigger every day. I don't know what ye feed him, Alice, but sure, he'll be the size of Sean McGuire and joining him in the ring before he starts school at this rate.'

Jerry laughed.

Alice, not so much.

'Here, Tommy, do something useful for once, would you, and hold this towel, please.' Alice sounded mildly perturbed.

She scooped Joseph out from the sink, clear of the water, his wet, elongated and slippery body making him look more like a skinned rabbit than the bonny baby he was. Then she placed him onto the waiting towel.

Well practised, Tommy quickly wrapped the towel around Joseph and, after placing a kiss on the top of his head, handed the warm fluffy bundle back to Alice.

'Have ye news, Tommy?' said Jerry.

'Aye, I have. Albert called in on his way home from the pub. Bill sent him over with a message from Maura. She and Kathleen will be back with Nellie tomorrow.'

Jerry was pleased; he missed his Nellie.

'What about Kitty?' asked Jerry.

Tommy frowned. 'Not a word. I wondered if ye had any news from Kathleen or Nellie?'

'No, we have none. I'm relieved they are coming home. It's often very hard to get Mammy back over here, when she's been visiting home, and Nellie is just as bad. I think they would both live there, given half the chance.'

His friend Tommy was worried. Maura had been very secretive about Kathleen's letter and had herself slipped away to Ireland under the cover of darkness. Tommy could well imagine the inevitable questions, should she walk down the streets in daylight, carrying a bag.

'Where are ye off to then, Maura, with no curlers in and yer lipstick on?' someone would be bound to ask.

'What's up with her?' one neighbour would say to another.

'She's been right odd, so she has, since all this business with the priest,' would be passed down the line in the butcher's shop.

'Aye, she has that. She hasn't washed her nets since it happened and I haven't seen sight nor sound of their Kitty,' Mrs O'Prey would mention to someone in the grocer's.

'That Tommy's been acting like a mental bastard,

threatening to bash McGinty's face in and giving pies to their Brian. The man has never in his life even taken a belt to his own kids, so he hasn't,' the men would say down in the Anchor.

'Angela Doherty has never stopped giving out about how she has to work now that their Kitty has done a moonlight flit,' the kids would say in the classroom.

And on it would go. Gossip, which would lead someone somewhere to jump to a conclusion.

'Would ye like a cuppa tea, Tommy?' asked Jerry as he rose from the chair. Tommy looked exhausted.

'Aye, thanks, Jer, I will. If I leave them little buggers long enough, they'll kill each other before I get back and that'll make things a bit easier in the morning.' They both laughed.

But not quite as much as they once might have done. Jokes about killing people sounded strangely hollow.

'I'm taking Joseph up,' said Alice, walking over to the fire with Joseph on her hip and his bottle in her hand. Joseph leant his head on Alice's shoulder and sucked his thumb noisily, half smiling at Jerry and Tommy.

'Say goodnight to Da and Uncle Tommy,' said Alice.

Joseph leant forward and bent down for another kiss from Tommy. Then he stretched out his arms to Jerry, who cuddled him and kissed his cheek.

'Night, night, little man. See ye in the morning for breakfast,' said Jerry, bathing his son in the most loving of smiles.

'I can't imagine what it must be like with only the little fella,' said Tommy. 'Me and Maura, we love our kids, make no mistake, but this week, Jerry, God, I'll tell ye this, I never knew my missus worked so hard, so I didn't, an' I never realized how much our Kitty did either. If Maura wasn't coming home tomorrow, I don't know how much longer I could cope. I've burnt the bloody letter from the nuns, complaining about Declan going to school with his ears blocked up with pobs. Jeez, Maura would have a fit if she saw that.'

He looked up at Jerry and, after a moment's hesitation, they both began to laugh as they imagined the sight of Declan with a bowl of pobs on his head.

The men sat and drank their tea, their anxiety gradually draining away. Once Tommy's mug was empty, he walked to the door to pick up his coat and said, 'Well, Jerry, I feel a million times better than I did when I arrived, so I do, and now I'm off to knock all their bleedin' heads together and get them into bed.'

The back door was closing and Tommy departing just as Alice returned to the kitchen.

Jerry was still grinning at the thought of Declan's ears being blocked with pobs as he grabbed Alice round the waist and pulled her to him.

'I think it's about time we went to bed and got an early night, don't ye think? We haven't had a chance yet to enjoy it, just being us in the house.'

'You go up and I will follow when I've cleared Joseph's bath things away.'

'I don't think so, Mrs Deane. Do ye realize, this is the last time we will have the house to ourselves before Kathleen and Nellie come back tomorrow? I think we should get in that bed now and make the most of it, don't you?'

As Alice walked up the stairs ahead of him, she realized this must be the last time. She would have slept with two men in two days, which was a recipe for disaster. As Jerry undid the buttons on the back of her dress and slipped his hands inside and cupped her breasts, she closed her eyes as a thrill of wickedness shot through her. She imagined it was Sean not Jerry who was caressing her. She focused her mind on Jerry's hands, which became Sean's, and the pleasure she felt as they roamed.

She either had to stop seeing Sean, or leave Jerry, she knew that, but for now, she would enjoy tonight knowing that when the morning came, she would have no idea which one she would choose.

The following morning, Harry popped his head round the kitchen door. 'I've left the babby in the pram by the out-house, Auntie Alice.'

'Thank you, Harry,' Alice replied quickly, so that he could hear her before he closed the door.

From the sink, Alice watched Harry, serious little Harry, with his purposeful walk and his head slightly bent. As he reached the pram, he straightened his cap and then lifted his green canvas army bag from the pram apron. He gave the pram handlebars a quick wiggle and slipped though the gate. As he closed the gate behind him, he saw Alice at the sink and gave her a smile before the latch clicked.

The Silver Cross pram bounced up and down in a gentle rhythm famous for sending babies to sleep within seconds.

The baby must be restless, thought Alice. She looked at Joseph, who had drifted back to sleep a half-hour since, and slipped into the yard. She pulled back the fly net and there was the baby with eyes wide open, blowing bubbles.

'You little tinker,' said Alice, smiling. 'Your mammy will be back later. Back to sleep now, or I'll be having a word with your daddy when he gets home from work. I have things to do today, miss.'

At that moment, Mrs Keating walked in through the gate, followed by a young woman Alice had never seen before.

'Morning, Alice,' said Mrs Keating, 'this is my niece from Cork, Finoula. She is staying with me while she writes after jobs. She's trying for work looking after babies, so she is, and I thought that, as Maura is away, she could get some practice in with the babby and could be a grand help to ye, an' all?'

Alice noticed that Finoula's hair was an unusual colour for an Irish girl. It was strawberry blonde, instead of flaming red or black. There were usually no in betweens; the Irish were one or the other.

'Well, that would be fine by me and I'm sure Maura wouldn't mind,' said Alice. 'But we are expecting Maura back tonight and I'm sure she will want the baby all to herself. You know what Maura is like. Would you like a cup of tea?'

For the first time in her life, Alice reached for the mop and banged on the kitchen wall for Peggy to come and join them. A visitor to the street was news.

Alice was becoming more Irish by the day.

Within half an hour, the kitchen was full. It was hard for Alice to concentrate on what the women were saying and she was glad that the conversation focused on Finoula, who was answering a barrage of questions about the news in Ireland.

Peggy had knocked on for Sheila and Deirdre. Alice began to understand that it was a very different gathering without Kathleen and Maura.

Her thoughts were wandering above the babble, not to last night with Jerry, but to the hotel, with Sean. As she remembered every second, a thrill of intense excitement shot through the pit of her stomach.

Where was Sean now? she wondered. Was he at work?

Brigid arrived at the back door with Mrs McGuire. Alice's heart sank. She had been avoiding them, not wanting to face either wife or mother.

The women round the table chorused, 'Brigid, Mrs McGuire, come on in, sit down for a cuppa.'

Alice felt resentful. She couldn't help it. She was uncomfortable with people treating her kitchen as though it were their own.

Peggy jumped up. 'I'll go and fetch a couple of chairs from mine,' she said. Then, 'Holy Mary,' she shouted from the yard, 'there are so many prams out here, I can hardly get back to me own house.'

'Shall I put the kettle back on, Alice?' asked Sheila, who didn't feel entirely comfortable doing so without asking first. She wouldn't have thought twice had Kathleen been there.

'Yes, of course,' said Alice, dragging her thoughts away from Sean. She could not erase him from her mind and she could not for the life of her stop thinking about their love-making. Was it really so different from what had happened with Jerry last night, she asked herself? No, it wasn't. And then, with the force of a train, it hit her.

She enjoyed sex with both men, but only one man dominated her thoughts to the point of distraction.

She was in love. She must be.

The laughter and the babble of the women faded. She had never felt like this before. She had thought of Jerry constantly, from the day she met him, but not like this. That was an obsession. This was love. There was an enormous difference. This made her feel happy and joyous, while her obsession with Jerry had made her reclusive and anxious, devious and mean. She had been cruel to Nellie and resentful, and she had made Jerry's life a misery.

God, I was a sick person, Alice thought to herself and, for a second, the sadness of the life she had led, and the person she had been, clouded her thoughts of Sean.

What am I going to do? she asked herself. What a bloody mess. What is the right thing to do?

'A penny for your thoughts,' said Finoula, sitting next to her.

'Oh, gosh. You don't want to know what my thoughts are,' laughed Alice. 'Even I can't work them out.'

She heard the dock klaxon sound as she finished washing the kitchen floor.

Jerry was working an extra half-shift, because the bar was full. Ships were waiting for a pilot to bring them into a berth. The pressure was on to unload as quickly as possible.

Finoula had taken both the baby and Joseph back to Mrs Keating's in the same pram. She had offered to feed them and take them for a walk. Alice was grateful for the break.

She loved her freedom and she wanted, more than anything, to be alone with her thoughts. To have space to dwell and think, without any interruption, about Sean and the time they had spent together.

At what point had she fallen in love with him? She had no idea, but she did know that, right now, her heart ached to see him.

As though she had willed him into her presence, the back door opened and Sean walked in. He looked round the kitchen. 'Are ye alone?' he asked.

'I am, yes.'

Within seconds they were in each other's arms. Within minutes, Sean had lifted her skirt up to her waist, and his hands, wild to feel every inch of her, were all over her body, down the tops of her stockings, across her back and over her breasts, seemingly at the same time. As he entered her, he had only one reckless thought: that he desperately, beyond any notion of reason, wanted either Brigid or Jerry to walk in at that very moment and catch them both – just as he claimed Alice as his very own.

There was no school for little Paddy. It wasn't his turn for the shoes. He was watching *The Flowerpot Men* on the black-and-white television when Peggy shouted to him, 'Paddy, go and get my kitchen chairs, there are two of them in Alice's backyard next to the gate. Go on now, do as I say.'

Little Paddy groaned.

Scamp sat up and looked at Little Paddy keenly, wagging his tail.

He placed his paw on Paddy's back and whined.

'OK, OK, I'm coming,' said Little Paddy, jumping up. 'Mam, I have no shoes to put on, so how can I?' he grumbled.

'Here, put my slippers on,' said Peggy, slapping margarine on the bread and then scraping it off again, for the meat paste sandwiches they would have for their lunch. Little Paddy wasn't the only one not at school; there were four of them watching TV, but he was the only one that Peggy and Big Paddy ever sent to run a message.

Peggy kicked off her slippers, the only footwear she possessed, and slid them across the floor to Little Paddy.

'Here ye are,' she said. 'Butties ready when ye come in with the chairs.'

The damp slippers were dirty and even Little Paddy could tell that they stank. He screwed up his face as he slipped them onto his feet.

Scamp ran ahead of him to Alice's back door. Scamp loved

Kathleen, who, like Brigid, always saved him stock bones and strips of bacon rind.

Little Paddy found the chairs next to the outhouse and began to carry them both to the gate.

'Come on, Scamp,' he said.

Scamp stood with his back to Little Paddy, looking up at the closed back door, wagging his tail furiously.

'Come on, Scamp,' shouted Little Paddy again, this time impatiently. It had been raining and the damp was soaking through the holes in Peggy's slippers, making his feet cold and wet.

He put down one of the chairs as he lifted the gate latch. Pulling the gate wide open, he leant against it as he attempted to pick up the chair and struggle through.

'Scamp,' he shouted again, angrily. The chairs were difficult to carry and he didn't want to have to put them down again.

Little Paddy looked up towards the kitchen window, to see if anyone had noticed him taking the chairs.

What he saw made him so scared, his knees felt weak.

Little Paddy went white and hissed under his breath as loudly as he could, 'Scamp, get here now, ye fecking eejit dog.'

Just at that moment, Scamp, growing impatient, scratched at the back door and barked loudly.

Paddy looked back to the window, but no one indoors had heard. Paddy saw that Alice's breasts were bare and that she was pulling her dress back over her shoulders. And Sean McGuire was helping her.

'Oh, fecking hell, I'm dead,' groaned Little Paddy, putting his hand over his eyes.

Chapter Twenty-one

IT WAS ALMOST midnight when Maura and Kathleen turned the corner of Nelson Street. They froze with astonishment at the sight that greeted them.

There was not a family in bed on any of the four streets.

Every parlour light was switched on. Front doors stood partially open, as light bled out onto the pavement. Children and women stood in the shadows, in huddles, whispering, and the men, having hurriedly left the lock-in at the pub, stood silently at the opposite end of the street, pint glasses still in hand.

As Maura and Kathleen stepped into the circle of street light, everyone turned to look at them. For a moment, frantic, panicky thoughts whirled through Maura's brain. She imagined her neighbours knew the truth about Kitty and were waiting for her, to scold and shout at her, to wag their fingers and to chase her off the street.

'Where have you taken your whore daughter then, eh? What have you done with her? Ye all so high and mighty and ye can't even teach yer own daughter to keep her knickers up.'

Kathleen took Nellie's hand and gently drew her close. Kathleen sensed danger and death running hand in hand, wild on the wind.

Maura's panic gave way to alarm when she spotted a large Black Maria police van outside Molly Barrett's house. Three more blue and white panda cars were parked in front of the Black Maria. A man with a camera in his hand stood on the opposite pavement.

'Hiya, love,' he shouted. 'Do you live on this street?'

'Yes, we do,' replied Kathleen. 'What's going on?'

'There's been a second murder,' said the man casually. 'An old woman, apparently, who lives in that house.' He pointed towards Molly's. 'She was found only a couple of hours ago. Do you know what her name was?'

Stunned into silence, neither Kathleen nor Maura could speak.

The man with the camera carried on. 'Seems like we've got a madman living around the dock streets. That's two murders. I'm from the *Echo*, queen. Anything you can tell me about the old woman?' He took his pencil from behind his ear and his notepad out of his pocket, conveying an air of expectancy.

At that moment, Harry and Little Paddy, with Scamp at his heels, came running up the street, wearing their pyjamas.

Maura said, 'My God, it's nearly midnight and Harry is not in his bed, *and look at Little Paddy's nose.*'

Kathleen slipped Maura a sideways glance. There had been a second murder on their own street and yet Maura was more worried about the fact that Harry was still awake and Little Paddy had been neglected.

Kathleen realized Maura's reaction was odd and inappropriate. She needed to move her indoors.

'How could any of the kids sleep?' she said, in a matter-of-fact voice. 'With a spotlight rigged up outside Molly's front door, how could anyone sleep?'

'Mam, Mam,' yelled Harry, throwing his arms round Maura. 'Molly is dead, her head has been smashed in. Annie O'Prey found her. Molly had been missing all day until Annie found her in the outhouse.'

The man from the *Echo* wrote down every word.

'Me ma says we aren't safe in our beds tonight, Auntie Maura,' said Little Paddy.

The end of his nose was cased in many days' worth of hard dried snot. Maura made a mental note to take him into her kitchen and soften it overnight with Vaseline, then she would help him clean it off in the morning.

Molly was dead. The street was in chaos and yet Maura fixed her attention on the things that kept her sane and grounded. The trivia of domestic life.

In the seconds that followed, an ambulance almost knocked them over.

'Molly might be alive,' said Maura, nudging Kathleen.

The man from the *Echo* dispelled that notion in a flash of the light bulb on his camera. 'Nah, that's the body trolley,' he said, matter-of-factly.

More adults moved out into the pool of light and joined the children, carrying cups of tea, smoking cigarettes and wearing their nightclothes. The boldest came first, with others following nervously, taking their cue.

An hour earlier, the entire street had been alerted by Annie's screams when she had found Molly. Anyone who hadn't heard Annie would have been woken by the sirens, not fifteen minutes later, as they fired down the street, announcing the arrival of the police. But by that time everyone already knew, on the four streets and far beyond.

A row of heads in curlers and hairnets began to line both sides of Nelson Street in a guard of honour. The lit upstairs windows filled with the faces of smaller children, not allowed out into the misty night air.

Silence fell upon the crowd as neighbours ceased talking in order to show their respect to Molly.

As the ambulance departed, a new feeling of fear descended upon the inhabitants.

Molly had been bludgeoned to death. Old fat Molly who made cakes and gossiped.

As the ambulance trundled down the Dock Road towards town and the siren faded into the distance, taking Molly further from the place where she had spent every day of her life, the women began to cry. The first and the loudest was Peggy. Then others followed suit until the air became choked with the wailing of frightened women.

Tommy and Jerry were walking up the street towards Kathleen, Maura and Nellie.

'Two murders, Tommy,' said Sheila to Tommy, as he passed. 'Are any of us safe in our beds, eh?'

Tommy couldn't answer. He touched his cap and walked steadily towards Maura, whose dark eyes radiated fear.

The only sound he could hear was that of Molly's cat, Tiger, howling on the back-entry wall.

Chapter Twenty-two

THE TACITURN NUNS led a sobbing Kitty upstairs to a room in the eaves. The floorboards were bare and each wall was lined with a row of wooden-framed beds. Upon each lay an uncomfortable looking ticking-covered horsehair mattresses.

On one of the beds lay a dark blue pair of long shorts, a dark blue top and a white apron.

'Put the clothes on, please, Cissy,' said a novice.

'I don't want to,' sobbed Kitty. 'I want to see my mammy.'

'You don't have that choice, I'm afraid.'

Kitty noticed that Sister Celia carried her leather bag. Kitty didn't want anyone else touching her precious belongings and so she leant down to take the bag from her.

'Ah, not so fast, thank you,' said Sister Celia. 'We take this. You can have it back on the day your family collect you. You are very lucky, young lady. If it weren't for the midwife, you might never see them again.'

Kitty was speechless. No one had ever spoken to or looked at her with such unkindness.

Sister Celia continued, 'There are rules here. You will speak to no one, ever. Do you understand?' Kitty could not believe what she was hearing. 'No one. Not a soul. We don't want the poor girls who won't be leaving to be upset by your good fortune in having the midwife as your relative. No one here is allowed to speak. Do you understand that? We have penitents here who will have no one to collect them. They atone for their sin fully and so we don't want them upset, now, do we? *Do we?*'

Sister Celia shouted and Kitty visibly jumped. 'Now, get those clothes on and we will take you over to the laundry.'

The nuns stood and watched her. Kitty stared back, waiting for them to move away and allow her some privacy. They didn't budge.

'Hurry up. Have you something different from the rest of us, Cissy?' Sister Celia sneered. 'Pity you weren't so shy when you were dropping your knickers for your five minutes of fun, eh? Not so shy then, were you? Get dressed.'

Kitty moved over to the bed. With her face burning and tears streaming, she removed her own clothes and put on the blue calico outfit that had been laid out for her.

The nun snatched Kitty's clothes from her aggressively as Kitty held them out in her shaking arms. To Kitty's utter horror, Sister Celia turned Kitty's still-warm knickers inside out and, holding them almost at the end of her nose, inspected them through her thick wire spectacles, squinting as she did so. She sniffed the gusset and, looking up at Kitty with a smirk on her face, she hissed, 'You dirty sinning whore. Not your fault, eh? Well, we've heard all that before and these knickers tell us differently, eh?'

She turned away with everything Kitty could call her own in her arms.

Kitty didn't know how she survived the day.

The work in the laundry was hard and there was no food until evening. She thought she would faint.

There were girls of her own age and many much older. Not one dared speak a word. Silence reigned the entire time whilst she plunged dirty sheets into the large sinks.

The laundry was filled with the sound of hissing steam and the noise of rollers and trolleys being wheeled in and out.

The only distraction arrived in the afternoon when the nuns, seemingly on the verge of hysteria, ran round the wash-rooms, demanding to know where a girl called Besmina had gone. No one knew, but Kitty noticed the looks that passed from one girl to the next.

Hours after she began work, a girl who seemed to be about her own age, with short red hair and freckles, passed her a wicker basket of dirty clothes. As she did so, she whispered, 'Don't cry so. Ye will make yourself sick. We will have a natter tonight, after they put out the lights.'

She gave Kitty's hand the gentlest of squeezes.

Kitty had finally lain down on the dormitory bed, having carefully watched and followed what the other girls did. Minutes after the nun had said a prayer and put the lights out, Kitty became aware of the noise of rustling sheets and feet pattering on the floorboards.

Then a kindly voice whispered, 'Come on then, shift up so we can get under yer blanket and have a natter.'

Kitty opened her eyes to a circle of girls standing round her bed.

They told Kitty about the routine and how they survived it. She learnt about the missing Besmina, who had been in the laundry for years. Her family had never returned to collect her, but every day she used to imagine that she saw her mammy, who had died years earlier, walking up the steps and knocking on the Abbey door.

'God knows where she is now,' said Aideen, the girl who had spoken to Kitty in the laundry. 'She was mad to escape and has tried so many times. She always ends up being brought back and then she gets punished so badly with the stick, poor Besmina.'

'I know my family will come for me,' said Kitty quietly. 'I counted the days today when I was washing. My mammy will be back for me. I know she will. I will count them down every day.'

They talked on Kitty's bed for over an hour.

'Not all the nuns are scolds,' said Aideen. 'We have new ones every now and then. They all start out nice.'

'Aye, but once they've been here a few months, they turn into fucking witches,' said an older woman on the end of the bed who had hardly spoken until that point.

Some of the girls had already birthed their babies, but had to stay, working without pay in the Abbey until the children were three years old, because they couldn't raise the one hundred and fifty pounds without which they couldn't leave. Kitty could hardly believe what she was hearing.

'I had my little lad two years ago,' said Maria, in a quiet voice. 'I have one more year with him and then he will be adopted and live with an American family. I pay my way here by working in the laundry and the parents in America will pay for his adoption. It's a win all round for the nuns. They use our baby money to buy their grand silver and Persian rugs, so they do.'

'Is Cissy yer real name?' asked Aideen.

Kitty was shocked. How did Aideen know?

Before she could reply, Aideen elaborated. 'We were all given different names on the day we arrived, and we can only be called by saints' names but, sure, it doesn't happen anyway.

We are only ever called by our last names. No nun has ever called me anything other than O'Reiley since the day I arrived.'

'My name is Maria but on the day I arrived they told me that my name is now Frances.'

'They can't take away your name,' said Kitty as she sat further up in the bed. She felt enraged at the notion that someone could have their name removed. She was only hiding her name; it wasn't being taken from her. She was still Kitty.

'Aye, they can and they do,' said Maria.

The older woman spoke again. Kitty thought that she looked the saddest. She later discovered that she had been in the Abbey for five years and that her baby had long since gone but that she had no home and no money. Ever since, she had remained in the Abbey, working twelve-hour days every day for no pay and at the mercy of Sister Assumpta's whim and temper.

'Just be sure to never speak,' she advised Kitty. 'Even if you are at the rollers in the laundry and ye think the noise will drown out what ye is saying, it won't. The witches have fuckin' good hearing, now they do. They will hear and ye will be sent to the Reverend Mother and when ye are, she will beat ye with a stick so bad ... See this.'

She pointed to a thin, bright-red weal down the side of her neck.

'And these.'

She held out her hands to Kitty, who inhaled sharply at the sight of the cuts across the older woman's palms.

'I got the stick because Besmina disappeared, like it was my fault. Besmina was put with me on the corridors and the bathrooms this morning. I'm just warning ye ...' She tailed off as she saw the look on Kitty's face. Kitty was appalled at the idea of a woman, the age of her own mother, being beaten.

The light from an oil lamp at the bottom of the stairs crept under the door. In seconds, everyone had fled to their own beds.

Kitty lay awake. The footsteps, belonging to the lamp-carrying nun, clipped away into the distance.

The gentle breathing of her roommates became deeper as they succumbed to exhaustion. Kitty heard the unfamiliar creaks and groans of the building as it moaned in objection to the wind buffeting it from all sides. Her eyes adjusted to the starlight shining in through the skylight opposite her bed, illuminating the faces of the sleeping girls.

She thought about the harvest, which might almost have happened weeks ago. Could it have been only yesterday that she met Aengus? She felt for the charm bracelet Maeve had given her. It was still there. She removed the bracelet and tucked it underneath her mattress in case a nun saw her wearing it and took it away.

As the faces of Tommy, Maura and her siblings filled her mind, she thought about home. She wondered, would the baby even know who she was by the time she returned? Everyone and everything felt as though it belonged to another life, a life she had left. Was it only this morning that she had arrived?

As she closed her eyes, she heard Sister Evangelista praising her English essay and remembered her pride when she had won a bar of Cadbury's chocolate, the class prize for reading. A feeling of utter homesickness overwhelmed her. Tears ran silently down her cheeks. She had never slept in a room with so many people nor ever felt so alone.

'Not long,' she whispered, as she scrunched the bed sheet

tightly in her hand, as though it were a rope holding her onto the edge of sanity.

After breakfast the following morning, a novice instructed Kitty to visit the Reverend Mother's office before she began work in the laundry.

There had been no talking at breakfast. Everyone remained silent while the nuns ate their bacon and sausages, and the girls their milky gruel.

Once the ordeal was over, the girls sat straight-backed on their wooden pews, hands folded in laps, waiting to be dismissed to the toilet before work. Kitty closely watched what they did and copied them, exactly.

Once the bathroom call was over, they were sent straight down to the laundry. Some were issued with house-cleaning duties, which meant having to scrub long corridors on their hands and knees. This was regarded as light relief after washing other people's dirty linen.

Kitty knocked on Sister Assumpta's door, the biggest she had ever stood in front of in her life, painted a glossy white with six tall panels. She stood with her hand resting on the large brass knob and strained to hear the instruction for her to walk in.

The word 'Enter' boomed towards her from across the vast room and penetrated the door with no difficulty whatsoever.

Kitty turned the knob and nervously stepped inside. The fading aroma of Kathleen's 4711 eau de cologne lingered behind the door, and ushered her across the acreage of pastel-green Persian carpet.

Kitty's heart leapt and then sank again. There was no one in the room other than Sister Assumpta, seated at her desk. As before, she was but a silhouette against the light flooding in through the window behind her.

Kitty hovered, not knowing what to say.

From what she could make out, Sister Assumpta was scrutinizing a letter. On her desk lay a long-handled, bone-and-silver letter opener.

In the absence of any acknowledgment or instruction, Kitty acted upon her own initiative and walked to the same chair in front of the desk on which she had been instructed to sit only yesterday. The dark wooden seat was upholstered in a beautiful, cream damask silk. Before she sat down, she glanced out of the window behind Reverend Mother and noticed that, on the front lawn, a long row of heavily pregnant young girls were on their hands and knees, picking at the grass with their bare hands.

Kitty watched for a moment, amazed that this was how the vast expanse of lawn was maintained. The girls crawled backwards as they shredded the grass, harvesting daisies. Following behind them were two more girls, pushing an enormous metal roller that was at least twice the size of them both, flattening the freshly picked grass.

'*Did I tell you to sit?*' the Reverend Mother roared with such ferocity, it made Kitty spring back to her feet.

She cupped her hands in front of her and stood looking down at them, for no other reason than she felt it would be impertinent to look directly at Sister Assumpta and she didn't know where else to look.

'Would you like me to send for tea, would you, Cissy?'

Sister Assumpta's voice was laced with sarcasm. Kitty lifted her eyes and could just make out that she was peering at her over her spectacles. She was not smiling.

'No, Sister, I have had my tea, thank you,' she replied with more confidence than she felt.

Sister Assumpta laughed. A hollow, unkind laugh.

'Have you, girl? Then, that's just as well, isn't it? I wouldn't like you to be thinking you could wander in here for a cup of tea at any old time of day, would I?'

Kitty knew she was being laughed at and remained silent.

'*Would I?*' Again the roar. Kitty was close to being afraid.

Her words wobbled on the edge of tears as she replied, 'No, Sister.'

Sister Assumpta stared at Kitty for what seemed like an eternity.

Kitty listened to the seconds ticking by on the grandfather clock in the corner and, with each second, her fear grew.

A fierce heat slowly crept upwards from her neck, under her chin and onto her face, as she looked down again, afraid of causing offence if she turned her eyes elsewhere.

'I have received a letter this morning, Cissy.' She stopped. '*Cissy.*'

Kitty's head jerked upwards. She looked bolder than she felt. In truth she was terrified.

'The midwife has written to say that she will be calling to see you. Now, that's very special treatment, isn't it, Cissy?'

Kitty didn't know how to answer but her heart skipped a beat.

She knew the midwife, Rosie, was a relative of Nana Kathleen.

'She will be here a week on Wednesday. I will see you again before she arrives. However, the reason I have asked to see you today is that I need to ensure that you always remember that many of the girls here are penitents. Just like yourself, Cissy, they are fallen women and have been placed in my care to help them find salvation through obedience and work. They do not have an esteemed midwife in the family, money, or indeed relatives gagging to take them out when the time comes. They will end their days here, seeking salvation and forgiveness from the good Lord. If you lived in Ireland, and had none of the privileges you do, you would likely be one of them, as you surely have their sinful ways, girl.'

She stopped talking and again stared at Kitty, waiting for a reaction.

Sister Assumpta was not happy that she had agreed to take in this girl. She had been given no back story and she didn't like that at all. She had not even received a letter from the girl's priest in Liverpool, which would have been the usual means of introduction. Something was not right with this situation. Kitty and her family were hiding something.

The Reverend Mother was no fool. However, she could not ignore the midwife, Rosie O'Grady. Since the hanging incident, it had been hard indeed to persuade a midwife to work at the convent under any circumstances. Rosie O'Grady was the matron at the women's hospital in Dublin where she had made a name for herself as the most senior in her profession in Ireland. She was not someone to be refused.

The most recent hanging had cast a grave shadow over the convent. The nuns had tried to keep it quiet, but bad news travels faster than any other. 'If only the stupid girls hadn't shouted out of the window for the laundry van drivers to help, we would have stood a better chance of keeping it quiet. We had managed it every other time,' Sister Assumpta often complained to Sister Celia.

She had to repair what damage had been done to the convent's good name.

News like this could stop the prison and the hotels sending their laundry out to the Abbey and that would be a catastrophe. The nuns would receive little help from Rome if their income dried up.

Refusing to take a referral from Rosie O'Grady would infer they had something to hide.

The Reverend Mother focused her attention on Kitty and noticed her tremble.

'I don't want you upsetting things and so you must not discuss your situation with anyone, do you understand me?'

Kitty nodded.

'*Do you understand me?*'

Kitty began to shake. She tried to not to, but she couldn't stop herself. The trembling began in her hands, travelled upwards through her arms and soon took over her entire body. Her teeth began to chatter uncontrollably. She could not stop them. But something unexpected washed over her. The knowledge that she was loved.

She was not alone. She was not friendless. She had people who cared about her who had brought her here out of kindness and, seemingly, at great expense.

A confidence she didn't know she possessed forced her to lift her head to look at Sister Assumpta straight in what she took to be her eyes.

'Yes, Reverend Mother,' she replied defiantly and almost slightly too loudly. 'I have committed no crime. I am not a penitent. I am here of my own free will, because this is the place my mammy and Kathleen chose for me, on Auntie Rosie's say-so. I'm glad Auntie Rosie is coming to see me next week. I shall be able to send a message home when she does and let them know I am all right.'

Sister Assumpta peered over her glasses in surprise at Kitty. Her mouth opened and closed like a fish and then, with a wave of her hand, she shouted, 'Oh, get out of here, girl. Get out and just remember, you are forbidden to talk. Everyone is forbidden, but you even more so.'

With a new-found and growing confidence, bordering on reckless, Kitty forced a smile to her lips. She looked straight at the blurred dark form in the midst of the light and said, 'Thank you, Reverend Mother,' and, turning on her heel, she moved towards the door.

Just as she pulled it closed behind her, she heard the voice booming impatiently behind her. 'And don't walk on the carpet.'

Once safely out of the room, Kitty whispered to herself, 'This must be what hell is like. I've been sent to hell. I'll bloody beat it, though.'

And, for the first time since she had arrived, she strode with her head held high.

Chapter Twenty-three

HOWARD KNEW HE would have to be especially kind when questioning Daisy. He was also keen to impress Miss Devlin.

'Have a heart, Howard. What can she possibly know? Sure, Daisy is a bag of nerves most of the time. This is freaking her out altogether, so it is,' she said.

Howard had popped into the school office to have a word with Sister Evangelista and afterwards had lingered, making pointless small talk, until Miss Devlin offered him a cup of tea.

Had he but known it, Miss Devlin was delighted to see him again.

She had taken to wearing her newly lightened hair in a fashionable short pixie style, in place of the ponytail tied up in a bow that she had sported since she was six years old.

Miss Devlin had recently celebrated the universally acknowledged spinster age of thirty. Alone. Reading *Madame Bovary*, with a pot of Earl Grey tea and a lemon puff. As far as she and most of the people around her were concerned, she was well and truly on the shelf. Howard's attention was an answer to her prayers. He wasn't a Catholic, but she was so keen, she was prepared to overlook this previously non-negotiable requirement.

Howard loved to stare at her soft powdery face, drowning in her liquid blue eyes with the first signs of crow's feet appearing at the corners. And now, as he became transfixed by her gently moving, cherry-red lips, he had trouble concentrating on what she was saying.

'Pardon?' he asked, as she finished speaking.

'I asked you, what could Daisy possibly know? She is simple and has been in the care of the sisters since she was born.'

Before he could answer, a loud metallic crash followed by a violent ping echoed across the room as the school secretary frowned over the top of her prim and proper, horn-rimmed spectacles. She was a click of a letter away from informing both Howard and Miss Devlin that she did not approve of flirting at work.

Miss Devlin frowned back. She made a mental note to inform the school secretary that in future she could take herself and her solitaire diamond engagement ring over to the convent for half an hour and leave them alone.

Howard could not tell Miss Devlin what Daisy was supposed to have confided in Molly. They needed to hear it for themselves. It was no use to them as hearsay and now that Molly was dead, they had to move quickly. They didn't want to be made fools of, yet again.

'We will be very careful with Daisy, you needn't worry.'

'What is it like down on the streets? Are the women anxious about the murder whilst the men are out at work?'

'It is bad,' Howard replied. 'Everyone is jumpy and who can blame them? They are all safe enough, though, we have officers everywhere.'

Howard didn't mention to her that he and Simon had a major headache. There was nothing he would have loved more than to have discussed it with her, but secrecy was a fundamental part of his job. In police work, he had to keep his own counsel.

They had been watching Tommy Doherty like a hawk since Molly Barrett had told them that Daisy saw Tommy murder the priest. But they knew it could not have been Tommy who killed Molly. He had been in his own house at the time.

Howard's superiors were convinced that whoever had murdered the priest had also murdered Molly.

Howard and Simon knew that, if what Daisy had told Molly was the truth, this just couldn't be the case and, besides, who would believe that? There had never been so much as a burglary on any of the four streets before. This community looked after its own, and yet he would be asking everyone to believe that there had been two random murders committed by two different people in a short space of time in one community. Even Howard knew that sounded incredible. Over and over again, he had quizzed the officers who had been on duty. Their stories were faultless. Not a crack in any of them.

Tommy had left Jerry Deane's house the evening of Molly's murder. He had returned home and walked in through his own back gate. He was seen closing his bedroom curtains and switching off the light an hour later. He never left the house again until the men knocked on for him the following morning.

Tommy Doherty had not murdered Molly Barrett. This was one of the very few facts in their possession. There had been a police officer in a parked car at the end of the road, close to Tommy's front door, and another car parked by the end of his entry all night. They had not stopped watching

Tommy since Molly's confession over the lightest sandwich cake Howard had ever tasted.

Molly's house was on the other side of the road. Whoever had murdered her had been calculating and audacious. Not one of the officers had seen or heard anything, but they did have one solitary clue. A Pall Mall cigarette filter had been found on the outhouse floor. Congealed in blood, but definitely a Pall Mall. They had taken good note. Tommy smoked roll-ups. Molly smoked Woodbines.

Until Molly's murder, Howard and Simon had thought that they had a solid lead. They had been waiting for Daisy to recover from her attack of nerves in the convent.

Now Molly was dead. And someone did it right under the noses of twelve of Lancashire's finest coppers.

There was a gnawing feeling in the pit of Howard's stomach that, somehow, he and Simon were responsible for Molly's death. That if they hadn't spent so much time in her parlour, drinking tea and eating cake, she might still be alive today.

There was only one person Howard knew who smoked Pall Mall and that was Simon. He made a mental note to ask Simon where in town he bought them to try and draw a link between someone in the streets and the filter.

Howard placed his empty cup on the desk beside Miss Devlin.

'I have to go. I'm off to brief Simon down at the station and run through the questions we have to ask Daisy.'

'It's a good job Sister has given permission for both me and Daisy to jump in the car with you at six tonight,' said Miss Devlin. 'I think Daisy will find it helpful having me there to hold her hand,' she added with a smile.

Howard grinned. ''Tis you who will need the chaperone if you are in a car with me,' he replied cheekily.

The typewriter carriage crashed and pinged and Howard flinched.

'Does she fire tin tacks out of that machine or what?' he whispered as he walked towards the steps.

'You cheeky thing,' Miss Devlin whispered back, tapping his arm playfully.

Howard's blue and white panda was parked at the iron gates. As he opened the door, he turned round and winked. She looked at him and they both smiled. A nervous smile. A smile that wished they were both in a different time and place, far beyond the four streets and the double murder investigation. A smile that made a promise. Soon. When this is all over.

Soon.

The interview was difficult from the start. Daisy had appeared nervous as they stepped into the large police station at Whitechapel, and now she had become quiet and non-responsive.

Even though the nuns had told her Molly was dead, she didn't appear to have taken in what it meant.

'It would have been better to do this in the convent,' Miss Devlin whispered to Howard as they descended the dark stone stairs to the interview room.

'We can't,' he replied. 'It has to be done on a tape recorder.'

To prove his point, Howard wound a thin ribbon of brown tape round one of the two wheels on the front of the machine that sat on the interview desk.

Simon, who had asked to lead the interview, came into the room behind them.

Howard reflected on how neither he nor Simon had ever before been involved in a case with so few clues and so little motive. This was the seventh murder case they had worked on together. Howard had been called up for yet another meeting in the superintendent's office that morning. He had explained that he could not find a single motive for either the murder of a much loved priest or that of an old woman, whose only crime was to have been in possession of a wicked sweet tooth.

The case had hit the news headlines yet again and put Howard's superiors in a bad mood. 'Police clueless over double dock street murders,' the *Daily Post* headline taunted them from the paper-sellers' stalls along the streets of Liverpool.

'No clues anywhere,' Howard said to Simon when he came back into the office. 'A motive is where our investigations usually begin. We have no motive. We have no beginning. All we have is simple Daisy.'

Simon removed his silver cigarette case from his trouser pocket and held it open in offering to Howard. A fountain of tobacco fell out over the newspaper Howard was reading. Despite their intense disdain for the press, they read every word of the article.

'Thought you smoked filters?' said Howard, flicking the tobacco away with one hand as he eased a Woodbine out of the case with the other. 'You are the only person I can think of, other than the murderer, who smokes Pall Mall. Where do you get them from? Where is the closest baccy shop to the four streets that sells them?'

'Dunno,' Simon replied. 'I decided filters are for queers and moved onto Woodies,' as he snapped the slim case shut and slipped it back into his trouser pocket. 'I gave myself a hernia tugging at the filters. I'll ask around the baccy shops, see if anyone knows, but you do realize, don't you, thousands of people in Liverpool smoke Pall Mall.'

Howard nodded. 'I know, that's why I say we have no leads.'

They both lit up. Enough said. Once again they both leant over the newspaper.

The basement interview room at the station was high and gloomy, lit by one light bulb, shaded by a bottle-green, glass pendant lightshade, and a single window that was protected by four vertical iron bars, sunk into the concrete.

The brick walls were painted brown to halfway up, then cream the remainder of the way up to the ceiling. The cream had turned a murky shade of brown, thanks to dense cigarette smoke, which, due to a lack of ventilation, hung around in the atmosphere, refusing to leave.

Grey light stealthily slipped in between the iron bars, but failed to reach even the table round which the four now sat. Daisy was constantly distracted by the sound of footsteps as people on the pavement outside walked past the window.

Howard bent to sweep a carpet of cigarette ash from the table with the cuff and lower arm of his jacket, and laid down two notepads and pencils.

'Gosh, seven o'clock already,' said Miss Devlin, with a false brightness.

'Yes. The time is moving on, sorry,' Howard said.

'Did you have a busy day today?' enquired Howard as she looked around.

'No more than usual,' she said.

Making small talk in a big space. That was what they were doing now. That and waiting for whatever Daisy would say to make a difference.

The tape recorder was ready. The table was ready. Everything was ready to begin.

Miss Devlin took a deep breath.

She felt as though they were sitting in a hospital waiting room, expecting a doctor to walk in and announce some life-altering news.

'It worked, he lives.'

'It failed, he died.'

Only no one would live. They were already dead and whatever Daisy revealed wouldn't alter that. Miss Devlin knew that what Daisy was about to say could possibly place someone's neck in a noose.

Someone else might die. Someone she may know.

She felt slightly nauseous.

It had begun to rain and the footsteps of passers-by became hurried. In a sudden downpour stilettos clicked rapidly along-side the steady clomp of solid brogues as in the twilit street the gutters filled. As they passed, cars sent up small tidal waves that splashed the pavement and soaked ankles, but never quite reached the basement window.

Daisy stared at the window and at the stockinged legs running past.

Simon had asked Daisy a number of the most subtle of questions but it was obvious, they were getting nowhere.

'So, what did you and Molly talk about?' asked Simon, gently, for the fourth time.

'Go on, Daisy,' Miss Devlin said, as she squeezed Daisy's hand, 'you aren't in any trouble. You're here because you are a grand help and a very important person.'

Daisy grinned. She didn't think anyone in her whole life had ever been as nice to her as Miss Devlin was, except maybe Molly.

'Go on, Daisy,' said Simon, 'we are all ears.'

The only noise in the room was that of the background hum of the tape recorder as the metal wheels swished round and round. From the street outside came the sounds of footsteps and trailing voices, the incessant patter of rain and beeping car horns. Life was moving on, whilst down in the Whitechapel basement they waited.

Daisy giggled at Simon. 'All ears! You aren't all ears, you only have two ears, doesn't he, Miss Devlin?' Her expression had softened. Daisy was beginning to enjoy the fact that they were interested in what she might have to say. They were interested in talking to her about her friend, Molly Barrett.

Daisy found her courage. She remembered that there were things she could say about Molly.

The memory of Molly sitting with Daisy at the Priory kitchen table came back to her. She was encouraged by a gentle pat on the arm from Miss Devlin, who with her delicate painted fingers lifted Daisy's fringe and pinned it back into her cross-clips.

'We talked about making cakes, me and Molly Barrett, and she always gave me some of the scones she had baked for the father and, oh gosh, she told me such funny stories about Tiger. That cat, he was the divil himself. Molly never knew what he was going to bring in through the door next.'

Daisy began to laugh. They laughed with her and then, as the laughing subsided, Daisy continued to smile at each one of them in turn. They all smiled back.

She had made them smile. She couldn't have been more pleased with herself if she had imparted a nuclear code. Daisy continued.

She talked about the neighbours. Especially Molly's nosy neighbour, Annie.

Simon shot Miss Devlin an earnest look.

She looked at her watch. Surely, something must happen soon.

Miss Devlin gave Daisy a big, false smile and nodded enthusiastically. 'Yes, go on, Daisy,' she said.

'She talked about all the people on the four streets because she knew them all, she did, every one of them. She didn't like Deirdre very much, because she never paid her bills and she said Sean McGuire was flirty. She even told me that once she saw Little Paddy nick a bottle of sterilized milk from Mrs Keating's doorstep. Can ye imagine? She was such good fun, was Molly Barrett, so full of stories. She used to make me laugh, so she did. I only ever laughed when I was with Molly. She was so nice and always said nice things to me, like, Daisy, you are the only person around here who can keep a house and a secret as well as I does. I used to love her coming, so, I really did.'

Daisy began to look sad and her voice cracked with distress.

'Molly was the only person who was really nice to me. I miss Molly now. I wish she was here and she could tell you all the things we talked about better than me. She was my only friend in the world, Molly was, and I miss her.'

Daisy began to cry. Miss Devlin began to cry. Howard took out his hankie.

Simon put his head in his hands in exasperation.

Things were not going well.

Howard rang the bell and a young officer carried in a tray of tea. He also brought a clean ashtray and removed the full one from the interview table.

'Have a cuppa, Daisy,' said Miss Devlin, pouring tea into the pale blue cup and saucer.

Howard decided to have a try himself and nodded to Simon to indicate as much. He had nothing to lose. He would have to put the words into her mouth and see what happened next.

'Daisy, did you tell Molly that you saw someone murder the priest?'

Miss Devlin was in the middle of wiping Molly's nose with her own lace hankie as Daisy answered.

'Oh, yes I did, I did see who did that,' said Daisy, 'and I'm not talking about the Priory, because I know I'm not allowed to talk to anyone about anything that happens in the Priory, but that was outside, an' so I told Molly when she came.'

Miss Devlin stopped wiping Daisy's nose.

Howard and Simon both put down their cups at the same time and leant forward. Howard gently asked, 'Who murdered the priest, Daisy?'

It was now almost dark outside. The Victorian street lamps lent their aid to the single bulb illuminating the room. The long shadows, banished to the corners by the central light, clambered up the walls and hovered over them all. Waiting.

Miss Devlin noticed that the rain had stopped falling and that the footsteps were now few and far between. The workers were home. She imagined her sister putting the key in the door, switching on the lights, picking up the post from the mat. Doing the normal things they did every day, sometimes together, and here she was, Miss Devlin, about to hear who had brutally murdered the priest. She was trying hard not to shake.

'It was Tommy Doherty, from number nineteen Nelson Street,' said Daisy. 'I saw him with me own eyes.'

Miss Devlin slumped back in the chair.

It was over. The suspense.

'*It failed.*

He dies.'

Simon motioned for Howard to follow him outside the cell.

'I just need a word with Howard, Miss Devlin. I will ask them to send you some more tea. Will you be all right with Daisy? We will only be a few minutes.'

'Of course,' Miss Devlin replied.

She was in shock. She knew everyone in the Doherty family and would even count Maura as her friend. This was a terrible mistake. It could not be true. She looked at Daisy who was tucking into an arrowroot biscuit with no idea of the bombshell she had just dropped.

'We will be all right, won't we, Daisy?'

'Eh, what?' Daisy said, looking up.

'Nothing, Daisy,' said Miss Devlin. 'It's fine, really, it's fine.'

'Right,' said Howard, 'do we arrest him now?' He had closed the interview door behind them. Simon paced up and down in front of him, rubbing his fingers through his hair. He appeared anxious.

'No, we bloody can't arrest him. There are just a few things here, Howard, that you may have forgotten. Tommy Doherty has an alibi. He was a witness for Jerry Deane and his alibi is the rest of the card school. Remember that? They were all at the card school, together with the rest of the fucking street. Have you seen the man? He wouldn't say boo to a goose. We have been watching him since Molly Barrett told us what Daisy said to her. We know he didn't murder

Molly Barrett. The super is very sure that whoever murdered the priest also murdered Molly. There is no way two entirely different psychopaths would have chosen the same street to have their fun on in such a short space of time. Add to that the fact that Daisy is simple and would be a nightmare in the witness box. Do you really think you should go to the super and get him to arrest Tommy Doherty, a man with a cast-iron alibi, on the back of that?'

Howard looked confused. 'I don't understand. When Molly told us what Daisy had seen, you were excited, you thought we had nailed him, and yet now you are telling me we haven't got anything?'

'No, Simon. What I am saying is that, until we began questioning Daisy, I didn't realize how simple she was. She is a sandwich short of a fucking picnic. With Molly Barrett alongside her, to stand testimony to Daisy's character and to what Daisy saw, we had half a chance. Without Molly and with Daisy that flaky, I'm not sure we have any chance at all. How was I to know that someone was going to come along and murder the old biddy? For fuck's sake, Howard, she was a harmless old lady and our only credible witness.

'Go and take them both home. I am off upstairs to phone the super to make sure he is free first thing in the morning, so we can ask him what he thinks. Go inside to those two and I will join you in a minute. Whatever we have, it has to hold water in a court of law and I don't think we have that here.'

Ten minutes later, when he went back into the interview room, Simon noted that Howard was deep in conversation with Miss Devlin, and Daisy was working her way through the biscuits.

'Well?' Howard enquired.

'I am seeing him in the morning. We can have a good night's rest ourselves beforehand.'

As they were gathering up their things to leave, Howard said to Simon, 'I will run the ladies home now, in the panda, if that's all right with you?'

Simon winked at Howard. 'That's fine by me,' he replied and then asked, thoughtfully, 'Daisy, what made you look out of the window that night if the place where the father was murdered isn't under your bedroom window?'

Howard fleetingly wondered why they hadn't asked that question when the tape recorder was running. How did Simon know which window was Daisy's?

'Oh, 'twas Bernadette,' replied Daisy cheerfully.

'Bernadette?' Howard looked at Miss Devlin. 'Who is Bernadette?'

'Well, I know of only one,' said Miss Devlin, holding on to her hat with one hand and removing her hatpin with the other, 'but she died a few years back now. She was Nellie Deane's mammy, so it can't have been her.'

Miss Devlin picked up her gloves and handbag from the table, ready to leave.

'Oh yes, 'twas,' grinned Daisy. 'She's there all the time in the graveyard. I often watch her. I see all the ghosts. I was never afraid of them. I am now, though. I don't want to see the priest. I don't want to see his ghost, ever.'

Miss Devlin was speechless. Howard and Simon groaned in unison.

Chapter Twenty-four

HARRY DIDN'T TELL Maura he had been picked to play Joseph in the school nativity play. She heard it from Angela. Despite the churlish way in which Angela imparted the news, Maura thought her heart would burst with pride.

'Our Harry is playing Joseph, is he? Our Harry? Well, isn't that just the best bit of news we have had for a long time now, eh, Angela?'

Angela looked at her mother as though she had gone mad.

'No, it isn't,' she replied. 'If I had been picked for Mary, now that would be the best news. Harry's a boy, so who cares what part he has in the play? All he has to do is put a tea towel on his head, wear the coat the sisters will make and carry a toy lamb.'

Angela continued to grumble, despite the fact that she could tell Maura had long since stopped listening.

'At last,' said Maura, flushed pink with pride, 'this is something we can hold our heads up and smile about.'

It had been too long. Excited at the news, Maura knocked on the wall for Peggy to kick off the jungle mops. This was something to crow about, although Maura knew perfectly well that it would last only minutes, compared with the constant speculation about who had murdered Molly Barrett, the question that had now eclipsed the previous one, who murdered the priest.

The news about Harry's starring role did not have the same joyous impact on Tommy, who fretted every single day about their Kitty.

'Try and be pleased for Harry,' Maura said to him that evening, once all the children were in bed.

'I am, Maura, I'm trying. It would be easier to be happy for Harry if we could write to Kitty and tell her that her brother is to play Joseph. That would help.'

'I know, but it is a long time off, Tommy. The school term has only just begun. There may be a chance, surely to God, somewhere between now and Christmas to get news to our Kitty. Rosie has written to say that, once Christmas is out of the way, Kitty will be back with us soon after. It will all fly past, Tommy. Our Kitty will be home soon, so she will. That is what I am holding on to.'

'Holy Mother!' Maura shot up from the arm of the chair. 'With all the excitement, I haven't marked off today on the chart.'

She walked over to the range and picked up the pencil hanging from a piece of string, tied to a nail next to a chart she had made with the days marked off until Kitty returned to the fold.

Not one of Maura's neighbours had questioned this, or even thought it was slightly odd. Maura was known to be a devoted mother and most of the women found it endearing how much she missed Kitty.

'Just so typical of Maura, it is, to send Kitty to look after her poorly sister in Mayo, when she is missing her so much back here. God, she is the paragon of virtue, that woman is,' said Peggy to Mrs Keating.

Standing on the doorstep, she leant out and snatched up two of her boys by the scruff of the neck as they ran past. She slapped both of them across the backs of their legs and ordered them into the house for their tea, never breaking her stride as she spoke. Mrs Keating didn't bat an eyelid.

'Aye, she is that, always has been,' said Mrs Keating. 'Any news, Peggy, about the murder? Did you get a chance to speak to that policeman, as you walked past? What did he say?'

'Well then, now.' Peggy leant in, folded her arms and lowered her voice. 'It definitely wasn't the bloody cat. Apparently, she had taken a chocolate sandwich cake out of the press and left it on a plate with a knife next to it in the kitchen. She didn't expect to die, did Molly. She thought she was going back in for a slice. The only clue they have is a ciggie butt on the outhouse floor, which isn't the brand Molly smokes. A Pall Mall it was. Who in God's name smokes Pall Mall? They don't even sell those around here.'

'A Pall Mall?' said Mrs Keating with a note of disbelief in her voice. 'They only sell baccy, Woodies and Capstan Full Strength in the tobacconist on the Dock Road. Pall bloody Mall? 'Twasn't anyone from around here, then?'

'Aye,' said Peggy, 'I know that's what I said, and a policeman wouldn't lie to me. It was definitely a Pall Mall.'

At the same moment they both spotted Sheila running towards the entry.

'Powwow in Maura's,' Sheila shouted down to them, as she shifted her toddler back into position on her hip.

'Maura has been knocking for ye, Peggy.'

'This is more like it, things getting back to normal,' Peggy said to Mrs Keating as they both wobbled along, Peggy's slippers squeaking and Mrs Keating's nose wrinkling at the rising smell.

'Only ye could describe gossip about a murder as getting back to normal, Peggy, shame on ye. I'll see ye in mass tonight,' said Mrs Keating as they both pushed in through Maura's back gate.

Later that evening, as Maura drew another line through another day on her chart, Tommy stood from his chair at the table and walked over to his wife. He put his arms round her and hugged her deep into his chest. 'I am proud of Harry, I am. I know it's Harry and the others keeping the show on the road. If it weren't for them kids, I'd be a dead man, Maura. Thank the Lord for our kids.'

'It has been a struggle, Tommy, but we are doing all right now. Things are getting better. We have more money to find and despite the promise from Kathleen and Jerry that they will provide when the time comes, we must pay it back.'

'We will, queen,' said Tommy. 'We will be paying it back for the rest of our lives, but pay it back we will, every half-penny.'

Maura kissed him on the lips and, putting a hand on either side of his face, looked into his eyes. She was now the stronger of the two. The news that Harry had been selected to play Joseph had picked her up more than any tonic could have. For Maura, the essence of her life was pride in her family.

'Not long now, Tommy,' she said. 'Tomorrow will be a busy day and then, soon enough, the days will fly by and she will be back home. On the day the children go back to school after the Christmas holiday, she will be nearly home. The Christmas holidays will whizz by, they always do.'

Tommy nodded. The way Maura put it gave him hope. It sounded not far away at all.

Tommy had never worried about a thing in his life, other than whether or not the horse he had placed a shilling on would come in for him. He now spent hours of every day worrying about the future. He was convinced a new and unforeseen disaster was heading their way and nothing Maura could say would disabuse him of this notion. His fear was rooted in guilt.

Changing the subject, he spoke again of the thought that constantly nagged him and which, in the darkness and privacy of their bedroom, he and Maura discussed every night.

Tommy lowered his voice.

'I can't stop thinking about poor Molly Barrett. Me guts tell me that her murder was connected with ours.' He dropped to a whisper. 'But we know it can't have feckin' been. What is going on, Maura?'

'I don't know. The women came in this afternoon after school. Peggy talks to the policemen, wouldn't she just! One told her they found a Pall Mall cigarette stub on Molly's outhouse floor.'

'A Pall Mall? Well, that means Molly's murderer was a bloody queer, or a woman. No man I know smokes feckin' Pall Mall!'

The back door latch clicked and Jerry stepped into the light of the kitchen from the black night outside.

Maura withdrew her hands from behind Tommy's neck and slipped them back into her front apron pocket.

'Eh, behave, put him down.' Jerry winked at Maura. 'I fancy a pint at the Anchor, you up for it, mate?'

Tommy looked at Maura who smiled her approval.

As he moved to take his jacket from the back of the door, Tommy said to Maura, 'Don't wait up, queen, you go to bed. I'll wake you when I get in, though.'

Maura winked back at Tommy and grinned. She heard the familiar, 'Ye lucky bastard,' from Jerry, as they walked down the back path.

Shortly after Jerry and Tommy had left for the pub, Kathleen arrived in Maura's kitchen.

'How are things?' she asked.

Casting her eye around, she could tell Maura had been hard at it, as usual.

The indoor washing pulley was suspended across the ceiling and from it hung a row of hovering white ghosts, wafting in the heat thermals from the range, masquerading as school shirts. As Kathleen looked up, she saw an array of children's clothes and nappies, steaming in the rising heat.

'No worse than usual,' smiled Maura.

She couldn't tell anyone of the horrible guilt she held deep inside. She was now happy to have left Kitty in the convent, happy that not a gossamer shred of shame would touch the family and that they had survived, intact in the eyes of her neighbours. She knew it would be tough for them all and she missed Kitty every single day. But hadn't she, Maura, been the one revered above the others as the wisest woman on the street? Wasn't hers the one house from which a child was likely to enter God's service? Wasn't it bad enough that everything she had striven for, all her married life, had been stripped from her by that man of the devil, without having to be publicly disgraced in front of her neighbours?

With the help of Kathleen, who was as good as family, she had come through and they were all safe.

Kitty would be home and then everything could be forgotten. Yes, she was relieved that she had left Kitty well cared for and looked after at the Abbey, but she knew Tommy would never understand. The Doherty family had not slipped from its pedestal. That was important.

'I am still in shock about Molly,' said Kathleen. 'What the hell has happened there, Maura? Everyone is saying it is the same person who murdered the priest. What the bleedin' hell is going on?'

Maura shook her head. If she had a pound for every time someone had asked her that question, she would be able to pay to take Kitty out of the convent on her own.

'Here,' said Kathleen, taking a bottle of Guinness out of each coat pocket. 'Put the poker in those coals and let's have a ciggie, too.'

Maura took two glasses down from the press and then shoved the poker into the fire, ready to plunge into the Guinness.

'Jerry nipped to the pub and picked them up before he came back for Tommy,' said Kathleen, nodding at the bottles. 'He's a good lad, is Jerry.'

Kathleen turned her head to watch the end of the poker turning bright red from the heat. She let out a huge sigh.

'Jesus, I'm worried about Alice, Maura. Do ye know where she is tonight, by any chance?'

'Alice?' Maura said with surprise. 'No. Is she not at home with ye lot?'

'She's not,' Kathleen replied. 'She went out after she put Joseph to bed at seven and said she was slipping down to Brigid's. But I just passed Mrs McGuire and told her to pass a message on to Alice, when she got back indoors, to say that I was nipping over to see ye and that Nellie was watching Joseph. Mrs McGuire looked confused. She said Alice wasn't there.'

'Well, maybe she went to the off-licence for some cigs on the way?'

'Aye, maybe, but she had a full packet before she left. I know, because I ran out and she gave me four Woodies from hers, to put in my packet.'

Maura opened the bottles, which let out a familiar welcome hiss, and slowly began to pour the Guinness into the glasses, which at one time had been the property of the Anchor.

'Where was Mrs McGuire off to?' asked Maura. 'Not the bloody chippy again? That woman is never out of there.'

Maura took the poker from the fire and plunged it into Kathleen's glass first. The sizzle of scorched Guinness filled the kitchen air, replacing the ever present smell of chip-pan fat.

Kathleen continued talking as Maura sat back in her chair. The dishes were done. The washing was drying. The boys' shirts were made of the new Bri-Nylon drip dry and didn't need to be ironed. She could relax without guilt.

'She said she had been to the boxing club to fetch Sean. Had a bee in her bonnet, she did, about how much training he is putting in. Said Brigid did too much and she was going to fetch him out, to come home and spend some time with his wife and kids. She's a tough woman, that Mrs McGuire. Mind you, there is no such thing as a soft woman from Galway. They don't put up with any nonsense. Not like us daft bats from Mayo.'

Both women laughed. Neither was daft. Both were back in control.

'But, Jaysus, she was giving out something wicked, she was. Had Little Paddy and Scamp to walk with her to the club, she said, being scared after Molly's murder an' all that, and Sean wasn't even there. She then started asking me, had I seen Sean? I thought, Holy Mother of God, here we are, two grown women, out in the streets, worrying about two kids who are supposed to be grown-up. I said to her, tell you what, if you find Alice first, send her home to me, will ye, and if I find Sean, I'll do the same with him. Kids!'

Maura and Kathleen both shook their heads and took a sip of their Guinness.

'Did ye walk all the way across yerself?' asked Maura. 'Because I don't think it's safe, so I don't. We don't know who the hell did that murder. It must have been a madman. Ye shouldn't come down the entry alone in the dark.'

'Are ye kiddin'?' said Kathleen. 'There are police cars everywhere out there tonight. The entire Lancashire police force must have come back from holiday, or summat, because I've never seen so many police cars in one street as there are tonight, other than on the night we got back from Ireland.'

'No?' exclaimed Maura in surprise as she rose from her chair and moved into the parlour to look out from the nets. Kathleen followed her and they stood together at the windows in the dark.

'I know it's weird and it's just all in me mind, but I feel as though they are all watching my house,' said Maura.

The two women walked back into the kitchen. As they passed through the hallway, both dipped their fingers in the holy water they had brought back from Ireland, which sat in a small ornamental bowl on a table under Maura's sacred heart on the wall, and crossed themselves.

Kathleen didn't want to confirm Maura's worst fears, but she felt the same. The police were indeed all looking at Maura's house.

'They say the cat's distraught,' said Kathleen. 'Annie has taken it in and is feeding it, but it keeps sitting at Molly's back door, making that crying sound, it does. I heard Annie shouting last night, "Tiger, come on, big boy, come and be good for Annie now, I have a nice treat for ye." Good job we know she's talking to the bloody cat. The police probably think she's some kind of wanton woman.'

Both women roared with laughter at the image of toothless Annie, as far from a wanton woman as one could imagine.

After a moment had passed, Kathleen smiled at Maura as she lifted her glass to drain the last drop of Guinness. The police might have been watching the house, but there was no way they could nail Tommy or Jerry for this. They would be all right.

Life was, in a very strange way, getting back to normal.

Jerry talked to Tommy all the way to the pub. Tommy hardly spoke at all, except to tell him he missed Kitty. His own, his favourite, little Kitty. She had patiently taught him to read and, in return, he had let her down so badly. His little Kitty was sleeping in a place where no one loved her best of all and that broke Tommy's heart in two.

'It's the last leg now, Tommy mate.' Jerry's words penetrated Tommy's thoughts. 'Once Kitty is home we can really begin to move forward and get back to where we were.'

They bought their drinks at the bar and took the table for two next to the fire.

The bar was busy and the noise and smoke erupted out onto the street as they opened the door.

Tommy picked up his pint of black nectar, closed his eyes and, tipping his head back, slowly let the balm pour down his throat, soothing his fractious mood. Putting his pewter pot down with a thud, he wiped the foam from his lips with the back of his hand before he spoke.

'Jerry, two of the McGinty kids are sat on the wall outside, again. That's the second time I've seen them out there. Is that man a fecking eejit? I told him what would happen if I ever found those kids shivering outside. I'm going to take them a couple of bags of crisps. They don't look like they've been fed tonight.'

Jerry wasn't surprised. The McGinty kids had a tough life. Their father, an alcoholic, was never out of the pub. They could be without coal for a week, if his wife didn't manage to catch him on a Friday night and rescue his pay money before it had all been drunk or gambled away.

Jerry watched as Tommy walked back out through the pub door. He could just make out Tommy's blurred form through the frosted windows, bending down to give the grateful and hungry kids their crisps. McGinty was in the bar, already half cut, and it was only eight o'clock. The children had been sitting on the wall since their mother had sent them down to retrieve their father, and what was left of the housekeeping, two hours since. They were still waiting, unable to extract him and too scared to return home without him.

Tommy strode back in through the revolving door, a look of fury on his face. He glared over at McGinty, who was propping himself up on the end of the counter.

McGinty saw Tommy looking at him and raised his cap in greeting. 'All right, mate?' he called across the bar nervously.

Tommy strode purposefully towards him.

'Tommy,' Jerry shouted, trying to avert any trouble, 'your pint's here.'

Tommy didn't hear him; his anger towards a man who would leave his children sitting on the pub wall, hungry and half frozen, was rising rapidly.

While he had been speaking to the McGinty kids, he could see his Kitty. The McGinty girl was half frozen, her hands were almost blue, with bright-red chilblains running down her fingers. Her large eyes were filled with tears from the biting wind. The lad, Brian, wore no coat and the girl had nothing more than her mother's shawl pulled tightly around her shoulders.

'Aye, I've asked everyone whose gone in to tell him, so I have, but he still hasn't come out,' Brian had said to Tommy when they walked past.

McGinty's reactions were too dulled by alcohol and too slow to anticipate what happened next. Tommy took him by the scruff of his neck and, marching him across the sawdust-covered floorboards, propelled him out through the door.

'How many times do ye need to be told to look after your feckin' kids?' he hissed.

McGinty's protestations were more of a squeak. 'What the feck are ye doing, yer mad bastard? Me pint, I have me pint on the bar.'

'Too fecking bad,' said Tommy, not wanting to raise his voice and scare the kids. 'Get fecking home to yer missus and take yer kids wit' ye.'

The two children were nervously walking across from the wall to their da.

'And if ye lay one hand on them kids, I'll smash yer bleedin' face in. Do ye get that, eh, McGinty?'

McGinty was nodding furiously.

'He had it feckin' coming,' said Tommy to Jerry as he re-entered the pub, picked up his pint again and downed what was left in one.

As he slammed his pint pot back down on the table, he looked at Jerry and said, 'I did that for our Kitty.'

Chapter Twenty-five

STANLEY AND AUSTIN met in the Jolly Miller. It was darts night and the pub was full.

They were downing a quick pint after work and then heading off to meet Arthur in a house in Anfield, an empty property belonging to a landlord friend of Arthur's.

Their instructions were not to drive, but to take the bus and alight at Lower Breck Road, then walk the rest of the way, down a small entry at the side of the house and in through the back door, which would be left open. Stanley assumed the landlord was in the ring, but he couldn't be sure, because he didn't even know his name.

Secrecy, and information that was shared on a need-to-know basis only, ensured they all remained anonymous and safe.

'Why does Arthur want to see us?' Stanley asked Austin, as he set his pint pot of mild down on the bar. The drink made Stanley feel better. It wasn't until he had put the drink to his lips that he realized how badly he had needed it.

He had told the doctor that his nerves were worse again. He couldn't stop the bouts of shaking.

'I'd have bad nerves, if I lived with your mother,' the doctor had said, writing him out another prescription. 'I've seen mothers like yours before. They keep a grip on an only son. You need to break free. It's not too late. Get yourself a wife.'

Stanley promised he would.

The only people who knew Stanley preferred little boys to girls were Austin and Arthur, plus some of the men they met up with, to exchange pictures and photographs. Quite excitingly, last month there had been a cine film on a camera and projector that Arthur had acquired, which they had all paid towards. But there had been no gathering since the priest, one of their ring, had been murdered. That had put the fear of God into them all.

The priest had been one of the few people running the group that were known to Stanley. He had been told there was a bishop too and some very high-up and important people, a politician even, but he didn't know who they were.

Stanley kept himself to himself as much as possible and only targeted the poor kids. They were easier to deceive, along with their pathetically grateful parents. Unlike Austin, Stanley took no chances.

'Right, drink up,' said Austin, 'and try to stop the fucking shaking. You will make the others nervous. They'll think you are unreliable. Here, I'll get us a chaser.'

Austin moved to the bar while Stanley took another of the pills the doctor had prescribed for him. He didn't want anyone to be worried about him. The circle was the most important thing in his life. He had to remain a part of it. It stopped him taking risks and kept him safe and out of prison.

Austin put the two shorts on the bar. 'Here you go, mucker, down in one,' he said.

Stanley had never drunk whisky before and he spluttered as it burnt all the way down into the pit of his stomach.

Feeling much stronger, they slipped out of the pub and into the dark, moonless night.

As instructed, they stealthily took the steps into the back of the large town house. It was almost pitch-black, apart from a trembling light provided by one flickering candle wedged into the top of a sterilized milk bottle, placed in the range grate.

Arthur was waiting, as were the others, hugging the shadows on the wall. Dark, sinister figures.

Stanley could not make them out. He pulled his cap over his brow and looked at his feet. 'No idea who the hell is here,' he whispered to Austin.

'I have,' Austin replied, 'but you don't fucking want to, believe me.'

Stanley nodded. He already knew one was a politician. He could hear him talking. He knew his voice from the news on the telly. Stanley and his mother watched the news together every single night.

A man began to speak. Stanley did not recognize the voice. His accent was refined, but mingled with a colloquial edge, Stanley couldn't tell what. It wasn't Irish. He guessed the man was attempting to disguise his voice, due to the scarf tied across his mouth.

Stanley and Austin squatted down with those who were sitting on the floor.

The man who was speaking stood next to Arthur. He was tall and, in addition to the scarf across his face, he wore a trilby hat, the kind worn by the men on Water Street as they strode towards their offices each morning. The collar of his long, beige gabardine mac was upturned, hugging his face and adding a further layer of disguise.

The mac provided some kind of illumination, as though it had absorbed the sun's rays during daylight hours and in a ghostly way was emanating a faded light back into the darkest of rooms. As the man moved, the gabardine static crackled and snapped.

'I know you were all nervous following the murder of the

priest,' he began. 'That has made you dammed jittery because he was one of our ring. And there has been the additional murder of the old woman.'

He stopped for a moment as though he was weighing up his words very carefully.

'Arthur has told me that you all have questions. He is worried that any change in your behaviour as a result of your nervousness could make you vulnerable and therefore pose a risk to the rest of the ring. Now, listen to me, all of you. Everything has been taken care of. There will be nothing to lead back to the group. You have to trust me on this. I know what I am talking about.

'It was a parent who murdered the priest.'

There was a sharp intake of breath from everyone with the odd 'Fucking hell!' hissed into the dark.

The man had voiced aloud a consequence that threatened them all. Their worst nightmare was to face the revenge of a parent. Give them the police, any day.

Stanley's eyes were adjusting to the light and he could just make out that there were about fifteen of them in the room.

The man continued speaking.

'The priest had become greedy. Too damned full of himself, and as a result he became slapdash and careless. A lesson to you all. I have no idea how the parent caught him, but I can tell you this: he doesn't want to hang for his actions and therefore won't tell anyone.'

The shadowy figures sitting on the floor tried surreptitiously to look at one another, natural curiosity getting the better of them. All they could see were the whites of eyes. It was enough.

'We know the parents have been very careful and have shipped the girl away. We believe that she may be pregnant, so they have done the right thing, going to great lengths to hide their connection to the murder.

'The old woman had to go. She knew who murdered the priest and, unfortunately, that could have opened an infernal can of worms, which may have been very difficult indeed.

'You may hear on the news tomorrow that a man has been arrested. Stay calm. I can assure you, you will be protected. He has a young family and has no intention of becoming acquainted with the hangman. He will not be making any confession and will be released without charge. You have our assurance of that. Now, any questions?'

There must have been ten of them sitting on the floor and five standing, in the darkest corner of the room. Stanley assumed the five were the group leaders.

Stanley shuffled his foot to a more comfortable position. With a nervous cough, Austin struck a match to light up his cigarette and, for a second, all of those seated round him.

The sudden squeak of a mouse shattered the silence as it scuttled across the floor through discarded and crumpled newspapers, disappearing into its nest at the base of the range. An owl hooted in the large garden at the rear and, from the road, they could hear the occasional car and the squeal of brakes on the bus, as it stopped outside the front of the house.

No one moved. The candle in the milk bottle began to splutter and spit as the wax reached the end of the wick.

Someone spoke, but Stanley had no idea who.

'What about the girl, Daisy? She was in the police station tonight, being questioned.'

The man who was speaking turned to another disguised man, who was rounder and shorter, as if asking for permission to comment.

'All organized I tell you; there is no need for concern. She will be sorted in an orderly way. The man who will be taken into custody will be released and, as soon as he is, she will be taken care of. You are all protected.'

A sigh of relief swept across the room.

They all believed him. He was right. One significant break-through in the investigation into the murder and it could all come tumbling down. The parent would talk. His child would talk; her friends would talk. There would be digging around and they would all be in danger.

Thank God, no one would know who they were, or what they did. They were free to continue as before.

Stanley wondered what 'taken care of' involved. It gave him a thrill. How normal everything sounded and yet, here they were, in a dark and dirty room, discussing a double murder. In their world, this was big time. Now that Stanley was reassured they were not in danger, he found the events exciting rather than threatening.

Austin punched him on the arm and with a grin said, 'Come on, mate, let's go. Time for a quick one?'

On the way out Austin whispered to Arthur, 'Back to our usual time on Saturday, Arthur. I've been saving up a stack of camera film I need developing.'

'Aye,' said Arthur. 'Back up and running. We have some great cine film on the projector for you, Stan, see you Sat'day, lads.'

As they turned the corner of the house and walked towards the bus stop, Stanley noticed that two of the men slipped into the back of a car, parked up the road, driven by the chauffeur.

'Don't look,' snapped Arthur. 'You know that's not in the rules.'

Ten minutes later they were back in the warmth and bright lights of the pub. Two happy men.

Chapter Twenty-six

S IMON KNOCKED ON the door and waited to be admitted. He could hear the super talking on the telephone but couldn't make out what he was saying. He then heard the click as the Bakelite handset was put down and the super called him in.

'Ah, Simon, my good man. How are things progressing? I take it no one is aware the ladies were downstairs?'

'No, sir,' Simon replied. 'The only people who know are Howard and myself, and one uniformed officer who I believe has received instructions directly from yourself, and the chaperone, Miss Devlin, who is also aware of the need for confidentiality.'

'Jolly good. Now, what has she said? Is it true she becomes very confused from time to time?'

Simon briefed the super on the interview with Daisy.

When he finished, the super swung round in his new swivel chair and, with his back to Simon, looked out of his window onto the noisy Liverpool street below.

It was rush hour and the traffic was heavy, he noted. People thronged the pavement, rushing and bustling backwards and forwards across the road like mice on the bottom of a cage. Buses queued and jostled to turn the corner. From his window he could hear bells ringing and bus conductors shouting. A constant source of irritation. He loathed the noises of the street. They reminded him of his wartime service, of the distant sound of enemy fire. He loved the peace and quiet of his garden in West Kirkby and resented every hour he spent in Whitechapel.

He turned back to face Simon.

'All right,' he said. 'Bring the fellow in for questioning, but don't arrest him. However, unless he drops an absolute corker, you had better let him go once you have a record on tape. Frankly, an unreliable witness is ten times worse than no witness at all. Neither of us needs the humiliation. We both know that whoever murdered the priest murdered the old woman too, and we know it cannot have been Doherty.

'If the housekeeper from the Priory struggled when being questioned by you and a chaperone, with kind words and tea, how would she cope with a Liverpool silk, far tougher than any silk from London and that's a fact?'

Simon nodded. He hadn't even told the super about Daisy's ghostly sightings, which would be laughed out of court. If he did, likely he would be laughed out of the super's office.

'Go and bring him in now. Do it with the minimum of fuss, there's a good chap. I will need to speak to the assistant chief constable over this. I'm playing golf with him today and will do it then. Keep the cars on the streets until I report back to you.'

Maura fed the baby in the kitchen while Tommy, in his string vest and long johns, took his shave at the kitchen sink, humming along to the Beatles on the radio. The fire in the range roared its morning high, as if waving its arms in fists of flames at the smog that huddled against the windows.

Only half an hour earlier the kitchen had been quiet and still.

The early light, thick and grey.

Maura thought how this first fire was the best of the day, the strongest, laying down the bed of hot ash for the remainder of the day's fires to simmer on. She could hear Peggy's voice through the kitchen wall, shouting to big Paddy to wake up.

She thought how normal everything looked and sounded.

Why then did she feel so restless? What had brought on this feeling of breathlessness? Although the fire roared, she felt cold.

'Them lads are doing well, aren't they, queen?' Tommy said with a nod of acknowledgment at the radio, as he rinsed out his shaving brush under the running cold tap, before shaking it carefully into the Belfast sink and rubbing it hard onto the block of pure white shaving soap in an old chipped cup. 'Remember when we saw them play in the pub, when Bernadette was alive? They was just kids then.'

'They still are,' Maura laughed, lifting the baby onto her shoulder to wind her.

Maura could smell flowers. Strong and heady. Definitely flowers. She put her hand out and pulled it back sharply. Despite the heat from the fire, it had passed through an icy breeze.

In half an hour exactly, she would walk up the stairs to rouse the kids for school and she couldn't wait to fill the kitchen with the melee of their routine.

'Aye, I remember that night in the pub with Bernadette,' she replied in a distracted manner as she rocked the baby from hip to hip. 'That was the best night out we ever had. The craic, it was fantastic. They were the days, eh, Tommy? What a laugh we used to have. We will never see the Beatles in the flesh again though, never.'

'We will again, queen. They will be going for years yet, those lads, and will be sure to play in Liverpool loads of times,' said Tommy, lathering his face in soap. ''Tis their home crowd, to be sure they will.'

This time there was no knock on the front door.

Neither of them heard a thing until suddenly the back door was quietly opened by a uniformed officer and Simon stepped into the kitchen. Both Tommy and Maura were stunned.

Simon wasted no time, as the officer took the razor out of Tommy's hand and passed him the shirt that was hanging on the chair next to the sink.

'Tommy Doherty, we are taking you down to the station for questioning, in relation to the murder of Father James Cameron.'

Maura tried to put the baby back into her box, but she couldn't. Her legs wouldn't move. Within seconds, they had gone. Tommy grabbed her hand as he went past and said just two words: 'Get Jerry.'

They had left the back door open and the wind howled round the kitchen, lifting Tommy's newspaper up from the table. Maura watched as it floated back down onto the floor.

The wind suddenly slammed the back door shut, startling both Maura and the baby, who began to cry.

'Sh,' she said, as she gently rocked her. They stood in the kitchen alone, with only the sound of the radio and the tap still running, pouring cold water all over her day.

Maura ran upstairs, told Angela to wake the kids up and ready for school, then she plopped the baby down on her bed and ran out of the house, down the back entry.

At Peggy's back gate, the men stood waiting for Big Paddy.
Maura just managed to reach Jerry before her knees gave way
and buckled beneath her.

'What the hell is wrong?' Jerry asked her urgently, but realized at the same time that he already knew, as he shouted to
Sean and Big Paddy to run with him to the police station.

'Pull yerself together and don't panic,' Jerry whispered
harshly in her ear, as he escorted her back to the gate. 'They
can't break us or our alibi. Ye have to laugh hard in the face
of this, Maura, do ye understand? This has to be the most
ridiculous notion the police have ever had and ye have to look
as though nothing could bother ye less, because ye know he is
an innocent man.'

Maura nodded. 'Aye, right. I will do that. The feckin' bastards, how dare they take my husband in.'

Jerry turned back to Maura; he almost laughed at the
irony but thought better of it as he made his way to rescue his
pal.

And, as if by a miracle, before teatime Tommy walked back
into the kitchen with Jerry.

'They had nothing,' said Jerry.

'Aye, he's right,' said Tommy. 'Nothing. Same questions as
before with the same answers. Nothing.'

As Maura felt the tightness she had carried around in her
chest all day long ease away, she began to cry.

'Look, Maura,' said Jerry, 'stop fretting. If someone saw
Tommy murder the priest, or they had a murder weapon, or
a motive even, we would worry. But they haven't, they have
nothing.'

'I have a feeling they will be knocking on for Big Paddy, to
take him to the station next,' said Tommy. 'Maybe they just need

to be seen to be interviewing every male on the street. 'Twas the queerest thing I have ever been through, to be sure. It was as if they wanted not to book me. Some queer posh nob with silver ropes on his jacket shoulder came in and asked me a few questions, but nothing I couldn't answer. He was more interested in how well I knew Molly and Daisy. Stop crying now, queen,' he said as he handed Maura the mop. 'Knock on for the women. If ye don't, it will look funny. Keep everything normal.'

And Maura did. Within minutes, her kitchen was full.

The neighbours had almost laughed when they heard Tommy had been arrested, assuming the arrest was in connection with the murder of Molly. Each and every one of them knew Tommy Doherty was the softest man on the street. He wouldn't harm a hair on a dog.

''Tis a joke and an act of desperation, all right,' Peggy had said to Sheila.

'Tommy Doherty? Even his own kids aren't scared of him!'

No one knew of the whispered conversation between Maura and Tommy in bed that night.

'Why did they call you in?' Maura had asked, terrified of earnest little Harry hearing her. 'They must know something, so they must, or why have they waited all this time?'

'I don't know, Maura, but I do know this. They had nothing, because if they had, I would have been arrested and in front of a magistrate. I don't want to be bold now, but I'm saying we are safe.'

And from that night on, each day had been lighter.

Chapter Twenty-seven

ROSIE DID PAY a visit to see Kitty, just as Reverend Mother had said she would.

One of the nuns collected Kitty from the laundry in the middle of the morning. Kitty was delighted beyond measure to remove her hands from under the cold tap of the huge long sink, in which she rinsed out the carbolic from the dozens of sheets she washed each day.

She walked along the corridor with the nun, rubbing her red hands dry on her calico apron.

Kitty had no idea where she was being taken and assumed it was to Reverend Mother's office, but as they turned up the stairs to where the girls slept, she realized she was wrong. She was being led to the labour room to be examined.

Sister Assumpta had initially objected to Rosie undertaking a prenatal examination. She held no truck with such things. The Holy Mother had managed without, so why should penitent girls and those with incontinent morals deserve more?

However, Rosie had put her foot down.

'It is important for Cissy to be familiar with the surroundings she will be birthing in, Sister. I am afraid I must insist.'

Sister Assumpta was keen that Rosie leave with a good impression of the Abbey and laundry, and so with very little grumbling she agreed.

Kitty had never before entered a room that truly terrified her, but this one did. The smell of Lysol assailed her nostrils as soon as she opened the door, reminding her of her hospital stay following the accident. It was the place where the baby in her belly had been conceived, in agony and humiliation.

White and stark, the room was cold, clinical and unwelcoming. It contained no feminine comforts whatsoever. A bed with no headboard stood away from the wall, in the middle of the room, with a pole on each end, with leather straps attached.

Almost at the base of the bed was a hole cut away and tucked underneath, out of sight, was a white enamel bucket with a navy-blue rim. Apart from a white enamel trolley covered with a small snowy-white sheet, and a fully stocked white enamel cabinet with glass doors, the only ornamentation was a plaster sacred heart attached to the wall and a wooden cross above the sink.

The sheets were white. The room was white. Virginal and cold.

Along one wall ran a long and shallow sink with elongated brass taps. Piled on the wooden draining board, folded and ready, lay half a dozen or so grey-looking towels. Not white.

The large small-paned window let in almost too much light and draught. The wooden floor was bare and the air was freezing cold. No Persian carpets in here.

Rosie avoided looking at Kitty as she set down her Gladstone bag on the only wooden chair and took out an apron and some gloves. She snapped the brass clasp shut and turned round with a look of irritation.

'That will be all now, thank you, Sister,' Rosie said to the nun. 'I will examine Kitty, er, sorry, Cissy, and then call you in when the examination is over.'

The labour room was tucked away in what had been an attic, far away from the rest of the house. No nun wanted to be disturbed by the screams of girls in labour, which regularly filled the corridor outside. The only room anywhere near was the girls' dormitory across the hall.

More often than not, babies were delivered in the middle of the night and it was a short step to the labour room, without inconveniencing the nuns.

There was a midwife who lived in. Her room was on the other side of the dormitory, with a wooden hatch connecting the two. If one of the girls went into labour, they would lift up the hatch and shout through to let her know.

It was a fact that most would rather have given birth alone than in the presence of the dour and unfriendly resident midwife, who most of them doubted was even qualified at all.

Fortunately, today she had taken herself off on her bicycle into town. Rosie wondered whether that was deliberate. Maybe she didn't relish the prospect of being questioned by a midwife tutor about her training or qualifications.

The nun, with Rosie's smiling stare fixed on her, backed out slowly and quietly, hovering outside the door for what felt like an eternity. Rosie placed a finger on her lips, mouthed a 'Sh' and smiled at Kitty. After a few seconds, the nun's footsteps could be heard gently descending the wooden staircase.

'Jesus, Mary and Joseph, that was hard work,' said Rosie, turning a warmer smile towards Kitty. 'Now quick, take off your shoes, stockings and knickers, Kitty, and jump onto the bed. Shuffle down so that you are comfortable and while I am examining you, you can read these letters I have smuggled in my bag. I will have to take them away with me, so you do need to read them quick now.'

Kitty looked at Rosie with eyes wide in shock, wondering whether Rosie had already read the letters.

'Don't panic, Kitty. I will speak to no one. Your secret is safe with me. I will take it to my grave, so I will. I see lots of girls and ladies in a difficult position. I am only here to help you.'

Kitty relaxed, her fear at the prospect of an examination being replaced by the sheer joy of reading a letter from home.

'Come on,' said Rosie, in a fractionally louder and slightly urgent voice. 'They won't give us all day, you know.'

Kitty slipped off her stockings and shoes and then carefully slipped down her knickers, without revealing any of herself.

Raped and pregnant, she knew the meaning of shame.

Rosie smiled kindly and once again thought to herself: poor, desperate girl.

'Jump up,' she said, 'and make sure your bottom is about here.' She tapped the middle of the bed and helped Kitty up.

'Pull your legs up like this,' she said, as she lifted Kitty's knee up, 'and now we let it flop, down to the side just a little.'

It hurt Kitty. The muscle on the inside of her thigh, unused to being stretched in such a manner, twinged with pain.

'I know this is hard, Kitty, but I need to examine you to see how far on you may be, so that I know when to expect this baby to arrive. I have to come from Roscommon if I am at home, so it will take me a little while. I could even be at the hospital in Dublin. Once I know when your due date is, I will spend some time at Julia's and if your waters broke when I was there, well, wouldn't that be a dream now, but in my experience, no baby ever arrived when it was wanted to.'

Rosie didn't want to tell her that it was imperative she reached to the Abbey as quickly as she could. She had no intention of leaving Kitty to the mercy of the sisters, or the resident midwife.

'Do you understand what I'm saying, Kitty?'

Kitty looked up at Rosie's face, which blotted out the single bulb hanging from the centre of the ceiling. The white lamp-shade appeared as a halo around Rosie's head, shining in a perfect circle.

The word 'angel' flitted, unbidden, across Kitty's mind as she stared at Rosie's moving lips. She felt vulnerable and scared but she trusted Rosie and she had letters in her hand to read. She had to do what Rosie told her and repress her panic. Tears prickled the back of her eyes. Rosie's kindness, fear of the impending birth, the mixed emotions that hounded her about the life growing in her belly and the letters: all over-whelmed her.

'This is how we do this,' said Rosie. 'Breathe in and out, deeply, and let your muscles relax. Then read as fast as ye can. They won't give us long before one of them is back.'

Kitty wiped her eyes with the back of her hand and, pulling herself together, began to read the first letter. It was from Maura and Tommy, but there were others, from Maeve, Kathleen and Nellie.

She pulled out Maura's letter first.

Kitty felt Rosie's hand slip inside her and, with a sudden, sharp intake of breath, she clenched the side of the bed. She dropped her precious letters, which slowly fluttered down onto the floor. Every muscle in her abdomen tensed. She was terrified.

'Breathe,' said Rosie, 'in and out, just breathe, come on, sweetie. In and out, in and out.' She pursed her lips and made a sucking and blowing noise. As Kitty copied her, she felt her abdominal muscles begin to relax.

Rosie picked up the letters from the floor and handed them to Kitty. 'God, child, ye will have to read fast now, to be sure.'

Within seconds, Kitty was transported back to Liverpool, to her home and her siblings, to her life on Nelson Street. There were messages from her school friends and even a little note from Harry, written across the bottom in his perfectly formed, neat hand.

Maura's letter was full of ordinariness. No mention of Molly Barrett, or the events that had shrouded the four streets in fear.

Kitty stopped for a second as once again she tensed and grabbed the side of the bed.

'How do my mother and the other women on the four streets go through this so often?' she gasped and then continued to puff and blow her way through the letters.

They heard footsteps ascending the stairs and the door gently opened, just as Kitty finished dressing.

Rosie was at the sink, washing her hands and arms.

'I'm thinking the beginning of January,' she sang out, pretending she hadn't heard the nun enter the room.

The letters had been well and truly packed away, back into the Gladstone bag.

'Were you around when your mammy had her babbies, Cissy?' Rosie asked, briefly looking over her shoulder at Kitty, as she rinsed her hands under the tap. God help her if she hadn't been, she thought.

Rosie didn't know how this girl had become pregnant in the first place. She had been so shy, so nervous and tense, throughout the examination. Surely it was as obvious as the nose on anyone's face: Kitty was no child of the world. Whoever had made her pregnant had done so with force.

Kitty nodded.

'Well, I suppose we must be thankful for small mercies. So you will know then what happens and that you will bleed for a little while afterwards?'

Again, Kitty nodded.

'I will bind your breasts until your milk dries up, so there will be no problem there. I imagine the sisters here are used to spotting the signs of labour, aren't you, Sister?'

Rosie threw a professional smile at the nun, who nodded without any hint of a smile in return.

'I think you will be calling me around the fourth of January, Sister, or thereabouts.'

Rosie had no intention of putting this shy girl through the embarrassment of asking when her last bleed had been. The examination told her early January and that was good enough for her.

Kitty looked at Rosie, who was now writing in a foolscap notebook. Kitty dare not ask her the question now burning inside her brain. She felt a sense of bitter disappointment that the nun was there and had returned so quickly. She knew if she did ask Rosie her question, it would get straight back to the Reverend Mother, who would not be happy.

Rosie, replacing her notebook and snapping the clasp of her bag shut, immediately understood the look.

'We will have you on your way back to Maeve for a few days, to recover almost straight after the delivery. She is expecting you. Then you'll be back on your way to Liverpool, a week or so later, just as soon as you finish bleeding and your stitches heal.'

They were both shocked when the nun's timorous voice piped up, 'We don't stitch here, midwife.'

'You don't stitch?' replied Rosie in a shocked voice. 'Why

ever not? What about bad cuts and tears?'

'Reverend Mother thinks the tear is God's just punishment ...' Her voice trailed off.

'Punishment?' said Rosie.

'The resident midwife is not allowed to stitch. Reverend
Mother won't entertain it. They all heal, eventually.'

For a short moment, Rosie was speechless and then she
retorted, 'Dear God, of course they heal eventually, but we
don't live in the bogs a hundred years ago, Sister. Sutures are
a fine way to improve healing and to prevent the woman from
suffering unnecessarily. Tears should be repaired hygienically
and efficiently.'

Rosie pursed her lips. Kitty had turned a shade paler than
she had been a moment ago.

'Don't worry, Cissy.' Rosie put her hand reassuringly on
Kitty's arm and winked. 'It will all be fine and well. You have
seen Mammy deliver often enough.'

By God, she thought, this would be her delivery and she
would manage it how she liked. She took a deep breath and
decided she would not pick an argument now, but would wait
until the moment came.

'Reverend Mother has tea waiting for you in her office,' the
nun said to Rosie. To Kitty, she said, with slightly less grace,
'Sister Celia is waiting for you in the laundry.'

Rosie smiled at Kitty and said, 'Take it easy now and I will
be back in a month to check up on you again.'

Kitty almost laughed. Take it easy! The hours in the
laundry were long and hard. So hard. Every day, Kitty saw
heavily pregnant girls who had been on their feet for nine
hours, crying in pain. But there was no reprieve. Not from the
sisters of no mercy. There was only more work to be done.

They shoved and wheeled in heavy piles of dirty washing,

374

and they washed, dried and pressed until it was placed in the large wicker baskets, mounted on wheels, and taken out to the vans that arrived from Dublin to collect them. For six days a week there was no let-up and no one finished work until the day's laundry was done. On Sunday, the nuns made the girls clean out their own dorms, change their bedding and wash their own laundry, as well as feed the nuns and clean their rooms.

And all day long, the arduous toil was undertaken in silence.

It occurred to Kitty that the nuns must be earning a great deal of money for the laundry that the girls heaved in and out through the doors.

Even knowing what she did about the Abbey, Kitty didn't imagine for one moment that the Reverend Mother would find reasons to refuse Rosie entry to the Abbey until she was due. Her biggest fear was that they wouldn't tell Rosie when she went into labour. She knew that was a possibility.

Kitty was scared.

Chapter Twenty-eight

IT WAS THE night before Christmas Eve. Tommy and Maura made sure they arrived at the school over half an hour early. They wanted to be at the front of the hall and bag the best seats, those behind the reserved rows at the front, which were a constant source of irritation to Tommy, especially if they were behind the seat reserved for Mrs Skyes.

Mrs Sykes lived on Menlove Avenue in the posh houses and provided regular donations to the sisters. Her husband, a shipping merchant, had died many years ago, since when Mrs Sykes had discovered that loneliness was the preserve of the poor. She quickly learnt that the gentle and careful disbursement of funds bought respect, position and somewhere to go. In a hat. To a seat marked 'reserved'.

Tommy never failed to grumble when he visited the school. He began the moment he walked in through the big double doors.

As he had spent his childhood in the shadow of his stable-hand father, schools made Tommy feel uncomfortable and inadequate.

If it hadn't been for their Kitty, he wouldn't even be able to read. The school reminded Tommy of all he had failed to achieve. His neck burnt red and itched.

As they walked into the hall, which smelt of lavender wax,

Maura heard Sheila call out to them both through the open hatch of the cavernous kitchen beyond. The two giant-sized Burco boilers were starting to steam and simmer. Huge dark-brown teapots stood waiting to be filled, just before the interval. Sheila was laying out cups and saucers at the hatch and pouring milk into the copper jugs.

A smell of stale mashed potato and gravy from lunchtime hung in the air.

'Keep us a seat, Maura,' Sheila called across, as Maura and Tommy walked down the hall between the rows of chairs that Harry and the other boys had taken down from the tall stacks and placed into position, ready for the nativity play.

'I will, queen,' Maura shouted back, as she and Tommy headed straight for the best seats at the front.

Under his breath Tommy muttered to Maura, 'If Mrs bleedin' Sykes has no kids at the school, why does she have a better view of our kids than we do?'

Maura was mortified.

Far too loudly, Tommy added, 'Jaysus, the size of that woman's hat. Is no one here going to ask her to take the feckin' thing off, eh, eh?'

They trotted down the hall in their rush to reach the front.

'Get behind the bishop, Maura,' Tommy said, 'at least he's bald.'

All four twins had a part in the nativity play. As Joseph, Harry was one of the stars of the show. The other Doherty boys were two sheep and a goat.

Little Paddy was in charge of the lights. He skilfully manned the dimmer switch as parents and children began to filter into the hall. Having looked up at the ceiling to check all was in order, he proudly scuttled back to his seat. Tommy gave him a wink as he passed.

'Good lad, Paddy, well done.'

Little Paddy grinned from ear to ear.

The lights on the Christmas tree at the side of the stage twinkled brightly, casting an iridescent glow across the hall. Watching them sparkle in the dark for the first time, the children gasped, their excitement beyond containment.

They were just hours from Christmas Eve and the hall was infused with an air of anticipation. Children who were used to behaving in an orderly manner, within the confines of the school, were now wriggling on their seats, whispering in loud voices, articulating their hopes and dreams for Christmas morning. Most of them were aware that an orange on the end of the bed would be their only luxury.

Kathleen arrived and sat down in the seat next to Maura. 'Where's Alice?' asked Maura.

'Not feeling too well,' Kathleen whispered back. 'Says she will come along in a while if she feels any better.'

The programme on the seats informed them that Brigid and Sean's daughter, Grace, was playing Mary.

Both Tommy and Maura felt their hearts crunch. They knew that Kitty had been Sister Evangelista's favourite. This year would have been her last year at the school. If Kitty were home, she would be Mary.

'Grand,' said Maura, in a falsely jovial manner, 'isn't that wonderful, Grace being Mary and our Harry her Joseph? Them knowing each other since they were babbies, like?'

She wanted to be pleased for Brigid and Grace, and fought with every ounce of good nature she had to sound more delighted than she felt.

'Are Brigid and Sean here?' Maura asked Kathleen.

'No,' whispered Kathleen, 'not Sean, he is in town for a

match tonight. It's a big one, apparently, good money if he wins. Brigid is on her way.'

'How good?' Maura's curiosity knew no manners.

'Five hundred pounds. Can ye imagine?'

Maura couldn't. She had never even seen that amount of money.

The remaining money needed to free Kitty seemed like a mountain to climb to Maura at the present, and there was Sean, who could be walking home with five hundred.

'Imagine that,' Maura half-whispered thoughtfully, more to herself than Kathleen.

Maura knew Jerry, with only one child, had saved a great deal and Kathleen had money from the farm, but it was obvious that even Kathleen was impressed by such an amount.

'Aye, imagine,' said Kathleen. 'And all he has to do is to beat the shite out of someone. My lads did nothing else when they were at school. If I had only known there was money in it, I'd have had Joe encourage them. Oh, here you go, sh,' she said, 'here they come.'

She waved to Brigid and Mrs McGuire, and pointed to the seats next to her. Brigid had the youngest baby tucked in her arms, wrapped in a crocheted blanket of many colours. Behind them was Peggy, ushering her brood into the seats. Big Paddy didn't attend school plays or parents' evenings. He had no interest in his offspring's activities and had viewed the nativity play as a good opportunity to escape down to the pub for a sneaky hour or two.

'Thanks for keeping the seats, Kathleen,' whispered Brigid, pulling a face at Mrs Sykes's hat, directly in front of her.

Peggy squeezed along and sat next to Kathleen, just as Kitty's teacher, Miss Devlin, appeared. Leaning forward, she whispered down the row, 'No more smoking now, please, ladies.' Lifting her hand up to her mouth as though to channel her words in a straight line: 'Mrs Sykes doesn't like it.'

Peggy turned to the others. 'Merciful God, she has to be fuckin' jokin', doesn't she? It's at least an hour until the break, once it starts. If yer allowed to smoke at the filums, why can't we smoke here? That's desperate.'

Mrs Sykes's hat wobbled in indignation. She had obviously overheard Peggy.

Maura put her finger to her lips and made the sound of a silent sh.

Peggy was having none of it.

'Mrs McGuire,' Peggy said, 'would ye mind swapping seats with me so that I can get out quick, like, in the break. I'm not even allowed to smoke in me own children's school now, so I'm not. Did ye ever hear of anything that took such a liberty?'

Anticipation fizzed through the air as Sister Evangelista appeared at the front of the school hall.

As she scanned the assembly before her with steely eyes, the children nudged each other sharply in the ribs. Like a gentle wave washing over the gathering, the chatter began to subside, starting at the front with those closest to her, until only Little Paddy's voice could still be heard.

'Me da will be here in a minute, he will, Declan, he's just gone to get his ciggies, he has so. Mammy, isn't me daddy on his way?'

The realization that the entire audience was listening to him dawned only as Sister Evangelista spoke. 'See me after the play, Paddy, and not another word now, boy.'

And then, as if by magic, her face broke into the brightest smile.

'Parents, ladies and gentlemen, special guests.'

'I suppose if I'm a parent, that means I'm no lady then,' said Peggy under her breath.

Maura and Kathleen looked at each other and smiled.

Kathleen reached across and gave Maura's hand a squeeze.

Kathleen hoped that Christmas would mark a turning point for Tommy and Maura.

Maura looked at Kathleen as she squeezed her hand, the best friend in all the world. Maura smiled back.

Sister Evangelista continued, 'Welcome to the St Mary's nativity play acted out by your children, in honour of the birth of our Lord, Jesus Christ. Before we begin, I have a little announcement to make. Many of you will know Daisy from the Priory.'

Everyone turned to look at Daisy who was at the hatch, quietly helping Miss Devlin to fold Christmas napkins for the interval.

'Well, tomorrow morning Daisy will be leaving Liverpool and returning to Dublin, to live with her family.'

For a second the hall fell quiet, apart from the odd sharp intake of breath, and then without warning or planning the audience erupted into applause.

Sister Evangelista beamed as she joined in, as Daisy flushed bright red and grinned from ear to ear. Miss Devlin gently placed her arm round her as the applause continued.

It had been a shock indeed when the bishop had called to see Sister Evangelista in a very agitated state.

'I have a letter from Daisy's family,' he announced indignantly. 'They are stopping the money and want her back.'

'Well, praise be,' Sister Evangelista had said, 'isn't that

wonderful news? I thought her parents wanted her cared for all of her life?'

'They did,' said the bishop, who was sweating profusely.

It crossed Sister Evangelista's mind that he was heading for a heart attack.

'The parents have died and the elder brother, a state solicitor, found out about the arrangement when sorting through the estate. He wants Daisy back. Here, read the letter.'

He thrust the letter into Sister Evangelista's hands. As she read it, her heart filled with warmth and happiness.

Her prayers were being answered: prayers for God's love and light to shine into their darkness, to banish to the shadows the evil that had lived amongst them for so long. Poor Daisy, she thought, she had been living in the midst of it all and none of them had known.

'But this is a wonderful outcome, Bishop,' she said, handing the letter back to him. 'He is a good Catholic, ashamed that his parents felt they couldn't raise Daisy, and they want to make amends. Surely this is wonderful news.'

The bishop grunted. 'He wanted to collect her from the convent but I have told them we will put her on the boat tomorrow, Christmas Eve. That way they can have their precious Daisy back for Christmas Day. I wonder if they have asked themselves where she would be if it hadn't been for us caring for her all this time?'

'Where would we have been without all that money, Bishop?'

Sister Evangelista asked the last question quietly. She knew how much they were paid. The family had obviously been very wealthy. She had often wondered to herself whether or not Daisy's family knew that their daughter was working as a housekeeper for so many years. She suspected not.

'Well, we shall send Daisy off with our blessing, Father. Only you and I know what that poor girl was living with in the Priory.'

In the midst of the clapping, the children began to cheer for Daisy.

And tears began to roll down her cheeks.

She couldn't believe what was happening to her.

She had made Miss Devlin read over and over again the letter her brother had written to her.

They had both laughed and cried together the first half-dozen or so times they had read it. Now she didn't need anyone to read it to her, because she could hear Miss Devlin's voice and the words. They were fixed in her mind. She wandered round in a daze as she went over and over them.

'*I am your older brother, and my wife and I want you to be back in your home and in the heart of your family, where you were meant to be, with your two sisters, your nieces and nephews, and me.*'

Daisy had barely been able to sleep since reading those words. She had a home and a family who loved and wanted her. She would never again see the bishop and never again have to endure him. She was going home to be safe.

Her only sadness was that she couldn't tell Molly, and so Daisy told her in her prayers instead.

Now, Sister Evangelista walked towards Daisy, with a present wrapped up in Christmas paper. All the children began chanting, 'Open it, Daisy, open it, Daisy.'

In front of two hundred children and their parents, and with the help of Miss Devlin, Daisy unwrapped the present and took out of a box a delicate hat. It was the most beautiful thing she had ever seen in her life. As everyone clapped again,

Miss Devlin, who was trying hard not to cry, reached up and placed it onto Daisy's head.

'Spare hatpin, anyone?' Miss Devlin shouted over to the parents who were all sitting hatless, in curlers.

Every pair of eyes turned on Mrs Sykes who, for the first time that night, smiled as she took a pin from her own hat and passed it along the row.

'We hope one day you will come back and visit us, Daisy,' said Sister Evangelista. 'We would all love to hear your news, once you have settled in Dublin, and you know that we will always be your family.'

Brigid leant over to Maura. 'Would Jesus have allowed reserved signs on chairs in a church, Maura? Would he?' she whispered, nodding towards the great and good in the row in front. 'And would he not have said big hats were barred altogether?'

Maura nodded and grinned. Sister Evangelista's voice faded away into a blur as Maura took in the scene around her.

For a second, her gaze alighted on her own children's shining faces. Sitting on their hands, wriggling in their seats, they fixed their eyes upon the stage, waiting, with pent-up anticipation, for the play to begin.

The lights dimmed further and their eyes, reflecting the bright spotlights shining on the empty makeshift stable in front of the stage, sparkled with excitement like stars sprinkled in a dark night sky.

Maura's gaze found Angela, sitting with her younger sisters, her arms folded. She was the only one not smiling, or covertly whispering and fidgeting. But even her normally grumpy expression had softened. Maura remembered what Kitty had been like at her youngest sister's age, barely able to keep still. Maura's love for her children was, as always, brimming under the surface. She took immense pleasure from watching them, when they didn't know she was looking, something she did all the time.

As she watched Angela and her sisters she thought to herself, no harm will come to any of ye. I have eyes in the back of me head now.

Six little ones from the primary class now took their seats at the side of the stage and picked up their triangles and tambourines ready for the carol singing.

As they tinkered with their instruments and Sister Evangelista peeped behind the curtain to see whether everyone was ready to begin, the spirit of Christmas swept through the hall and touched all in its way. Maura noticed Angela smile as one of her sisters took her hand and stretched up to whisper in her big sister's ear.

She looked at Peggy, who was checking for ciggies in her pocket, so that she could make a run for the door in the break.

Maura, who had thought that this Christmas would be a miserable affair, unexpectedly felt a nostalgic pull from all the Christmases past, familiar and comforting.

Nothing any of them said or did tonight was out of the ordinary or unexpected, and that was just how she wanted their lives to be forever more. Ordinary.

Everything was as it always was and always had been. Almost.

Tommy squeezed her knee and smiled at her. The spirit of Christmas had touched him, too.

Suddenly, the hall burst into applause. Sheila's eldest was pulling hard on a big rope at the side of the stage and the curtain began to lift slowly. Maura watched as her precious Harry walked into the pool of light at the front of the stage.

The tea towel was his headdress.

A striped dressing gown his cloak.

A pared branch his staff.

Maura's eyes filled with tears of pride.

Kitty wasn't here. Things weren't right, but they were better.

They were still in the darkest tunnel, but she could see the light at the end and there was her Harry, standing in the middle.

It was seven o'clock sharp as the curtain went up. Miss Devlin walked from the back of the hall to the front foyer and closed the large wooden doors to the school, prohibiting further entrance. Lateness was intolerable, both in children and in adults. Pity the parent working late.

There would be no room in the hall.

As the large bolt slid across the door, Alice emerged from the shadows of the high convent wall opposite.

A few moments earlier, she had felt an overwhelming urge to walk towards the light that poured out of the school doors and tumbled down the steps to the playground.

She felt an ache, deep in the pit of her stomach, that made her long to be a part of the warm laughter. The temptation to belong was almost irresistible.

For seconds, she teetered on the brink of running into the school hall and confessing everything to Kathleen. Kathleen, the older woman who had saved her. The mother she had dreamt of having, all through her childhood nights, and whom she now truly loved. The only woman who for years had ever shown her kindness.

Kathleen had ripped away the memories that tied and bound Alice to her past.

Kathleen, her saviour.

Alice wondered if she would ever be forgiven for what she

was about to do, but she knew the answer was probably not, ever.

Tall Victorian street lamps lined both sides of the road that sloped gently down towards the town.

Alice moved to stand underneath one, imagining that some warmth might penetrate her frozen bones. She looked again to catch sight of the bus. Maybe he wouldn't catch the bus to the school. Maybe he would alight at the stop before, so as not to be seen, and walk the rest of the way.

Alice laughed out loud. What would it matter?

'Oh, please let him win,' she whispered to herself, noticing her frozen breath hanging in the air and wondering at how dramatically the temperature had dropped in the past hour.

The wide cobbled road had been built to accommodate shire horses and carriages, pulling flat-bed loads from the docks to the processors. It was quiet and eerie now. Nothing had passed by for the past ten minutes.

From the shadows cast by the wall, Alice had silently observed the sisters as they crossed the road from the convent to the school, excitedly chattering to each other as they bustled in to see the nativity play, a highlight in their calendar year.

The biting cold now cut through to the bone as Alice pulled her coat tighter. Her eyes began to water as, full in the face of the icy northerly that lifted up from the river, she stared down the hill, willing him to come quickly.

Flinching from the rising wind, she turned towards the classroom windows.

Inside would be the desk and chair where one day soon Joseph would sit. She conjured up an image of his dark hair and his freckled face as he looked at a blackboard and then wrote earnestly in his notebook. Alice knew, she could tell already, Joseph would be bright. He was as inquisitive as he was funny. Joseph, the little man she had come to love.

She imagined his short legs dashing down the steps with his brown leather satchel flying in the air behind him and his face beaming as he ran to someone. Who is it? Alice thought, looking eagerly at the gate, now shrouded in darkness, where during the day the mothers stood waiting and chatting. Many arrived early to engage in the school-gate gossip. Whom will he run to? Who will it be? There was someone at the gate, she thought, moving back into the deeper darkness – but she couldn't make out who it was, waiting to greet the excited, laughing Joseph.

The icy wind slapped her across the face and made her eyes sting. She closed them for a second.

In her own darkness, she saw herself in Joseph's bedroom. He was fast asleep, his little head lay on the pillow, Nellie's old and threadbare teddy tucked under his arm. One thumb, half in his mouth, having slipped out as he had fallen into a deep sleep. His soft, flannelette, blue-and-white striped pyjamas kept him warm. As always, he had kicked off the pale blue cot-blanket that Kathleen had knitted and the beautiful, hand-made, white lace cover his Auntie Maeve had sent across from Ireland.

She could smell his powdery, sleep-filled room.

Her heart felt as though it were in a vice as in her mind's eye his angelic face softened with the laughter of a dream.

She saw her boy, waking up on Christmas morning, every room in the house smelling of the turkey Kathleen had slowly roasted in the range overnight.

She saw Joseph running into the bedroom to wake everyone, in his haste to open the presents under the tree.

The previous Christmas, Jerry had made Nellie wait on the stairs as he held the door to the kitchen closed, pretending that Father Christmas had forgotten her.

'Has he been?' said Jerry, peeping through the door, opening it just a crack, pretending he could see the tree. 'Oh, no, I don't think he has, Nana Kathleen. I think Miss Nellie can't have been a very good girl this year.'

They drove her crazy as she playfully pummelled Jerry's back with her fists, in an effort to push past.

Alice replayed the scene in her mind. She had stood at the top of the stairs, watching, smiling, not really a part of what was happening. Observing in her usual way, from the edge.

Will he think of me? she asked herself. Will he remember who I am? Will he run home from school with the others and wonder where his mammy is?

She began to shiver with the cold and then she felt it on her skin, the first snowflake of Christmas. She looked up into the wind. It was as if the angels had opened a trapdoor. The snow fell heavy and fast. In less than a minute, the pavement on which she stood was white, her shoulders were heavily dusted and, despite the swirling wind, it began to settle.

Once more, she glanced directly down the road, into the wind and through the snow. Still no sign.

When she had explained her plan to him, he hadn't wanted her to wait at the school.

'Don't go out, Alice,' he had said. 'Just say you're unwell and stay at home. I will come straight there.'

But she couldn't. She was compelled to leave. She hadn't wanted to see them getting ready. She couldn't bear to kiss Joseph goodbye. He would have been full of excitement at being taken to the big school for the play. Joseph was always beside himself with delight when in the company of other children.

Alice had made an excuse about having dreadful toothache and said that she would take herself off to the dentist in town.

'Oh, that's just desperate now, ye poor thing.' Kathleen's face had instantly become a picture of love and concern.

'I will be fine, Kathleen. It's happened before. I may be a while, though, and I won't feel like going to the school afterwards. I will just come home and go straight to bed.'

'Best thing, queen,' Kathleen had said as she busied about making an early tea before they left.

Alice had hidden in the shadows and watched them all arrive. Nellie had pushed the pram up the hill and Kathleen had held onto Nellie's arm.

'Ooh, I'm blowing for tugs,' she had heard Kathleen gasp.

Alice had felt like a ghost. She could see and hear all but she was invisible.

She had seen Peggy, smoking as she walked, with a gaggle of children round her, nervously squealing and jumping up and down, running ahead of Peggy, up the steps to the entrance. It seemed as if every young woman from the four streets had filed into the hall, chatting in that companionable way that had always eluded Alice.

She knew that Joseph was now inside the school hall, happy and warm, sitting on Nellie's or Kathleen's knee, and here she was, back where she had begun, on the outside looking in.

She had tried to explain her feelings to Sean.

'My marriage to Jerry was a symptom of my illness and of the person I had once been. I want to leave that person behind.

I am whole now. I have fallen in love all by myself, without manipulation or deceit and it feels the most amazing thing. I cannot stay and live a lie and nor can you, but what is worse is that if we do, we have to carry on with our old lives and see each other every day. I could not bear that.'

Alice looked down at her shoes. They were buried in snow. The school door and the windows of the classroom opposite had taken the full force of the wind and both were plastered in the white powder.

On each pane of the sash windows, a hand-made paper Christmas decoration peeped through the snow. Soon, one of them would have 'Joseph Deane, Class 1' written on the back.

But Alice would never see it.

She felt her insides crunch. The school gate was still shrouded in darkness and yet the feeling that she wasn't alone was stronger than before.

Applause suddenly reverberated through the school doors and then, after a short time, she heard voices. Children were singing the beautiful haunting first notes of a carol she recognized from her own unhappy school days. 'Silent Night'. And it was. A very silent night.

She doubted now if she could do it. Maybe Sean was right. Maybe meeting him at the school had been the wrong thing to do.

Already the pain of missing Joseph was intense. She would never hear or see him sing 'Silent Night' with his school friends.

The strains of 'Little Donkey' followed, pouring out into the snow-filled air. Was Joseph trying to sing? He would be looking up at his Nellie and trying his best to join in. A child in a hurry to grow up. His world was perfect, his routine stable. He was surrounded by people who loved and adored him, but she wasn't there. She knew he would be looking for her. He would turn his little head to the door when he saw a fleeting shadow pass. He would look seriously at Nellie when she said to him, 'Mammy may be here soon, if she's feeling better.'

Pain and doubt ripped through her heart.

She turned and saw his figure emerge over the brow of the hill, walking slowly towards her, his head bent against the driving snow. His hands were thrust deeply into his pockets and his long overcoat kicked out before him.

When he reached her, she saw his face in the lamplight. One eye was closed and filled with blood. She had never seen him look so bad.

'Sean,' she whispered, 'oh my God, are you all right?'

Sean looked at her frozen face. Her hat was covered in snow and if he hadn't been in so much pain, he would have laughed. 'I'm fine,' he replied. 'You won't even know I've been in a fight a week from now.'

'Did you win?'

Alice almost didn't want to know. If he hadn't won, nothing would have altered. Half of her felt a sense of relief at that prospect, the half that wanted to stay with her son and to watch him grow into manhood. The other half, that loved Sean to the point of pain, willed him to have won his fight. If he had, they would take the morning passage to New York.

'I won,' he said, placing his hand on her elbow and looking around. 'I have put an envelope with money on the mantel for Brigid and I have already left both our bags at the hotel. We can do it, Alice. We can sail to America in the morning.'

Conflicting emotions tore through Alice. She wanted to shriek with excitement at the prospect of realizing her dream and also to cry with grief at all she was leaving behind.

Tears poured down her cheeks.

'Have ye changed your mind?' asked Sean.

Their future hung on her answer.

They had agreed that if they didn't take passage to America together, then their illicit affair must stop and they would both spend the rest of their lives in agony, each knowing the other was only yards away, under a different roof, married to someone else.

Neither of them could bear that thought. It would be impossible. Alice thought she would rather die than have to live through that kind of misery.

Sean put his arm round her shoulder and turned her towards the brow of the hill. 'Come on, Alice,' he said, kissing her on the temple. 'We have to, before anyone leaves and sees us.'

They both turned and walked into the wind and drifting snow. Alice was now sobbing quietly. Sean understood. The pain he felt at leaving his daughters was intense, but he thought that Alice's heartache as a mother must surely be worse.

'As soon as we are settled, we will send for them to visit us, or we will sail back and see them. We aren't leaving them for ever, Alice.'

She turned her head to look back at the school.

'Little Donkey' was reaching an end. She could hear applause yet again and laughter, and then she saw a movement at the gate. Someone else had been there all along. Who could it be?

The snow was driving into her eyes and forcing herself to blink, but she saw her. It was definitely her.

Against the frosty whiteness, Alice could not doubt the wild red hair swirling in the midst of what had become a blizzard. Bernadette. The dead wife and mother whose place Alice had stolen, with deceit and lies. Bernadette looked at Alice and her gaze was one of deep sadness, deeper than anything Alice had ever known.

She stood rigid in shock.

'Alice, come on, we have to hurry,' said Sean urgently. 'Come on, queen, what's up? Ye look like you've seen a ghost.'

The moment the the singing stopped and the clapping began, Peggy took herself to the front of the school and tried to push back the bolts on the wooden door.

Little Paddy had done his job of turning up the lights and everyone was gathered round the school hatch for their mince pie and cup of tea.

One of the classrooms had been opened up and orange squash and mince pies were being served to the children. For some of them, those whose parents often skipped mass and spent their wages in the pub, it was the only treat they would enjoy all Christmas.

Once Little Paddy had finished his chore, he ran to help Peggy open the door. Sliding back the bolt, they both gave a gasp of shock as they saw the snow, already over an inch deep.

Little Paddy grabbed the sleeve of his mother's coat. 'Do ye see that?' he yelled in surprise. 'It's snowing!'

'Merciful God, we could do without that, all right,' said Peggy, grudgingly putting her foot onto the first step. 'Here, Paddy, give me yer hand.'

Little Paddy put out his arm to help his mother down the steps.

Peggy was wearing her usual old slippers with no stockings. She had neither the time nor the money to be fussing with stockings and suspender belts.

'Just another thing to wash,' she would say to anyone who troubled to ask.

Within seconds, the cold had made the varicose veins around her ankles protrude like bunches of black grapes.

'Holy Mary, it's fecking cold out here, Paddy,' she muttered, as they negotiated the steps. 'I'll stand here, lad,' she said, once they got to the second step. 'It's far enough away from precious Mrs Sykes.'

Little Paddy left his mother as quickly as he could and ran into the classroom, yelling, 'It's snowing outside!' Within seconds, Peggy was engulfed as children flew down the steps on either side of her.

'Oh, would ye look at that,' said Nellie, running to Peggy's side. Peggy smiled. The front yard was full of children shouting and throwing snow into the air.

Nellie crouched down beside Peggy to make a snowball, but the snow just crumbled into powder in her hands. Peggy looked up and down the road to see if there were any buses running.

It took her a minute to make out what she had seen, but once she was sure, she knew.

As Nellie stood up, Peggy spoke to her. 'Nellie, would ye run back inside, queen, and ask Nana Kathleen to come outside to me.'

'Now?' said Nellie.

'Yes please, queen,' said Peggy, 'now.'

Peggy knew they would be over the brow by the time Kathleen reached the front door, but she wanted to protect Nellie. Fetching Kathleen had been a ruse.

'Well, well, well,' said Peggy, out loud. 'My lad's not a liar, after all.'

Peggy pondered as she watched Alice and Sean disappear into the town; what should she say and to whom.

They were walking briskly down the candlelit corridor to Compline. Kitty felt uncomfortable. She had been lost in her own thoughts, recalling Rosie's words. Some time in January. She could be home in just a few weeks. The tightening round her waist now began each time she walked, but the girls had warned her, it was just her body rehearsing, preparing her muscles for the delivery.

As she looked closely at Aideen walking along beside her, it occurred to Kitty that she would soon miss her friend. How could she help her to leave this horrible place? she wondered. Surely there must be a way? Her thoughts were distracted as, once more, her abdomen clenched.

Later the following morning, Aideen and Kitty were both in the laundry, ironing shirts. Sister Celia, who watched over them to ensure there was no talking, had taken herself away for a moment, reprimanding Aideen as she went for not pressing the collars crisply enough.

'Probably gone to stuff her face with another slice of cake,' Aideen grumbled as the laundry-room door closed. 'God, that woman is a scold. She never stops bellyaching at me. We will see that cake sat on her fat arse when she comes back in.'

Kitty laughed, but she didn't know how she had done it. The baby she carried was so heavy and she had been on her feet for hours. She felt as though the baby would just drop out, so great was the pressure.

'Will ye be able to get out of this place soon, Aideen?' she asked, looking up from her ironing. Beside her stood a large wicker basket on wheels, only half empty. Kitty's job was to iron the whole lot before the day was over.

'Well, I would, if I had the money to buy my way out.'

Once again, Kitty felt lucky that she had people who cared for her. Aideen was looking at spending at least three years of her life in the laundry. It was worse than a prison sentence.

Aideen was not going to waste the advantage presented by Sister Celia's absence. When the opportunity arose, the girls spoke twice as fast as normal, making up for lost time and hours of imposed silence.

'Sure, some who've been sent by the government are here for ever, so they are, and some lucky ones leave when they have paid with three years' work in the laundry and have somewhere to go to. The bitches still charge the Americans for the adoptions, though. The poor kids get taken from their mammies when they are three. The tears and the wailing on those days would rip yer heart out, it's shocking, so it is.'

Kitty knew, she had heard it. At first, as she was one of the girls who was never allowed to visit the nursery and, as there was no conversation permitted, she had no idea what was happening until it was one of the girls in her own dormitory who had her little girl taken.

Kitty folded her shirt neatly, placed it on the pile and then took another out of the large wicker basket.

She was wondering why the girls didn't escape like the one called Besmina.

The Gardai had been to the home twice. The girls had gathered from the whispering nuns that Besmina had not been found.

'It's the reason we aren't allowed to speak. The girls who are here for ever, who have been sent by the government, have done nothing wrong. Some are just orphans and, God knows, one was sent here because she was so gorgeous, the lads in the village kept whistling at her. She's in the asylum now. I saw them take her myself in a van, strapped up. Some of them even get pregnant whilst they are in here. Now tell me, how the fuck does that happen?'

Kitty whispered back, 'They can't have done nothing, they must have done something wrong. It's illegal to lock someone up for nothing.'

'Oh, sure it is, Kitty, yer right about that,' said Aideen. 'This place is feckin' illegal. That's why we aren't allowed to talk. The nuns are getting bloody rich on the back of girls who are sent here by the authorities and ending their days here as slaves, for nothing more than being raped by their own brother or the feckin' priest, which was beyond their own doing.'

Kitty almost dropped the iron. She stood for a second and put her hands inside the pocket of the apron she was wearing. There were other girls here who had been raped by a priest? She wasn't the only one?

Aideen, who hadn't noticed Kitty's shock, continued, 'Some of them are got pregnant by the priests whilst they are in here and no one says a fucking thing. It's as though they are invisible. One of the older women in here has had three babies in twenty years. Either the immaculate conception is common in places like this or Father Samuel is having his end away and no one gives a fucking flying shite.'

Kitty put her hand on to the side of the ironing table to hold herself up.

'Are ye all right?' asked Aideen.

'I'm OK, I just felt a bit weird, like,' said Kitty.

'Sit down then, for feck's sake, ye look as white as that shirt.'

Kitty could hardly believe what she was hearing. She had been sent here because of a priest. She had thought he was the only one in the world to behave in that way and yet here she was, being told by Aideen that, even in the Abbey, no one was safe from a predatory priest.

At that moment, Sister Celia walked back into the room. The telltale signs of cake crumbs clung to the front of her black habit.

'Are you two talking?' she shouted. 'What are ye staring at, girl?'

Kitty was wearing an odd expression. Her mouth was open and her eyes looked wild, but she made not a sound.

Kitty thought the room suddenly seemed much brighter and hotter than it had before. And then it came. A pain that felt as though someone had placed a band of metal round what was once her waist and was slowly, slowly, tightening it, relentlessly, in a painful contraction.

Kitty heard a piercing scream coming from somewhere in the room. And then she realized the scream was her own. Without warning, a gush of warm water cascaded down her legs and formed a large puddle on the floor. At the same time, the metal band began to slowly, slowly loosen its grip.

Kitty began to sob. She had no idea what she was saying, but she knew she was crying for help.

Aideen rushed forward and took both of her hands.

'Get the disgusting thing out of here,' Sister Celia screamed at Aideen.

They both knew, without asking her to explain, that the disgusting thing was Kitty.

Sister Celia then shouted to one of the girls from across the room, who were now looking over the top of a sink, 'And stop yer gawping, you filthy lot, and get this mess mopped up.'

Sister Celia hated it more than anything else on earth when the girls went into labour in the laundry. She would avoid it at all costs. Sometimes she even pleaded with the nuns who worked on the other sections of the laundry, not to send her the girls who were far gone. She had had no choice with Kitty.

God alone knew why they had accepted that girl. The Reverend Mother had been on pins since the day she had arrived and Besmina had escaped. Reverend Mother hated anyone knowing the Abbey's business. Sister Celia had been stuck with the girl. And now her worst fear had been realized and, God knew, she hated it.

The screams, the pain, the mess: they were the audible and visible manifestation of sin. Sister Celia became agitated. She was surrounded by sin, breaking free and setting itself loose in her laundry. It leaked, it oozed, it ran and it smelt. Sin escaped.

And, God forbid, now sin was laughing at her, sat in a puddle on her laundry-room floor.

Chapter Twenty-nine

THE WOMEN STOOD just inside the school entrance, whilst the children ran and screamed in the playground, full of excitement at the arrival of snow. And on the night before Christmas Eve.

Sister Evangelista would normally be irritated by the delay. Tonight was different. She even huddled up with the rest of the women, an unlikely member of the gang. The icy wind whistled in, bringing with it light dustings of snow lifted from the playground. Once in through the door, they dropped and immediately melted. Even in the short time that the women had waited and despite the appearance of muddy puddles on the highly polished, parquet floor, Sister Evangelista remained in a good mood.

She was happy with how the evening had gone.

Brigid and Mrs McGuire moved tentatively down the steps to the playground, and began rounding up the McGuire children and shook the snow off the pram apron. Brigid carried the baby in her arms.

'Holy Mother, would ye look at this,' she exclaimed, brushing the inch of snow from the pram canopy and lifting out the pillow to give that a shake, too.

'It'll not last long, it never does in Liverpool. Sean says it's because of the Gulf Stream. I've only ever seen the river meself.'

'It was still here in March last year, Brigid. I hope this isn't it for another three months,' said Mrs Mcguire.

'Will I go to the chippy, Brigid?' Mrs McGuire asked hopefully. She saw the frown on Brigid's face. She knew Brigid had mashed potatoes and gravy waiting for supper.

'Oh, go on, it'll be a little snow treat for the children now. It's not every day it snows and you know I like to treat them, when I'm here.'

'I'd rather that the children looked to your heart, Mrs McGuire, not your hand,' chided Brigid, but they both knew Mrs McGuire would win. 'Oh, go on then,' she said. 'Take Patricia with ye. I will start getting the others changed and ready for bed. Don't forget Sean, he might have something to celebrate tonight.'

Mrs McGuire was feeling confident. If Sean won tonight, he would surely persuade Brigid to move to America and join their Mary and Eddie, wouldn't that be just fantastic. With his own money and not dependent on others, he would be free to travel over first and then send for his family very shortly afterwards.

Mrs McGuire had it all planned out. She would travel over with Brigid and the children, and they would all settle in Chicago together.

Sean had always agreed with her but, over the past few weeks, she had found it impossible to engage him in conversations about America in the way she used to.

She had put it down to the big fight he was having tonight.

The big Liverpool Christmas fight, on the same night as the nativity play.

Mrs McGuire knew her son. He was a secretive one, all

right, always had been. Only she knew how desperate he was to reach Chicago. Liverpool was too restrictive. The tales of big wages he had heard about in Ireland before he arrived were out of all proportion to the reality.

In Liverpool, if you arrived poor, you stayed poor. This was not the case in America, as their Mary and her husband had demonstrated. America was full of opportunity.

Mrs McGuire linked arms with Patricia, so that she didn't slip in the snow, and they strode off together towards Jonny Chan's, smiling and happy.

Jerry took hold of Nellie's arm and Kathleen shuffled in beside Nellie, wheeling the pram. Nellie thought she would attempt to ice-skate, like she had seen on the black-and-white television last week, and within seconds was flat on her back on the pavement. Jerry and Kathleen roared with laugher and Joseph, with his face peeping out from his hand-knitted bala-clava, clapped his hands in excitement.

Kathleen smiled. 'I've never, in my entire life, seen a baby laugh and smile as much as he does, Jer,' she said.

'It warms my heart every day, so it does, to see how great Alice is with the little fellow.'

Jerry put his arm round his mammy's shoulder and placed a kiss on the top of her head.

'Get away with ye, Jerry, are ye going soft altogether?'

Nellie laughed. They were all three full of Christmas cheer.

Kathleen held onto the pram; Nellie held onto her nana; Jerry, on the outside, held Nellie's hand.

A warm glow wrapped around them.

The deep companionship of the three. Virgin snow that sparkled like glitter on the pavement. The sound of the children's breathless laughter. The crisp freshness of the air. The promise of a white Christmas Eve to wake up to. The beautiful, loving baby boy grinning at them from the warmth and comfort of his pram.

They walked in companionable silence aware that they would remember this night for ever.

When they reached Nelson Street, Maura and Tommy turned and waved goodnight to them.

'Nana, it won't be long until Kitty is home, will it?' said Nellie.

Kathleen squeezed Nellie's hand and smiled at her. Trust Nellie to be always thinking of others, she thought.

'Aye, I know, queen, and a blessing that will be, for sure.'

As they reached their door, Malachi ran past, screeching at the top of his voice, as he chased Harry and Little Paddy, with a ball of snow in his hands, ready to shove down the back of both their necks.

Older neighbours, who hadn't been to the school, were peeping round their net curtains to see what all the noise was about. The news of snow was heralded by excited cries.

'Da, Da, save me,' Harry squealed as he ran past.

Maura had stepped indoors. Tommy stood in the middle of the road, not daring to run, yelling at the top of his voice, 'Malachi, get here now, or I'll give ye a good hiding!' Everyone who heard him knew that was a lie.

Jerry reached out and caught Malachi by the collar, lifting him clean off the ground.

Malachi's legs pedalled furiously as his temper flapped at his heels.

'Put me down,' he screamed, 'put me down.'

'Come on, Malachi,' said Jerry, laughing. 'Come on, Harry. Yer safe, lad.'

'Mam, put the kettle on, and tell Alice I'll be two minutes, if she's up. I'll just help Tommy, the big soft lad, with these little scamps.'

Kathleen and Nellie, both laughing out loud, turned into the entry.

When Brigid stepped in through the back door, she was surprised to see that the main light had been switched on. She knew she had switched it off when they left and she wondered, was Sean home?

Relief flooded through her as she realized that he must be.

She had regretted letting Patricia accompany Mrs McGuire to the chippy and wished she had sent one of the younger ones instead. It was difficult, though. Mrs McGuire and Patricia had a special bond.

Brigid was the youngest of fourteen and so the notion surprised her that Patricia, as the eldest, had a different place in the family from all the rest.

Sure, wasn't she the most organized of any of her siblings? Didn't she run her house with absolute order and control?

Her house was immaculate.

Brigid had a great deal to be proud of. She still wished she had told Patricia to stay, though. Having to get five under the age of five ready for bed, never mind the others, was hard work and Patricia was a grand little help. Brigid was exhausted. However, she hadn't told Sean yet she was pretty sure there was another McGuire baby on the way.

This one made her more tired than she ever had been before and her face was flushed and burning, not signs of early pregnancy that she remembered from her previous babies. She could hear her heart beating in her eardrums and had fallen asleep during the nativity play. Never mind, she thought. If Sean has a win tonight, a pregnancy will hold off any talk of a move to America for a while.

As soon as she took off her coat, she put the kettle on and reached for the nappies she had left to warm on a shelf next to the range.

'Ooh, warm as toast,' she said to one of her toddlers, pressing the warm nappy on her ice-cold and bright-red little cheek.

Brigid shouted up the stairs to Sean. No response.

That's funny, she thought to herself.

She filled a small enamel bowl with warm water, took down the towel and pyjamas, and began changing the toddlers and the baby.

When she had finished, they jumped up and, one by one, piled onto the sofa in front of the TV. The older girls came down into the kitchen, all changed and ready, carrying their shoes with them.

'Clothes all folded neatly on the press for the morning, girls?'

Each one nodded.

'Shoes by the back door now,' she said. 'Was Daddy upstairs, Emelda?'

Emelda shook her head as she slipped onto the sofa with her siblings.

Brigid sat at the table and looked at the row of red heads, watching *Coronation Street* on the television. They didn't really understand it but they all knew that being up this late was a treat and not one of them was about to complain or misbehave. Besides, Nana and Patricia were gone to the chippy.

'Isn't this just the best night of the year?' little Emelda said. 'We've had the play, treats at the school, snow and the chippy too. This is the happiest night in me life, Mammy.'

Brigid felt her heart fill with love. Making her children happy was a bonus. Keeping them clean and fed, and running an orderly home, was her job. None of Brigid's children missed a day from school, ever, not unless they were truly poorly. Brigid was a good mother. She and Sean did things the right way.

'Is it now, you gorgeous thing?' Brigid's face suffused with a warm and loving glow as she looked at her daughter's tooth-less grin. 'It's mine, too.'

At that moment, they all heard Mrs McGuire and Patricia walk up the path and the back door opened.

'Mary and Joseph, would ye close that door,' Brigid shouted, rubbing her arms to counter the cold blast.

The kitchen filled with the smell of newsprint soaked in vinegar.

'Here we are, all,' said Mrs McGuire, 'chips and a saveloy each.'

Mrs McGuire loved pronouncing the word 'saveloy'.

'Pass the big plate down from the mantel, would ye, Brigid. It's nice and warm and we can put it all in the middle of the table for them, what do ye think?'

'Aye, that's grand, thanks, Mrs McGuire. I think maybe Sean nipped back earlier, but he's not here now,' Brigid replied thoughtfully with a hint of concern in her voice.

The children had dived off the sofa and were dutifully piling onto the chairs round the table. Grace fetched forks out of the drawer, and the plates from the neat and tidy row along the back of the press.

Emelda had removed the muslin used to keep the flies away, taken the breadboard and knife from the press and placed it on the table. Now she began helping the smaller ones up onto the chairs. They were all chattering away excitedly, salivating at the smell of the chips. Chair legs scraped across the stone floor, cutlery and plates banged loudly on the table, and the kettle whistled impatiently on the range while Emelda set the table.

Little Paddy's dog, Scamp, scratched away persistently at the back door. He had followed Mrs McGuire all the way home from the chippy and was now letting Brigid know he was there. Brigid was begrudgingly kind to Scamp. She felt for him, having to live at Peggy and Paddy's, and often threw him a bit of raw sausage.

Brigid reached up for the big meat plate from the mantel-shelf above the range and immediately saw the envelope. She recognized the handwriting as Sean's. He had never, in their ten years of marriage, written her a letter.

A feeling of dread crept slowly into the room and her expression became one of fear, as she ripped open the envelope and extracted the single sheet of notepaper. It had been torn from Patricia's school book and with it was a wad of ten-pound notes. Brigid's first thought was one of irritation at his having taken paper from Patricia's school book. Brigid kept her own pad of usable scrap paper, with a slip of string through the corner to hold it together, in the press drawer.

On the television, Ena Sharples was giving out to Minnie Caldwell. Someone took the kettle off the range to silence its persistent whistle.

Brigid couldn't hear what they were saying. The noise from the television and the children's chatter had merged into a low background buzz.

She felt her blood drain into her boots within seconds, as happiness, laughter and hope for her future left.

Mrs McGuire bent down to turn up the television and the closing theme music from *Coronation Street* began to fill the room.

'Merciful Mary, it was that flaming queue, Patricia. We've missed it,' she exclaimed in a bitterly disappointed voice.

Brigid stared at the letter. The meaning of the words washed over her slowly in rhythmic waves, becoming stronger and more painful with each second. Her mind, shielding her soul, refused to absorb the truth at once, but held at bay the realization of all the things she had suspected – had known, really, but had suppressed and ignored in the midst of her busy life.

No morning kiss. Distracted. No talk of America. No desire for sex. Already gone when she awoke. Never home when she went to bed.

Her heart began to race and pound in her chest as the adrenaline swam out to shield her. Tears swarmed in her eyes, blurring the words, washing them away, saving her from the pain of reading them again, for now.

Mrs McGuire turned from the television to look at Brigid and saw it happen.

The moment when the words seeped through, hit Brigid's heart and, shred by shred, tore it apart.

Kathleen thought it was very unusual that there were no lights on in the house and that the fire had gone out.

'Jesus,' she cried, as they stepped into the kitchen. 'I didn't bank the fire up, because I thought Alice would be back to do it and the flamin' thing has gone out, on the very coldest night of the year. Would ye believe that? Nellie, Alice must be feeling very poorly indeed. Let's get a pot of tea mashed and then we can take her one up and see how she is. You see to Joseph, while I get the fire going.'

'I'm going up to the cot, Nana, to fetch his pyjamas,' said Nellie.

Kathleen had dropped to her knees, raking the range fire and muttering to herself.

'Aye, there's enough life left in here,' she said with relief, whipping an *Echo* out from underneath the seat cushion and screwing it up tightly. Within a minute, the kitchen glowed orange and the reflected flames danced up the walls. Kathleen carefully placed one piece of coke after another on top of the burning paper and then closed the range doors.

The crêpe-paper garland decorations that Kathleen, Alice and Nellie had patiently glued together over a week of evenings, and then strung across the ceiling, shuddered and crinkled above her as the heat rose from the fire, lending the festive decorations a life of their own.

Kathleen leant back onto her haunches and wiped her hands down the front of her apron. 'Thank the Lord for small mercies,' she whispered, looking up at the statue of the Virgin Mary, and crossed herself.

It wasn't the statue Jerry and Bernadette had bought. That one had mysteriously broken some years back, when Nellie was just a toddler. Nellie had asked her only the other day where it had come from.

'The first one was bought before Jerry and Bernadette were married. I remember, they bought it from a lady in the little shop in Crossmolina, when they were at home on their holidays. This is the second one, though, and I have no idea where that came from, or even how the first one broke.'

All that seemed such a long time ago. As she stared at the holy figurine, Kathleen murmured, 'Ah, Bernadette, ye loved Christmas like no one I have ever known before or since.'

Kathleen crossed herself again. It must have been the emotion of Christmas, of having a moment here on her own, in front of the fire, in an empty kitchen, because as she waited to see if the coke had truly caught, something suddenly touched her. They hadn't switched the lamp on yet and, apart from the fire, the room was dark. She thought about life and its ups and downs. How different her life would have been if their Bernadette had lived, if she had been here with them tonight at the school. The pain of her memory and the acuteness of her loss stabbed Kathleen straight in the chest. It always did.

Kathleen took her handkerchief out of her apron pocket.

'Ah, get away, ye daft old sod,' she said, wiping her eyes and lifting up the poker, ready to open the range doors.

She suddenly felt cold and yet she was kneeling in front of the range, with the flames already roaring up the chimney. She held her hands out to the door to feel if it was hot. Yes, of course it was, she could see that, couldn't she?

An icy shiver passed over her. She rubbed her arms and looked around, confused.

'God in heaven,' she said to herself, 'have I a chill?' And leaning back, she pressed the back of her hand to her forehead, which felt normal.

Nellie walked slowly down the stairs. She had dressed Joseph in his pyjamas as if on automatic pilot. Her inclination had been to scream and to run down to the kitchen, but she didn't. She held on.

She had thought that they had been burgled. The press drawers were open, along with the wardrobe door. Alice's apron, and a few of her clothes, were strewn around the room. Everything else that had belonged to Alice had gone.

Everything, except for Joseph.

She had looked in the wardrobe first. The hangers on the side that belonged to Alice were empty. The drawers in the press, likewise, and her few bits of make-up, her hairbrush and curlers, which lived on the top, had also disappeared.

Her shoes. Her boots. Her coat. Her hats. Her gloves. Her everything. Gone.

As Nellie came through the door at the bottom of the stairs, holding Joseph in her arms, she stopped dead in her tracks.

Joseph put his thumb into his mouth, silently laid his head on her chest and stared at the scene in front of him, sucking slowly and steadily. The kitchen was still dark. The fire had now reduced from its initial roaring blaze to a softer, quieter flame.

There was Kathleen, kneeling in front of the fire, and next to her knelt Bernadette. There was not a sound in the kitchen. When the coke in the fire slid down onto the grate with a sudden crunch, Nellie almost jumped out of her skin, but nothing altered.

Bernadette's hair had absorbed the warm light from the fire and radiated a red glow that wrapped itself around them all.

Kathleen wiped her eyes and Bernadette put her arm round her shoulders. Nellie heard Kathleen talking to Bernadette, but she couldn't hear what she was saying.

Nellie wasn't scared at all of Bernadette, her mammy, whom she loved without ever having known her. But she knew something was shifting, altering, that she was in their midst and that whatever was happening was beyond their control. Something was very wrong. Why else would Bernadette appear, and so openly too? But this feeling, in the kitchen, this was special. It was like magic. It felt like heaven.

Nellie kissed the top of Joseph's warm head and as he nuzzled in deeper, she hugged him. She felt an ache, very deep inside. A yearning. A longing. A need to be the one her mammy was hugging. A desperate loneliness flooded her and her eyes filled with pain, as she quietly sobbed and, for the very first time in her life, she cried the word 'Mammy' out loud.

After what seemed like many minutes but was in fact only seconds, the spell was broken by the sound of Jerry lifting the latch of the back gate and the noise of Peggy and Little Paddy, shuffling along behind him in the snow, urgently shouting, 'Jerry, Jerry, will ye wait. Come here while I tell ye.'

Before the back door had even opened, Kathleen was on her feet and Bernadette had vanished.

It was Christmas Eve.

Daisy wanted to stand on the deck of the boat and stare as hard as she could until she saw the coast of Ireland and her family waiting for her.

She had so many images in her mind of what they would look like and what they would say when they saw her. She had been told that her older brother, his wife and his eldest son and daughter would be there to greet her. Miss Devlin had said that when Daisy's sister-in-law had spoken to Miss Devlin on the telephone, she had become so full of emotion and excitement at the prospect of Daisy being with them at Christmas that both she and Miss Devlin had been blubbing like a pair of eejits.

They had made Miss Devlin promise that she would visit in the school holidays and, of course, she had said she would.

After all she had been through, Daisy now had a family of her own and a friend in Miss Devlin.

Miss Devlin had put Daisy on the boat and asked two elderly sisters who were also boarding, and whose names she discovered were Edith and Elsie, to keep a watch on Daisy.

They assured her that they would and Miss Devlin explained that Daisy's own family would be right at the gate when they docked, waiting and ready.

She had asked the ladies if they would show Daisy where the toilet was, and help her to buy a cuppa and a biscuit to settle her stomach.

The ladies, who were both from Dublin, were as kind and friendly as any Irish grandmother would be.

'Of course,' they had said, 'no problem at all, you just stick with us, Daisy.'

But Daisy hadn't wanted to sit in the café inside. Daisy had spent almost her entire life inside. She wanted to gaze at the sea and watch for her family.

The ladies had brought Daisy a cup of tea on deck. 'We will be back out with another cuppa in half an hour,' said Elsie kindly.

Daisy had smiled and thanked her. Daisy knew her manners. She could count on one hand the number of times anyone had ever made her a cuppa, but that didn't mean she didn't know the right thing to say when someone did.

She hadn't stopped smiling since Miss Devlin had first read her the letter from her family. Tonight, she didn't mind being alone. She had so much to look forward to. Daisy would never be alone again. She reached her hand up and stroked her felt hat, which had been presented to her at the play. It felt so soft. Daisy could barely believe her luck.

It was as she bent to place the empty teacup onto the bench behind her that Daisy saw the man approach.

'Hello,' she said with a big friendly grin, as she stood upright. She recognized him immediately. 'Are you going to Dublin too? Well, fancy. I am off to meet my family. I have a family, you know. My brother, he's the state solicitor and he wants me to live with him and his wife. Can ye imagine that? I don't want to go inside. I want to wait here. I don't care about the cold tonight. I don't really. I want to be the first to see my family waiting for me when we arrive in Dublin. Miss Devlin tells me they will be at the very front, waiting for me at the gate.'

Daisy looked over the rail and across the sea as she giggled at her own words. She was beyond excitement. For the past twenty-four hours she had been seized by a euphoria that manifested itself as a new calmness and radiance. Everyone had noticed.

'She cannot keep the grin from her face,' Miss Devlin had said to Sister Evangelista.

'I have noticed!' the sister replied. 'Sure, she is radiant indeed. Let's pray to God that smile stays there forever because if anyone deserves to be happy, Daisy does.'

Daisy felt the man's hand on her back and turned to face him. 'Will someone be waiting for you, too?' Her smile was open. Friendly, happy, questioning. Simple.

'Yes, they will. Daisy, your family, they have asked me to escort you. I am taking you to meet your brother, Daisy. You have to come with me now. Let's move down to the front of the boat to be ready, so that we can be the first away.'

Later that evening, Simon was on duty and had arranged to meet the super at his golf club where he was hosting a family celebration.

The bobbies were becoming agitated. They wanted to be at home with their families, not sitting in police cars, doing absolutely nothing at all on the four streets.

Simon stood in the glass foyer and lit a cigarette. He watched the doorman enter the restaurant and inform the super that Simon was outside.

The super half stood, waiting for the waiter to remove his chair, and patted his mouth with his napkin. He cast a glance through the door to Simon and then, seeming to apologize to his guests, walked out into the foyer.

'I'm sorry, sir,' said Simon, 'but it's Christmas Eve and the men . . .

'Not at all, I am delighted you are here,' said the super. 'Look here, this is a good time to shut things down. The papers are on holiday and everything and everyone has gone terribly quiet. I have spoken to the chief, who agrees that we should keep the file open and stand the men down until something or someone comes forward. Best thing to do. Let the men go home.'

'Thank you, sir,' said Simon. 'I will tell them straight away and let Davies know.'

'Good man. Merry Christmas.' And without another second wasted, the super walked back into the club dining room and returned to his party.

'Yes, thank you, sir, Merry Christmas,' said Simon to his retreating back.

Simon left the club via its large revolving door and lit another cigarette. It was his last. As he slipped into the driver's seat, he threw the red and white packet onto the ground.

On his drive back to the four streets he called in to the station to make a call.

'Investigation abandoned,' he said in a low voice into the phone.

'Are you sure?' came the reply.

'I'm certain,' said Simon. 'We are all safe.'

As he replaced the receiver, he took a packet of Pall Mall out of the top drawer of his desk and headed back down to the four streets to send the officers home for Christmas.

As he sat in his police car, he looked into his rear-view mirror and, flinching, he ripped off the Elastoplast dressing on the back of his neck, squealing as he pulled away some of the downy hair.

'Bleeding cat,' he hissed as he turned the key in the ignition.

As Simon drove past the Grand on to Lime Street, he stopped at the pelican crossing outside the Shamrock pub to allow Alice Deane and Sean McGuire, their heads down, to run across the road. Sean was carrying two suitcases and they were both heading down towards the Pier Head. Neither noticed as they passed in front of his car. The snow on the main roads in town had turned to slush and his rear wheels slipped slightly as he accelerated away.

As he drove down Church Street and then onto the Dock Road, he wondered how long it would be before he was summoned to investigate a missing passenger on the Dublin ferry.

And then, letting out a deep sigh, he grinned as he turned left and headed up towards the four streets.

Christmas morning.

She had only Aideen to comfort her when her son made his arrival into the world. The snow had begun to fall at exactly the moment Kitty's labour pains seized her. Within no time at all, the solitary overhead telephone cable fell and lay buried under a carpet of crystal-white snow. They were stranded from the outside world.

Aideen almost chased the nuns out of the room when they arrived to impart the news that there was no telephone to contact the midwife and no way of getting a message into the village. She felt that, for some reason, the nuns were nervous, almost scared of what they said and did around Kitty. Aideen, who was sharp as a knife, took full advantage of this.

Kitty was the only girl anywhere near her due delivery date and the resident midwife had taken herself home to Dublin for the Christmas break. As she slammed the front door behind her, her last words had been, 'That girl's not my responsibility.'

Despite having chased the nuns from the labour room and having witnessed plenty of her own mother's births, Aideen was terrified.

Pain wrapped itself around Kitty's waist like a metal band and each time its grip became longer and harder to bear. She heard screams filling the room but was too far gone to feel shame or embarrassment.

'God, help me,' she screamed over and over. 'Mammy, help me.'

Aideen held Kitty's hands and walked her round the room. She sat next to her on the bed when she could persuade Kitty to lie down. She mopped her brow with cold water and gave Kitty sips of water. And all through the evening and into the night, the baby showed no sign of making an entry into the world.

The girls from the dorm had sneaked bread into their apron pockets and slipped into the labour room to hand it to Aideen.

'Fucking hell,' said Aideen. 'Did not one of them mean bitches think one of us could do with the disgusting slop they give us as soup? She has no energy. How is she going to push this thing out?'

Juliette, one of the older girls, looked concerned as another contraction took hold of Kitty.

'Would ye like me to take over for a while, Aideen? Maybe we should take it in turns to stop with her?'

Aideen looked at Kitty, soaked in sweat and almost delirious.

'No, thanks, I will stay and see the job done. I feel close to this poor girl.'

Juliette nodded and left the room. She understood. They all felt close to her. She was a sweet kid and, God knew, the faces she had pulled at the nuns behind their backs had all but creased them up with laughter at times.

'I'll see ye later then,' whispered Juliette from the door with a glance at Kitty who was oblivious, in a world of intense torment.

By four o'clock in the morning, following hours of pain and screaming, Kitty had given up. She felt calm and no longer tried to respond to Aideen's instructions to push. 'No,' she whimpered, 'I can't, I don't want to do it.'

It was now Aideen's turn to begin to scream.

'Push, ye fucking bitch,' she shouted at Kitty. 'Do ye think I'm wasting my night in here for you to decide you can't be bothered to push? *Push*, now.'

There was no response from Kitty. She wanted to die, in a place of her own, somewhere distant from the room and Aideen. She had had enough.

'It is the perfect thing,' she muttered in her delirious haze. 'It is the perfect answer if I die. There will be no trouble for anyone and no problem. I just so want to die.'

The slap across Kitty's face hurt almost as much as the contraction that quickly followed. Aideen was yelling into her face to push.

She had climbed up behind Kitty, dragged her up the bed and forced her to sit upright, resisting Kitty's urge to lean back and lie down again.

'Don't let the fucking witches win. Don't let the child's bastard father beat you. Don't let him win.'

Aideen was now scared. She could see Kitty had disappeared somewhere and she didn't know where. She was terrified that Kitty was indeed about to die.

'Do you want the bastard father to win, do ye?'

Kitty could hear Aideen. She was aware of her hands prodding and pushing her heavy, flaccid body. She was aware of Aideen's words penetrating though her fog.

The bastard father beating her? Was that what Aideen had just said?

Kitty began to laugh.

'For fuck's sake.'

Aideen climbed back down from the bed. 'What in God's name? Why are ye laughing now?'

Kitty snapped back from the place where she wanted only to close her eyes and sleep. She didn't want this baby. She didn't want to be here. She didn't want to work in the laundry. She hadn't wanted to be raped. But none of that mattered. Kitty didn't want to live, she wanted to die, but she didn't even have that. Aideen wasn't going to let her. Aideen was going to make her live and have this spawn of the devil himself. Aideen thought that, in this way, Kitty would be winning. She wasn't even going to let Kitty choose whether or not she died.

It made Kitty laugh again, almost in hysteria.

'Push,' yelled Aideen, as the pain once again seized Kitty's abdomen with an intense ferocity and made it harden like a rock. With all that she had left, Kitty pushed again.

Following sixteen hours of screams and chaos, the labour room suddenly fell silent, apart from the tiny snuffles from deep within a white knitted blanket, which Aideen had found in the layette of baby clothes Rosie had left behind when she had visited to examine Kitty.

An hour later, once she had managed to clear up the after-birth mess and had washed down Kitty and the baby, Aideen suddenly felt giddy and sat down on a chair, before she fainted herself with exhaustion.

Although Aideen had switched off the light, hoping that both she and Kitty could catch an hour's sleep before morning, the room was lit with a vivid bright whiteness, reflected from the snow-laden sky and the newly covered trees.

'Would ye look at him,' said an exhausted Kitty as she lifted her new baby up to show Aideen. 'Isn't he just gorgeous?'

Kitty now had no recollection of not wanting to have this baby. As she first laid eyes on him, no thought of rejection crossed her mind. He had brought his own love with him.

As Aideen had finally delivered his thin and slippery body, without warning Kitty had been swamped by emotion. Since the second he had been born, she had been unable to take her eyes off him.

Aideen gave her a look of concern. 'Aye, he's sweet enough, all right, but in days he will be the child of a rich and fancy American couple, so don't forget that and go getting all attached.'

Without speaking a word, Kitty brought the bundle up to her face. She felt the warmth of his body lying against her own and nuzzled her face into the dark downy hair on his head.

'He looks like me da,' she whispered to Aideen in the dark. 'Can I give him a name?'

Aideen looked at her. 'Aye, but I'm sure his new mam and da will want to choose his own name. What were ye thinking?'

'John,' Kitty whispered into her baby's warm cheek where she had laid his first kiss, 'his name is John.'

There was a tap on the door as the girls from the dormitory tiptoed in one by one.

'Would ye believe it,' said Juliette as she came into the room. 'Sister Virginia is first up. I told her about the awful night with no midwife an' all and she gave me the key to the kitchen and said go and fetch the girls a tray of tea and some toast. Ye have certainly spooked them, having a Christmas baby, sent them all of a dither, that has, and it being you an' all, Kitty. Would a sinner give birth on Christmas Day? In a right state they are!'

Kitty looked up as the girls slipped in. The room filled with the smell of hot buttered toast and Juliette began to pour the scalding hot tea into cups.

One of the girls, who, like Aideen, had to stay at the Abbey for the full three years and had already had her baby, handed Kitty a bottle of formula milk.

'Did ye forget about the baby?' she smiled at Aideen.

'No, not at all, he just hasn't bothered looking for a feed yet,' Aideen replied. 'I was just getting over me shock. I swear, God was holding my hands through that because I had no idea what I was doing.'

Kitty was no stranger to feeding a baby a bottle and she expertly fed John, who latched onto the teat in a split second.

'Look at him,' Kitty laughed, 'he nearly has it drained already.'

The laundry-room girls cooed over John and Kitty, and chattered quietly, something they were never, ever allowed to do.

Kitty had noticed that some of the girls, who had been in the Abbey for a longer period than most, spoke almost like the deaf little girl on the four streets. So unused were they to talking that, when they did, it was as if their tongues had forgotten how to form a word. When they did speak, it was slurred and difficult to understand.

One of the girls sat on the edge of Kitty's bed, smiling at her and gently rubbing John's back. 'A Christmas baby, can ye imagine? That will make him very special indeed.'

Kitty didn't know what to say. He would be special, but she wouldn't see it. Dawn was breaking and there was an atmosphere in the room. The Christmas baby and hot buttered toast were having an effect.

'I'm not wasting having the key,' whispered Ann. 'I'm off to make more tea and toast. There was enough bread in that kitchen to feed a fuckin' army.'

And she giggled as two of the other girls tripped down the steps with Ann to make a further raid on the kitchen. 'It's a blessing that ye are here, Kitty, ye have made Christmas for us with the toast.'

As Kitty sat up in the bed, with her baby laid on her chest and a cup of tea in her hand, she looked round at the other girls chattering. Letting no thoughts other than those needed for that moment come into her mind, she smiled the first smile of happiness since the day she had arrived at the Abbey.

I will remember this, she thought to herself. My days of imprisonment here are nearly over.

And then as though he could read her thoughts, her little bundle wriggled his tiny feet in objection and kicked her tender tummy of raw jelly and, once again, she bent down to kiss his head.

Breathing in deeply, she allowed her nostrils to fill with his smell and held on to it, not breathing out, willing her mind to remember. She rubbed his back slowly, aware of her every move. She bent to look at his face and his blue eyes locked onto her own. She burnt the image onto her memory and into her heart. This was all she would have to remember. These moments, bathed in snow and dawn light.

Aideen began to pour the second round of tea. There was no laundry work today; none of them would return to bed now. She looked at Kitty and worried. Kitty, just a girl and full of motherly love.

'Maybe it's better that we get three years with them,' Aideen whispered to Ann. 'That way we have more to hold onto and remember.'

'Three years or three days, it's all cruel,' Ann replied harshly. 'One day these witches will get their comeuppance and I for one cannot wait.'

They turned back to look at Kitty. The dawn had broken as the first robins perched on the snow-covered branches of the plum tree outside the window. The Abbey bells began to ring. Kitty's son lay in the crook of her arm with his head tucked under her chin. Both were fast asleep.

Sister Assumpta was relieved that Kitty had given birth. The sooner she could get that child out of the convent, the better. The nuns, all of a fluster that a baby had been born on Christmas morning, had been almost beyond her control. She could hardly believe her ears when she had been informed that the girls had been handed the keys to the kitchen.

'God in heaven, what next?' she had screamed at Sister Celia. 'He's a baby born in sin and out of wedlock, he isn't Jesus Christ and she is certainly no Holy Mother!'

As she silently climbed the stairs to the labour room, the Reverend Mother had already decided to send a message to

Rosie to collect Kitty as soon as was physically possible. Although how she was going to do that in the snow, God alone knew.

The girls scattered when she opened the labour-room door and stepped into their midst. She noted that the electric fire had been switched on without permission and the detritus of breakfast lay scattered on the tray.

'Get down to prayers, all of you, they started ten minutes ago,' she spat at them in a voice that contained no hint of Christmas cheer.

The girls flew out of the room and down the stairs towards the chapel. Aideen kept her eyes lowered and cheekily snatched the last piece of toast from the tray as she hurried past.

The noise woke Kitty, who opened her eyes. Aware of the baby lying across her chest and the old rolled-up nappy Aideen had placed between her legs, she shuffled herself painfully up the bed, using just one elbow as she gripped the baby with her other hand. Sister Assumpta watched in stony silence and offered no assistance. The cramps sweeping across Kitty's belly and her breasts, although nothing compared to the labour pains, were bad enough to make her wince as she attempted to move. Aideen said she had torn quite badly and she knew the warm feeling between her legs was blood oozing out onto the rags with the effort of moving.

Sister Assumpta showed not the slightest concern, only irritation, as she glanced at the baby. The more attractive the baby was, the happier the new parents in America would be when he was handed over. This one would be leaving soon and he definitely was very attractive. She would not keep a baby born on Christmas morning in her convent for a day longer than necessary.

'The snow won't be here for long,' she said crisply as she

walked to the window and cast her glance over the carpet of glistening white lawn. 'It will be just a day or two before the midwife is here and I am sure we all agree it is for the best if she takes you back to your family as soon as possible. You can stay up here in this room. There are no other deliveries due and I will have food sent up to you. You have no further work to do. Just stay on this floor and don't come down into the Abbey until the midwfe arrives.'

Despite her huge discomfort, the tiredness, the burning pain in her belly and the fact that her legs felt as though they wouldn't work even if she tried to walk, Kitty felt a huge relief. It would be at least two days before Rosie would reach her. Two whole days with her baby. Two days of memories. Two days in which to smother him with a lifetime of love.

Regardless of her best effort not to, Kitty's face broke into a loving smile as she shuffled her baby up into her arms.

Sister Assumpta turned away from the window and she saw the smile. She blinked. Within seconds, she had assessed the scene. Her face set, hard. In a voice devoid of emotion, she spoke.

'I will send up a novice directly to collect the baby. He will live in the nursery now until his new parents land at Shannon airport.'

Before Kitty could utter a word in protest, she glided out of the room on the wave of her own destruction.

Kitty had only minutes with her baby as she heard the bells peal the end of prayers. There was no time to think or plan, no point in pleading. She knew the coldness, the evil, that resided in the heart of the Reverend Mother. Evil was no stranger to Kitty.

'Wake up, little fella,' she whispered urgently as her tears ran onto his downy hair. 'Wake up.'

And he did. He woke and scrunched up his newborn red face. Lifting both of his tiny clenched-up fists to his cheeks, he scratched his own delicate skin with a papery fingernail and began to whimper in complaint.

Kitty held him out in front of her and shook him gently as she heard heavy footsteps ascend the stairs and knew this was it. Her last moments. Sister Assumpta had wasted no time.

'I love you, do ye hear me?' she whispered to him urgently. 'Can ye hear me?'

He opened his deep-blue eyes, level with her own, and, once again, stared deeply into hers. His perfect lips, tinged white with milk, opening and closing. He knew her. Her smell. The sound of her voice. He ceased to whimper. She had all of his attention. He knew her as he knew himself. The physical cord cut, but the bond remained intact.

'I will find you one day, I will. I will find you,' she whispered desperately between her sobs. Her salty tears fell onto his newborn face and his eyes narrowed as if in concern.

Her lips were pressed against his soft and warm temple as she spoke, holding him tight. Repeating the words, 'I will find you, I am Kitty. I am your mammy, only me, no one else,' pressing them deep into his soul. Hiding them there. For ever.

Acknowledgements

I write this as I lay down the final words in book three of the trilogy, *The Ballymara Road*. If there is one thing I have learnt, it is that writing a book is a team effort. I have many people to thank and should start at the beginning, with Vicki Field and my agent, Piers Blofeld, as without their generous words of encouragement it is unlikely I would ever have written past the first chapter of *The Four Streets*.

I owe a huge debt of gratitude to my family, to my three daughters, Philippa, Jennifer and Cassandra, and to my mother, who between them have kept me grounded and in touch with the things that matter in a way only the women in my family could. Also to my wonderful partner, Chris Hammond, who has fed and soothed me and taken charge of every practical obstacle in order that nothing prevented me from writing, in the few hours I had spare each week.

To family in Ireland, with their wonderful ways and my Aunty Jean and Uncle Terry in Liverpool, I am prouder of all of you than you ever could be of me.

My editor, Rosie de Courcy, has never failed to inspire me with wonderful ideas of her own and, in addition to mentoring me, she deserves huge thanks for having had to put up with an author who knew absolutely nothing whatsoever about writing a book or, as it turned out, three books, and for that I also have to thank the publishing legend, Anthony Cheetham, who believed in me. Thank you to the entire staff at Head of Zeus who have never once raised their eyebrows or rolled their eyes at me, the novice.

My friends and their kind words were the balsam on the days things didn't go so well. I couldn't write this page without mentioning Alison and Alan, Lynn and Giles, Carol and Les, and Anna; they are the people I drown my sorrows with and who I know are always there for me, when and if I need them. And there are those who shared my joy as if it were their own and for that I would like to thank Stewart Jackson MP, Douglas Carswell MP, Andrea Gordon, William Joce, Budge, Iain Dale and my late friend, Anne Rayment, who downloaded *The Four Streets* but couldn't stay long enough to read it. Her husband, Andy, has been a sage and wise mentor, and I would especially like to mention my very close friend, the lovely Tim Montgomerie, for his endless love, support and kindness.

I would also like to thank Darina Molloy at Mayo Library, for going the extra mile, and the staff at the Museum of Country Life in Eire.

And last but definitely not least, the amazing characters who played a significant role in my extraordinary childhood.